praise for dust devil on a quiet street

D0814906

dust devil on a quiet street

dust devil
ON A QUIET STREET

Richard Bowes

Lethe Press
Maple Shade, New Jersey

Dust Devil on a Quiet Street

Published in 2013 by Lethe Press, Inc.
118 Heritage Avenue, Maple Shade, NJ 08052 USA
lethepressbooks.com / lethepress@aol.com
ISBN: 978-1-59021-297-4 / 1-59021-297-5
e-ISBN: 978-1-59021-169-4 / 1-59021-169-3

This novel is a work of fiction. Names, characters, places, and incidents are products of the author's imaginations or are used fictitiously.

Set in Warnock, ITC American Typewriter, Bilbo, & Shaun of the Dead.
Cover and interior design: Alex Jeffers.
Cover art: Juan Santapau.

LIBRARY OF CONGRESS CATALOGING-IN-PUBLICATION DATA
Bowes, Richard.
 Dust devil on a quiet street / Richard Bowes.
   pages cm
 ISBN 978-1-59021-297-4 (alk. paper)
 1. Bowes, Richard--Fiction. 2. Authors--New York (State)--New York--Fiction. 3. Greenwich Village (New York, N.Y.)--Intellectual life--Fiction. 4. Autobiographical fiction. I. Title.
 PS3552.O8735D87 2013
 813'.54--dc23
                    2013013380

For Chris, with all my love.

Acknowledgments

Fourteen previously published stories were used, in altered form in this novel.

Stories were nominated for Nebula and World Fantasy Awards, won the International Horror Guild and Million Writer Awards, and were included in many Year's Best anthologies.

They appeared in the online magazines *Sci Fiction*, June 15, 2005, *Clarkesworld*, February 2008, and on the *Mumpsimus* blog on June 28th, 2009.

Stories appeared in the print magazines *Postscripts*, Spring 2005, *Subterranean*, Issue #7, 2007, *Icarus*, Fall 2011 and *The Magazine of Fantasy and Science Fiction*, December 2009, March/April 2010, July/August 2010 and November/December 2010.

Stories appeared in the following anthologies: *Salon Fantastique*, 2007, *Lovecraft Unbound*, 2009, *The Beastly Bride*, 2010, and *Haunted Legends*, 2010.

My thanks to the editors: Terry Windling, Nick Mamatas, Matt Cheney, Peter Crowther, Steve Berman, and most especially to Ellen Datlow and Gordon Van Gelder.

Years ago a friend everyone called Major Barbara and I noticed the whirls of debris and dirt raised by a sudden stray breeze in the gutters of a quiet street in Greenwich Village.

"Dust devils," she said.

"Local ghosts and small gods," I replied. We were young and we were amused. I saw faces in the swirl. Years later when we were no longer friends she denied having seen anything.

For most of my life I've lived in New York. When I say New York I mean Manhattan and when I say Manhattan I mean the Villages East and West. Here I've seen rent boys riot and burning towers fall, made friends for life, been haunted by ghosts of old boyfriends and even girlfriends.

As a child I went to bed worried that the me who fell asleep would disappear in the dark and not be remembered by the me who woke up. I've never wholly lost that. It's one reason I write these stories.

Chapter One

WEDNESDAY 9/12

On the evening of the day after the towers fell, I was waiting by the barricades on Houston Street and LaGuardia Place for my friend Mags to come up from SoHo and have dinner with me. On the skyline, not two miles to the south, the pillars of smoke wavered slightly. But the creepily beautiful weather of September 11 still held and the wind blew in from the northeast. In Greenwich Village the air was crisp and clean with just a touch of fall about it.

I'd spent the last day and a half looking at pictures of burning towers. One of the frustrations of that time was there was so little most of us could do about anything or for anyone.

Downtown streets were empty of all traffic except emergency vehicles. The West and East Villages from Fourteenth Street to Houston were their own separate zone. Pedestrians needed identification proving they lived or worked here in order to enter.

The barricades consisted of blue wooden police horses and several unmarked vans thrown across LaGuardia Place. Behind them were a couple of cops, a few auxiliary police and

3

one or two guys in civilian clothes with I.D.s of some kind pinned to their shirts. All of them looked tired, subdued by events.

At the barricades was a small crowd, ones like me waiting for friends from neighborhoods to the south, ones without proper identification waiting for confirmation so that they could continue on into SoHo, people who just wanted to be outside near other people in those days of sunshine and shock. Once in a while, each of us would look up at the columns of smoke that hung in the downtown sky then look away again.

A family approached a middle-aged cop behind the barricade. The group consisted of a man, a woman, a little girl being led by the hand, a boy being carried. All were blondish and wore shorts and casual tops. The parents seemed pleasant but serious people in their early thirties, professionals. They could have been tourists. But that day the city was empty of tourists.

The man said something and I heard the cop say loudly, "You want to go where?"

"Down there," the man gestured at the columns. He indicated the children. "We want them to see." It sounded as if he couldn't imagine this appeal not working.

Everyone stared at the family. "No I.D., no passage," said the cop and turned his back on them. The pleasant expressions on the parents' faces faded. They looked indignant, like a maître d' had lost their reservations. She led one kid, he carried another as they turned west, probably headed for another check point.

"They wanted those little kids to see Ground Zero!" a woman who knew the cop said. "Are they out of their minds?"

"Looters," he replied. "That's my guess." He picked up his walkie-talkie to call the checkpoints ahead of them.

Mags appeared just then, looking a bit frayed. When you've known someone for as long as I've known her, the tendency is

richard bowes

4

not to see the changes, to think you both look about the same as when you were kids.

But kids don't have grey hair and their bodies aren't thick the way bodies get in their late fifties. Their kisses aren't perfunctory. Their conversation doesn't include curt little nods that indicate something is understood.

We walked in the middle of the streets because we could. "Didn't sleep much last night," I said.

"Because of the quiet," she said. "No planes. I kept listening for them. I haven't been sleeping anyway. I was supposed to be in housing court today. But the courts are shut until further notice."

I said, "See how with only the ones who live here allowed in, the South Village is all Italians and hippies?"

"Like 1965 all over again. Except now everyone's old."

She and I had been in contact more in the past few months than we had in a while. Memories of love and indifference that we shared had made close friendship an on and off thing for the last thirty-something years.

Earlier in 2001, at the end of an affair, I'd surrendered a rent-stabilized apartment for a cash settlement and bought a tiny co-op in the South Village. Mags lived as she had for years in a rundown building on the fringes of SoHo.

Living a few blocks apart we saw each other again. She's never read anything I published, which bothered me. On the other hand, she worked off and on for various activist left-wing foundations and I was mostly uninterested in that.

Mags was in the midst of classic New York work and housing trouble. Currently she was on unemployment and her landlord wanted to get her out of her apartment so he could co-op her building. The money offer he'd made wasn't bad but she wanted things to stay as they were. It struck me that what was youthful about her was that she had never settled into her life, still stood on the edge expectantly.

Lots of the Village restaurants weren't opened. The owners couldn't or wouldn't come into the city. Angelina's on Thompson Street was, though, because Angelina lives just a couple of doors down from her place. She was busy serving tables herself since the waiters couldn't get in from where they lived.

Later, I had reason to try and remember. The place was full but quiet. People murmured to each other as Mags and I did. Nobody I knew was there. In the background Resphigi's *Ancient Airs and Dances* played.

"Like the Blitz," someone said.

"Never the same again," said a person at another table.

"There isn't even any place to volunteer to help," a third person said.

I haven't had a drink in years. But Mags, as I remember, had a carafe of wine. Phone service had been spotty but we had managed to exchange bits of what we had seen.

"Mrs. Pirelli," I said. "The Italian lady upstairs from me. I told you she had a heart attack watching the smoke and flames on television. Her son worked in the World Trade Center and she was sure he had burned to death.

"Getting an ambulance wasn't possible yesterday morning. But the guys at that little fire barn around the corner were there. Waiting to be called, I guess. They took her to St. Vincent's in the chief's car. Right about then, her son came up the street, his pinstripe suit with a hole burned in the shoulder, soot on his face, wild eyed. But alive. Today they say she's doing fine."

I waited, spearing clams, twirling linguine. Mags had a deeper and darker story to tell; a dip into the subconscious. Before I'd known her and afterwards, Mags had a few rough brushes with mental disturbance. Back in college where we first met, I envied her that, wished there was something as dramatic and hip that I was able to talk about.

"I've been thinking over what happened last night." She'd already told me some of this. "The downstairs bell rang, which scared me. But with phone service being bad, it could have been a friend, someone who needed to talk. I looked out the window. The street was empty, dead like I'd never seen it.

"Nothing but papers blowing down the street. You know how every time you see scraps of paper and dust swirling around now you think it's from the Trade Center? For a minute I thought I saw something move but when I looked again there was nothing.

"I didn't ring the buzzer, but it seemed someone upstairs did because I heard this noise, a rustling in the hall.

"When I went to the door and lifted the spy hole, this figure stood there on the landing. Looking around like she was lost. She wore a dress, long and torn. And a blouse, what I realized was a shirtwaist. Turn-of-the-century clothes. When she turned towards my door, I saw her face. It was bloody, smashed. Like she had taken a big jump or fall. I gasped and then she was gone."

"And you woke up?"

"No, I tried to call you. But the phones were all fucked up. She had fallen but not from a hundred stories. Anyway she wasn't from here and now."

Mags had emptied the carafe. I remember that she'd just ordered a salad and didn't eat that. But Angelina brought a fresh carafe. I told Mags about the family at the barricades.

"There's a hole in the city," said Mags.

That night, after we had parted, I emailed friends, though the connection was shaky. On the static-ridden phone I talked to my family, reassured my mother up in Massachusetts that I wasn't in danger. My sister Lee here in the city and Polly up in Massachusetts, their husbands and kids were fine. My brother David was angry that people were making so much about this. My brother Gerry in Brooklyn wasn't having good days and this wasn't much worse than others.

Then I was in bed watching but not seeing some old movie on television, avoiding any channel with any kind of news, when the buzzer sounded. I jumped up and went to the view screen. On the empty street downstairs a man, wild eyed, disheveled, glared directly into the camera.

Phone service was not reliable. Cops were not in evidence in the neighborhood right then. I froze and didn't buzz him in. But, as in Mags' building, someone else did. I bolted my door, watched at the spy hole, listened to the footsteps, slow, uncertain. When he came into sight on the second floor landing he looked around and said in a hoarse voice, "Hello? Sorry but I can't find my mom's front door key."

Only then did I unlock the door, open it and ask her exhausted son how Mrs. Pirelli was doing.

"Fine," he said. "Getting great treatment. St. Vincent was geared up for thousands of casualties. Instead..." he shrugged. "Anyway, she thanks all of you. Me too."

In fact, I hadn't done much though I wanted to. We said good night and he shuffled on upstairs to where he was crashing in his mother's place.

Thursday 9/13

By September of 2001 I had worked an information desk in the university library for almost thirty years. I live right around the corner from Washington Square and just before ten AM on Thursday, I set out for work. The Turkish-run souvlaki stand across the street was still closed, its owner and workers gone since Tuesday morning. All the little falafel shops in the South Village were shut and dark.

On my way to work I saw a three-legged rat running not too quickly down the middle of MacDougal Street. I decided not to think about portents and symbolism.

The big televisions set up in the library atrium still showed the towers falling again and again. But now they also showed workers digging in the flaming wreckage at Ground Zero.

Like the day before, I was the only one in my department who'd made it in. The librarians lived too far away. Even Marco, the student assistant, wasn't around.

Marco lived in a dorm downtown right near the World Trade Center. He'd seen someone jump from the WTC roof. Then the students were evacuated without much more than the clothes they were wearing. Tuesday, he'd been very upset. I'd given him Kleenex, made him take deep breaths, and got him to call his mother in California. I'd even walked him over to the gym where the university was putting up the displaced students. He'd kind of clung to me when I had to go back to work and it felt like I'd abandoned him.

Thursday morning, all of the computer stations around the information desk were occupied. Students sat furiously typing email and devouring incoming messages but the intensity had slackened since 9/11. The girls no longer sniffed and dabbed at tears as they read. The boys would jump up, hurry to the restrooms and come back red-eyed and saying they had allergies.

I said good morning and sat down. The kids hadn't spoken to me much in the last few days, had no questions to ask. But all of them from time to time would turn and look to make sure I was still there. If I got up to leave the desk, they'd ask when I was coming back.

Some of the back windows had a downtown view. The pillar of smoke wavered. The wind was changing.

The phone rang. Reception had improved. Most calls went through. When I answered, a voice, tight and tense, blurted out, "Jennie Levine was who I saw. She was nineteen years old in 1911 when the Triangle Shirtwaist Factory burned. She lived in my building with her family ninety years ago. Her spirit found its way home. But the inside of my building has changed so much that she didn't recognize it."

"Hi, Mags," I said. "You want to come up here and have lunch?"

A couple of hours later, we were in a small dining hall normally used by faculty on the west side of the Square. The university, with food on hand and not enough people to eat it, had thrown open its cafeterias and dining halls to anybody with a university identification. We could even bring a friend if we cared to.

Now that I looked, Mags had tension lines around her eyes and hair that could have used some tending. But we were all of us a little ragged in those days of sun and horror. People kept glancing downtown, even though we were inside and not near any windows.

The Indian lady who ran the facility greeted us, thanked us for coming. I had a really nice gumbo, fresh avocado salad, a soothing pudding. The place was half empty and conversations again were muted. I told Mags about Mrs. Pirelli's son the night before.

She looked up from her plate, unsmiling, said, "I did not imagine Jennie Levine," and closed that subject.

Afterwards, she and I stood on Washington Place before the university building that had once housed the sweatshop called the Triangle Shirtwaist Factory. At the end of the block, a long convoy of olive-green army trucks rolled silently down Broadway.

Mags said, "On the afternoon of March twenty-fifth, 1911, one hundred and forty-six young women burned to death on this site. Fire broke out in a pile of rags. The door to the roof was locked. The fire ladders couldn't reach the eighth floor. The girls burned." Her voice tightened as she said, "They jumped and were smashed on the sidewalk. Many of them, most of them, lived right around here. In the renovated tenements we live in now. It's like those planes blew a hole in the city and Jennie Levine returned through it."

"Easy, honey. The university has grief counseling available. I think I'm going. You want me to see if I can get you in?" It sounded idiotic even as I said it. We had walked back to the library.

"There are others," she said. "Kids all blackened and bloated and wearing old-fashioned clothes. I woke up early this morning and couldn't go back to sleep. I got up and walked around here and over in the East Village."

"Jesus!" I said.

"Geoffrey has come back too. I know it."

"Mags! Don't!" This was something we hadn't talked about in a long time. Once we were three and Geoff was the third. He was younger than either of us by a couple of years at a time of life when that still seemed a major difference.

We called him Lord Geoff because he said we were all a bit better than the world around us. We joked that he was our child. A little family cemented by desire and drugs.

The three of us were all so young, in school or recently out of it and in the city. Then jealousy and the hard realities of addiction began to tear us apart. Each had to find his or her own survival. Mags and I made it. As it turned out, Geoff wasn't built for the long haul. He was twenty-three. We were all just kids, ignorant and reckless.

As I made excuses in my mind Mags gripped my arm, "He'll want to find us," she said. Chilled, I watched her walk away and wondered how long she had been coming apart and why I hadn't noticed.

Back at work, Marco waited for me. He was part Filipino, a bit of a little wise-ass who dressed in hip downtown black. But that was Monday 9/10. Today, he was a woebegone refugee in flip-flops, an oversized magenta sweatshirt and gym shorts which had been made for someone bigger and more buff.

"How's it going?"

"It sucks! My stuff is all downtown where I don't know if I can ever get it. They have these crates in the gym, toothbrushes, bras, Bic razors, but never what you need, everything from boxers on out and nothing is ever the right size. I gave my clothes in to be cleaned and they didn't bring them back. Now I look like a clown.

"They have us all sleeping on cots on the basketball courts. I lay there all last night staring up at the ceiling, with a hundred other guys. Some of them snore. One was yelling in his sleep. And I don't want to take a shower with a bunch of guys staring at me."

He told me all this while not looking my way. I understood what he was asking and was touched by his trust and vulnerability. He'd read a novel I'd written about addiction and being a gay boy in Boston. He'd told me he'd been abused sexually by an older kid and I know how it seeps into everything.

"You want to take a shower at my place, crash on my couch?"

"Could I, please?" Marco had been by my apartment a few times to fix my computer. I'd let him stay one night when he managed to lock himself out of the loft he had sat that summer.

This could be a pain. But everyone in the city was looking for some way to help in the disaster. Remembering Geoff and seeing Mags, I wanted to do what I could for someone else. The kid's pride and confidence had been broken and it would be painful to see him hurt any further.

So I took a break, brought him around the corner to my apartment, put sheets on the daybed. He was in the shower when I went back to work.

He woke up that evening when I got home. In the back of my closet I'd found hospital scrubs dyed black and too small for me. I thought they'd be pajamas for Marco. He loved them, wore the scrubs when we went out to eat. Hip twenty year olds do not normally stick close to guys almost three times their age. This kid was shaken.

We stood at the police barricades at Houston Street and Sixth Avenue and watched the traffic coming up from the World Trade Center site. An ambulance with one side smashed and a squad car with its roof crushed were hauled up Sixth Avenue on the back of a huge flatbed truck. NYPD buses were full of guys returning from Ground Zero, hollow-eyed, filthy.

Crowds of Greenwich Villagers gathered on the sidewalks clapped and cheered, yelled, "We love our firemen! We love our cops!"

The firehouse on Sixth Avenue had taken a lot of casualties when the towers fell. The place was locked and empty. We looked at the flowers and the wreaths on the doors, the signs with faces of the firefighters who hadn't returned and the messages, "To the brave men of these companies who gave their lives defending us."

The plume of smoke downtown rolled in the twilight, buffeted about by shifting winds. The breeze brought with it for the first time the acrid smoke that would be with us for weeks afterwards.

Officials said it was the stench of burning concrete. I believed, as did everyone else, that part of what we breathed was the ashes of the ones who had burned to death that Tuesday.

The shifting wind brought swirls of dust, pieces of burned Trade Center paper in the gutters and up onto the sidewalks—ghosts and little gods.

Bleecker Street looked semi-abandoned with lots of the stores and restaurants still closed. The ones that were open were mostly empty at nine in the evening when we walked home.

Marco's eyes were tearing. I hugged him. Getting him through this was what would get me through it. "It'll be okay."

I don't drink anymore and Marco was underage. But I figured a little booze wouldn't hurt him. I asked, "If I buy you a six-pack, you promise to drink all of it?" He nodded.

At home, Marco asked to use the phone. He spoke in whispers to a guy named Terry and a girl named Eloise. In between calls, he worked the computer.

I played a little Lady Day, some Ray Charles, quite a bit of Haydn, stared at the television screen. The president had pulled out of his funk and was coming to New York the next day.

In the next room, the phone rang. "No. My name's Marco," I heard him say. "He's letting me stay here." I knew who it was before he came in and whispered, "She asked if I was Lord Geoff."

"Hi, Mags," I said. She was calling from somewhere with walkie-talkies and sirens in the background.

"Those kids I saw in Astor Place?" she said, her voice clear and crazed. "The ones all burned and drowned. They were on the General Slocum when it caught fire."

"The kids you saw in Astor Place all burned and drowned?" I asked. Then I remembered our conversation earlier.

"On June fifteenth, 1904. The biggest disaster in New York City history. Until now. The East Village was once called Little Germany. Tens of thousands of Germans with their own meeting halls, churches, beer gardens.

"They had a Sunday excursion, mainly for the kids, on a steamship, the General Slocum, a floating fire trap. When it burst into flames there were no lifeboats, the crew and the captain panicked. By the time they got to a dock over a thousand were dead. Burned, drowned. When a hole got blown in the city, they came back looking for their homes."

The connection started to dissolve into static.

"Where are you Mags?"

"Ground Zero. It smells like burning sulfur. Have you seen Geoffrey yet?" she shouted into her phone.

"Geoffrey is dead, Mags. It's all the horror and tension that's doing this to you. There's no hole..."

"Cops and firemen and brokers all smashed and charred are walking around down here." At that point sirens screamed in the background. Men were yelling. The connection faded.

"Mags, give me your number. Call me back," I yelled. Then there was nothing but static, followed by a weak dial tone. I hung up and waited for the phone to ring again.

After a while, I realized Marco was standing looking at me wide eyed, slugging down beer. "She saw those kids? I saw them too. Tuesday night I was too crazy to even lie down on the fucking cot. I snuck out with my friend Terry. We walked around. The kids were there. In old, historical clothes. Covered with mud and seaweed and their faces all black and gone. Terry couldn't see them but I could. It's why I couldn't sleep last night thinking I'd gone crazy."

"You talk to the counselors?" I asked.

He drained the bottle. "Yeah, but they don't want to hear what I want to talk about."

"But with me..."

"You're crazy too. You understand."

The silence outside was broken by a jet engine. We both flinched. No planes had flown over Manhattan since the ones that had smashed the towers on Tuesday morning.

Then I realized what it was. "The Air Force," I said. "Making sure it's safe for Mr. Bush's visit."

"Who's Mags? Who's Lord Geoff?"

So I told him a bit of what had gone on in that strange lost country, the 1960s, the naïveté that led to meth and junk. I described the wonder of that unknown land, the three-way union. "Our problem, I guess, was that instead of a real ménage, each member was obsessed with only one of the others."

"Okay," he said. "You're alive. Mags is alive. What happened to Geoff?"

"When things were breaking up, Geoff got caught in a drug sweep and was being hauled downtown in the back of a police van. He cut his wrists and bled to death in the dark before anyone noticed."

This did for me what speaking about the dead kids had done for Marco. We got to talk about our ghosts.

Friday morning two queens walked by with their little dogs as Marco and I came out the door of my building. One said, "There isn't a fresh croissant in the entire Village. It's like the Siege of Paris. We'll all be reduced to eating rats."

I murmured, "He's getting a little ahead of the story. Maybe first he should think about having an English muffin."

"Or eating his yappy dog," said Marco. A bit of the wise-ass was back. He wore the black scrub suit, said he'd see me later.

At that moment, the authorities opened the East and West Villages, between Fourteenth and Houston Streets, to outside traffic. All the people whose cars had been stranded since Tuesday began to come into the neighborhood and drive them away. Delivery trucks started to appear on the narrow streets.

In the library, the huge television screens showed the activity at Ground Zero, the preparations for the President's visit. An elevator door opened and revealed a couple of refugee kids in their surplus gym clothes clasped in a passionate clinch.

The computers around my information desk were still fully occupied but the tension level had fallen. There was even a question or two about books and databases. I tried repeatedly to call Mags. All I got was the chilling message on her answering machine.

In a staccato voice, it said, "This is Mags McConnell. There's a hole in the city and I've turned this into a center for information about the victims Jennie Levine and Geoffrey Holbrun. Anyone with information concerning the whereabouts of these two young people, please speak after the beep."

I left a few messages asking her to call. Then I called every half hour or so hoping she'd pick up. I phoned mutual friends. Some were absent or unavailable. A couple were nursing grief of their own. No one had seen her recently.

§

That evening in the growing dark, lights flickered in Washington Square. Candles were given out and lighted with matches and Bics and wick to wick. Various priests, ministers, rabbis and shamans led flower-bearing, candlelit congregations down the streets and into the park where they joined the gathering Vigil crowd.

Marco had come by with his friend Terry, an elfin kid about his age who was staying with someone he didn't like. We went to a 9/11 vigil together. People addressed the crowd, gave impromptu elegies. There were prayers and a few songs. Then by instinct or some plan I hadn't heard about, everyone started to move out of the park and flow in groups through the streets.

We paused at street lamps that bore signs with pictures of pajama-clad families in suburban rec rooms on Christmas mornings. One face would be circled in red and there would be a message like, "This is James Bolton, husband of Susan, father of Jimmy, Anna and Sue, last seen leaving his home in Far Rockaway at 7:30 AM on 9/11." This was followed by the name of the company, the floor of the Trade Center tower where he worked, phone and fax numbers, the email address and the words, "If you have any information about where he is, please contact us."

At each sign someone would leave a lighted candle on a tin plate. Someone else would leave flowers.

The door of the little neighborhood Fire Rescue station was open, the truck and command car were gone. The place was manned by retired firefighters with faces like old Irish and Italian character actors. A big picture of a fireman who had died was hung up beside the door. He was young, maybe thirty. He and his wife, or maybe his girlfriend, smiled in front of a ski lodge. The picture was framed with children's drawings of firemen and fire trucks and fires, with condolences and novena cards.

As we walked and the night progressed, the crowd got stretched out. We'd see clumps of candles ahead of us on the streets. It was on Great Jones Street and the Bowery that suddenly there was just the three of us and no traffic to speak of.

When I turned to say maybe we should go home I saw for a moment a tall guy staggering down the street with his face purple and his eyes bulging out.

Then he was gone. Marco whispered, "Shit, he killed himself." Terry looked around unable to see what we did. Over the years I've gotten used to stuff like this. But usually I keep it at bay.

At some point in the evening, I apparently had said Terry could spend the night in my apartment. He couldn't take his eyes off Marco. On our way home, way east on Bleecker Street, outside a bar that had been old even when I'd hung out there as a kid, I saw the poster.

It was like a dozen others I'd seen that night. Except it was in old-time black and white and showed three kids with lots of hair and bad attitude: Mags and Geoffrey and me.

Geoff's face was circled and under it was written "This is Geoffrey Holbrun, if you have seen him since Tuesday 9/11 please contact..." and Mags had left her name and numbers.

Even in the photo, I looked toward Geoffrey who looked towards Mags who looked towards me. I stared for just a moment before going on but I knew that Marco had noticed.

Saturday 9/15

My tiny apartment was a crowded mess Saturday morning. Every towel I owned was wet, every glass and mug was dirty. It smelled like a zoo. There were pizza crusts in the sink and a bag of beer cans at the front door. The night before, none of us had talked about the ghosts. Marco and Terry had seriously discussed whether they would be drafted or would enlist. The idea of them in the army did not make me feel any safer.

Saturday was a workday for me. Getting ready, I reminded myself that this would soon be over. The university had found all the refugee kids dorm rooms on campus.

Then the bell rang and a young lady with a nose ring and bright red ringlets of hair appeared. Eloise was another refu-

richard bowes

gee, though a much better organized one. She had brought bagels and my guests' laundry. Marco seemed delighted to see her.

That morning all the restaurants and bars, the tattoo shops and massage parlors were opening up. Even the Arab falafel shop owners had risked insults and death threats to ride the subways in from Queens and open their doors for business.

At the library, the huge screens in the lobby were being taken down. A couple of students were borrowing books. One or two even had in-depth reference questions for me. When I finally worked up the courage to call Mags, all I got was the same message as before.

Marco appeared that afternoon dressed in his own clothes and clearly feeling better. "You were great to take me in."

"It helped me even more," which was true.

He paused then asked, "That was you on that poster last night wasn't it? You and Mags and Geoffrey?"

When I nodded, he said. "Thanks for talking to me about that," and hugged and kissed me. It felt like I'd accomplished something.

§

I was in a hurry when I went off duty Saturday evening. A friend had called and invited me to an impromptu "Survivors' Party." In the days of the French Revolution, the Terror, that's what they called the soirées where people danced and drank all night then went out at dawn to see which of their names were on the list of those to be guillotined.

On Sixth Avenue a bakery that had cupcakes with devastating frosting was open again. The Avenue was clogged with honking, creeping traffic. A huge chunk of Lower Manhattan had been declared open that afternoon and people were able to get the cars that had been stranded down there.

The bakery was across the street from a Catholic church. And that afternoon in that place, a wedding was being held. As I came out with my cupcakes, the bride and groom, not real young, not glamorous, but obviously happy, came out the door and posed on the steps for pictures.

Traffic was at a standstill. People beeped "Here comes the bride," leaned out their windows, applauded and cheered, all of us relieved to find this ordinary, normal thing taking place.

Then I saw her on the other side of Sixth Avenue. Mags was tramping along, staring straight ahead, a poster with a black and white photo hanging from a string around her neck. The crowd in front of the church parted for her. Mourners were sacred at that moment.

I yelled her name and started to cross the street. But the tie-up had eased, traffic started to flow. I tried to keep pace with her on my side of street. I wanted to invite her to the party. The hosts knew her from way back. But the sidewalks on both sides were crowded. When I did get across Sixth, she was gone.

Aftermath

That night I came home from the party and found the place completely cleaned up with a thank you note on the fridge signed by all three kids. And I felt relieved but also lost.

The Survivors' Party had been on the Lower East Side. On my way back, I had gone by the East Village, walked up to Ninth Street between B and C. People were out and about. Bars were doing business. But there was still almost no vehicle traffic and the block was quiet.

The building where we three had lived in increasing squalor and tension over thirty years before was refinished, gentrified. I stood across the street looking. Maybe I willed his appearance.

Geoff appeared in the corner of my eye, his long ringlets of dark hair, his smooth face dead white, staring up, unblinking, at the light in what had been our windows. I turned toward him and he disappeared. I looked aside and he was there again, so lost and alone, the arms of his jacket soaked in blood.

And I remembered us sitting around with the syringes and all of us making a pledge in blood to stick together as long as we lived. To which Geoff added, "And even after." And I remembered how I had looked at him staring at Mags and knew she was looking at me. Three sides of a triangle.

The next day, Sunday, I went down to Mags' building, wanting very badly to talk to her. I rang the bell again and again. There was no response. I rang the super's apartment.

She was a neighborhood lady, a lesbian around my age. I asked her about Mags.

"She disappeared. Last time anybody saw her was Sunday, 9/9. People in the building checked to make sure everyone was okay. No sign of her. I put a tape across her keyhole Wednesday. It's still there."

"I saw her just yesterday."

"Yeah?" She looked skeptical. "Well there's a World Trade Center list of potentially missing persons and her name's on it. You need to talk to them."

This sounded to me like the landlord trying to get rid of her. For the next week, I called Mags a couple of times a day. At some point the answering machine stopped coming on. I checked out her building regularly. No sign of her. I asked Angelina if she remembered the two of us having dinner in her place on Wednesday 9/12.

"I was too busy, staying busy so I wouldn't scream. I remember you and I guess you were with somebody. But no, honey, I don't remember."

Marco was much involved with Terry and Eloise. When I asked if he remembered Mags' phone call, he did but maybe didn't want to think about that.

Around that time, I saw the couple who had wanted to take their kids down to Ground Zero. They were walking up Sixth Avenue, the kids cranky and tired, the parents looking disappointed. Like the amusement park had turned out to be a rip-off.

Life closed in around me. A short-story collection of mine was being published at that inopportune moment and I needed to do publicity work. My old lover and best friend Marty Simonson made it a point to come back and visit New York in its crisis and we spent some good time together.

Mrs. Pirelli did not come home from the hospital, but went to live with her son in Connecticut. I made it a point to go by each of the Arab shops and listen to the owners say how awful they felt about what had happened and smile when they showed me pictures of their boys in Yankees caps and girls in jelly shoes.

It was the next weekend that I saw Mags again. The university had gotten permission for the students to go back to the downtown dorms and get their stuff out. Terry and Eloise and Marco came by my library office and asked me to go with them. So I volunteered.

Around noon on Sunday 9/23 a couple of dozen kids and I piled into a university bus. It was driven by George Robins, a Jamaican security guard who had worked for the university for even longer than I had.

"The day before 9/11 these kids didn't much want old farts keeping them company," Robins said to me. "Now they all want their daddy." He led a convoy of jitneys and vans down the FDR drive, then through quiet Sunday streets and then past trucks and construction vehicles.

We stopped at a police checkpoint. A cop looked inside and waved us through.

At the dorm, another cop told the kids they had an hour to get what they could and get out. "Be ready to leave at a moment's notice if we tell you to," he said.

Guard Robins and I as the senior members stayed with the vehicles. The air was filthy. Our eyes watered. A few hundred feet up the street, a cloud of smoke still hovered over the ruins of the World Trade Center. Piles of rubble smoldered. Between the pit and us was a line of fire trucks and police cars

richard bowes

22

with cherry-tops flashing. Behind us the kids hurried out of the dorm carrying boxes. I made them write their names on their boxes and noted in which van the boxes got stowed. I was surprised, touched even, at the number of stuffed animals that were being rescued.

"Over the years we've done some weird things to earn our pensions," I said to Robins.

"Like volunteering to come to the gates of hell?"

As he said that flames sprouted from the rubble. Police and firefighters shouted and began to fall back. A fire department chemical tanker turned around and the crew began unwinding hoses.

Among the uniforms, I saw a civilian, a middle-aged woman in a sweater and jeans and carrying a sign. Mags walked towards the flames. I wanted to run to her. I wanted to shout, "Stop her." Then I realized that none of the cops and firefighters seemed aware of her even as she walked right past them.

As she did, I saw another figure, thin, pale in a suede jacket and bell-bottom pants. He held out his bloody hands and together they walked through the smoke and flames.

"Is that them?" Marco had been standing beside me. I turned and found him staring at Mags and Geoff. Terry was back by the bus watching Marco's every move. Eloise was gazing at Terry.

When I turned back Mags and Geoff had disappeared into the hole in the city.

"Be smarter than we were," I said.

And Marco said, "Sure," with all the confidence in the world.

23

Chapter Two

Gradually I gave up the search for signs of Mags Mc-Connell. None of her friends had seen or heard from her since before 9/11. She was listed as missing, presumed dead. Her family wouldn't talk to anybody—especially not to someone whom they remembered from bad times past. That winter her landlord cleaned out Mags apartment.

Maybe I'd seen ghosts. Maybe I was just an unreliable witness. But Marco had spoken to Mags on the phone, glimpsed her and Geoff from a distance. We shared a certain eldritch strain and he remembered what he'd seen and heard.

Marco found a better job on campus and left the library. We stayed in touch, went out to lunch. Things with Eloise and Terry were strained. When he talked about that I felt for the kid and had my own memories to deal with.

In spring, on the first afternoon when the sun held real warmth, I was in the Farmers' Market at Union Square. Bright flowers were on sale. People strolled without coats and white boys were back in shorts.

I saw two heads of flowing hair, one light, one dark, gauzy clothes floating on the breeze. My first thought was Mags and

Geoff but these two evoked memories from before Geoff or even Mags. The words "Witch Girls" sprang from wherever they had hidden in my memory.

By the time I focused, they had crossed 14th Street and blended into the crowd without giving any sign of having noticed me. But images from deep in childhood came flowing back.

All these years later I can still see them gliding over the grass amid the fireflies of a July evening when I was four. The summer of 1948 is the first piece of time I can remember as a coherent whole and not just a series of disconnected images. That evening I saw magic and told no one.

A couple of my parents' friends ran a summer theater in Ithaca in upstate New York. They hired my father as box-office manager and he, my mother and I spent a summer there. My mother had stopped acting by then and my brother Gerry hadn't yet been born.

My bedroom window that summer looked out on a backyard with trees. Where we lived in Boston my third-floor window overlooked an alley and beyond that a barn for the Hood's Milk delivery horses. On an embankment behind the barn were the New York and New Haven railway tracks.

One night that summer in Ithaca crickets chirped, the trees sang in the wind and women in long chiffon dresses walked silently over the grass. I knew they were the Witch Girls and stayed very still so they wouldn't see me.

Those figures were a memory that popped up later in my childhood to jerk me awake as I fell asleep. From as early as I can remember, while drifting off, I'd be afraid that the me who awoke would be a different person with no memory of one who'd fallen asleep.

In my early teens the Witch Girls returned when I drank or got stoned and had started to doze. They remained a minor chill in a life that had some good-sized ones and weren't a thing I much dwelled on until my last year of college. The first person I told about them was a psychiatrist, Dr. Maria Lovell. She was French. Her husband was a controversial electronic music composer. Many of her patients were artists.

It was the winter of 1965. I'd just turned twenty-one and was in my second to last semester of a somewhat dented college career.

"I remember when I was four years old looking out my window one night and seeing these women in diaphanous dresses drifting across the lawn under these old trees," I said.

Dr. Lovell was a Jungian and so actually displayed some interest in what I told her. "Who were they?" she asked.

"When I first saw them they were characters in a play called *Dark of the Moon* that got put on in a summer theater my parents were with. It's about a witch boy who's in love with a human girl and becomes human to marry her. They used a lot of old folk songs in it."

To illustrate this, I sang a verse I'd recently re-learned, set to the tune of "Barbara Allen." When I came to the line "Pining to be human," Maria Lovell gave a quizzical smile.

"There were two witch girls who wanted to break up the marriage," I said. "That's who I saw under the trees. Even though I knew the actresses who played the parts and had been in their dressing room and everything, this was very scary."

"You dreamed this when you were small?"

"No, I saw it out the window when I was small."

"Your parents were in the theater?"

"When I was small."

"Do you remember other things from that summer?"

"I remember all the plays in the repertory. One was *Abe Lincoln in Illinois*, which is about his life before he went to Washington. There was a scene where Lincoln read to his youngest son Todd. The kid who was supposed to be Todd got sick or something and they wanted me to do the last performances. All it involved was sitting on Lincoln's lap.

"The actor was a man who went on to play the father in *Lassie* on television. He was nice but I didn't want to do it. My parents were okay and didn't force me. But there was this fire engine I wanted, all red and plastic with little firemen hanging on the back and a ladder that went up and down.

"So that was how it came about. I sat on the actor's lap and he read something aloud. I wore a costume with long stockings that itched but I didn't scratch my legs. I was supposed to have a line but instead of me one of the kids playing my older brothers said it. I sat and didn't look at the audience just like I'd been told. And the last night when the curtain came down for that scene, the stage manager had the fire engine for me."

"Was that before or after the Witch Girls?"

"They were at the start of that summer. Abe Lincoln was at the end, as I remember."

"So you made your debut."

"My only performances; I've never set foot on stage since."

She made a note. "Next week at this time?" She never asked where I got the money to pay her and I never told her.

My writing teacher had referred me to Dr. Lovell after I told him that I'd secretly dropped compulsory ROTC and gym. Without four semesters of each I couldn't graduate from college.

On my first visit Dr. Lovell asked why I'd done that and I said, "Because one day in the gym last spring, the cadet officer of my ROTC platoon and his friends jumped me as I came out of the shower, called me a faggot and slammed me against my locker. Guys I knew stood around watching! I can't go back."

"It is all right to cry, you know," she said and pushed a Kleenex box across her desk. My eyes burned and I blew my nose but I didn't cry in those days.

"Those young men's problems with their own sexuality led them to attack you while you were nude and vulnerable," she said. "How did you come to study to be a soldier?"

"That's what happens to boys who lose scholarships at good schools. When I flunked out of the first college I attended it got decided that a couple of years of close order drill would straighten me out. The alternative was getting drafted. I know I'm supposed to serve, all the men in my family did. But I don't think I'd survive a week in an army barracks."

"I've seen many soldiers," she had said, shaking her head, "You are not one."

Friday afternoons that winter, without telling my family, my friends or anyone else, I came into Manhattan from Long Island and talked to her. At that time a psychiatrist on one's schedule was a sign of sophistication.

Her office was in the East Seventies. Walking fast, I headed down Third Avenue in my black winter raincoat, chinos and penny loafers. After I flunked out of my first college, first my old man and then the Army Reserves had kept me in extremely unhip crew cuts. Now I was growing my hair like an English rocker. But freedom felt precarious.

Boston where I'd grown up was a town compared to this city. Third Avenue was a cruising zone on a Friday afternoon. Guys stood casually on street corners, paused significantly in doorways, gave sidelong glances. Eyes tracked me from the windows of the bird bars: *The Blue Parrot, The Golden Pheasant, The Swan.*

I went into a place in the mid-Fifties. It was dark and quiet before the weekend began. Piaf sang on the jukebox. A couple of men in suits at the far end of the bar stopped talking when I came in. The bartender was big and bald. He looked me over and said in a weird little girl voice, "You should try Rhonda's."

"I have a draft card." The legal drinking age was eighteen but in straight bars I always got carded. Sometimes they refused service because they thought my card was phony and I was underage. Gay bars were much less fussy and the patrons could be generous.

The first gay bar I ever went to was one in Boston called something like the Sugar Bowl. A couple of friends talked me into it so I lied to my parents. I was sixteen and the Boston drinking age was twenty-one. They wouldn't serve me but didn't care if guys gave me their drinks. The place got raided. I was slapped around by the cops but not arrested. My parents pretty much locked me up when I got home.

Five years later, I said, "Scotch and water," and reached for my wallet.

He waved the card aside and watched me put the whiskey away in a swallow. When I went to pay for it, he shook his head and poured me another. "You're new?"

I nodded.

"Honey, I'd love to have you around but management doesn't want kids in here."

I hit the street a bit later with a glow on and the bartender's telephone number in my pocket.

Down the Avenue at Fifty-Third and Third was a world famous chicken run. Boys, some a lot younger than me, stood in canvas sneakers and thin jackets, waited under awnings. Hostile and wary, they stared at me out the windows of Rhonda's Coffee Shop and knew just who I was. I had done what they were doing: got run up against walls by guys who wanted sixteen year olds who looked thirteen.

That afternoon I'd told Dr. Lovell about the Witch Girls because they'd been on my mind lately. It was also to turn the conversation away from the scary stranger with unblinking eyes who had stopped me in a South Boston subway station when I was thirteen.

On my second visit she'd asked me when my sex life got started. So I told her how the stranger took me to a place he knew, opened my clothes, blew me as I stood transfixed, gave me five dollars, said I was a good kid and to forget this had ever happened.

The next time I saw his face was on the front page of a newspaper. He had killed two brothers a little younger than I was. The last time I saw him was in the papers when he got murdered in jail.

Dr. Lovell constantly came back to the imprinting that had made sex a habit like drugs and booze. This stirred up anger and pain that deeply disturbed me.

At Grand Central I caught the crosstown shuttle, took the A train down to vast, doomed Penn Station which was already slated for destruction and half deserted.

Then I headed back to school in a Long Island Railroad car full of ladies with shopping bags from Macy's and Bloomingdale's.

The plays I'd seen that summer in Ithaca at age four were clearer in my memory than ones I'd been to that semester.

My Sister Eileen had two women from Ohio living in a cellar apartment in Greenwich Village. At the last-act curtain the brick fireplace collapsed and a man wearing a miner's helmet with a lighted lamp on it poked his head out of the debris and said the Sixth Avenue subway was going to be built right through their living room. One matinee I was brought into the back of the playhouse just so I could see the marvelous fireplace fall down one last time.

At the train station I caught the shuttle bus to the campus. The commuter school was mostly deserted on that February evening. A few lights burned in offices. A stray faculty member with a briefcase walked to his car. A pair of uniformed cadet officers strutted past. Guys like them had tried to make it impossible for me to graduate.

Suddenly I was back in the mire of a strange and seedy commuter college that had both a major drama department and two years compulsory ROTC and gym for all male students. I turned a corner and lights were on in the playhouse; rehearsals were underway.

The Witch Girls, one dark, one fair, stood on the front stairs smoking and shivering in the chill. Each had her long hair tied back and wore a black leotard, a scarf and a diaphanous black top that flowed about her when she moved. The Theater Department's main stage play for March was going to be *Dark of the Moon*.

They waved when they saw me. The girl playing the dark witch and I found each other amusing. "You a Witch Boy," she called in a low, sexy voice, "and you always gonna be one."

Mags McConnell was the Fair Witch. She watched my approach through slitted eyes. "I got ways," Mags said in the phony Ozark accent everyone had started using on stage and off and blew smoke in my face. "I can turn you into a human boy." We all laughed.

Mags was a star drama student. She and I had known each other since I began hanging around the Theater Department on my lonely first semester at the college.

At first her disdain was monumental. I'd heard she called me "a little boy in ROTC drag." Mags amused friends by pointing me out when I had to run sprints in gym shorts or wear a humiliating freshman beanie because I couldn't transfer enough credits to be a sophomore. But I understood she was watching.

I dropped gym and ROTC and people began saying she had the hots for me. Mags was a year and a half older and a girl going after a younger guy of uncertain sexuality was an oddity even in the Theater Department.

But she was campy, sex with a woman was something I could do and the idea of a girlfriend seemed safe when other things didn't.

That night inside the theater, work lights shone on the stage. Cast members sat scattered throughout the house. Professor Cortland, the Drama Department chairman, who was directing this production, stood down front talking to the techs.

Marty Simonson sat towards the back of the house. Cortland had made sure the cute boys in small parts were all barefoot and in bib overalls with the legs rolled above the knees. "God, you look fetching," I whispered just to see him blush.

Cortland looked my way briefly as I came down the aisle and up onto the stage. "So glad you could join us," he said.

I picked up the prompter's copy of the script. The theater was the only interesting spot on campus. To get credit for a drama minor, I had to do things like this each semester. The first time I read the play I'd been startled by the power of my childhood memories.

Cortland said. "Places. Rehearsal starts in five minutes."

The first scene has John, the Witch Boy, asking the Conjure Man, a kind of backwoods wizard, to turn him into a human. The Witch Boy was a tall senior with a dazzling smile who went on to star in several popular cigarette and deodorant ads on television.

The Conjure Man was Carl Ryman who even at twenty-one was losing his hair but who owned whatever stage he stood upon. Five years out of school he would have his own Off-off Broadway repertory company of transvestites and manly women in a rat-infested loft on Lower Second Avenue.

The Conjure Man repeatedly says that John is a Witch Boy and always will be and is never going to change even if he marries a human girl. Everyone in the company but Professor Cortland, so deep in the closet he didn't get the joke, now said Witch Boy and Human Boy instead of gay and straight.

Holding the script through a dozen rehearsals had stripped away most of the magic. But at moments like Carl's performance or when the spiteful Witch Girls were on stage I was four years old and sitting enthralled beside my mother.

I tried to stay slightly ahead of the cast, gave them lines when one occasionally glanced my way. But my mind wandered and sometimes when the actors blew a line, I missed it too. Cortland was not happy.

After rehearsal I sat in a student beer bar between Mags and Marty, laughing as Carl Ryman said, "The barest hint that you're a Witch Boy and Cortland will take you on a camping trip to the Catskills so he can show you how the birds and the chipmunks engage only in Human Boy behavior."

Mags took my hand and I let her. I'd have held Marty's hand under the table if he'd offered but he didn't and I never made the first move with guys. Mags had to leave early. I walked her out to her car. In her freshman year at Swarthmore she had a nervous breakdown and spent a few months in a hospital. This college specialized in bright, damaged kids like us who washed out at the good schools where we started and had to transfer here.

"You want to get together Sunday afternoon?" she asked as we kissed good night. I shook my head. It drove her crazy that I'd never say why I wasn't available Sundays. "We could invite Marty," she said. "He's almost as good-looking as you." She gave me a Benzedrine tablet, which I washed down with the beer I carried.

Quite a bit later Marty drove me home because I currently had no car. He'd been a last minute transfer to the college because tuition and board for Penn State disappeared when his mother and stepfather split up.

I'd seen him on his first day at school, this beautiful kid newly divested of his hair and civilian clothes, wearing that ugly uniform and a lost, scared look.

I fell for him but in those days guys had to proposition me and Marty was eighteen and naïve. So we stayed friends.

We stopped in a secluded back road along the way and shared a joint. "Mags wants to turn both of us into human boys," I said and cracked up at his wide-eyed expression. The joke between us was that because he was taller and needed to shave more, people mistook me for the innocent one.

Apparently he drove me home because I found myself making my way around to the back door of my parents' split-level.

I shared a bedroom with my younger brother in what otherwise would have been the rec room next to the garage.

As I turned the corner into the back yard I saw figures in flowing garments. They moved towards me across the lawn. By the light of a big Long Island half moon that looked just like a stage contrivance, I saw that they had no faces.

I gasped and sat up in bed in my Jockey shorts. My brain was still soft with booze and drugs. In the other bed Gerry stirred and turned over in his sleep. He'd kicked off his covers and lay in his briefs. Everyone said we looked alike. Maybe this was like seeing myself asleep. I got up and covered him. Still asleep he said, "Thank you."

Five years younger, Gerry was now taller than I was. A couple of years before a woman in a store had said, "You're twins, right?"

Happy at being taken as my age he replied, "Yes, but not identical."

The woman asked, "Who was born first?"

Not nearly as happy, I said, "It was a difficult birth. I came out five years before he did."

A light was on upstairs in the kitchen. I smelled cigarette smoke. One of my parents was awake.

I hoped it wasn't my father. On a snowy Sunday morning that January I awoke in bed bare-assed with no memory of how I got there. According to Gerry I'd staggered in at three in the morning so encrusted with snow, so stoned and incoherent that our father had pulled the clothes off me, smacked me around and dumped me in the bed.

Embarrassing, but at least I didn't remember it. My old rust bucket, though, had died for good a half a mile from home and things were still cold and distant between my father and me.

Tonight my clothes were strewn on the floor, which meant I'd gotten myself undressed. Chances were it was my mother awake. So I put on a robe and went up to the kitchen. She sat at the table doing the *Times* crossword puzzle. The clock said it was just past four. She glanced at me, quizzical, unsmiling, and beautiful. It seemed to me that she must understand exactly what I'd been up to.

"Couldn't sleep?" she asked. "I heard you come in about an hour ago." That I'd awakened her was unspoken but a given. She slept lightly.

"Who were you with?" she wanted to know.

"Marty drove me. You've met him."

She said nothing, drew on her Phillip Morris. My parents smoked but I didn't much—not cigarettes anyway. Again she gave me the look.

"I was thinking about Ithaca," I said and kept my voice low as I tried to change the subject. My father, my sisters Lee and Polly and my youngest brother David were asleep upstairs. "Especially the Witch Girls," I added.

She nodded and finally half smiled. "You loved them. You didn't understand much else in that play but when anyone talked about it, you'd say, 'Oh, them Witch Girls!' Everybody loved you doing things like that."

"Did you want to come and see *Dark of the Moon*?" I asked my mother. She never went to see plays anymore. Rarely went out.

"Not if you don't have a part in it," she said and turned back to her puzzle.

"I'm writing now," I said and she nodded. She wrote too—had done scripts for local television back in Boston when I was a kid. My parents had moved down here the fall I started college. When I bombed out of school I joined them and became a city kid lost in the suburbs.

Saturday morning, I was up on a few hours sleep amid a maelstrom of brothers and sisters who needed rides to friends, to art or music lessons. I had to beg for a lift to my part-time job as a stock boy in a shopping center, a bothersome child who couldn't grow up. That with my late hours and short answers earned me dark parental looks.

I remembered that faraway summer when they were in their twenties and we three were walking on a quiet Ithaca street. They were joking about something and my mother pretended to run away. My father first mimed pursuit and then, shrugging, gave up.

Both of them laughed and when they did, I laughed too. They turned to look at the windows of the surrounding houses, saw someone who had been watching duck back behind a curtain and burst out in laughter again.

Sunday afternoon after I'd had to go to church and sit through family dinner, I hitchhiked over to Will's place in Massapequa. Even when I had a car I traveled that way. He liked the idea that I wasn't old enough to have a driver's license and was saving money to enter college.

When I'd met Will on the Fire Island ferry the summer before last I'd told him a story about a strict father and the military school I attended. When I said I was a sophomore he assumed that meant high school and I hadn't contradicted him.

Sometimes looking young bothered me and I felt trapped in perpetual childhood. But usually I played to it.

His house was in a development kind of like the one I lived in. Will was maybe forty and seemed safe. His camera was all set up on a tripod. A photo of me on that ferry in short pants and a striped jersey was up on the wall. Certain guys noticed when I wore clothes my mother bought me.

"Get everything off," he said as soon as I was in the door and helped me do that. Even when expected, forced nudity made me go away mentally. Everyone from my father to Subway Man to the army knew instinctively how to run this game on me.

From some remote place I saw Will make this kid with an erection and blank expression put on a pair of hi-top Keds and hold a basketball. I watched like it was a stranger's school nudity nightmare.

Once Will had the snapshots, the action moved to the couch. He rubbed my neck, took his time, and ran his hands over me.

I thought of Marty and Paul Newman while Will worked my cock, got off between my legs but not in me. He went down on me, but I didn't on him. I could set limits because my story was I was underage and not gay.

All of a sudden he flipped me over and began slapping my ass hard. He'd started doing this recently. It was way too close to my actual life. I yelled and managed to squirm away.

He was amused, paid an extra ten dollars. "Your daddy doesn't give you birthday spanks?" It was dumb to get dependent on him. But I had the money I needed and a bit more.

§

That Friday Dr. Lovell asked, "What is your earliest memory of violent assault? I don't mean sexual necessarily."

The question surprised me. I thought about it and an image came to me of an August evening with the light going away.

"That summer I told you about, the summer at the theater, is the first time I remember aggression. A kid hit me with a rock.

"I was with some kids my age playing and one pointed up and said, 'Look!' I looked and coming slowly down the slope from the yard behind was this boy who had been sneaking up on us."

Dr. Lovell asked, "Who was he?"

"A kid who, I guess, was a year older than me, a big deal when you're four. His father was the local District Attorney. Our parents wanted us to be friends. Until that summer I'd never been let out to play with other kids. My playmates were all my parents' friends—actors, grad students. None of them had children. They'd sing, act out stories, do funny voices, listen enraptured when I talked.

"To me this boy was sinister and I shied away from him. Kids, like all animals, sense fear in others and he came walking down the slope from the next yard, slowly, smiling this big scary smile. I think he had the rock in his hand already.

"The twilight was behind him. I stood, rooted. Maybe he expected me to run and when I didn't, he stopped a distance away. Still uphill from me he let fly. The rock hit me on the top of the head."

I rubbed the spot. "It still feels like there's a scar."

Dr. Lovell got up and came around the desk. She was a tiny person and made me lower my head to look and touch. "The fontanel, your skull bones, would have closed by that age," she said. "This seems like a normal skull contour. There is, though, on the spot you touched, a small patch of almost white hair. What happened next?"

"I ran inside crying. I was awake that night and it felt like the inside of my mouth was swollen. Once I must have dozed and saw my father at the end of a long hall with a cartoon whirl of cats and dogs fighting like a wreath all around him."

She leaned back against her desk directly in front of me. "Before I left Europe I was a pediatrician. Were you taken to a doctor?"

"Yes. I remember the waiting room and feeling like everything, the toys and kids and mothers were spinning. I behaved badly, crying and not wanting to be touched. He shot something into my butt, I remember, and said I had a concussion."

"Childhood concussion is hard to diagnose. But that is what I would have said." She sat behind her desk again. "And later you saw the Witch Girls."

I thought for a moment. "All that happened after I saw the Witch Girls, not before."

"And did you see them again that summer?"

"No. Not once that play had ended its run." Then I told her about the recent dream in which they'd had no faces.

"Those Witch Girls could be what we call your Anima," she said, "Your vision of your female unconscious, in a way your soul. I'm sorry you don't see their faces."

That Saturday night was the final performance of *Dark of the Moon*. The party afterwards was at a bungalow on the water in

Long Beach. Rents were cheap in the off-season and lots of the theater kids lived there.

Dietrich and Lenya sang on the record player, the bathroom was thick with marijuana smoke, only same-sex couples were allowed to dance. Mags had Marty off in a corner. His ears were bright red. He cast looks my way like he wanted me to save him.

Mags then talked to another woman and took me aside. "Janette says she and Claudia are going away tomorrow and we three can have their place in the afternoon."

"I'm busy," I said.

"She was really mad," Marty said later, trying to be cool.

"We'll make it up to her." Because I was stoned, I kissed him and he almost steered off the road.

§

Sunday was drizzling and cold. A nice boy, bareheaded and thumbing, appealed to motorists. I got picked up and driven almost to Will's door. It was early when I flicked drops off the top of my hair and rang his bell.

I heard footsteps, thought I heard voices and knew enough to be wary. Will greeted me, started to pull my raincoat and everything else off. But that would mean I couldn't leave. On the coffee table was a barber's clippers, a pair of frilly panties, handcuffs and other stuff. Intended for me, I knew.

I backed up. "Who else is here?"

Will grabbed my belt. The door to the kitchen opened and a big guy in a sweat suit, smoking a Marlboro, stood looking at me like I was a lamb chop.

I heard him say, "Will thinks you're a naughty boy who lies about his age." His laugh sounded like an old car engine trying to start. He moved my way fast, "Time we turned you into a nice girl." My belt got unbuckled.

But I still had the door open behind me. I butted Will and bolted backwards, broke his hold, got out on the porch. "Come back here, little boy!" the guy said as I stumbled down the walk, pulling my pants up. "We'll make it worth your time."

Walking home in the rain, I was angry that they thought I was that stupid and angrier still that I probably was. A nice old lady driving a 1950 Nash Rambler, the kind that looked like an upside-down bathtub, drove me all the way to my parents' door. She warned me never to go out without an umbrella and rubbers.

§

That Friday I had just enough cash for one more session with Dr. Lovell. She asked me why as a kid I never told my parents or anyone else what had been done to me. The answer that came blurting out was, "I knew they wouldn't love me if they knew."

"A compartmentalized life is one of the penalties that come with keeping so many secrets," she told me.

"I have a girlfriend now," I said. "There's a guy I really like. I think I'm going to be okay." I didn't tell her how I lost the source that paid for the visits or how horny that had left me.

She doubtless knew more of what was going on inside me than I did. "You almost epitomize the molested child. Some aspects of life you know very well. In others you are immensely naïve. We will stay in touch. I will give you a letter when you need it for the army. We will meet here again before long."

§

That night I was more than available when Mags asked if I was busy Sunday. Her friends let her have their apartment and I brought along Marty.

We were all a bit dazed and amazed by booze and grass. We all lost our clothes and started giggling. Mags and I got turned on by the scene but Marty was shy. We each tried to lead him but he was uncomfortable.

That spring Mags and I fucked just often enough that I thought I might be partway human. Marty and I kind of stopped talking.

That May on the Saturday night after the end of the semester the family was asleep and I was down in the cellar sipping a beer, chewing a couple of Benzedrine, pounding the old Royal typewriter. This was my father's office and I was allowed to use it when he didn't. I wrote:

The Kid's eyes were dead from the camera sucking the soul out of him even before the cameraman hit him on his bare ass with the spike-load of junk so he was cold cocked and helpless when the shining metal recruiting sergeant came into the room and dragged him away from the bright lights and the Kid's head lolled back as he moved and he saw all the pictures of boys like him upside down on the walls before and after they got stripped and stunned.

One photo of a boy still in leathers and jeans looked just like the Kid and the eyes in that photo watched as the two men gagged and bound the Kid like a piece of meat wrapped him in a roll of canvas and carried him out to the van that waited in the garage. As they did that the boy in the photo shook himself loose and came sliding down the wall like a small grey ghost that got bigger as he moved across the shooting floor drew a blade that did not reflect the light and was human size as he headed after the men making off with his physical body.

Mags had graduated and was apprenticing at a regional theater in Minnesota. Marty was working out in Montauk that summer wondering, as he told me later, why I only liked Mags when he had such a crush on me. But he did begin sending me postcards.

My parents were delighted that I'd gotten on the Dean's List and helped me buy a little blue Plymouth Valiant. I had a cashier's job at the World's Fair.

Problems loomed but they were months away. Right then the night was mild and to someone raised in New England, Long Island was almost the tropics. Around here college boys wore shorts a lot and I was in them for the summer.

This always pleased my mother. I think she believed my problems started when she let me wear long pants. Out in the yard I walked barefoot on the grass. It seemed like a moment for the Witch Girls. But they never came when I expected them.

richard bowes

Chapter Three

By the end of the spring semester of 2002 the World Trade Center had begun to be part of New York's mythology and things started to get dated as having happened before then or after 9/11.

Around then Marco came around while I was at the Science Reference desk to say goodbye. He'd done his time in New York, things with Eloise and Terry hadn't worked out and finishing school in southern California seemed attractive.

At a university you get used to kids leaving but this was more of a wrench than most. I was losing a bit of my past, my last living link to Mag's and Geoff's ghosts. As we kissed goodbye he whispered, "Thanks for showing me that being a little off the beat is not the end of the world."

Work at a public service desk for as long as I did and you become a kind of landmark. I was about to tell Marco how much I'd miss him when a woman appeared and said, "They were sure downstairs that the white-haired guy up here could help me. Are you him?"

Marco laughed and told her, "Yes, he is. And this is how I want to remember him."

About then I was asked to contribute to an anthology of original speculative-fiction stories. The editor hinted that a New York setting would be appropriate.

I recalled an image I'd seen in maybe my first visit to the East Village. My last year of school, I was in the city a lot.

Greenwich Village was old and full of legends and ghosts. Across town in the East Village the myths were just taking shape, ghosts-to-be still lived and walked the streets.

The remembered image was a girl, real young, looking anxious and eager, sitting on the curved metal stairs that led from the pavement to the second floor of a building on St. Mark's Place.

Instinct told me she was waiting for a boyfriend and I got turned on imagining what it would be like to have anyone want me as much as she obviously wanted whoever it was.

A few years later, she was famous as the girl in *the* iconic East Village sex, drugs and rock triangle. By then she'd become a minor hobby of mine and we were briefly, not intimate, but close enough that she told me parts of her story, including what she was doing that fine spring day.

Later on she used other names: Judy Light, Judy Icon. But when I first saw her she was still Judy Finch. Back then she was growing up on St Mark's Place, which is kind of an alias for the three blocks of Eighth Street between Third Avenue and Tompkins Square Park.

Writing her story, I used a mix of research, remembrance and improvisation: to stuff she told me I added things I heard, things I witnessed and things I guessed.

On that spring day in 1965, Judy was fifteen and had what she thought of as her first real boyfriend. She was blue eyed and what we called dirty blond when I was a kid. The boy who called himself Ray Light had dark hair, brown eyes, was a year older and a bit taller. But their hair was the same length and some days, without planning it, they dressed almost identically.

Sitting on a sunny neighborhood stoop they blended into each other, his head resting on her shoulder, her denim-clad legs draped over his, one passing their last cigarette to the other.

Ray Light was not his real name. He'd chosen it just after running away from home. When he talked about that, Judy saw him sitting on the edge of a loading dock in Ohio, waiting for a guy, any guy, to start him on his way to New York City.

What little I know about telepathy, I mostly learned from Ray and Judy. And I can see how on first encounter it's easy to mistake for personal insight or that special connection we have with someone we love. Judy thought that being able to see into his mind was another sign they were a couple.

Before death and afterwards Ray fit a pattern, a style I shared in some ways. And I could pretty easily fill in his iconic first trip to this city.

The thin, jumpy man, who picked him up first, before getting down to business, asked his name. Instead of boring Jonathan Duncan which he'd been called since birth, out came Ray Light. Later it occurred to both Ray and Judy that this had been prophecy.

Ray came from a nice suburb of Cincinnati. His family hadn't expected a son who wore long hair and wanted to paint, to dance, to play music. It varied from day to day.

When he talked about this, Judy thought his plans were kind of hopeless. She had some idea how these things worked. Her father was the conceptual sculptor Jason Finch. Her mother was the essayist and critic Anna Muir. She was going to study acting.

Ray lived with a guy he called the Man who locked Ray out of his loft on East Fourth Street every morning as he went to work and let him back in when he came home. When she thought about his situation, something deep inside Judy ached.

Ray had just said, "I'm going to ask the Man to lend me the money to buy a guitar," when she looked up and found this other kid standing there waiting for them to notice him.

"You got a match?" the kid asked and wiggled an unlighted Camel. Ray handed him matches and looked right into his face. Judy gave him the once-over.

He lighted up with a little flourish, handed back the book of matches and said, "The name's BD." They told him their first names. He said he'd just moved into the neighborhood and wanted to know where he could hear music. They told him there were hootenannies in Washington Square and folk rock in little cafés in the East and West Village.

When he asked, "Is there some place I can score grass?" they both shook their heads, and when he didn't walk away they got up and did just that.

Later they compared notes and both knew immediately that this kid was from the halfway house. His institutional haircut, washed out T-shirt, sneakers and jeans were like a uniform.

The halfway house on St. Mark's Place near First Avenue was a place for teenage boys whose parents were enmeshed in the legal system or in the hospital or somehow couldn't or wouldn't take care of them. They followed a type—white, skinny, a little in shock—and they got held there until they could finish high school and go on to college or more likely the army. Vietnam was just starting to heat up.

"Is he a narc?" Judy wondered.

"If he's not in the halfway house, he's got one hell of a cover," said Ray.

They walked by Judy's place. Her father's studio occupied the ground floor of a building on the south side of St. Mark's near the corner of Second Avenue. A few years later Judy showed me the interior. The first floor had once been a barn when it was a tradesman's house, and a horse and cart were kept there. The barn doors had long ago been cemented shut and had windows cut into them.

Her mother was away a lot. She was in Madison that week leading a seminar on the works of Kate Chopin. Because her father's studio was too crowded to give him the needed space, he had started to spend a lot of his time upstairs in the living room. He'd rolled up the rug to expose the gleaming parquet floor and had a row of bricks toppled like dominoes in an S-formation. He was working out the exact shape and dynamics of the fallen bricks. There were scrapes on the parquet floor. The building had been bought with her mother's money.

Today Jack Moore, from the Museum of Modern Art, was there, smoking a cigarette and sipping a scotch. He smiled and said hello to Judy, looked twice and nodded at Ray.

Jason Finch was forty and looked thirty. He wore a denim work shirt and work boots. When he worked with bricks, with electric wiring, with pipes like in his last piece, Jason Finch always began to act and sound like a blue-collar worker, a union man doing what he got paid to do.

"Hey," he said to Judy while scribbling notes on the back of an envelope. "Did you do that science paper?"

"I finished it in study period and handed it in," she said though she hadn't and Jack Moore, with his broken nose, chuckled.

I knew Moore by sight. In fact late in his life I refused an offer of money to lure him to his doom. Finch I met at a party some years after that. The subject of his daughter didn't come up.

"We're going to watch television," she said. Her father nodded vaguely. One rule bound Judy and Ray's time in the house. She couldn't have him in her room with the door closed.

Ray let her take the lead. They kissed long and hard, as on the screen an actor dressed like a mailman talked to a clown who spoke by holding up voice balloons with words written on them. She switched channels and in another city in the late afternoon, a bunch of boys in three-button jackets and narrow ties and girls in short skirts and long hair danced like it was Saturday night.

The two of them danced a little, giggled and ground against each other. Her father and the critic laughed in the living room.

Another rule limited their time together. Ray had to leave a little before six to be home for the Man. Judy found this tragic and romantic. She usually walked him over to Fourth Street.

That day he wanted to leave a little early and chose to take a roundabout route. Usually Ray never wanted to go near the halfway house. That evening he insisted they walk down St. Mark's Place.

Against a brick wall in the twilight, neighborhood boys—some still in parts of their Catholic school uniforms—played handball, Ukrainians against Poles.

Across the street kids from the Halfway House leaned on the railings in front of their building and watched. They didn't even speak to each other, much less form teams of their own. Each stood apart from the others and watched the passersby. Behind them, through the ground-floor windows, Judy could see lights on in the dining hall. Ray glanced their way casually but Judy knew he was looking for BD.

The Man lived over on East Fourth Street between Bowery and Second Avenue on the top floor of a loft building that was still mostly factories. Judy, when she first met Ray a couple of months before, would go by there at night and look up at the lights in the windows. That evening they kissed and hugged a few doors down from the place where he lived.

"You were looking for BD," she said.

"I think he's a spotter," Ray told her.

"What?"

"Someone who looks for runaways," he said, gave her one last kiss and went inside to ring the bell and be allowed upstairs.

Judy stared after him not breathing. She'd never heard him refer to himself as a runaway. For a moment when he'd said it, she'd seen an image of a figure running down the middle of a highway late at night, headlights blasting past him in both directions. And she knew that was his image of himself.

Walking along thinking about that, Judy let herself float on the surface of the city, on the deep smoke of a Ukrainian sausage factory, on a tall woman in tights, a dance skirt and straight black hair carrying dry cleaning in one hand and a trumpet case in the other, on fire engines blasting up the avenue and the feel of a stray evening sea breeze that hadn't yet picked up city soot and grease.

She was on St. Mark's Place, walking past the Dom, the big old Polish wedding hall, when someone said, "Hi." And there was BD right in front of her with a cigarette in his mouth.

Judy told me that it occurred to her later he probably followed them to where Ray lived and then doubled around to casually encounter her there.

"You're going to be late for dinner," she said, indicating the halfway house.

"As long as I'm on time for lights out they don't care," he said not missing a beat nor in any way surprised that she knew where he lived.

They stood for a moment amid the Slavs and Spanish who came out of the rumbling subway and off buses on their way home from work, students and poets and shambling winos and a pair of old hookers with minds like confetti walking to their beats up on Fourteenth Street. The guy who called himself Mr. William Shakespeare and who dressed in a velvet doublet and red tights went past them speaking blank verse to himself.

BD said, "You live around here?" and she nodded vaguely in the direction of her house. "With your parents?"

The way he asked made her feel for him a bit. She said, "Mostly with my father, right now."

"What does he do?"

"These days he's mostly a bricklayer."

"That's good work," he said. "My father worked delivering The Daily News. He got sick and died and I had a choice of living with family I don't like or coming here."

Judy was surprised that he spoke better than she'd heard him do earlier and that he told her about himself like that. Afterwards for a long time she would never fully trust him. But right then, she said goodbye and once indoors thought quite a few times about how his nose was just a little flattened and his T-shirt read in faded letters Police Athletic League Golden Gloves.

She attended the Quaker high school on Stuyvesant Park, eight blocks up Second Avenue from where she lived. Next afternoon when she came out of there at the end of the day, Ray stood across the street.

He had one foot up behind him and leaned against the antique iron spiked fence that ran around the park, smoking a Marlboro, glancing at passersby. Seeing him in that hustler pose it struck her for the first time how lost he looked.

Judy remembered when she'd just met Ray and he'd talked about the Man. She had seen through his eyes a tall open window. Felt the handcuffs on his wrists, the cold cement window sill on his bare feet, the terror of the eight-story drop and the cement below.

She crossed the street and took Ray's arm as they walked through Stuyvesant Park. She thought about how he always waited for her to take the lead and imagined this was what he did with the Man.

"That guy BD isn't in the halfway house," he said. "I went by there this morning and asked, and none of the kids had heard of him.

"I knew I was taking a risk. One of the counselors spoke to me. Acted like he thought I'd come in looking for shelter. He's queer. Told me they took in runaways. Tried to stop me from leaving and started dragging me to the showers before I got away." Judy saw it all as he spoke.

They went arm in arm past the Eastern Rite church and strange little stores that shipped packages to Eastern Europe, and stayed on the other side of Tenth Street from the gang of psycho, speeding Italian kids who hung around that corner.

He was shaking. They sat on a bench in the St. Mark's in-the-Bowery churchyard and she held him. "They know I'm here," he said. "This morning when I left the house I saw BD, whoever he is, right down the street. They're going to try and take me back home. My father will institutionalize me."

Ray didn't want to hang around the neighborhood that afternoon. So he and Judy walked in a wide loop over to Greenwich Village, through Washington Square, past coffee houses and Italian clubs, down streets lined with buildings full of sweat shops, past garages and places you could buy live chickens to kill. I could see it all when Judy told Mags and Geoff and me the story.

All the way, he talked about what he was going to do. He'd tell the Man what happened, get as much cash as possible and split. He'd call her when he was on his way and maybe she could meet him and they'd say goodbye.

It was like the center of her world was about to disappear. She offered to hide him in her house, to get her parents' friends to help him.

But he refused. She saw Ray reflected in a mirror wearing just a bathrobe and with his head shaved standing in what looked like a hospital or prison corridor. It was the first time Judy had seen his future. They both knew this was what could happen to him.

Both were crying and it was almost dark when they set foot on his block. Nothing was happening: a woman pushed a baby carriage, a super hauled trash to the curb, a couple of drag queens sashayed toward the Club 86 near Second Avenue.

They walked to his door and he turned to kiss her. "I've never known anybody like you. You're part of me. You can see what I'm thinking. You're the only reason I've stayed here."

The door to the building opened and a guy who had been waiting in the hallway came out and grabbed Ray. The car must have been right around the corner because it appeared and stopped directly behind them. The men were big but they didn't hurt anybody. Two of them cuffed Ray and carried him despite his yelling and thrashing to the back seat of the car.

The third blocked Judy from interfering. Deflected her hands, booted aside her kicks. "You shit-head," she screamed.

"Now, miss, you shouldn't talk like that," he said and grinned. Then he turned and jumped into the car and they tore off down the street.

Judy ran after the car, tried to remember the license but couldn't. She felt Ray's rage and fear. His face was shoved into the seat, his pants got pulled down. A needle was stuck in his butt.

After that he slipped like water through her fingers as she stood on the corner and tried to hold him in her mind and heart. For an instant she had a glimpse, a vision, of three figures against a background of what looked like Technicolor amoebas writhing under a huge microscope.

Judy became aware that a background noise was a man screaming, "I'll kill you sons of bitches! Bring him back! He's radiant! He's the future!"

People on the street who had barely noticed the abduction, stared up at the building. She looked and

richard bowes

saw a guy with wild hair and eyes, leaning out his window staring at where the car had gone. Judy knew this was the Man, remembered her glimpse of Ray naked on the window sill and hated him with everything she had in her.

She ran home wanting to lock herself in her room, and her mother was there. So were Randolph Crain and Evelyn Killeen, an old married couple, stage actors whom Judy had always liked.

Her father was down in the studio and there was the sound of an electric saw. Her mother was standing on the stairs telling him to come up because they had guests and it was rude. Randolph and Evelyn were saying they understood. And Judy went past them with her hands over her face, ran upstairs and slammed the bathroom door.

Her mother tried to talk her out. "Honey, I know I've been away and you felt abandoned. But tell me what's wrong so I can help you."

"I'm not your child!" she yelled.

Her father tried next, all quiet emotion as befit an honest workingman. "Judy, tell me who it was that hurt you."

"You couldn't see the one I love when he was in front of you!"

It was Evelyn Killeen who came so silently to the door that Judy didn't know she was there until she spoke. "You lost your young man, honey." Her voice was uncannily youthful. "I read that in you when you rushed past me just now."

Some years later Judy found exactly those lines when she read for the part of Norah, the older sister, in the 1930s romantic comedy September Fancy.

That night though, bundled up in her bathrobe, she told her story to all of them amid tears and hiccups.

Later she heard her mother downstairs in the living room say clearly, "You let her hang around where she could get kidnapped."

Then her father mumbled something unclear. And her mother said, "Your family. They're deranged enough. Your parents told me I was unfit to be a mother."

"<u>My</u> parents! Your old man looked like something out of the wax museum."

"His money was good enough to buy this damn place."

The next morning when Judy was on her way to school, her father was heading out the door at the same time as if by coincidence. And, like it was the most normal thing imaginable he walked to school with her.

And she was so lonely because Ray wasn't there that she let him do that.

BD was on the corner of Second Avenue. The sight of him angered Judy so much that she told her father who he was and how she knew he had turned Ray in.

That afternoon her mother came to the school and took her daughter out of study hall. She had packed two suitcases and said Judy was going on a little vacation with Randolph and Evelyn at their house out in Buck's County.

She was too surprised and distraught to properly protest. Next came her parents' filing for divorce, then a move with her mother to Cambridge, Massachusetts, after which Judy found herself in school in Vermont. It was a couple of years before she heard from Ray, and even longer before she got more than a glimpse of St. Mark's Place.

Chapter Four

The summer Ray and Judy each went into captivity was my last as a student. Just before Labor Day, I was summoned to the ROTC building to explain how I intended to deal with my course requirements. In the building I found a bunch of my fellow shirkers stripped, shorn and looking ready for their sacrifice to the Volcano God.

Cadet officers yelled at me to come back in a regulation haircut. Scared and angry I stormed out the door of the building and realized I was being followed. I turned and found Freddie Ayers, a sophomore I'd met in a playwriting class.

He shook his head at the trap he'd almost fallen into but was a bit overawed that we were in the same boat. I was a senior and an object of curiosity and gossip. Freddie had dark hair too fine to lose, a nice build and tan, a bit of a Greek vase profile.

"We can find better stuff to do," I told him and led the way to a student hangout. We had a few beers and he explained that he'd managed to dodge his obligations with doctors' notes but now was out of excuses.

In the parking lot we smoked a little grass and took my car back to the house. My brother Gerry was at work. That week my parents had taken my sisters and little brother off on a tour of some historic site. Gerry and I both had jobs and got to stay behind. Mostly we behaved ourselves.

Freddie was hot and interested but unable to lead. Visits to Fire Island had gotten me past that and in short order he was in the rec/bedroom out of his clothes and on the bed. He was impressed with my full-body tan. It was mostly boy sex: cock play and the dry hump.

My brother came home to find us sacked out and had no problem with it. The Beach Boys played high summer music on WABC. We made a messy dinner and got even more stoned. We showed Freddie the South Farmingdale District water tower looming over the rooftops, lights flashing like a dozen pairs of big red eyes blinking.

"We're going to make a movie," Gerry said. "Rock the camera back and forth and it will look like the thing is moving."

Gerry slept upstairs on the couch. Freddie and I had the bedroom. Next morning with the Kinks playing in the background, Freddie, an only child, watched wide-eyed as my brother and I laughed, joked, straightened out the house before we dressed. The family would return later that day.

Especially he watched Gerry. Driving him back to his car I said, "My little brother is straight," smiled and made it a joke.

He nodded. "I know but I'd give anything to have a brother or sister, especially one like that. You are so lucky." I just shrugged because I was cool.

§

That autumn a letter from Dr. Lovell got me past both the college psychiatrist who was very nice and a U.S. Army colonel who chewed me out but waived two semesters of ROTC. I celebrated by driving to a deserted beach and snorting half a bag of heroin.

Freddie Ayers had seen enough of the college and transferred to NYU. He was living on Avenue A in the East Village.
I started crashing with him weekends, buying grass and speed
and selling them at school.

One Saturday night in the short days of December I awoke
in what I was told was St. Vincent's Hospital in Greenwich
Village with no wallet or I.D. and no memory of who I was or
why I was there.

In the small hours of the night an old nun came around and
talked to me about how Dylan Thomas had died on the floor
just below the one we were on. She said, "I wonder if you too
are a young man who has an uneasy relationship with death."

She scared me enough to jump-start my memory. Things returned—like when they asked if I had a doctor, I remembered
Marie Lovell's face and then her telephone number and gradually other stuff came back. But I never caught a recollection of
how I'd gotten the cut on my head or how the police found me
mostly undressed on a cellar floor. Luckily I also had none of
the drugs Freddie later told me I'd been carrying.

Family and friends appeared but Marty was the big surprise.
He volunteered to come into the city and drive me and my car
home. Marty found my little Plymouth and helped me into the
shotgun seat.

"I grabbed this chance even though you don't want me
around," he said and looked like he was afraid I'd tell him to go
away. I surprised us both by laying my head on his chest and
crying. My breath came like I'd run a race.

What we did was fast, intense and very Long Island winter—
in cars on lonely roads with the lights off, the heater running
and our bodies tangled in the back seat. Sex was a bit different
with someone I knew.

That February, I graduated and the diploma came in the mail.
In those simple days, a few stories in the college magazine, a
chaotic draft of a novel about a young kid who talked like
Rimbaud and wrecked the life of an academic poet, a recom-

mendation from my writing teacher, got me a literary agent though not a publisher.

My parents talked about moving back to Massachusetts but I knew what I wanted. With the diploma and a temporary draft deferment I wrangled a job as an apprentice fashion copywriter in the Garment District. Then I sold my car and moved into the city.

Marty drove me and my stuff to Freddie Ayers' place but looked unhappy, like he'd lost me forever. We were in the doorway, it was getting dark. I glanced around to see if anyone was watching then turned and kissed him hard. The first time I'd kissed a guy in public.

Marty I loved, but Freddie seemed more in keeping with my role as urban sophisticate. He didn't offer a lot of personal involvement. Maybe for the same reasons I didn't.

After I'd told him about my childhood he said, "My Subway Man was Mr. Bledsoe, a friend of my parents who ran the local boys' club. When I was ten, he started taking me in his office for 'private training.'"

I asked when it ended and he shook his head sadly, "When I hit puberty." Sharing our histories did not bring us together. Inevitably we quarreled and I moved into Anise's Place, a rambling crash pad/commune on East Tenth Street.

Five or six other people besides Anise and me stayed there. Psychedelics were the driving force. Trebizond the cat had achieved a high level of cosmic awareness and effectively ruled the place. At Anise's I managed to outrun the letters from my draft board.

My job meant that five days a week I dragged my ass out of the East Village smoke and madness and up to Seventh Avenue. In the Garment District the insanity was organized. Old copy editors smelling of cigarettes and gin snarled at me, "Cut fifteen characters out of the body, schmuck!"

Buyers shouted, "Double stitching is not as big a selling point as the sleek mod look, understand?" Randall, the art director,

richard bowes

a generous older guy, took me under his wing and asked for my company and night-work once or twice a week.

My agent wasn't much older than I was and mainly wanted someone to go with her to parties. All her plans for my writing career involved prominent writers who were looking for boyfriends.

That summer at a book party at Scribner's on Fifth Avenue, she introduced me to James Baldwin. The bubble eyes which looked so strange in his photos were riveting in real life. He was charming and we kissed but left separately.

At the end of summer my parents moved back to New England. Gerry got a scholarship at NYU and stayed in the city.

That fall my Selective Service notices caught up with me and one bleak morning I found myself among several hundred other potential draftees shivering in our briefs at the Induction Center on Whitehall Street in Lower Manhattan.

The halls stank of tension and fear. For hours we got poked and prodded, gave up blood and urine, stood in lines. The army knew just how to screw with my head. I tried to keep in mind what I had to do and not turn passive. But it felt like I was in a car sliding endlessly out of control on ice.

I had letters from Dr. Lovell. If they didn't work I'd be shipped to Fort Dix that night. My clothes would be sent to my parents and the process of erasing me would begin.

Then I stood before a psychiatrist who sat behind a desk and read about the Subway Man and me, about how I had suffered incidences of traumatic head injury both as a child and just the year before and might have neurological damage, how I was a conflicted homosexual, a compulsive alcoholic and drug abuser—the story went on.

Dr. Lovell had described the contents to me, "To save you the trouble of opening the envelope and discovering you can't understand the jargon."

The shrink sneered as he wrote the permanent deferment and I wondered just how much he got off on having an endless

59

succession of scared, nearly naked young guys come through his door.

Afterwards in the locker room, my hands shook so much I had trouble getting dressed. A legend of the draft physical was the guy who flipped out to fool the army and ended up permanently crazed. I couldn't stop thinking about how someone else would have to go to war in my place.

Outside it was evening rush hour. I was too dazed to find the subway and wandered through unfamiliar streets. In the middle of a block a panhandler sat on the sidewalk looking at me with crazed eyes. For a moment I saw myself a few years down the line.

I called Randall, the art director and my sugar daddy, from pay phones until he got home and told me to come by. He opened and rebuttoned my clothes, which were on all askew, brushed my hair, took me out to dinner and got me gently but deeply drunk.

The next morning Randall decided I needed a shave, which in those days I really didn't. So I let him, which was kind of how things worked between us. He stood with his arms around a naked kid, who leaned into him as both stared at the lathered reflection in a mirror.

He found clothes that fit me and I was at my desk writing catalog copy at nine AM. But the feeling I was in a car sliding on ice stayed with me.

§

"Your description of me in that letter was awful," I told Dr. Lovell that Saturday morning.

"Understand that I put your problems in the worst possible light for the army. Now that bad episode is behind us we will begin work to make you better. What do you have to show me?"

I took out the creased notebook that was my journal and read. "Last night I had a dream I've had before. In it I came into the tiny cubbyhole that's my room and discovered a door

richard bowes

I'd never noticed. I pushed it open and found this large room with a view of a big backyard with trees."

Dr. Lovell waved her hand and smiled. "Darling, everyone in New York has dreams like that. It means only that you want a bigger place to live. With your new freedom you must get out of that drug commune."

She wanted me to cut down on my drinking, to stop doing drugs and find someone to love. Half witch, half grandmother was how I described her when people asked.

At a party in the Chelsea Hotel on a Friday night when I'd started drinking at lunch the day before, my agent introduced me to Arthur C. Clarke. He was British and was about to write the screenplay for a Kubrick movie. But he'd already found a young Asian boyfriend who was relatively sober.

So I ditched that party and went off with a couple of gay Australian rock musicians. The next thing I remember was being awakened at Anise's late Monday morning by an angry call from work asking where I was.

Dr. Lovell's office was on the ground floor of a big East Sixties co-op where she and her husband had an apartment upstairs. One Saturday morning after staying up the night before for a nine AM appointment, I arrived early and sat in the small waiting room.

It seemed there was a patient ahead of me. I heard a man in the office say, "It's utterly idiotic that I should be held accountable for every mistake some stupid sales clerk made. I signed the bill, thinking I was being charged the correct amount."

Her answer was too low for me to hear.

"And it infuriates me that you're taking their side," he said. The door to the inner office flew open and a beautifully dressed middle-aged guy with grey hair brushed back like a symphonic conductor's emerged. He carried a little dog under his arm.

Apparently unbothered that I might have overheard, he gave me one disdainful look and was gone. I recognized Ma-

61

ria Lovell's husband, the composer Reynolds Strand, and felt pretty sure his anger had been an act.

"Come in," she said and smiled when I did. "You see, my dear, that all relationships have problems from time to time."

At that session I told her, "The night before last I had the soldier dream again. It was pretty much the way I've told you before. I know in the dream that I'm a soldier and I carry a rifle but I'm wearing jeans and a sweatshirt. I'm in a neighborhood of old houses with big lawns that looks like the town outside Boston where my family moved. But there's no one around, no enemy, nobody. I'm on patrol and I know I'm alone on patrol all the time."

I paused. She said nothing so I added. "I understand that it's because I dodged the draft."

She nodded slightly. "We've talked about your feeling of guilt. Part of you feels worthless for being gay and for not letting the army take you. I know your father and all your uncles served. But I don't believe you would have emerged from that intact."

I said, "Yesterday, on my way to work, I went through Astor Place. There are people lined up along the wall of the Cooper Union panhandling. And I saw this bum I first saw on my way back from the physical. He was in rags, with overgrown stubble and crazed eyes. And I realized he's the kid in the dream except old and beaten."

"You mean you dreamed this? Or that you had seen this street person before and that he then appeared in a dream?"

I shrugged to indicate I didn't see what difference it made.

"An inability to distinguish between dreams and reality is called delusion. It can be fueled by psychotropic drugs and amphetamine. You must stop taking them or there is nothing that I can do for you!" Her voice rose. She looked angry.

"If the soldier in the dream, that lost kid in a deserted world, is me now," I said, "The guy on the street is me if I had been drafted."

"Yes," Dr. Lovell said quietly. Then she remembered she was angry. "You must stop doing drugs and drinking or that will be you in any case. What abuse did was to drive a wedge between you and your emotions. I am trying to help you reconnect and you are fighting me."

I agreed and looked contrite because I wasn't entirely sure what I'd seen and what I'd dreamed.

Something I didn't say was that I thought of her as a bit magical and somewhat out of a dream. I'd been told her story: she was a French doctor who fled to England in 1939 just ahead of the Nazi conquest of France. She wanted to get to the U.S. and couldn't until she heard about the actor Peter Lorre who was in London.

He was a junkie and the *Queen Mary*, on which he was to sail back to the U.S., insisted there be a medical person along to administer his morphine. She signed on for that and got to New York. Once here she married the composer Reynolds Strand, who was fourteen years her junior and already a bit famous.

If I could accept her as something out of an Ingrid Bergman movie, I didn't see why she had so much trouble with my dreams spilling over into my waking life.

I didn't stop doing drugs or drinking. I got fired after many warnings. Randall, my patron, shook his head and told me, "Honey, even I can't save you this time, but let's go to the American Ballet tomorrow."

We did. *Coppélia* with Carla Fracci and Erik Bruhn was as close to a gay event as was possible in the days before Stonewall. Dozens of rich, older men and the boys they escorted were in attendance. I was enthralled by the boy dubbed "The Downtown Ganymede." We slipped away to a men's room and had to be dragged apart by Randall and Danzig's patron, the critic St. Just.

After a week-long drug and booze marathon, I awoke, broke and unemployed, to the smell of morning grass at Anise's.

Randall helped me land a copywriting job at Flying Dutchman Promotions for much less than I'd been making. It was a bottom-rung agency with a brutal boss.

I stiffed Anise for my share of the rent and got on the wrong side of Trebizond the cat. I wound up in the Hotel Betsy Ross, a notorious old fleabag. The Betsy featured hot and cold running speed freaks, drag queens and Billy B, the son of a famous junkie writer.

Around then Randall had a heart attack. He'd been good to me and probably needed me around more than ever. But I was the wrong boy at the wrong time and wasn't there for him as much as I should have been as he died.

People rotated like distant planets right then. "I guess I'm not a very good ad for avoiding the army," I told Marty when he graduated and let himself get drafted.

My brother Gerry lived in a college dorm nearby. When we got together I knew my little brother was worried about me. But it was like I was drowning. Freddie Ayers reviewed for the *Village Voice* and moved in art circles. He liked Gerry but ignored me.

Then on Avenue B on a perfectly clear afternoon, someone said, "Hello, Witch Boy!" Mags McConnell had just moved back to New York and we fell into each other's arms.

In her apartment near Avenue A in the East Village she introduced me to her roommate. Geoffrey Holbrun was twenty-two when we met, a bit willowy, hair in ringlets, cute, funny and officially bisexual.

He went wide-eyed. "I've heard all about you. Miss Thing himself! You know where the drugs are, where the gay is!" There was no hint of tragedy on that wonderful day. I saw immediately how it would work: I was smitten with Geoff, he loved Mags and she loved me.

Within a couple of days I'd moved in. We were an East Village triangle in the summer the legendary one got assembled.

Chapter Five

Decades later, writing my version of the story of Judy Finch, Ray Light and BD the undercover led me to wander around the East Village. St. Mark's Place by the early twenty-first century had become a Japanese neighborhood. As yet no plaque marks the building where Judy, Jason Finch and Anna Muir once lived. Over on East Fourth Street nothing identifies the building where the Man once kept Ray Light in captivity. The city's best stories often are not what the city wishes to commemorate.

A couple of years after Ray's abduction but before I knew his story, that same man gave me what I still remember as the worst night of my life. As I stood on the corner looking up at what had once been his window, dust and debris swirled in the gutter. Looking down I thought I saw familiar faces, including mine.

Seeing the building on Tenth Street where Mags, Geoff and I had lived, I remembered the second time I saw Judy. It was late in the summer of 1968. The three of us had done acid with a bunch of people on Saturday night and sat the next morning smoking dope on our front stoop.

A stir made me look up at what I thought was a guy in black jeans and boots. I did a deeply buzzed double take and realized this was a girl, Geoff knew her, said, "Judy Finch!" in an awestruck whisper. We'd all heard bits of the tale of love and abduction.

Now the kid I'd once glimpsed on St. Mark's Place was back in the neighborhood, dressed like her old boyfriend. Their story wasn't over at all. She sat on the stairs. A small crowd gathered and she told us the private cop who fingered Ray Light was back in the East Village.

When she pointed him out later on I realized I'd already seen the guy called BD walking his dog. Over the decades I read enough and heard enough to add to what I'd seen and make the second part of the story about him.

§

That fall, BD returned to the city where he'd been born and raised, working in a neighborhood which he knew quite well. His cover name was Bobby Danton, simple and easy to remember.

BD was twenty-three, looked a couple of years younger, and could if necessary shave close, wear a shy smile, and pass for nineteen or even eighteen. It was a handy talent in his line of work.

So far his hair was only down to his ears. He'd grown a beard and mustache because it was hip and because he had worked here before and needed to hide his face.

Bobby Danton's stash of grass was top grade and he was generous with it. His employer had rented him an apartment in a second-story walkup on Seventh Street around the corner from Tompkins Square Park.

One Monday that October, he was having a little morning-after toss in bed with Rachel, a waitress from the Dom Bar on St. Mark's. They'd met the night before. He did some grunting, she moaned, and the noise attracted the attention of Marlene, the six-year-old German shepherd, who scratched at the door and barked three times.

When he came back from giving Marlene food and water and promising her a good long walk, Rachel was sitting up and lighting a joint. This morning she looked a little older than he'd guessed. "Your dog's a jealous bitch," she said but smiled nicely.

Aside from the big, second-hand bed, the room contained nothing but a used dresser with a lamp on it and a night table with a clock and a radio. "You don't go in for decoration," she observed, looking around and toking. "Most guys would put up a poster; maybe have a record or two lying around. This is what the artists call austerity."

He remembered that Rachel, with her curly dark hair and ripe body, was also an artist's model. In fact that's what had first made him interested in her. "You know Jason Finch?" he asked. "He does sculpture."

"Jason doesn't come around much any more. All the artists are up at Max's Kansas City. The Warhol crowd too. Last year Warhol rented that Polish wedding hall upstairs from the bar.

"He called the place the Exploding Plastic Inevitable. The Velvet Underground and Nico and all his other freaks were all over the place. Then, poof, he lost interest and they all went uptown. We still got plenty of freaks, just not those ones. How do you know Jason?"

He wanted to say "I knew his daughter," but realized that would be stupid. Part of BD's cover was that he studied architecture at Cooper Union. So he said, "We talked about him in class."

She nodded and pulled her stuff together, got up and went into the bathroom. She was heftier than he liked, a little older. But beer and gin and grass and a hit or two of hash laced with opium had smoothed the way.

While he waited for his guest to depart, he scratched Marlene's ears the way he'd learned she liked and listened to mandolins and guitars on a distant stereo and car horns blasting on the street outside.

Thinking about Judy Finch reminded him of his last tour in the neighborhood. Back then BD was twenty and just finished with his hitch in the army. The halfway house where he'd ended up when his family dissolved one day had been good preparation for barracks society.

College didn't interest him. He stopped by the house and a counselor who had known him when he was a resident said a private detective agency was looking for someone they could use for undercover work.

That was BD's job the day he was trailing Jonathan Duncan. Little Jonny had changed his name to Ray Light and started living with a chicken-hawk. He was sitting on a stoop making out with what looked almost like his twin but turned out to be a girl. They had an aura BD could still feel but couldn't describe even to himself. He was surprised they hadn't drawn a crowd.

When Rachel had gone, BD slipped a camera into his jacket pocket, clipped the leash onto Marlene's collar and left for work.

It was a beautiful morning with a lingering chill in the shadows and warmth in the sun. Marlene was almost prancing at the end of her leash. He had inherited her from another agent. They got along well and walking her was a great cover for being out and around.

On Avenue A, just inside the gates of Tompkins Square Park, was a lithe girl with vacant green eyes, in a ballet skirt, halter, sandals and maybe nothing else. She called herself Krazy Kid and he'd seen her couple of nights before at a loft party on Avenue C.

"Hey, dog man," she said.

He gave Marlene a sit command and she allowed herself to be petted. "How come your parents
named you Krazy Kid?" he asked and the girl
laughed quietly. He guessed that she was, maybe,
sixteen and he didn't even know her real name and
had no reason to believe that anyone was looking
for her.

All he knew was that she was sweet and the guy
he had seen her hanging onto was a scumbag. He
liked to imagine himself rescuing people.

For the last couple of years while his face faded
from local memory, his employers, Guardian Lamp
Investigations ("Lost and runaway children our
specialty and our mission"), had him out on loan to
a private eye firm in the upper Midwest.

The last place he'd worked was St. Paul, where
his name was Danny Bremmer and he was a clean-
cut army deserter, a simple boy from Erie, Penn-
sylvania, hiding out because he didn't want to go to
'Nam. One crash pad passed him along to the next
like he was a sacred relic and kids got snatched up
and returned to their families in his wake.

The Yellow Pages ad for the Midwest firm was
a drawing of a figure in what might almost have
been a cop's uniform shining a flashlight into an
alley where a teary-eyed, scared little girl huddled.
In fact, the last runaway child he'd helped return
(to a family of wealthy aluminum manufacturers
terrified of scandal) was a seventeen-year-old,
three-hundred-pound blob of fat with an insatiable
appetite for methedrine and for whores who'd sit on
his face.

When Krazy Kid said goodbye to the German
shepherd and then to him, he went to the dog run
and let Marlene off the leash. She bounded forward,
stopped, seemed to watch a slightly stubby dog with
some Doberman in him.

A little further down the fence, staring through
the dogs and trees and iron lamp posts of this
ragged-assed old fashioned park, looking like he

was gazing into the navel of the universe and was not pleased by what he saw, was a skinny black man with grey hair. He was dressed in ratty pin-stripe dress pants and a turtleneck jersey. On his head was a broken-down velvet Borsalino that must once have belonged to a pimp.

BD guessed that at one time Chambliss had been that man. Right now though what he did mainly was deal, shoot junk, and climb fire escapes to break into the apartments of people who went to work during the day.

BD moved down the fence, keeping his eye on Marlene like that was his concern. When he was close, Chambliss, without shifting his gaze, without moving his mouth, said, "That one you was interested in? Calls herself Aurora?"

Marlene was racing in an improvised pack up a dirt mound and down the other side. A woman called, "Regal!" to the Doberman mix.

Chambliss said, "She's in a political commune on Avenue B and Sixth Street, Southeast Corner. There's some commie dyke runs it. They got pictures on the windows of Chairman Mao. I seen Aurora out shopping at the bodega around the corner. She does that every morning."

A group of kids barefoot and in tatters came by ringing cowbells and chanting "Hare Krishna". A police cruiser sped across Seventh Street with its cherry-top flashing. The kids all screamed, "Pig!" and gave the cops the finger.

Chambliss said, "I gave you the lead. You owe me twenty."

"Friday." BD just breathed the word but compared to the other man's voice it felt like he was shouting. That was company policy; Chambliss got paid for the week on Friday.

Chambliss was silent for a long moment but BD knew he was going to speak again. He listened to the chants fading, to distant sirens, to the occasional yip and snarl from the dog run.

Then he heard, "I hear some queer dude last night was asking about undercovers. Says he knew one was working the neighborhood a few years back disguised as a halfway-house boy, calling himself BD. Wants to know what became of him."

BD always kept a twenty folded thin in his pocket. He had it in his hand as Chambliss pushed away from the fence. The guy seemed as if he might have something more to add.

Before BD could ask what that was, Marlene, bothered by Regal the Doberman mutt, took a bite out of the dog's shoulder as the two of them began snapping and snarling. The mutt's owner yelled her protest. As BD looked that way, Chambliss ambled past, his hands hung at his side. When he snapped up the twenty it was too fast for a human eye to follow.

§

BD's living room had a sofa and chair from Goodwill, a telephone, and not much more. Late that afternoon he sat on the couch with his feet resting on the chair and talked to his boss. He rolled a joint as he spoke.

"Aurora Sun?" he said. "Formerly Marilyn Friedberg of Greenwich, Connecticut? She's living at 93 Avenue B. I started charting her daily routine this morning.

"Yeah, I'm sure. She's stopped washing her hair and wearing dresses but it's her. The photos are on their way up to you."

BD paused, twirled the joint in his fingers and said, "I got a question. About an old case from early sixty-five. You remember a queer rich kid named Jonathan Duncan who called himself Ray Light? We put a snatch on him, returned him to the bosom of his family. I've got reason to think the little freak is back."

Marlene was stretched out on the floor. She raised her head and BD scratched her ears as his boss searched the files. It turned out that as far as Guardian Lamp Investigations knew nobody was looking for Jonathan Duncan. The boss wondered if BD had fond memories or something.

That made BD angrier than he expected to be. He said, "It was my job to return him. And I did it. I just wonder if he's back here and trying to fuck up our operation."

Again he listened to his supervisor. "I am sticking to business and not letting things get personal," he said. "Aurora will be packed for shipping by Wednesday. Thursday at the latest."

After he hung up and fired the joint, BD thought of Ray Light and Judy Finch on the stoop. He remembered how he'd risked blowing his cover for no reason at all when he went up and asked them for a match.

Later, on the day they'd planned to do the snatch, he'd tailed the two of them, called in his location from pay phones as they sat on benches with her holding him, traveled arm in arm in a wide arc through the city. He forgot to breathe sometimes, watching them.

Then they turned back toward Fourth Street and he knew they were headed to the spot where the snatch was set to go down. For a moment he wanted to catch up and warn them, to run off with them and be part of what they were. He'd rarely felt like that about a woman and never about a guy until then.

Instead he made the call and Ray Light got taken off the street, right on schedule. The next morning Judy's father walked her to school. The day after that she was gone.

That had been his first assignment. He was a lot more professional now and nothing like that had happened since. Tuesday he was up early staking out the address on Avenue B, confirming what Chambliss had said about Aurora Sun's morning schedule.

By that evening the Friedbergs had seen the photos of a barefoot waif in an oversized muumuu and confirmed that this was their daughter. The snatch was set up for the next morning. It was all going smoothly.

He started drinking that night at the Annex just up Avenue B from Tompkins Square Park. There he met some people he kind of knew and ended up at a loft party where the air was so full of pot and incense smoke that it felt like you needed to part it like beaded curtains. Something had been added to the grass. The walls were moving.

Then he saw what appeared to be Ray Light looking just as he had the day he got snatched. With Light was a crowd of very thin, pale and amused people who stared at him and made kissing mouths. All this I saw first-hand.

BD stared, wide-eyed, as Ray stepped forward. Only when the figure was right in front of him did he realize it was Judy Finch.

"How's it going, BD?" She was taller than he remembered and much thinner.

"The name's Bobby Danton," he said.

"Cut the shit, BD," she replied and smiled. "You've been asking about me. You want to know where I went? After you kidnapped Ray and then starting hanging around in front of our house, my parents thought I was going to be snatched. They were getting divorced and to keep me safe I got sent to an all-girl's school in fucking Vermont. Two and a half years of sub-zero hard time. Thanks to you."

She spoke in a loud clear voice that everyone around could hear over the music. Later he found out she was studying acting. The pupils of her eyes were like pinpricks.

"Doing a lot of meth?" he asked.

"Uh-huh. Another thing you need to answer for. Brought up in the East Village and the most I'd done was a couple of tokes of grass and a sip or two of daddy's booze. One semester at school and I had an extreme speed need."

She took out a matchbook, stuck it in his shirt pocket, and said, "This is Ray Light's number. He always talks about you being in that vision he had of our future. You need to call him." By the time he could react, she and everyone with her were gone.

A few years before when Guardian Lamp snatched Ray Light, BD was around the corner in a phone booth. He'd just made the call that set the operation in motion. The car with the kid face down in the back seat sped right past him.

For an instant it was as if BD was in Ray's head. In that moment he saw three figures: one in denim and short hair, one in leathers, one in flowing robes. They stood on a stage amid bright light and flowing color. He knew the three were Ray and Judy and him.

§

The next morning, BD and Marlene watched from a block away as Aurora walked to the local bodega. He gave the signal and a woman from Guardian Lamp came up behind Aurora while a man stepped in her way. She didn't even yell when they hustled her into the car that rolled up the street.

Then someone appeared and snapped a picture of them. A woman shouted, "Kidnapping pigs!"

"Nazis!" yelled a man and threw a beer bottle against the front window as the car jumped a light and sped away.

"Hey, Dog Man," said a familiar voice. BD turned and someone took his picture. Krazy Kid and her sleaze of a boyfriend were there. She spat at him. The boyfriend had a camera. He took another shot. BD went at them. Marlene snarled. They ran but not before getting one last shot of him and his dog.

When he got home, somebody waited across the street and watched him go in the front door. BD packed everything he owned into two suitcases. He looked out the front windows and saw a couple of guys standing in doorways on the block. He called Guardian Lamp.

"Someone talked," said the boss.

"Chambliss," said BD. The whole thing was a setup. He should have known that from the moment Chambliss said someone was looking for him.

"You trusted him too fucking much," said the boss. "I'll send a car around to pick you up. We got stuff to discuss."

The issue of the East Village Other with pictures of BD on the front pages and "Undercover Cop" in headlines hadn't yet hit the street and been reprinted in hippy enclaves everywhere. But BD knew that his career was over.

He waited downstairs in the front hall. When the car pulled up, he came out the door of his building. A guy stepped up to him saying, "Press. I'd like to talk to you." But Marlene with one growl and an aborted lunge took care of that.

No one else came near them. BD put his luggage in the trunk and got in the back seat with the dog.

A woman shouted, "That's him!" as the car pulled away. Someone took a picture. He took the matchbook with Ray Light's phone number out of his pocket.

BD remembered what Judy had called Ray's "vision." He knew like in a dream that the three figures were Ray Light, Judy Finch and him but wasn't able tell which one of them he was. BD understood that he was about to find this out.

Chapter Six

One midnight shortly after we met Judy Finch, Geoff, Mags and I were part of her entourage. We went up to Max's Kansas City to hear the Velvet Underground play. We three came in ripped and got nicely plowed.

Then I saw Frankie the Bug Boy who dealt the meth of death. I knew Frankie from when we both lived at the Betsy Ross Hotel and it struck me that this would be a nice way to top off the evening. As I approached him I recognized the one Frankie was talking to.

Previously I'd only seen Reynolds Strand in photos and when he was putting on a show in Maria Lovell's office. Now his face was flushed, his eyes glistened. He had his arm around a very beautiful young woman, my age maybe.

She looked European, slightly glazed, and bored. I watched the Bug Boy's hand go into and out of Strand's pocket to deposit a pack of powder, and extract a bill.

Then Frankie moved my way and we made a connection. Mags, Geoff and I snorted in the women's room and buzzed in the infrared glow of the light sculpture in the back room.

A few nights later Judy Finch invited us and a bunch of people to a loft party. She told us that BD the undercover would be there. When she confronted the famous pig, Mags, Geoff and I each realized we'd seen him in the neighborhood and got a bit turned on.

Next day we watched him get driven out of the neighborhood. Shortly after this, Judy Finch disappeared. To rejoin Ray Light rumor said. I didn't speak to her for almost forty years.

§

A couple of weeks later the three of us were naked and floating on junk. Geoff stood before the front windows of the apartment. Sunlight framed his head of shoulder-length curls.

"A nicely endowed angel comes with a message from heaven," Mags said.

He was beautiful. Geoff looked towards Mags lying nude on the bed and she smiled a smeared junk smile at me, with a hard-on despite the drug.

Around then, talking about Geoff I told someone, "I can't believe I'm part-owner."

It was a way my father used to talk about me: "Ashamed to say I owned you." Twisted affection might be the kindest way to describe it.

It got back to Geoff. "I thought Mags and I took you in off the street," he said. At different times each of us secretly thought he or she was the only one holding us together. It came up in the increasing number of fights we had. At least once a week, usually more often, one or another of us went out the door for good and came back the next day.

§

That autumn Dr. Lovell told me, "I believe that your involvement with this boy and this woman with all its trauma and quarrels is your effort to knit some kind of coherence in your life. You are going about it in absolutely the wrong way."

I'd thought the same thing. But I just shrugged and said, "It's fun."

"Young man, fun is an American word. I never heard anyone in Europe say anything like it."

Each morning the walk down the blank morning streets through Astor Place to the subway grew colder. Often the change for my subway fare was the only money I had on me. The madman I worked for fired me dozens of times and re-hired me ten minutes later.

Then one morning when I was falling out at my desk he told me to get my coat and he and the nephew who worked for him escorted me to Flying Dutchman Promotions' door. The boss handed me two weeks pay in cash and said, "You need to get better. Go in the hospital or something. Don't ever come back here."

My first reaction was that I was rich. The second was that I didn't have to get up in the mornings. My situation didn't twist my gut until a bit later when the hit of junk that had gotten me to work wore off.

When I couldn't find another job, Dr. Lovell stopped charging me for my visits. Once when she said my personal life lacked any reality I saw in my mind Remington Strand kissing a girl much less than half his age.

§

Geoffrey had stopped going to school. Mags got hand-outs from her family. I peddled drugs in places the Bug Boy didn't want to go, cruised the theater johns on East Fourth Street.

One day that winter there was no heat in our building and we were all so jumpy and strung out with our three full-grown joneses that we couldn't even stay in the big bed together for warmth. I stood in the doorway and screamed at Mags be-cause she had accused me of taking five dollars she'd intended to use to buy food. "You owed it to me. It was mine. I turned you on last night and all this week."

And when Geoff said, "She's the only one who wants you here, asshole," I slammed him against a wall once and did it again for good measure. Then I stormed out and didn't return that night.

When I stumbled back there the heat was on again and I was so high that I had even saved enough junk to get both of them off too.

"If you will not stop doing drugs, I can no longer treat you," Dr. Lovell told me. "They are not my patients, but I can't imagine that your Geoff and Mags are in any better condition than you. If you love them, you all must stop living together and get treatment."

And I said, "I think you're living in a threeway just like I am. I saw your husband with his girlfriend. Does Reynolds Strand ever bring her by here?"

She was silent, looking at me. I couldn't tell what she was thinking. "Yes, I know my husband has a mistress and I have seen her. He is very careless and I'm sorry you saw that. I regret that I have done you so little good. Obviously we cannot continue. But when you are ready to seek drug treatment, I will give you the referrals that you need."

She stood then and escorted me out of the office and through the waiting room. I was in a kind of shock. I don't tower over many people but I did with her. She looked up at me. "And you *will* become ready and you *will* be back."

§

She was right but it took a bit more than a year and a day. By the time that happened Geoff had killed himself while in police custody. His parents lived upstate and we couldn't get to the funeral even if they'd have allowed us in.

Mags' family had her put in a hospital and they were not anxious to have her hear from me. I hit the street and thought that if I'd just gone to Vietnam and died none of this would have happened.

My brother Gerry was living in the East Village and tried desperately to stay in contact. I remember him calling out to me from across Avenue C while I was making a heroin buy. I ran to escape him.

Marty Simonson was back in New York. He'd spent his army time in Germany. It was he who found me crouched in the shadow of the Cooper Union building.

Marty held me, talked to me, made me drink coffee. "I thought of you every day," he said. He phoned my brother. In Gerry's bathroom mirror I saw the wild-eyed panhandler with overgrown stubble that I'd seen on the street or maybe dreamed about.

I needed help shaving because my hands shook. I thought of Randall and burst into tears. Every nerve in my body twisted. My legs and arms jerked. Gerry collected painkillers from friend's medicine chests. They cut a bit off the edge of my withdrawal.

The last time I saw Maria Lovell was the next morning, a Sunday that carried a hint of spring. Desperate, I'd called her at dawn and left Gerry's number with her answering service.

An hour later the phone rang. "Are you able to travel?" she asked. When I said I was, she told me, "I will see you at nine o'clock."

My spine vibrated. I got off the couch where I was crashing, tried to get myself cleaned up, borrowed money for the subway. Because I was strung out, I kept spilling the coffee Gerry had made.

I got to the office early. The doorman was a big German who didn't like the looks of me. "The doctor is walking her dog and says you are to wait."

I had a pain in my guts. After a few minutes Dr. Lovell came into the lobby with her little dog. In the time since I'd seen her she seemed to have grown old. She gave me the once-over and gestured towards her office. I saw her give a little nod to the doorman as if to say this was okay. Inside, she turned on the lights and indicated I should sit on the waiting room couch.

"How much heroin a day are you doing?"

"Twenty dollars."

She looked at me appraisingly. "Thirty, perhaps?"

"Maybe."

She went into the office and came back with a glass of water. "Take these." She opened her other hand. It held two large pills. As I washed them down she said, "In a few minutes they will have an effect."

The dog came over to me trailing its leash. "I assure you Kublai is not this friendly to everyone." Kublai jumped into my lap and I held him. Whatever she'd given me came on strong. My aching bones became something going on out in the hall.

"What has happened to you?" Dr. Lovell asked.

I tried to tell her but all I could say was, "When I looked in the mirror the face was that guy I told you I saw begging outside the Cooper Union." When I tried to tell her about Geoff and Mags I began crying and couldn't stop.

"I'm sorry your growing up has to be this hard," she said. Then she went back into the office and made a phone call. I heard her talking as I patted Kublai.

When she came back, Dr. Lovell turned off the office lights and I knew her time with me was almost over. She had a couple of prescription slips with names and addresses on them. "Beth Israel is near the East Village. They will admit you today. You will speak to the doctor whose name is written here. I will call him tomorrow to make sure all is well. Do you have money for the subway?"

She went towards the door. The dog leaped up and I followed. In the lobby she turned to face me. "This will be the last time I see you. I did you a great disservice as your doctor when I grew too fond of you." She reached up and I bent down. She kissed me on the forehead. "It is my belief that you will recover. Do not disappoint me."

She turned and went down the hall to the elevators. Only Kublai was watching me when I paused at the door and looked back. Outside the bright day hurt my eyes.

§

That night in the hospital someone screamed until the nurses shut him up. On the ragged border between methadone and agony I wondered if the Subway Man had spared my life because he saw himself in me.

For a moment I dozed and it was dawn or dusk and I was alone. Gliding in and out of the shadows were the Witch Girls.

I closed my eyes and they must have approached because I felt their cool hands on my forehead. They straightened my bedclothes, dried my tears, sang the pining song I'd heard when I was four.

When I opened my eyes they were gone. I understood that what I'd done and what had been done to me were the misfortunes that come to a Witch Boy trying in all the wrong ways to be human.

richard bowes

Chapter Seven

When people talk about the notorious riot that was the East Village circa the 1960s, they devote time to the Summer of Love and shy away from the dark that followed. The last days of Lord of Light, though, usually get attention. Writing my East Village story I checked sources and had the timeline and movements for Ray Light's last weekend on earth. I had also shared images directly from his mind.

§

Early in 1971 on the chill, drizzling Sunday night of the weekend Lord of Light played the Fill-more East, Ray Light was interviewed in a booth at the Odessa, the blowsy old Ukrainian restaurant on Tompkins Square Park.

Judy had taken him there once when they were kids. That day had been bright, new leaves danced on the trees in the park, the streets were crowded. Now a few streetlights shone through the dark, people scuttled by in the late winter drizzle. Ray had spiked his coffee heavily with cognac from a flask.

Lord of Light was on an upward track floating on a twisted reputation. Things so far had gone according to the signs Ray had seen. His sightings of the future were erratic, a stray vision here and there. But they were signposts and they had always come true. It began his first time in New York. He'd caught images of himself locked up and tortured. Abducted, he saw himself, Judy and the undercover on stage. In the mental hospital when he wanted to kill himself, he had glimpses of freedom and revenge.

"I understand you once lived here," said the Village Voice's rock critic. This was a second stringer—not Bangs or Goldstein. But then Ray was still a new talent and Lord of Light was an opening act at the Fillmore—not the headliner or even the number two band. The critic made statements instead of asking questions. He had hair that came down like a curtain to his shoulders without a curl or twist but with some grey strands.

Ray recognized him as a failed graduate student who'd blown out his frontal lobes in the battle for cosmic consciousness. Not someone with whom he could make mental contact or wanted to.

He said, "Almost six years ago I lived here until my family had me kidnapped. This is where I met my soulmates: the girl I loved and the private eye who snatched me."

He planted this information in each interview. His bright smile gave it an eerie quality. Judy had taught him that trick.

"You were nearly seventeen when you were returned to your family," said the interviewer.

The guy had done his homework and Ray believed this was going well. "They opened up my mind back there," he said. "Shock treatment is better than acid."

"You once said that the doctor who treated you later cut his own throat."

Ray kept his face blank. "Yeah, that's what I heard."

"And you've talked about your father's suicide."

"With all the guns he had around." A shrug. "Maybe he felt bad about what he did to me." Even without being able to enter the other man's mind Ray knew what was coming.

"It's being said you were once close to Phillip Marcy, the art dealer. He jumped out the window of his loft Friday morning."

Ray was kind of pleased that people were already making that connection but he frowned and paused like he was trying to think how best to put this. "I mostly called him the Man. Close? Well he kept me handcuffed to his bed. We kind of lost touch. In lots of ways he was a monster. But he taught me stuff."

The reporter raised an eyebrow, seemed a bit uneasy about asking what kind of stuff got taught.

Ray Light told him, "The Man said that if you don't make your own story out of your life, someone will make his story out of your life. I guess he couldn't take his own advice."

Even as he had read the newspaper account of the Man diving off the windowsill of his loft Ray couldn't decide for which reason he hated him more: the way the Man had taught him to touch minds or the fact he hadn't taught him enough.

The interview was winding down and Ray indicated he had an appointment. The reporter said, "This was fascinating," but seemed anxious to escape, which was perfect. "Your show was the best thing I've heard since the Doors," he remarked and got away.

That Friday night before the band's first set Ray had stood in the wings of the Fillmore East and looked through a peephole at the crowd filtering into the seats that soared towards the roof of the old Yiddish theater/movie house turned concert hall.

Here Joplin had shouted and moaned as the red and yellow plasma of Joshua Light Show exploded on the screen behind her and the packed balconies screamed back. Now Joplin was gone and sightings of her ghost were starting to get reported. Tonight's main act was not going to fill the theater and there was a rumor the Fillmore was going to close. The crown was in the street. Nobody knew who'd be the next Monarch.

The sound check had been done. The emcee was warming up the crowd. Ray's drummer and bass player, steady guys who kept to themselves, waited behind him in the wings.

Judy came up beside Ray and put her hand on his arm smiling. She could play keyboards and sing backup like Emmylou Harris. BD appeared barefoot in a long silk robe and carrying a tambourine and looking as if he still couldn't figure out what had happened to him.

"And now the Fillmore East is proud to present Elektra recording artists Lord of Light."

There was good applause and some cheers as they made their entrance. The audience saw what had flashed through Ray's mind as he was taken into captivity years before. He wore black leather from head to toe. The first song would be "Dollar a Day Boy," about the girl who loved him and the cop who busted him. The girl now called Judy Light had a blond crewcut and a Marlboro in her mouth. In silk robes and with hair to his waist, the ex-private cop moved like he was in a trance.

Hendrix's gift while he lived was to stand on a stage amid the smoke and reverb and for a solid hour enfold ten thousand minds inside his own.

Ray could touch the consciousness of a few people. The trio paused and looked out at the audience and immediately went into "Just a Boy Without Wings." The lyrics described a twisted wizard torturing a runaway, forcing him to reach out and reach the wizard's mind with his. Ray had made sure that the Man heard the song before he jumped out his own loft window and that pleased him.

Now the Man, Phillip Marcy, was part of Ray's story. A mythology was getting built. There were whispers, rumors; people called the group "Lord of Darkness."

The Odessa was shutting for the night as Ray pulled a cap down over his hair, turned up his collar, stepped out into the light, cold rain and crossed the western end of St. Mark's Place. On his right the lights were sparse in Tompkins Square Park.

In the streets around the park were patches of black where street lamps were broken, storefronts boarded up, buildings abandoned. It had always been a tough neighborhood. Now speed and junk ruled and graffiti sprouted everywhere: death's heads and Black Panther symbols, swastikas and cult signs.

People mourned the death of the East Village. Ray knew the good part was just starting. This time and place needed its own myths and he was prepared to provide them.

He had once asked a guru in Taos, a psycho-analyst who had done much mescaline and lost his license to practice, about his gift. The old man had looked right through him and said, "You are a diver in the gestalt sea where there is no then or now or will be. You are your own guide."

So far that had always been true. But Ray had seen no images of anything beyond the Fillmore performances. Over the years he wondered if his visions were self-fulfilling prophecies. But he missed them acutely now that they'd dried up.

He felt like he was again standing bare and handcuffed, on the sill of a tall open window with an eight-story drop to the concrete below. That's how the Man had tortured and trained him.

Ray turned east at Tenth Street and walked down Tompkins Square North. He spotted the van outside the building where Lord of Light was staying. A figure in jeans and leather with a knit cap pulled down on his head stood next to it. Dressed in male street clothes, BD awaited him.

When Ray, snatched off the street, had a vision of the future, BD was the third figure on stage with Judy and him.

Between shock-treatment sessions in the hospital he saw BD in tears and with no place else to go standing naked before him. He saw how he and Judy put this cop in a dress long before they actually did it.

Since then he'd seen BD at the wheel of the car that drove him away from his father's house well before the night Ray showed his parent what was on both their minds. He saw BD with him in the Man's loft and knew that both of them would watch the Man step out into space rather than stay in Ray's presence.

He and Judy let BD join them in bed. But Ray was never able to look into the guy's mind. He didn't even talk to him much. So it came as a surprise when BD suggested after their last set late on Saturday night that the two of them go out the next night and visit some low places BD knew about.

"Judy says you seem down," BD said. "She's going to be visiting a friend and thought it might take your mind off things." It aroused Ray's curiosity and he agreed. Maybe BD had magic and more revelations left in him.

As they were about to set off, a passerby, a guy in a battered leather jacket and boots who maybe had been touched a little too hard by the street, recognized them and stopped. Ray looked his way, read him in an instant.

The guy had seen Lord of Light's last performance on Saturday night. When Ray reached out to the audience during the song "Just a Boy Without Wings," the guy received a jolting reminder of a junk-clogged night a few years before. Like Ray he'd once stood handcuffed on the sill of an open window

above East Fourth Street with the Man screaming
at him to read his mind or die.

After the concert this stranger had gone home
and written the stream-of-consciousness narrative
of a kid who was part him and part Ray Light. For
him Sunday night's encounter with BD and Ray on
Tompkins Park North seemed like destiny. A breeze
kicked up the dust. He felt it swirl around his legs.

Ray looked and saw this one's sad world of a
dead lover, drug programs, menial jobs, living off
the generosity of relatives and friends. The stranger cringed under his contempt, felt like a bug about
to be snuffed out.

BD put his hand on Ray's arm and broke the
contact. The stranger backed away and maybe was
the last person Ray Light touched on what turned
out to be his last night alive.

§

That guy, of course, was me in the dark, low years after
Geoff and Mags. I saw BD and Ray get into the van and drive
off.

The next morning the East Village and the rest of the world
found out BD had killed Ray and hanged himself. Any proper
legend has murder and mystery at its core. Books got written,
a couple of movies played around with the details. The general public was entertained. Those who'd known them were
haunted.

It would be years before I'd turn my attention to Lord of Light
again. By then Judy was reading my words aloud in theaters.

Chapter Eight

Ghosts and godchildren were on my mind in the aftermath of the first 9/11 anniversary. I wrote stories about uncanny ghost-spotting detectives and became the long distance godfather to a sweet kid in Ohio, a young writer named Chris. Playing parent gave me lots of pleasure and he was patient enough to let me.

Deep into autumn my friend Barbara Lohr phoned. When we were young she and I discovered the nature of Dust Devils. Everyone calls her Major Barbara or just the Major because of her height, bearing, and commanding British accent.

"I told you Eddie Ackers' funeral was last week," she said. She had but Eddie and I were never close and fortunately I had work as an excuse.

"It was way up the Hudson. You should have seen the Dutch church and the graveyard where Eddie was laid away—utter Sleepy Hollow. None of his wives and rather awful children was interested in his effects. His sister's sweet as can be but getting on in age as we all will and can't come down to the city.

"I've been rounding up the old Flying Dutchman gang. We'll pack up his personal possessions Sunday afternoon. And after we've done the right thing, we may all go out and get a bit sentimental."

My memories of Flying Dutchman Fashion Promotions and our boss, Bud Van Brunt, are far from pleasant. It was an end-of-the-line ad agency and I'd been fired. Van Brunt and Eddie Ackers had literally shoved me out the door. But the Major seemed anxious that I rejoin the old crew for an afternoon.

She talked while I searched for the perfect alibi. I was at my computer and this email popped up: "See you at the Eddie Ackers bagging party?" It was from my old friend Joan Mata. We had met at Flying Dutchman and stayed close. I'm the god-father of Selesta, her only child.

So that Sunday afternoon I joined a gathering at Ackers' apartment. The Major and I had met at the agency. She and I and Jay Glass the critic whom I occasionally run into and little Mimsey Friedman were all copywriters. Mimsey still has a column in *Harper's Bazaar* and is on television during fashion week. The other half dozen volunteers had worked for Flying Dutchman before or after me. I awaited Joan Mata.

The Major organized the sorting and boxing, ordered pizza, and set us to work. "Ceremonies for the dead, such as this, are the only real rituals in circles like ours," she announced. "The rare birth is preplanned. Weddings, well, they're pretty much just place markers in this day and age. But death, oh death, my dears, that's often a surprise and usually final." Major Barbara writes long, critically celebrated fantasy novels and it shows.

We rolled through Eddie Ackers' possessions: bagged clothes for the Salvation Army, boxed kitchen appliances, golf clubs, and trout-fishing equipment to be shipped to his sister. We tossed away magazines with names like *Man Eater* featuring young ladies wearing lion and tiger masks and nothing else. Everyone took a good look.

Talk as we worked centered on our old boss, the legendary horror Bud Van Brunt. "Satan in a Brooks Brothers suit," the Major said.

"The scent of sulfur barely hidden by the Vitalis aftershave and gin breath," I added. In my mind Van Brunt's round, flushed face and big bald dome turned into a pumpkin lit from within by flames.

Eddie Ackers hardly got mentioned at all. "Poor Eddie," someone remarked, "kind of an empty life."

"He was a relative of Van Brunt's. A nephew-in-law, or something," I said.

"He endured a decade or two of Uncle Bud," replied Jay Glass. "And when Van Brunt finally got dragged off to hell Eddie took over the business. Well worth the price of his soul."

At that moment Joan Mata appeared, elegant in a suede jacket and a scarf that caught the green of her cat eyes. She did freelance artwork at Flying Dutchman when we met and from about that moment we knew we'd be friends.

Back then she too lived in the East Village. On front stoops and fire escapes we talked about sex and parents and trauma. Joan could sit on railings and never lose her balance. She was only a year or two older than I was but knew so much more. Her mother was a civil-rights lawyer; her father was Antonio Mata, the Mexican painter who did surrealistic works that looked like cartoons. He signed himself "Margay," which is a tree cat. We did a few drugs and shared our strange secrets. Hers had topped mine.

"Perfect timing," said the Major, as we kissed and hugged. "We're just ready to adjourn."

"Where to?" someone asked.

"The Knickerbocker Holiday," she said, "or 'Knicks' as they call it now. It's where dear Eddie breathed his last."

"Isn't that a little macabre?" Mimsey Friedman asked.

"Not at all! He may even be waiting for us." Mimsey flinched but the rest of us chuckled.

"It's always a celebratory occasion when you've beat the reaper," I told Joan.

Ackers lived not far from where Broadway crosses Sixth Avenue and forms Herald Square. In the middle of a block of low buildings the wreckers have passed by stands an ancient four-story, wide-front building with a huge neon *Knicks* sign hanging out front.

When we were young and Manhattan was all wonderment, the Knickerbocker Holiday Tavern on the outskirts of the jumping, vibrant Garment District was an oasis for junior copywriters and assistant art directors. Back then the Knickerbocker had a colonial motif and waitresses in Dutch bonnets and wooden clogs that we'd all found delightfully campy.

Now the District and its streets choked with racks of clothes are a fading memory. And all that's left of Dutch New York is an occasional street or building with a name like Gansevoort, Stuyvesant, Roosevelt, Astor, or Vanderbilt.

We stood on the sidewalk and read the brass plaque that now flanked the door. "On this site in Colonial times was a roadhouse and coach stop. Aaron Burr and Benedict Arnold are said to have slept there."

"Together?" we all wanted to know.

Inside all was leather and steel. One large-screen television showed the Giants playing football in West Coast sunshine. The other had guys in blazers with network emblems working out the meaning of the baseball playoffs. The sound was off. Sunday evenings were obviously a down time, the place was big and kind of empty.

Our server, a dark young lady with long black hair, announced herself as Benicia and took our drink orders. I ordered club soda. Major Barbara asked her, "By any chance were you on duty when there was an unfortunate episode with a patron a couple of weeks ago?"

"Yes," Benicia's head jerked in surprise. "It was creepy but I'm sorry for him. He came in and went right past the hostess. Happy Hour is crowded. The guy was flushed and he was walking funny like he was already drunk. The manager came out to talk to him but the customer went flat on his face. They called EMS but he was dead. How did you hear about it?"

"We knew him. His name was Eddie Ackers."

"I'm so sorry," the server said.

"Where did he fall?" asked Major Barbara.

"Right about where you're sitting." The major seemed pleased.

"How's Selesta?" I asked Joan.

"I'll bet you've talked to your godchild more recently than I have."

"Oh dear."

"So let me ask you, how's Selesta?"

"Fine. We had lunch, went to the Whitney the other week." Joan sighed.

"What on earth led Ackers to come here to die?" someone wanted to know

"The perfect spot for a Van Brunt relative. I'd guess it has the strongest magic in the neighborhood," said the Major.

"Magic?" people asked, "Where?"

"Just because a sacred place has been defiled does not mean it's without power."

Joan and I shook our heads.

"Poor Eddie," Mimsey remarked. "Remember how Van Brunt used to ream him out in front of everyone?"

"Was there anybody the Flying Dutchman didn't do that to?" I asked. "I recall him sticking his face into mine and saying, 'Make the suit copy read like a man wrote it, you little pussy.'"

"I was in there maybe two days a week and he fired me a dozen times," said Joan, massaging my neck like she had back when that was happening.

Van Brunt's specialty was hiring cheap: kids in need of experience, people on the skids. He described the company as "An Agency on Seventh Avenue and in the Heart of the U.S." We provided fashion promotion to dreary little department stores in the places we'd run away from.

Everyone in the business called Van Brunt "The Headless Horseman." His temper, even in an industry whose foundations rested on argument and insult, was a legend.

Jay asked, "Remember how he'd end a phone conversation by screaming, 'It'll be hard for you to walk with my size-eleven shoe lodged in your fucking colon!'"

"Dear God, what a bottom feeder he was," the Major remarked. "And we were what he fed on."

The drinks arrived and for a couple of minutes there was silence.

"Remember," said the Major, "when we discovered that Brom Bones, the bully in 'The Legend of Sleepy Hollow' who chases Ichabod Crane out of town, was based on a character named Van Brunt that Irving had heard about."

"Bud talked about that in his rants," Mimsey said quietly. "How his family had money and Washington Irving had envied them and made up the story about his ancestor stealing Katrina Van Tassel. On the other hand, maybe 1980 or so I was told he had died in the mental ward of a hospital and what he said could just have been insanity."

She looked troubled and I remembered the open secret back in the day that she and the Dutchman were having an affair. It was easy to imagine how awful that must have been.

Jay Glass said, "The Headless Horseman was a legendary Revolutionary War Hessian officer who rode out each night to find the head he lost to a cannonball."

This reminded me of a night Van Brunt had me working late trying to squeeze copy onto mock-up catalog pages. The top of his bald head was the bright scarlet it turned when he got smashed.

Vietnam was at full boil and he asked, "How did you dodge the draft, pervert?" He knew I'd lied about getting deferred for physical reasons. Sharp as the moment it happened, I remembered how he stuck his face near mine and whispered low like this was a seduction, "You worthless faggot, drug freak, coward."

He was baiting me and coming on to me at the same time. I needed the money or I'd have cut him with the scissors on my desk.

Just then, another part of his brain opened up. He began talking about Russians and the red menace: Hessians leaping out of sewers with bayonets, commies parachuting out of the skies to conquer New York. This, too, was scary as hell and evoked dark riders and pumpkin eyes lighted by candles.

We'd all heard him do this stuff. Past and future looped over the present like a skater making a figure eight on the ice. I told the rest of the table, "Once I heard the Dutchman say that communist Mohawks were going to come down from Canada and take back New York. Impressive paranoia."

"He'd had a very bad war," someone said. I doubted he'd had a bad war. My guess was he'd enjoyed every bloody, bullying minute of it.

"And peace wasn't very satisfactory either," I added.

Then Benicia was back with another round of drinks and plates of chicken wings and fried mozzarella. I got up to look for the restroom. Joan was on her feet also and we wandered past the bar.

"At first glance, with his red face and head, Van Brunt looked like a jolly burgher in an old painting," she said. "But the monster inside was always waiting to emerge."

She went past the end of the very long bar and looked in a corner. "Hey, remember this?" On the wall was a picture that had hung behind the bar in the old Knickerbocker Holiday. It showed a roadhouse/inn, circa 1790 to judge from the clothes, a two-story building with an attic and weathervanes.

A coach had pulled up in front. The coachman flirted with the barmaid, birds flew about in the trees, and passengers filed through Dutch doors. A country church, a few scattered houses, a store, and a blacksmith's constituted a village just off Broadway, some miles north of the little town at the tip of Manhattan Island.

Staring at it, I noticed again that in the midst of all that summer light, the two center second-floor windows in the inn were both pitch dark.

"We used to sit here and wonder what lay behind those windows," she said, "imagined exotic Dutch voodoo."

We parted at the restrooms. The men's was well lighted and with forced air to dry your hands. The old one had featured oaken stalls that could have accommodated carriage horses and urinals so tall and deep you could fall in and never be found.

Waiting for Joan, I looked at the picture again and remembered a dream that had come back when the Major called about Eddie Ackers. In it I stood outside the two-story tavern. It was night and the only light was a lantern flickering over the door.

Then another light swung in the dark. Three toots of a horn and a night coach came rolling down Broadway. Lights went on in the two dark windows at the inn and a pumpkin head with candles flickering behind its eyes stared at me from the coach.

Joan just nodded. She knew about my dream.

When we got back to the table, the Major told us, "This has become a group therapy session."

Jay said, "I remember the day he insulted my copywriting, my manhood, and my taste in socks. Then, of course, he fired me. I left and never came back." We all applauded.

Little Mimsey Friedman downed a colorful drink. "I'd left a great job in the promotions department at Lord & Taylor to get married. Then my first husband lost his job and never found another one, ever. To support us both I had to go looking for work. And there was *nothing*! Except, of course, for

Van Brunt! A day he didn't drive me to tears was a day he considered wasted."

Everyone drank to that. Aside from her favored position, Mimsey also knew more about fashion writing than everyone else at Flying Dutchman combined.

Back then she provided a weekly column, "Cut on a Bias," with fashion commentary, mild gossip and plugs for clothes. Client stores could publish it whole or in part as advertising in local newspapers. It was the start of her long career.

Since I was next to her all eyes turned to me as I sipped seltzer water. "I was the hippie/faggot/junkie. No office was complete without one in those days." A couple of people chuckled. "Work for me was a constant round of abuse. What kept me coming back day after day was that compared to the East Village, Flying Dutchman Promotions seemed calm and orderly."

The major said, "You would have been the very life and soul of the party if the Flying Dutchman had been a party. Compared to London, New York was expensive. I was working at *Harper's Bazaar* for almost nothing and thought everyone in advertising made tons of money. Van Brunt said he loved my accent and ridiculed me every day I worked there because of it. After a couple of years of this I sold a silly murder mystery series to a publisher, walked into the office, and quit." We all cheered.

The Sunday evening crowd, such as it was, had thinned out. Customers were sparse. The bartender and the server looked bored.

Jay Glass, waving a scotch and soda for emphasis, was saying, "I think Van Brunt had a curse handed down from Brom Bones, maybe earlier. But he reveled in being a complete and utter monster."

The others nodded with sage, tipsy understanding.

Mimsey Friedman spoke up. "I saw Van Brunt, maybe eight years ago." I was about to say he would have been dead for some time. Then I saw her tearing eyes and shut up.

"My marriage to Joachim had finally crashed and burned," she said and I remembered hearing she had broken up with a European designer about then. "Boris and John were wonderful to me. They have a lovely little farm on the Hudson near the Mohawk Valley and I stayed there a lot that summer.

"There are gardens and a small herd of sheep, grey ones with lovely black faces, quite decorative, that graze in the fields. They had geese in a pond and an old retired New York City Police horse named Crispin, the gentlest animal in the world.

"A local man came by and took care of the animals. I never much noticed him—he was quite anonymous. Then at the end of the summer, he had to be away and got someone to take his place. I remember it was a hazy August afternoon. There was thunder up in the mountains but no lightning or rain.

"I saw a figure walking across the pasture and Crispin shied away from him. Something about him was so familiar. He noticed me at the same time, paused and turned to look my way. It was Bud Van Brunt and he stared at me for a long moment. He wanted me to know he was there.

"I packed and left that day. Boris and John eventually persuaded me to come back and I never saw that man again. But it wasn't the same. Even Crispin seemed jumpy..."

She paused and stared horrified. A door behind the bar had swung open. A figure, big and bald, was backing through it, carrying a crate. He turned and for a moment, like Mimsey, I saw Van Brunt and froze.

But that only lasted until the guy realized all of us were staring at him wide-eyed. He was very young and looked bewildered in ways Van Brunt never did.

"I wonder," whispered Joan, "if he's the manager Eddie Ackers saw the night he staggered in here to die." At that moment, Benicia the server came over to the table and said, "Folks, I'm afraid we're closing a little early." It was just past midnight but we were about the only customers.

That broke the spell. Quite quickly for people in late middle age and in many cases half smashed, we tallied the bill and got out of there. Mimsey was crying.

Sunday nights are the one time Manhattan really does seem quiet and almost deserted. Everyone said their farewells, grabbed cabs, hurried off to subways and Path trains assuring each other that they'd be in touch.

Joan put her arms around Mimsey who was taking large gulps of air. The major stood with me. "That poor kid was so desperate to support herself and her worthless husband and Van Brunt got a bit of her soul. At Eddie's funeral she told me some of what we heard tonight."

I looked back at Knicks and instead saw a night coach, lights going on in the roadhouse windows and the flame-eyed pumpkin.

She looked down at me, "I wanted you here tonight because you were the other one I worried about. I remember how disturbed you were all those years ago about Van Brunt—we'd call it sexual harassment today. I remembered you back then talking about your dream and thought perhaps Van Brunt had his hooks into you as he does with Mimsey."

I must have been staring wide-eyed. I shook my head but the roadhouse and pumpkin remained. I shook it again and *Knicks* reappeared in neon.

"Thanks for your concern. But I got over him some time ago," I managed to say, "Maybe it's because I've got no soul. Maybe it's because he was just one nasty drunk and not some creature of dark magic and mystery."

She looked down at me. "Back in the old days your sense of the uncanny was more acute. You had no trouble recognizing the evil in Bud Van Brunt." She sounded disappointed.

The major raised a hand and stopped a cab. Then she gathered up Mimsey and took her away. Joan and I watched them drive off. "Mimsey really thinks Van Brunt is after her," Joan said. "The major was worried about you."

"I was just a minor character," I said.

"Me too," she said, "we lucky bystanders."

Chapter Nine

Not to boast, but I'd say I'm pretty good as a godfather. As an actual parent, I'd doubtless have been a disaster. But I have six godchildren and I love all of them. One should not play favorites but Selesta, Joan's daughter, is my favorite.

One Friday afternoon that spring Selesta drove me out to Long Island. We were spending the weekend with her mother and grandmother at the House That Ate the World.

Since Joan and my evening at Knickerbocker Holiday I'd been looking for ways to bring her and Selesta together. Selesta was twenty-three, an artist like her mother and grandfather.

When she was real small, three and four years old, I had Mondays off and Joan would leave Selesta with me while she kept appointments with her design clients in the city.

That's when Selesta and I first talked about cats. Back then I had an apartment on Second Avenue in the teens. On the ground floor of the building facing mine was a row of small shops each of which had a cat. Selesta took a great interest in them, perhaps just because she couldn't have a cat of her own.

The Italian deli had a majestic tricolor cat named Maybelline. As a deli cat she had plenty of food, numerous admirers whom she allowed to pet her as she sat in the sun by the front door, and mice to keep her busy at night.

The Russian cobbler next door had a thin grey cat with a truncated tail that twitched back and forth. A shoe-repair shop has no food and probably few mice. The cobbler was thin and grey himself and once when I asked him the cat's name he just shook his head like he'd never heard of such a thing. So I decided to call him Hank and Selesta agreed with me.

The third store was a Vietnamese nail and hair and massage shop with neon signage. It employed a trio of exotic ladies with elaborate nails and one very silly man. Their cat was a Siamese named Mimi or something like that. Mimi had a wardrobe of exotic sweaters and collars and even booties.

She was usually carried by one of the ladies. When she passed by, the other cats' noses and ears twitched as if they could sense a cat nearby but couldn't tell where it was.

To amuse ourselves, Selesta and I made up stories about the three cats and their adventures. Once they all went out to find a pair of red striped socks for Hank on his birthday. Another time they went to the moon, which was run by a bunch of gangster mice.

Maybe I should have discouraged her interest. However, I believed Joan had asked me to be the godfather of her only child because we went back so far and shared so many secrets.

Eventually Selesta's parents moved to Hoboken, she started school and our Monday afternoon adventures of the store cats were no more.

It was a few years later when she was eight or nine that Selesta first asked questions about Joan and me and the old days. It was the Wednesday after her birthday and I'd just taken her to see a matinee performance of *Cats* on Broadway. That had been her wish and her mother had no objection.

The kick in bringing a kid to the theater is seeing and sharing their unbridled wonder. Afterwards we discussed the show and let the crowd carry us to the subway. I noticed that Selesta now had her mother's green eyes flecked with gold.

"My favorite part was the end where the cat goes up to heaven," she said.

"On the old rubber tire," I replied. "That's the way it always happens with cats."

"My mother says she has allergies so I can't have a cat or dog."

This sudden swerve in our conversation took me by surprise. "She *is* allergic, honey," I said automatically and immediately regretted it. Kids are uncanny. Selesta knew I had lied just as she suspected that her mother was lying.

She followed it up by saying, "Once when I was little you told me you lived in a house with a mystery cat. Like Macavity in the play."

Macavity, the villain of the musical, seemed to me too over the top to be very scary. The animal Selesta referred to had been very quiet and quite real.

"It was long before you were born or even thought of," I said as the matinee crowds carried us down the subway stairs.

I had a vague recollection of having told her about the cat at Anise's crash pad.

"What was the cat's name?"

By then we were waiting amid a crowd of commuters at 33rd Street for the PATH train to Hoboken, New Jersey. I began the story and as I did she listened with the exact same rapt expression she'd had at the show.

"He was called Trebizond. That was an ancient city far away on the Black Sea. Anise was a lady who had started to get a doctorate in history before she became a hippy and decided to run a commune."

"You were a hippy! Was my mother?" The idea intrigued her.

"I guess I was. You'd have to ask your mother if she was."

"What was Trebizond like?"

"He was a big old orange cat who seemed very smart." I didn't tell her that the people living in that apartment had achieved a rarefied degree of psychic awareness and mind expansion which Trebizond shared.

"It seemed he always had a favorite. When I first came to stay there, he spent every night on the chest of a very quiet stranger, a kid from the South who slept on the living room couch. Anise joked that the cat had adopted him.

"All of a sudden, every time a newcomer entered the apartment, the cat would get off his chest and sit and watch. The kid would take off all his clothes, kneel down on the floor in front of the new arrival and kiss his or her feet."

"He kissed your feet?" she was fascinated.

"It was creepy and embarrassing. But I noticed other people were pleased when it happened. Like they said to themselves, *'Finally people are kissing my feet!'* And Trebizond acted like an owner whose pet had done a clever trick.

"I guess word got back to the kid's family because one day his parents appeared and took him home."

"What did Trebizond do?"

"Found someone else who lived there, a dreamy kind of girl who was studying to be a dancer. The cat slept beside her in this bed in a little alcove near the kitchen. We called her the Flower Girl because she brought home the single roses that gypsy ladies sold in bars and little sprays of lilies of the valley, potted geraniums.

"Then it escalated. She began coming in with bridal bouquets, with boxes of red carnations, huge bunches of violets. The crash pad began to look like a funeral parlor. Trebizond prowled among them, chewed the ferns, and batted the petals that fell to the floor.

"The Flower Girl started to look furtive, haunted. One time she came home with two shopping bags full of yellow daffodils. Another time it was orchids. Stuff she'd probably stolen.

She'd put them on the floor around her bed and Trebizond would lie there like it was his altar.

"Eventually the police nabbed her as she was ripping off a bank of tulips from the Macy's garden show. With her gone, Trebizond began to notice me and I knew I was next."

The train arrived right then and we didn't get seats. I held onto a pole and Selesta held onto me. We sang scraps of the songs. She knew a lot of the lyrics. The other passengers pretended we weren't there.

I hoped my goddaughter would forget what we'd been talking about. But as soon as we hit the platform of Hoboken terminal Selesta asked, "Did my mother know Trebizond?"

Hoboken back then was still such a compact old-fashioned working-class city that in my memory it's all black and white like a 1940s newsreel. We walked from the station to Newark Street where a sign in the shape of a giant hand pointed its finger at the Clam Broth House.

Cats and Joan were a delicate subject. But I'd already lied to this child once and wasn't going to do it again. I had told Joan about the cat.

As we walked I said, "One day I brought your mother home. Trebizond sat in the room where I slept and stared at me. Your mother gave one look at Trebizond and he ran and hid in the kitchen."

What Joan had actually done was let out a low growl. Trebizond's reaction was like that of the cobbler's cat and the deli cat when Mimi was carried past. His nose and ears twitched; he looked around, scared and confused like he sensed a cat but couldn't see one. But I didn't think I had to add that.

Trebizond never came back out of that kitchen. Anise knew something was wrong, but she and the cat were both afraid of Joan.

"Why didn't Trebizond make my mother allergic?" Selesta asked.

Before I could think of a reply, a voice said, "The allergies developed later, honey." Joan Mata stood smiling at the front entrance of the sprawling block-long maze of dining rooms that was the Clam Broth House.

Her husband and Selesta's father, the architect Frank Gallen, was away on business. Their townhouse was like a showcase for his work and hers. Some part of it was always being rebuilt or redesigned. That week it was the kitchen.

So we ate at the restaurant, which Selesta always loved. When we were seated Joan put on her glasses to glance at a menu. They always seemed to alight on her face like a butterfly.

Selesta recounted scenes from the musical and chunks of our conversation. "And he said he was a hippy but he didn't know if you were."

"Your godfather has it backwards," said Joan. "He was the one with the regular job. I was the hippy freelancer!"

Selesta asked, "What happened to Trebizond?"

Neither of us knew. "I imagine he had a few lives left." Joan said.

Selesta left us briefly, reluctantly, for the ladies' room, knowing that in her absence secrets would be discussed.

"She asked and I told her a little bit about the cat and you."

"That's perfect. She's getting curious and I'm glad it happened like this and with you."

"Shouldn't you tell her about your father?"

She sighed. "She'll ask and I'll tell her."

That night for the first time in our friendship, I questioned her judgment but said nothing.

§

Driving east on Long Island with Selesta thirteen or fourteen years later I watched the uncanny light you get on that thin, low strip of land late in the day as sunlight reflects off the Atlantic and the Sound.

Selesta was slim but not painfully thin as she'd been in middle school when her parents divorced. She was cured of her bulimia and led a tightly scheduled life the point of which, maybe, was to prevent her pondering too much about who she was.

Lots of times over the years, we had talked about her mother. We'd even discussed cats. That day in the car she asked, "You know about ocelots?" I nodded and had a good idea where the conversation was going.

"They're small; their bodies are a couple of feet long, with a tail almost that long. They have beautiful coats," she said. "They live all through South America and Mexico. Whenever I go anywhere if they have a zoo I check and see if they have ocelots. San Diego does and Cincinnati.

"Ocelots are shy," she said. "And, of course, they're getting scarce because of their fur and the forest disappearing.

"Obviously, though, what I'm really interested in is the margay, a kind of cousin with the same markings. You know about them."

"They live and hunt in trees," I said. "They're nocturnal, very, very shy and getting rare."

"You know that because my mother talked to you about this, didn't she? Back when you were kids. She knew about all this, about her father. You know Margay was his nickname? I first got interested in them when I was about twelve and heard about Grandfather Margay from Grandma Ruth.

"Ruth took me to Mexico a couple of times. We went to the town where Antonio Mata was born and grew up. There were still people who knew him. We made a special visit to Belize because of this amazing zoo they have. It's away from the coast with lots of space. More like a nature park with all animals from Central America," she said.

"I waited outside the margay enclosure and at dusk I saw one on a high tree branch. Its eyes reflected the light. Other people were there but it looked at me. Then it was gone."

As we rolled along the flat prairie that is the Island's center, sunlight made long shadows and gave a kind of magic to the endless strip malls, the buildings with signboards listing dermatologist and dentist offices, the used-car lots.

Selesta said, seemingly out of nowhere, "Trebizond may have been possessed, but the way he acted with my mother is how a domestic cat reacts to a wild one."

I realized that Joan must never have talked to her about any of this. "You're right, honey," I said. "That's what it was like."

Keeping her eyes on the road, she reached over with her left hand and pulled down the shoulder of her blouse. There was a small patch of tawny fur with a touch of black.

"How long have you had that?"

"A few years. It was just a speck and then it grew. I knew what it was when it appeared. I shaved it at first and was afraid someone would find out. Lately I've let it grow."

I watched her in profile, tried to see a cat shape in her head. She glanced my way and for a moment her eyes did catch the light.

"Your mother had the same thing when I first knew her. She had to get rid of it with electrolysis. Painful stuff."

"My mother never volunteers information about things like this. When I first got the fur I asked her what it meant. She mentioned her father briefly, then told me about laser treatment.

"But you didn't want that."

"I want to remember. Maybe understand something."

We drove in silence for a while. Then Selesta said, "She was about the age I am now when you met. How much did she know?"

"She had just figured out what had happened to her and to her brother Luis. She was mad that your grandmother hadn't been able to tell her more. But I think Ruth must have been in shock herself back then. I think your mother was too. Maybe that's what made them so dedicated to their work."

"Look in that portfolio," she said and indicated one stuck in between our seats.

It contained photos. The first few were of her grandfather, Antonio Mata. As a young man he was thin and poised. Maybe his head and face seemed a bit streamlined. But I might have been seeing that because of what I knew. He was with a group of young people in one picture at a country house in Mexico. I recognized Frida Kahlo in the crowd. In another picture, Antonio Mata in his shirtsleeves painted on a canvas.

I had seen these before. Joan had shown them to me when I first knew her. There was one of Antonio Mata and Ruth, Joan's mother, which I remembered having seen. They made a handsome couple. Ruth wore shorts and a man's shirt.

After her husband's disappearance Ruth went to Columbia Law School, married the civil-rights lawyer Harry Rosen and became a legal counsel for Amnesty International.

"Look at the next one," Selesta said.

This one was new to me. Antonio Mata lay stretched out on the branch of a tree looking at the camera with cat's eyes.

"And the next."

The picture had probably been taken at dusk on a porch. A light was on inside the house. Mata was a bit older than in the other shots. He was poised with his hands on the rails as if he was going to leap into the gathering dark. He looked like he was trapped. I recognized the porch and the house.

"Your mother gave you these?"

"My grandmother. She took them."

The next picture was of three children standing on the front porch of the place that Mata called "The House That Ate the World." They ranged in age from nine to maybe three. The oldest was a very serious boy who seemed to be looking at something in the distance. This, I knew was Joan's brother Luis. The youngest was Joan's sister Catherina smiling and holding a doll up to the camera with both hands. Joan was right in between. She gazed up at her brother.

"I'd never seen a picture of her brother."

"There aren't many. They say he was very shy around strangers. A true Margay. Just look at him! Those eyes!"

"He died very young."

"Eighteen," she said. "Drowned in the Great South Bay a few years after his father disappeared back into Mexico. Water killed the cat. Everyone knew it was suicide."

It's tough when a friend you love and respect is doing something you think may be dumb and wrong. "Your mother was still torn up about that and about her father's disappearance when I first knew her," I said like I was pleading her case. "She really had no one to talk to."

Selesta drove in silence. The sun was going down. I looked at the pictures of the Mata paintings that she had in her portfolio. I found the House That Ate the World.

It's the house in the old rural Hamptons in which Antonio Mata had lived for some years with his wife and children. In the painting it's distended, bulging. Through open windows and doors flow furniture and phonographs, tennis shoes and radios, refrigerators and easy chairs.

Out of the house and onto the lawn in front and the meadow in back they tumble: cocktail dresses and ice buckets, strollers and overcoats, the possessions of an American household circa 1948.

"Kind of quaint compared to what's inside an American house today," I said.

"I don't think it's about materialism so much as about wariness and curiosity," Selesta said. "And maybe fear. He's a feline in human territory."

"Are you afraid, honey? Like he was?"

"Sometimes I am. I think it's good to be a little afraid sometimes."

We drove for a while before she asked, "Was my mother ever afraid?"

"Not that I saw when she was your age. She only seemed to get scared after you were born."

111

We talked a little more about her family. Brief bursts of conversation took place amid stretches of silence.

It was dark when we parked in the driveway of the House That Ate the World. Lamps were on inside but Joan stood on the unlighted porch and smiled as we approached.

"She can see us in the dark," muttered Selesta. "She just shrugs when I ask her about it."

We all embraced and Joan asked, "How was traffic?"

"No problem," said her daughter stepping past her. "How are you?"

By night, it could almost still be the cottage of fifty years before. I caught the tang and murmur of the ocean. A few hundred yards away the tide was coming in.

Through the open windows I saw the easel in the living room with the half finished painting. Bulbous circa-1950 American cars bore down on the viewer. Antonio Mata had disappeared without finishing it.

"A cat's eye view of the highway," I murmured.

Joan looked at me and then at her daughter, who smiled. Neither said anything but they moved down the hall to the kitchen, not touching but walking together.

When they were alone, Joan would ask her daughter what she and I had talked about on the way out here. I was glad to have given them that opening.

"Hello, Richie," said a familiar voice behind me. I turned and standing at the back porch door was the woman from the 1950s snapshots. Then Ruth Mata Rosen moved and that illusion disappeared. Decades obviously had passed and now she walked with a cane.

Ruth had called me Richie the first time we met many years before. There was no reason for it that I've ever been able to discover. Nobody else in the world has ever used that nickname for me.

"They're alone together?" she asked.

"In the kitchen," I said.

112

richard bowes

"No yelling? No screams?" she asked. "I don't necessarily hear. Especially things I don't want to hear."

"Quiet so far."

"At first, with my background in negotiation, I tried to arbitrate their dispute," said Ruth. "What I discovered was that when you spent nine years married to the cat man and never asked some basic questions, you're not dealing from a position of moral authority or common sense."

"We've all done things like that."

"Truly have you ever done anything quite like that?"

"Well..."

"No. I was naïve and bedazzled and just plain stupid. And a lot of misfortune came from that."

"You did something fine with Selesta."

"I'd been back to the place where Antonio was born a couple of times. There are still people who remember him as a kid. A few of the locals had folk tales about tree cats who can take human form. Rumors run that his grandmother was one.

"Poor Joan," Ruth said. "When she was Selesta's age and wanted so much to find out about her father, there was a travel ban in that area. It was a dangerous place. The government was killing student dissidents. And right then I was busy."

The kitchen door opened. Selesta emerged and then Joan. A kind of truce seemed to have been arranged.

"Is anyone else hungry?" asked Ruth.

"Yes," said Joan. "But the sad thing is none of us can cook."

Selesta narrowed her eyes and flashed her teeth. "I can probably rustle up something fresh and tasty from outside."

Joan winced but I chuckled. Ruth said, "Suit yourself. However, there are take-out menus on the refrigerator door. I thought maybe Thai would be nice."

Chapter Ten

The first library suicide occurred the day after the second anniversary of 9/11. It was late in the afternoon of the first Friday of the Fall 2003 semester. I sat in my office chatting on the phone with Marty Simonson, listened to his problems with a production of *Buried Child* that refused to come together and an ex-partner who wouldn't go away. "I want a whole bunch of closure," he said.

When he said that what came to mind was Mags and Geoff. Those two, especially Geoff, seemed to wait for me behind every corner. But when it was my turn I talked about my brother Gerry sick with hepatitis C. Marty knew him from back in the East Village. To take our minds off our problems I told him about Selesta and about Chris out in Ohio.

Marty was amused. "The Fairy Godfather!"

We detoured into gossip and nostalgia. In what I later saw as more uncanny than coincidental, we talked about the guy who called himself the King of the Big Night Hours.

Years ago I used to get Marty into the library and the gym as a guest. "Is the gym still open late?" he asked. "That's when and where I remember the King!"

"It's not open as late and it's not the same without him." The King was a big West Indian who did a lot for the university security uniform he wore. His bearing defined him as much as his looks.

As I remembered that, shouts echoed in the atrium and I heard a large, hollow thud like a quarter ton of wet laundry had hit the marble floor. I did not immediately rush out to see what had happened. The library hummed with kids and I thought it was one more damn student thing.

In fact a kid had just jumped into the atrium from the tenth floor. The screams got me off the phone and onto the ninth-floor balcony.

The center of the university library is a twelve-story atrium. Balconies line each floor and flying staircases connect each balcony with the ones above and below it. Railings of four-and-a-half-foot-tall vertical brass spikes were all that separated those balconies and stairs from the wide, empty interior space.

Right then those railings were lined with spectators who stared down in silence. The atrium floor is polished marble decorated with in an intricate grey, white, and black geometrical pattern. A body lay sprawled face down on the marble surrounded by a splatter of impact blood.

Seeing him, I visualized his downward path, saw the floor flying towards his face. From above, the design can create the illusion it's coming at you even if you're just standing there. Staring down at that still body, the pattern seemed to fill my vision. I managed to turn away before I was mesmerized.

At times like these, it always helps to have a function, something to do. Some of the students who stared were wide-eyed, hypnotized by what they had seen. Right then, acting on impulse, violating university protocol, I touched the students, tapped each one on the back, then put my hands on their shoulders and turned them around. "Don't look," I said. "It doesn't help."

Sirens sounded outside. Uniformed police and EMS came through the front doors with their radios blasting.

One kid whom I'd turned around stared straight ahead looking horrified; tears stood in her eyes. "I was on the stairs talking on my cell phone," she told me. "And I saw him climb onto the railing up on the tenth floor. I yelled at him, 'What are you doing?' Then he went over the side. I could have run up there and stopped him."

She repeated this a few times. She told me her name was Marie Rose. Glancing down, I saw the medics at work on the body. I kept telling her I knew how she felt and that she had done everything she could.

When the silent crowds on the balconies stirred I looked again and saw they had the jumper on a stretcher. Everyone watched in absolute silence as he was rolled across the atrium and out the door.

"Come sit down," I said.

Yellow crime-scene tape was being strung around the area with the spattered blood. A nursing student who came upstairs said she had heard the EMS say the kid's heart had stopped but that they had gotten it beating before they took him away.

The Science Reference desk where I usually worked was through a glass door that opens onto the ninth-floor balcony. The librarian who had been on duty through the whole incident badly needed to get away for a while.

So I sat at the desk with Marie Rose and asked about her studies. She was taking a masters in French lit and I got her to talk about that.

While she did, I found myself wondering what would have happened if I'd jumped up at the first shouts and gone out on the balcony. Could I have gotten to the kid before he went over the railing? Had the first mention of the King been a sign that I should start moving? How easily I fell into magic.

Police began to appear on the upper floors. A couple of detectives went through the building asking for witnesses. I looked to Marie Rose. She nodded and went over to them.

A very young uniformed cop had been sent upstairs to find the jumper's personal effects. I took him to the tenth floor and we looked at piles of books and papers, backpacks abandoned as people ran out to see what had happened. Many of them had yet to return. Nobody was even sure if the jumper had been studying on the floor.

The cop was nervous and a little pale and I wondered if maybe he'd been given this assignment because he was having trouble with the blood downstairs. After a while, we found a blue backpack with a bunch of suicide poetry: books by Anne Sexton, Robert Lowell, Sylvia Plath. And I said, "I'm afraid this is what we're looking for."

When I was back at the desk, a young man asked me very quietly, "Is there another way out? I want to leave but I don't ever want to cross the atrium again." Flashes came as the technicians took pictures of the spot where the body had landed. Looking down I could see reporters at the front door questioning the people who left.

I asked aloud who wanted to go out the back way. Half a dozen patrons responded and I brought them down in the freight elevator and out past the trash and garbage on the loading dock.

Guard George Robins was leaning back against a wall with his hand over his eyes, breathing hard. He'd driven the NYU jitney when I went to the downtown dorms with Marco and company. It occurred to me as we passed him that Guard Robins had also known the King.

I had worked in the building since it opened almost exactly thirty years before. Even though it was against university regulations, no one thought to stop me when I opened the back door and let out everyone who had followed me.

When I got back upstairs, another bunch of students wanted to leave and I took them down too and let them out. Robins by then was drinking coffee one of the secretaries had brought him. He'd been the first to get to the body. "I just heard he's dead in the emergency room," he told me. This was not the moment to ask him about the King.

By then the police were through with the site where the kid had landed. I stood at a door that led into the atrium. The building-maintenance foremen spoke in Spanish to one of the porters who refused to look at him.

Hector was the porter's name and he trudged out onto the floor with a water cart and a mop and started to clean up the blood. It was obvious this bothered Hector.

I saw the head of Reference standing with other administrators and went and told her I'd been letting people out the back way. She said it was fine. I had been there so long that when I did things like this it was assumed somehow I was following precedent.

University grief counselors appeared just as they had on 9/11. Staff members stood in clusters around our information desks mulling over the timing of this death. I made sure Marie Rose got to see the counselors but I didn't go myself.

The one who died, as we learned more about him and a photo was found in the university system, turned out to have been someone I half remembered, a silent guy who sometimes used the computers on my floor.

Just before the reference desks shut down for the evening, a big, goofy kid who I recognized as a regular rushed in and wanted to know, "Did anyone see my backpack?"

When I asked what was in it, he said, "My notebooks, a calculus text. And books for a twentieth-century American poetry class I'm taking." I told him the police had it.

The suicide's personal effects, when we found them, were in a basement study area. They were piled neatly and clearly identified as his, as if he was making things easier for us before he went up to the tenth floor and jumped.

Then work was over and there was nothing more to be done. Almost always when I left for the day, I left work completely behind. That evening walking through the atrium I felt like threads still connected me to the building.

I was supposed to attend a reading at the Nuyorican Poets Café but I skipped it. I went home and first sat down, then lay down, aware that I was in a kind of minor shock from the blood and the body.

A bit later that marble floor came up and hit me in the face with a dull smack and I jerked myself awake in my bed. It was after nine o'clock, too early and too late at the same time.

Over the last year or two I'd had a mini-affair, some one-nighters and weekenders, a call boy or so. I thought of dialing a friend, then thought of something better. I grabbed my bag and got to the university gym just before nine-thirty in the very heart of the Big Night Hours.

The place is often half deserted at that time on Fridays. Passing through the lobby I looked down on a few swimmers doing laps in the pool. A couple of three-on-three basketball games were almost lost on the vast gym floor. From somewhere in the distance I heard a racquetball ricochet and for a moment I almost expected to see the King leaning against a wall taking everything in with a little smile on his face.

The spell was broken in the locker room. Students were pulling on their clothes. Their talk was all chatter about missed shots, a girl someone knew from high school and just met again today, an accounting exam, the frat party on Saturday night.

These straight kids are very modest. They rarely take off their garish, shapeless boxer shorts and wrap towels around themselves before they do. Mostly they go back to their rooms to shower.

Some of my friends complain that these boys are puritanical. I think they're just polite and trying to ignore certain activity taking place around them. At times I feel like I'm part of an alternate world, semi-invisible but occupying the same space.

In this other world some of us are older and some are still students. It is a world of fleeting encounters in stairwells or steaming shower rooms, appointments to meet again outside.

Here men walk to the showers with nothing but the towels around their necks, whistle Sondheim, check each other out. In this other world when one catches a glimpse of a bare ass, one turns casually to see more, meets a wide-open gaze.

I was looking for other guys who had been around for a while. I found Ben and walked the treadmill next to his. Kenneth was riding a stationary bike. The last time I'd noticed, those two were an item. Now it seemed it wasn't so.

Just after eleven, we were drying off from the shower. Ben is about my age, a tenured professor in the School of the Arts. Kenneth is much younger, a poet, working on a doctorate and teaching freshman composition.

In the distance someone yelled, "Closing time."

"Today on the phone, a friend and I talked about the King of the Big Night Hours," I said.

"Oh, my," said Ben. "Your friend must be so old. I barely remember the King."

"Who?" Kenneth asked.

"Once upon a time when this was a sweeter scene and stayed open later, everyone was hot and available and there was this incredible guy," I said.

"Some Jamaican security guard who managed to get himself assigned here on the evening shift," Ben said in a bored tone. He pulled on white briefs and black trousers, ducked his shaven head into an Hermès sweater. "He was the one who cleared out the men's locker rooms and the showers at closing and did it slowly and very...selectively. He had this smug little smile like this was his game preserve."

It bothered me that Ben was so dismissive. I remembered the King holding me and how comforting he was.

"You called him the King of the Big Night Hours," Kenneth said. "Why?"

"It was his joke. One to four were the wee small hours, Sinatra territory. Around here, when the King ran things, nine to twelve were the big night hours." As I said this, I realized that nothing about this scene now evoked the King.

Just then a youngish man, a Russian experimental film director with piercing eyes and several days' worth of facial stubble, glanced Ben's way.

Ben who lives right around the corner said, "Excuse me, I see my ride home." He stepped into Gucci loafers and followed the Russian.

Kenneth looked a little lost but not surprised. "I heard what happened in the library today," he said. "I taught the kid who jumped."

We sat for some time in an all-night coffeehouse on Mac-Dougal Street. A few years before Kenneth had taught the suicide freshman English. He said the boy was straight, a little withdrawn and quite smart.

"I suppose I should have been able to spot something," he said.

"His friends, people who saw him earlier this afternoon, had no idea," I said. But I was getting tired of being reassuring. I wanted someone to try to make me feel better. When I got home, the caffeine meant I couldn't sleep much. But considering my dreams of falling, it was also a bit of a plus.

Saturday was still a work day for me and I was mildly stupefied as I crossed the atrium the next morning. The whole floor had been cleaned. I couldn't pick out the exact spot where the kid had landed.

The place was quite empty. The students were staying away. Various administrators were on hand to greet the staff as we arrived and ask us if we were okay. I told them Hector was very upset about having to mop up the blood and that they needed to be nice to him.

When I got up to the ninth floor, I went over to the balcony and looked down. Great long windows cover the front side of the building. The light that morning was soft. The patterned floor stayed where it was.

I remembered Dr. Maria Lovell. When I talked about suicide, which I sometimes did back then, she had said, "My dear, there's no future in it."

When the library was being built in the early seventies, the university was still poor. Construction went on for years: funding problems caused shutdowns; the quarry that provided the sandstone exterior went bankrupt and had to be bailed out.

My brother Gerry worked for the university. After I went through drug treatment he got me a job with the libraries. I was in my twenties and adrift, drank heavily with relapses into drugs, kind of expendable.

They used to send me over to the half-finished building to measure out spaces for offices. Inside, I wore a hardhat. The stairs weren't finished; the passenger elevators hadn't been installed. Work elevators open on all four sides rose and descended in the atrium, carried me up to balconies without railings where I'd hop off.

The building had no electricity. Sunlight came through the long windows, turned silver in the brass and marble atrium. Once I came into the building when a broken pipe on the sixth floor had created a sheet of water, which poured down like a miniature Niagara Falls. The construction workers paused to admire the sight.

When the place first opened, I gave tours. Most of it was by rote: "The pattern on the ten-thousand-square-foot floor is based on the design of the floor of a Renaissance church."

More often than not, when we were up on one of the top floors looking down, someone would ask if there had been any suicides. And I would say no and there had been no reported attempts. I'd point out the bronze vertical railings all along the balconies. I'd mention the security guards on patrol on the upper floors and the fact that in the week, the month, the semester since we had opened, there had been no trouble.

I wouldn't mention the university employees who were unable to work on the upper floors when we moved into the building. There were people who had vertigo each time they got off the elevators. They had to sidle along near the walls, careful not to look over the edge and see how the glass and brass interior swept down to the marble floor. Some got used to it. Some were unable to continue in their old jobs.

Among the tour groups, some thought the geometric marble patterns made the floor appear to come towards them. I would retell the university-approved legend of how the geometric patterns were intended to appear like spikes and pyramids and how this was supposed to dissuade anyone from wanting to jump.

I would not mention the campus folk tale, the one in which those same shapes would draw you in if you looked at them too long.

Giving tours was a task they could find for a long-haired young guy in a leather jacket and boots who had a minimal academic background and a bad attendance record. It was known that I led a tumultuous private life, packed a switchblade. Even after Gerry left the university for a job in publishing I was granted many second chances. People who remembered my brother loved him still.

Around me, things were changing. The dozens of little libraries and departments stuck in various spots around the campus had been consolidated into the main building when it opened. And all of us who had worked in those small and idiosyncratic situations had to find new places for ourselves in this huge building.

Eventually I was sent up to the brand-new science library on the ninth floor. The staff was a librarian who stayed in her office and me out at the information desk. Thirty years later the department had grown and I had an office but my job was much the same.

By then I was a kind of anomaly, a clerical who had written books which were in the collection, someone who was thought to have institutional memory. One use they had found for me over the years was as the token non-professional, the union member at the table of faculty and administrators.

The week after the suicide there were email memos reminding us of the grief-counseling services the University offered and announcing the formation of various committees. I didn't go for counseling but I was appointed to a panel examining what the library could do to improve student life.

On the committee were a serials cataloger and a programmer, a documents librarian, an assistant dean, a brand new paraprofessional from electronic resources, and a woman from the personnel office. We sat around and conjectured about student alienation and loneliness. I think I was the only one in the room who had actually dealt with the patrons. Certainly I was the only one who had spoken to the one who killed himself.

A week or two after she saw the kid jump, Marie Rose came to see us at the reference desk. Marie Rose's last name was Italian. She was a pleasant young lady who told us how the Saturday after the suicide she had to go to the wedding of a cousin in New Jersey and be happy and cheerful when all the while she was seeing the guy hit the floor. She thanked us and said she thought she was okay now.

§

Exactly four weeks after the suicide, I was on my way back from lunch when I met library staff and patrons walking away from the building quickly, looking straight ahead, never glancing back. They told me someone else had jumped a few minutes before.

This time it went almost by rote, like everyone knew their parts. The EMS and police were already rolling him through the front door on a gurney when I arrived. His face, what I could see of it behind the breathing mask, had a dark flush like the skin was full of blood.

He too had jumped from the tenth floor. Just as with the first suicide, he was still alive when they took him out but he died in the emergency room.

This time there was very little blood. And this time Hector's supervisor came along and helped him clean it up. Then the dean thanked them. Etiquette was being worked out.

Later in the day I saw the jumper's picture and stared at the face. He was very young. He had only been at the university for a few weeks and I doubted we'd met. But he reminded me of Marco and dozens of other students past and present whom I had known.

That night the kid fell past me in my dreams, looked up with large doomed eyes and Geoff's face as I stared over the balcony and he fell onto the marble patterns.

Saturday I went to a grief-counseling group session held right in the library. Everyone said where they were and what they saw when the boy jumped. A very serious young woman from the Legal Council Office on the eleventh floor spoke in tears about hearing him scream as he fell. I told about my dreams of the floor coming up to smash him. The therapist led us in breathing exercises, tried to get us to let go of memories and dreams like the young woman's and mine.

The next week at the committee meeting, we read reports and safety protocols for suicide prevention at large universities around the country. It seemed as if each jumper marked a failure on the part of our community.

Privately though, I began to wonder about the building itself. The architect, an American, had been a Nazi sympathizer and had lived in Germany in the thirties. Speaking about his past at the time the library opened, he said he had been young and foolish and had been fascinated by the uniforms.

The benefactor who had donated millions for the construction of the library bearing his name was a pharmaceutical tycoon, a self-made man. He had helped Nixon into the White House. The president himself was supposed to dedicate the building. But by the time of the official opening, he faced impeachment and was not making public appearances.

Many years later, one of the benefactor's granddaughters picketed in front of the library claiming he had molested her. Back and forth in all weather she went, carrying a sign. It was something everyone got used to. Then she was gone. Some said he had settled money on her, others that she had been hospitalized.

Recollecting things like these made it easy to spin stories of a building that killed kids. But the unease fueling my dreams involved personal and more elusive memories, ones on which I wasn't willing to dwell.

The students stayed away as if they knew the place was accursed. It was half deserted in the middle of the day. Staff working the reference and circulation desks, hauling book trucks in the stacks, editing the computer records, cataloging books, listened for the screams and the muffled thump.

All the available security guards were in the building. They patrolled the upper floors, stood on the flying staircases, warned students away from the rails and discouraged anyone from hanging around on the balconies.

Some of them were normally on duty in other parts of the university and I'd not seen them before. Others I'd gotten to know over the years. Guard Robins was up on my floor one day and I found a chance to talk to him. He had been in the army and in hotel security in Jamaica. My brother had helped one of his kids get into the school and he remembered Gerry fondly.

"Lots of overtime but it all goes in taxes," said Robins. "I will not die rich, I am saddened to say."

Robins and the King of the Big Night Hours had been friendly. I'd often seen them talking long ago.

He was older and liked a bit of formality so I still addressed him as we'd been told to do when I first started work.

"Guard Robins, you knew someone from a while back. Fortnum was his name."

Campus Security in its own small way is a police unit and as such is closed and secretive. There was a distance between us now that I'd asked this. "Charles Fortnum?"

"Yes. Someone was asking what happened to him."

"We came from the same town in Jamaica, Fortnum and I. He was younger and I didn't much know him there. But his mother knew my family and when he came here, they asked me to recommend him for a job.

"When he got sick, he went home to his mother. My old aunt was a nurse and she told me when Fortnum died. It must be fifteen or twenty years ago."

So now I knew what had happened to the King and it wasn't unexpected. He was very much a part of my reaction to the young jumpers. But I was poking around the periphery of my memories, reluctant to think about the two of us and what had brought us close.

Something in my expression made Robins add, "Unless it's in my job, I do not meddle in what others do."

In the days after the second death, men and women in suits and with blueprints stood in the atrium and on the upper floors and talked to men in work clothes. Then it was announced that tall, clear plastic baffles were going to be put up on all the balconies and stairs. No one would ever again have access to railings.

While this work was happening, all the balconies were closed except for those on floor seven. The elevators operated by security guards went directly there. Patrons would then be escorted into the stacks by staff. From there they could go to the cement fire stairs buried inside the walls of the building and get to whatever floors they wanted.

The first Saturday this construction was underway, I sat almost alone in the Science Reference Center. The doors out to the balconies were all locked. Muffled drilling and workers' shouts could be heard from the atrium. An occasional student would climb the fire stairs and emerge onto my floor.

Marie Rose was one. She made her way upstairs to tell me, "I wanted to say goodbye. I'm not coming into this place ever again. My friend Julie has agreed to come here and take out any books I need. I'm transferring out next semester."

It seemed to me Marie Rose might well have been one who had looked down from these balconies and thought of death.

What I said, though, was, "I'll be sorry to see you leave." And I realized how bound I was to this place and how when I was gone nothing would remain but one or two people asking, "What happened to the white-haired guy who used to sit at this desk?"

"After the second death," she said, "I started seeing the first one go over the side again."

Looking for something to say, I told her, "Julie sounds like she must be a wonderful friend."

"She is," Marie Rose nodded

"You have that, you're solid," I said.

In the strange weeks following, crews worked twelve to eighteen hours six or seven days a week. Slowly metal frames and plastic baffles grew along the balconies.

On the seventh floor, the elevator doors would open and a guard would step out. Patrons would be guided off the elevator and into the stacks where library staff would direct them.

Staff would also line up the patrons who wanted to go downstairs, and when an empty elevator was ready they were herded aboard. None of them got to walk unescorted out onto the balcony.

Because people weren't asking reference questions, I signed up for this duty and stood on the seventh floor for hours each day. Often, late in the evenings, it would be just one security guard and me. The trickle of patrons mostly looked unhappy and wanted to know why we were doing this.

Once in a while that autumn, in no pattern or rhythm I could discover, I would fall from an immense height and jerk myself awake as I smashed into the floor. The breathing exercises the counselor taught me helped. I refused the offer of sedatives.

Finally one day in my office, I talked to Marty Simonson on the phone. "What made you think of the King of the Big Night Hours?" I asked. "You were talking about him just moments before the first kid jumped."

"You brought it up out of nowhere as I recall," said Marty. "Suddenly asked me if I remembered him. I hadn't thought about the guy since the last time I saw him all those years ago."

When he said this, I remembered sitting at this desk as we had talked a couple of months before and feeling hands on my back. It had been so real I'd looked around and found no one else in my office. I'd been reminded of a time the King had done that and that's when I had asked Marty if he remembered him.

Realizing all this brought back a memory of standing on a high balcony one night not too long after the building first opened. Everything felt black. An affair with an East Village drug dealer's younger brother had gone very wrong.

A front tooth had gotten chipped when a gun was shoved in my mouth and I got a severe cut on the back of the head. My knife, leathers and long hair were gone. Now I wore a Mets cap over a crewcut, sneakers and hand-me-down clothes.

Remembering I fell silent on the phone. Marty asked, "Are you okay?"

I said, "I wonder if all the fucking uncanny I find in my life is real or the result of head injuries."

And he asked, "It can't be both?" And when I didn't respond, he said, "Listen, I'll come to New York this weekend and we'll see some shows."

I didn't tell him not to bother. But I did think of myself as having survived for a long time and to no real purpose.

When I was young I read Graham Greene's account of playing Russian roulette as a kid. When he was in a black depression, he'd get the revolver out of his father's desk. Each time he spun the barrel and pulled the trigger and lived the depression cleared.

It had seemed such a simple and reasonable thing to do back then that I kind of filed it away as a survival tip.

The guard on duty with me for my stint on the seventh floor that night was young and seemed uncomfortable in his uniform. He told me he wasn't used to it. He took classes at the university and looked so much like one of the students that they mostly had him in plain clothes.

I would be sixty in a few months and wasn't used to standing for hours on end. It had begun to catch up with me, and my legs ached. While he talked, I looked around the atrium at the places where they still didn't have the baffles up.

After work, I considered going to the gym. Instead I sat on a park bench in the big night hours, stared at the huge lighted front windows of the library and thought about the time I'd stood with my hands grasping the rails.

Then I went back to the building. It was after closing time and Guard Robins was on the front desk. I told him I had lost my house keys and had a spare set in my office.

I know he watched me cross the atrium and go to the fire stairs. The climb up all the flights was brutal, but I didn't care. I went out onto the seventh-floor balcony and then went up the stairs. Earlier, I'd spotted a place on the eighth floor where the railings were still exposed.

Work had halted for the night. No one even noticed me go to the eighth-floor balcony. This might be the last time I could do this.

Thirty years before, broken and humiliated, I stood with my hands on the brass spikes just as I did now. I saw no place for myself in the world. In the East Village everyone had heard what happened to me. At work they were tired of my absences and surliness. I'd alienated anyone who'd ever taken up my cause.

On tours when someone asked whether anybody had jumped I had always say no. That night decades ago I grasped two of the brass spikes and pulled my weight up. My palms would get slashed as I vaulted over the side but that wouldn't matter when the marble floor rushed up.

Right then I had felt a tap on my back. Two huge hands grabbed my shoulders and turned me a hundred and eighty degrees. When I focused my eyes, I saw the King step over to an open elevator door and beckon me.

Thirty years later, remembering all this, I heard the elevator behind me and felt as if my ritual had evoked the King. When the door flew open I turned and saw the familiar uniform.

"Get in here, you stupid bastard," said Guard Robins. "You know the kind of trouble you would get me in?" he said as the elevator descended. "You have no thought of that? What is it in you people that you all want to become dead?" I knew he meant the King and the jumpers and me and wanted to tell him I hadn't been going to jump, couldn't even have scrambled over the side.

I wondered if the ones who jumped had been enacting their own ritual. Had they tried to see how far they could go before hands reached out to hold them?

"At your age," Robins said, "You should know that it will happen soon enough that we don't need to hurry it."

He saw me out the door. I knew he wouldn't report this since it would implicate him. Walking home, I felt alive, revived. My legs didn't hurt.

I thought about when the King of the Big Night Hours had found me at the rails. Ben was right that the King always looked pleased with himself. But I felt he had reason.

He moved so quickly for a big man, kept his hand on my back guiding me along to a little empty office in the sub cellar. The throne room, he called it. He had a key. The place, I remember, smelled like spice. As did the King himself. He laughed once when I asked what cologne he used. "It is my essence," he said.

Without the uniform, he looked even larger than with it. There was a silver scimitar of a scar along his rib cage. "A mean old man did that when I was young," he told me once when I asked.

If I got naked now and screwed on an old wooden desk I'd be crippled for the rest of my life. But I was gay and the Seventies were a bacchanalia. Death avoided or at least postponed made everything vivid and exhilarating. When we were finished he stood over me and said, "If you do anything like that again, I will keep you locked bare ass in my throne room for good."

We got together many other times but it lacked the intensity of that first encounter. In an era of abundant opportunity we faded out of each others' lives. Possibly neither of us wanted to drain all the magic from the moment. While we were seeing each other I turned thirty and that year I finally kicked drugs and booze.

When I noticed the King was never around it was years later in the plague time. The ones I asked only said he was back in Jamaica and I didn't want to follow that any further.

Maybe the King had returned to the university after death. Or some part of him had never left. Had he tried to reach me in time to save the jumper?

If so, he failed or I did. But enough of him got through that I had known to tap those shoulders and turn those kids around when they stared agape. Minor good deeds like those may help his soul and mine.

On the weekend Marty came into the city and stayed with me. I was really happy to see him but my crisis had passed. Later, Kenneth, the poet I'd known from the gym, called and we got together.

When the grief therapist contacted me, I said I felt fine and thanked her. I was glad to see them erect the last baffles and seal off the atrium.

The job got finished early. One afternoon in late fall it was over. The elevators started to work again and we could walk safely on the balconies and stairs.

The sun now reflected off the plastic panels. This changed the light in the atrium, made it seem far duller. It felt as if the building had been tamed.

Remembering the King had reminded me that there was no need to hurry death. Kenneth and I were having a minor affair. By the time the new semester began I had decided I didn't need to die in this place. Privately I set a date for early retirement.

It was a bright winter morning when I reached my decision. I was walking to work when I saw Marie Rose with a plump dark young lady.

Seeing my surprise, Marie said, "Julie and I decided it made no sense to run away."

"You're going to stay and I'm going to leave," I said and told her about my plans.

"We'll miss you," she said. "But I'll remember you." And in this business it's all one can hope for.

Guard Robins was on duty that day. Our eyes never met now and we hadn't spoken since the night he ordered me off the balcony. Each time he ignored me I felt bad about what had happened.

Now I often think about the King but I haven't felt his presence since that September afternoon. Maybe nothing has happened that would bring him back.

Chapter Eleven

On a rainy March morning I thought about how a life can wind in and out of yours. Lovers don't stay with me but friends and siblings do. I'll never have a child but people lend me theirs. That morning I started an SF story about someone whose life was tied to mine when I was five years old.

The Times of My Life (a story in progress)

Every version of the world that's ever been or will be has a way of dealing with its wild boys and bad girls. The army recruiter, the sweet-talking ponce, the press gang at the harbor, each takes away his share.

In the sorry-ass place I came from, I was an immature punk with something to prove and no future I could see. Back there, people were afraid of the Dark. Kids quite often and even adults on occasion went out into the night and never came back. Usually it was something you heard had happened two towns over or in Europe. But a girl in our town had disappeared and rumor was the Dark had taken her. So kids had a curfew complete with the CP, the Curfew Patrol.

We called them the Ceepers and acted out with
them the usual rituals of Authority and Youth. The
inevitable result of that was that some of us ended
up getting chased straight through the night and
out into the light of another world's day.

Then I saw the clock and realized I had to leave my cozy
apartment for work. The March rain was wind-driven and I
had a short but wet and chilly walk to the university library.

As I dumped my umbrella in my office wastebasket the
phone rang. My sister Lee was on the line, telling me that our
brother Gerry, broke and uninsured, was waiting to go into
the emergency room at St. Vincent's Hospital. His body had
suddenly become bloated with sixty pounds of excess liquid,
the result of a failing liver.

Rearranging my schedule, taking early lunch I walked
through Washington Square Park and along Greenwich Avenue over to the hospital and got wet again as I did. The park
and sidewalks were deserted. Even the streets felt bare of traffic. It seemed like a dream, a memory of the empty London of
Antonioni's *Blow Up* or the deserted San Francisco of Hitch-
cock's *Vertigo*.

St. Vincent's, the Greenwich Village legend, was where I had
awakened with no memory of who I was in 1965 when I was
twenty-one. It was where in 1974, after Gerry was stabbed and
died and brought back to this world, his one remaining kidney
had been made to function and his life had been allowed to
continue.

When I got there, Gerry had been registered and sat in the
waiting room of that blowsy, good-hearted old institution.
"Man, I'm glad to see you," he said.

His face and his upper body seemed normal enough. But his
legs were swollen; his pants legs looked like water balloons.
Hepatitis C had destroyed my brother's liver.

I sat with him waiting for a bed in the emergency ward to open up and trying to look at anything except his legs. The color on the television set in the waiting room was blurred.

"Jerry Springer's interviewing radioactive mutants," he said, looking at it.

"Crossdressers with death-ray eyes who think it's okay for both partners in a marriage to have affairs on the side," I told him. He was amused, but distant and worn.

Then a nurse called his name. I saw Gerry through the swinging doors of the emergency room, made sure the nurse understood what was wrong and walked back to work. Above Sixth Avenue, the hands of the clock on the brick gothic tower of the old Jefferson Market Court House stood at a quarter past two.

Sixth Avenue had been the hub of the old Village. It had existed in the shadow of an elevated train line. The El had gotten torn down in the 1930s. But a lot of the buildings along Sixth in Greenwich Village are still low and naked looking.

The corner where Greenwich Avenue crosses Sixth and turns into Eighth Street was once an active sleaze pit. A few traces of that remain but you only see them if you know they're present.

As I rarely do now, I stopped at the Grey's Papaya stand on the corner for a hotdog and orange drink. Besides myself, there were a Spanish and an Asian queen behind the counter, and a couple of junkies, one white, one black. It reminded me of old times.

The white kid stood unmoving, staring out at the Avenue. The black kid paced up and down, his eyes fierce, withdrawal already making him jumpy. Their faces, framed in baseball caps and sweatshirt hoods, reminded me of Gus Van Sant's line, "Both possess a certain painful down-and-out handsomeness of a street hustler."

For a moment I found myself looking through their eyes, straining to catch sight of the connection coming through the rain. Then I threw my paper plate and cup in the trash and walked out.

In Washington Square Park only the grass dealers stood, revolving slowly, chanting their spiels, nodding to me as I strode past, water finally getting through my boots and onto my socks.

Back at the library, I sat at my desk for a couple of minutes. On the bulletin board of my office was a poster created a few years before to celebrate my thirtieth anniversary at the university. A black and white photo of me from early in my time working there had been found and blown up.

I kept it as a reminder. Long-haired, somewhat vulpine, the stranger in the photo is handsome enough and more than a bit painful. He sits in an office with his elbows on a typewriter looking at something off camera. The me in the picture was almost a stranger, someone I'd look at twice if we passed on the street but would know better than to cruise.

That photo evoked another image that was somewhere between dream and memory. In it, a woman in a dress and boots, face craggy almost like a man's, sat in what was called an "old law" New York kitchen, the kind where the toilet was out in the hall and tub was there in the kitchen.

This one, though, was clean and homey, well kept up. She had a kitten in her lap and stared, eyes wide but not amazed, at what had just come through her door—a black man was dragging in a white guy's naked body.

If I could have had a photo of this memory or dream, it would have been up on the bulletin board next to the one of me. Because the guy in that photo was the one the woman saw being dragged in the door.

The why and how of this I couldn't pin down. But I knew that I could see myself like that because when it had happened I was dead.

After all those years I could go through my work routine without serious thought. When I walked back to the hospital afterwards, it was evening and rush hour. The wind and the rain had died down.

Crowds of people came out of the subway, lighted windows and headlights cut through the dusk. I looked in Grey's Papaya as I went past. The hustlers were gone, the place was busy. I scanned the faces, imagining I was still the guy in the photo, waiting for a john, looking for the man.

They let me into the emergency room to see Gerry. He had been admitted to the hospital and was waiting for a bed to become available. They had him on painkillers and he was much happier. He was calling the nurses "darling," talking to them in the big, fake Irish brogue that he put on sometimes.

When I was sure he was going to be well taken care of, I said good night and left. The rain had stopped completely by then. On my way home lights shone on the wet streets and I thought about Gerry and myself.

§

My brother's path to the St. Vincent's emergency room began on a Saturday night and Sunday morning in the summer of 1974.

I had been out late. That year, I was thirty years old and embarked on a great adventure. The West Village was a fantasy park and these nights I was having sex without drugs or booze for the first time since shortly after I met the Subway Man.

Everything seemed dramatic. Over on the Hudson, some guy I held on a rotted pier got illuminated by the moonlight shining through the holes in the aluminum roof above, by the city light reflected on the oily river water. Our clothes were half off; he had a dark buzz cut and his eyes were closed. I took his prick and wished he was the first guy I'd found that night.

At around three when I got home to the East Village, the phone started ringing as I turned my key in the door. When I answered, a cop was on the line asking if I had a brother named Gerald. When I said yes, he told me he was calling from the emergency room of Metropolitan Hospital up in Spanish Harlem.

Gerry had been stabbed and was in critical condition. The doctors needed me there to approve what they had to do.

When I reached the hospital, a Pakistani doctor no older than I was told me, "He was stabbed in a street incident. One kidney has been perforated."

Gerry was laid out on a gurney. We, both of us, are light-skinned but he was dead white.

He saw me. "Hey, man. They brought me back here. It's all like flowers and fire." he said.

"He was stabbed," the doctor said as if anxious to set the record straight. "His signs had failed when he came in. We revived him."

"I'm in the flames and I'm going to die," Gerry said.

"No, you won't," I said. Later, in an age of AIDS, I became more adept at telling people who were dying that they were going to be fine. This was my first time. "You're going to live and have to listen to me tell this story again and again."

Gerry smiled. "I was in the palace," he said. "It was all lighted up. Then they pulled me back here."

The doctor led me outside. He said Gerry had large amounts of cocaine and alcohol in his system. They needed to remove the damaged kidney. With the condition my brother was in, that would be dangerous. But they saw no other choice. Another doctor, a resident a year or two older, stood with him, nodded his agreement.

With no idea what I was doing, I signed something. I was numb.

The doctors went back inside and I sat in the waiting room on that Saturday night. A stretcher rolled in with paramedics and cops around it and a patient with an oxygen mask on his face and cuffs on his hands.

Two men, completely ordinary looking, suddenly appeared and introduced themselves as homicide detectives. They wanted to know what I knew about my brother and what he was doing that night up in Spanish Harlem.

I had a good idea that drugs had brought him there but I thought it best to tell the cops I didn't know.

They said there had been a street altercation. A bottle had been thrown. A knife used. They were as good as certain about who had done that. Listening, all I could think was that they were going on the assumption Gerry was dead.

Behind them, the door of the operating room flew open and the doctors, kids I'd see them as now, came out excited, slapping each other's backs in celebration. They had removed the damaged kidney without killing Gerry.

When that happened, the homicide cops disappeared. Gerry had died briefly on the operating table but came back and was still alive. My brother wasn't a homicide case any more. The precinct detectives I spoke to had no ideas about who had stabbed him; were more interested in the drugs in his system.

Waiting there that night I kept thinking of how he'd almost made it to the palace. At dawn he was admitted to the hospital itself, on the critical list but alive.

My brother had lost a kidney and the other one didn't function. Metropolitan Hospital was a great place to go if you'd been stabbed. But there was no follow-up. Friends of our parents pulled strings. Gerry was transferred downtown to St. Vincent's, which had a special kidney wing.

That first time in 1974 when I told people at the library what had happened, the ones who knew him would say, "I pray for him," and "I pray for you both."

And I would say, "Thank you." I don't think I ever prayed for Gerry. Or for anybody in all my life. Oh, maybe when someone pointed a gun at me or I was in withdrawal and felt like I was going to die: brief, involuntary religious spasms.

Gerry died again on the operating table that first time at St. Vincent's as they put a shunt into his wrist to give him dialysis. Again he was brought back to life.

141

"A genuine resurrection artist is what you've become," I said when they let me talk to him. "You try to fly to the palace again?"

"It's a garden, but all lights. Instead of plants, lights. And I was like some kind of insect compared to it. Then I heard a woman calling, 'You get back here!' It was the nurse, this West Indian lady. When I woke up, she said, 'You're not getting away from us.'"

Gerry had a science-fiction book with him. I think it was one of the Terry Carr anthologies. He held it up. I saw that his hands, his wrists were covered with raw wounds, places where he'd been stabbed and sewn up, places where shunts and needles had been stuck into him.

"There's a story in here," he said. "About two beings on this planet. One is an explorer, an astronaut from earth who crash lands, and the other is a native species who's like a sentient tree. The author doesn't quite say that, but that's what it's like.

"And this tree-like thing takes care of the explorer and loves him. And he loves it, but he doesn't understand that right away. Then he's rescued and they take him to the hospital ship and he's protesting because he doesn't want to leave this tree. At the end he comes back..."

"...and the tree has been chopped down to make splints for his broken bones."

He started to laugh. "Kind of. You read it?"

"Just a wild guess."

In fact, I'd thrown in the joke because I found the symbiosis between the explorer and the tree a little uncomfortable and sticky, a bit too much like our own.

It reminded me of something Vincent Tracy, the addictions counselor I was seeing, had told me about how relationships got turned on their heads, not only by someone drinking, but by someone going on the wagon.

Mr. Tracy said, "Say there's a drunk who is entirely out of control. And there's a partner, a friend, a relative, who likes to take a drink or two, but has a life that's relatively in order and who's done everything in his or her power to help the other person.

"The drinker goes on the wagon, maybe, becomes a bit self-satisfied and self-righteous. And suddenly the other person becomes the one with the drinking problem."

Only when I stopped doing hard drugs and any kind of alcohol earlier that year did I become aware of Gerry doing things like going to East Harlem to buy coke. Did my going clean somehow remove a prop, a purpose, from his life?

At St. Vincent's in 1974 Gerry's remaining kidney began to function. His powers of recovery amazed the doctors. He got better fast.

When I came by, we'd talked about the past, about that room we shared out on Long Island when I was in college and he was in high school. We evoked Boston and the neighborhood in Dorchester where we'd lived.

"Thick with Irish: a community whose main industry was producing Catholic children," he said.

"Remember Crusher Casey, that ex-wrestler, had a bar downtown and the biggest house in the neighborhood?" I asked, knowing the answer.

"I knew his son. Crusher had these cauliflower ears. Proud of them too; if you asked he'd flap the ears for you. Nice guy."

At St. Vincent's, that first time, they saved his life and, though nobody understood it back then, quite possibly wrecked it. In that simple and ignorant age, the blood supply was hopelessly compromised. Gerry received several transfusions. And that perhaps was when he contracted the Hepatitis C, which, over decades, silently, relentlessly destroyed his liver.

In September of 1974 he got out of the hospital long before the doctors expected. I rode with him in the cab back to Brooklyn and his wife. He had a couple of the Zelazny Amber novels. Those books about nine semi-immortal brothers locked in a bloody struggle for possession of cognate reality fascinated us both.

"Brooklyn is Amber, the one true world," he said and smiled. "Everything else is its pale shadow."

"That's ridiculous," I said. "Manhattan is the center of the universe."

We agreed it was stupid for brothers to fight and decided to divide reality between us.

It was all autumn sunshine as the cab went over the Brooklyn Bridge. Gerry was alive and I was sober and everything felt very big and possible.

THE TIMES OF MY LIFE (A STORY IN PROGRESS)

Way after dark my brother and I made our way home, fast but careful, on the watch for the Ceeps, the Curfew Patrol. We went down alleyways and over back fences. All the shortcuts we'd found at seven and ten were there when we needed them at fourteen and seventeen. Then it had been a game pure and simple, now it was a game with real sharp consequences

Three years younger and just as big as I was, Brad was the perfect younger brother. Not once did he complain, or even mention that all this was because I sat in the cellar we called a clubhouse and ignored the warning bell, the curfew whistle because I couldn't resist one last toke, one last hit of beer, one last Benzedrine. Instead of appreciating that and loving him, I was eaten up inside because people told us we looked like twins, like clones. I didn't want to think I still looked like a goofy little kid.

Brad and I climbed as one up a chain-link fence and over the flat roof of the Muellers' garage. We dropped down from the roof and moved fast along the narrow driveway, invisible to anyone behind the lighted windows in the houses.

Those lights only shone a short way into the night. Inside, parents with all their children safe at home could relax thinking they had them safe. People like that didn't understand that the Dark didn't reach out and take their kids. What I already sensed was that, by restricting our lives, turning us into outlaws, our parents were driving us into the Dark.

We paused in the shadows waiting for a safe moment to dash across the street. I could hear the Muellers' radio playing dance music. The Castros next door had a television on and a studio audience was laughing it up.

A car drove by slowly, old man Kreel's DeSoto. I didn't think Kreel would turn us in, but I drew back, pulled Brad with me.

A Ford truck sped past in the opposite direction. Then the street was empty. "Go," I whispered and we crossed it diagonally, ran neck and neck through the Fitzgeralds' yard and over the old stone wall that lay behind their house.

Beyond that was the wide corner lot on the next street from ours, the most open ground on our run. We could see the lights on in the back windows of our house. Maybe being so close to home made me careless. As we came off the dry October grass and set foot on the sidewalk, headlights caught us. A Ceep cruiser pulled out of a driveway and was headed our way.

At that moment I gave back something for the years of undeserved devotion I'd gotten. "Go," I yelled and Brad was off, running straight for home. I don't know how far he got before he realized I wasn't with him. All the way, I hoped. He was a smart kid with a clean record.

If I got caught it would be the third time for me and that meant jail or the marines. Not much waited for me at home. My parents had about had it with me. For getting my brother in trouble they'd probably turn me in themselves.

I didn't know what I was doing until I did it. As Brad took off, I turned and ran down the sidewalk right past the Ceepers. They went into reverse trying to catch me and I ran headlong for the Woods.

What we called the Woods was a vacant lot, trees and undergrowth, broken glass and flattened beer cans. When we were younger the Woods had been the Far West, Sherwood Forest, Omaha Beach.

Lately it was the subject of rumors; a place where talk had it that kids disappeared. A few weeks before, coming past it at night, I'd seen, out of the corner of my eye, a slash of sunlight dancing. I'd been spooked. But somewhere in my mind I must have decided that if I had a chance of escape, it lay in that light. And if it killed me, so be it.

Oncoming traffic got in the Curfew Patrol's way. With sirens wailing, lights flashing, they did a U-turn. I could hear other sirens; see cherry-tops converge as I plunged into the Woods.

The Ceepers were out of their cruisers and after me. I must have planned this subconsciously, set up a situation this desperate. Probably a thousand miserable kids wanted to leave for every one like me who did.

All I know is, flying on beer and bennies, with nothing to lose, I ran through the Woods. When I saw the light, I turned towards it. When I saw it again, I turned again then again.

And the light got brighter as I twirled, until it was late morning and I was tumbling on green grass. Before me was a grove of trees and a temple, half white and half black. People in white robes encircled me, each one clasping the hands of the ones on either side. Interrupted in mid-dance, they pointed, amazed at my sudden appearance.

In the years, the decade, that followed my brother's stabbing and recovery, we actually did kind of divvy up our corners of cognate reality.

When Gerry got out of the hospital the job in publishing was still his but he wasn't interested. Instead he bent heaven and earth to become a bartender in Brooklyn. It was like the old neighborhood in Boston reached out, asked, "How is it you think you can escape?" and reclaimed him. He and his wife had a kid, bought a house. It made sense if you saw it in the context of his becoming one with his own private Amber.

Me? I stayed in Manhattan, worked for the university, had a series of one-night stands, a few longer-lasting relationships. With a guy I met in the Village I started to design and sell board games. I began writing for the first time since college, trying to make some kind of sense of my lost teens and twenties.

Gerry and I met off and on. One night, I think it was in the early '80s, for reasons I no longer remember, we were in an Irish cop bar over on Third Avenue in the teens. I drank seltzer. My brother was doing Hennessey and telling me and a bunch of guys I didn't know a lot of not quite connected stories about the bar world of Brooklyn. "He's the fucking Borough President and he's standing there begging for someone to find his car keys."

Gerry introduced me to an off-duty cop with a bright whiskey gleam, Sergeant Joey Somebody. "We know each other from Park Slope," he explained, like it was a far shore or a famous battle.

"This is my brother," he told the Sergeant. "He designs games. Where we grew up in Boston was wall-to-wall Irish bars and churches, nuns who smoked cigars, priests in big cars, altar boys drunk on the sacramental wine."

He was off on a monologue about a neighborhood that wasn't entirely recognizable. It felt like he was slipping away from me.

Talking over Johnny Cash on the jukebox, I told my brother, "Listening to your description is like hearing someone who grew up on an alternate world."

He looked a little hurt, like he too understood we were losing touch. I felt bad. He deserved to have grown up in a world where he had a better older brother, one who had maybe taken fewer whacks to the head. Maybe the drugs and booze had been my addiction and I had been his. Not an idea that made me feel really swell.

We talked a bit that night about people we both knew, trying to knit ourselves together again. He told me, "Freddie Ayers says hello." And I remembered that he and my sometime boyfriend had become friendly first at school, then in the East Village and in publishing. They still talked.

A couple of years after that conversation on Eighth Avenue in Chelsea, at about five in the last morning of a Memorial Day weekend, I encountered Freddie Ayers.

Since that brief time when I was first in New York and we lived together, we'd run into each other on occasion. In the flexible way of that era in gay New York we'd put aside bad memories and done a few one-night stands over the years.

After a long tour of duty on the docks, I felt and probably looked ragged-ass and empty. Freddie was thin, saint-like, with dark shadows under his eyes. I'd come to be wary of that look. We kissed, spoke briefly and he asked about Gerry. I knew it was stupid but I still resented their friendship; felt somehow betrayed.

Shortly afterwards, as one often had reason to do in those days, I added up my physical contacts with Freddie Ayers. He'd been diagnosed with AIDS. What had started out as boy sex had gone on to full exchange of bodily fluids. In total it amounted to an intense two-week fling spread out over seventeen years, none of it really recent.

The next time I saw Freddie was a year or so later in Roosevelt Hospital. He was attached to a ventilator with tubes running out of him. I had learned by then how to keep it light and reassuring, talking of Sondheim and rumors of new treatments.

At the Science Reference desk, though, I kept careful watch on AIDS/HIV research and knew there were no breakthroughs.

I actually made him laugh a little. But at one point, he said, "You know, it was your brother I really wanted. I know he's straight. Sex wasn't the point. I envied the way you two were so easy with each other in that room you had in your parents' house.

"We were in college and the East Village at the same time but I really got to know him when he was doing fine and working in publishing. You were over the edge, having an affair with that dealer's kid brother. Then someone saw the kid wearing your clothes and was told you got killed by the gang.

"So I called Gerry and he said no, friends of his had found you. He had just moved to Brooklyn and had to come into Manhattan at four in the morning and bring you to the emergency room and then to his place.

"He was home in bed but when they called he responded. I wondered if anyone in the world would have done that for me. I was more jealous of you than I've ever been of anybody."

When Freddie described my brother rescuing me something popped out of my memory and I saw the woman in the dress and boots with her face almost like a man's sitting with the kitten on her lap in the old law kitchen with the tub. I saw it all like I was floating in the air above her but there was no sound.

She stared, eyes wide but not amazed, and that's when I saw what she saw. A big, black guy came in hauling the body of a white man—me—all naked and banged up. The black guy had me under the arms with my feet dragging on the floor, my head lolling.

Everything else in the kitchen was in color but the body was black and white. The hair on the head and crotch and the couple of patches of blood were dark, the skin was pale.

The woman rose, laid aside the sleeping kitten, took hold of the long hair and pulled the head up. The face was the one in the picture I later kept on my office bulletin board, but slack now, dead.

The bathtub was empty and they put me face down in it. She parted the hair on the back of my head and there was a bloody wound, a hole smashed in the base of the skull.

She stroked the wound and stroked it and I could see she was talking, but I couldn't hear. Then gradually I heard her repeating, "They bring me this dead meat but I will make it alive," like a prayer, a spell. And then I was back in my own body face down in the cold enamel tub.

It was so real that it seemed like something I had managed to forget for the prior ten or so years. And, once it was evoked, I couldn't get it out of my head that something like this had happened.

On my next visit to the hospital, I tried asking Freddie what else he remembered Gerry saying. But he was having a very bad day. They were mostly bad after that. AIDS could be quick back in the beginning.

Then I got sick too, as I had expected I would. It got worse and worse. Since I believed there wasn't much that could be done, I thought about it as little as possible.

I was writing an SF novel, *Warchild*, about time travel, telepathy and alternate worlds. When I finished it and finally went to a doctor, he found out I didn't have AIDS but I did have colon cancer. I was hysterical with relief and terror.

Gerry came and stayed with me for a few days. I told him about the woman in her kitchen.

"It was Marixia and her boyfriend who found you that night you got robbed, pistol-whipped," he said. "I'd known her when I lived in the East Village. You met them too but probably forgot."

"I got left in the street naked."

"Nah," he smiled. "I think you still had your socks and turtle-neck jersey. Marixia was sort of a witch, I guess, or wanted to be. Like half the people in the East Village. She cleaned you up and stuff before she called me.

"Remember, I brought some clothes, got you to the Beth Israel emergency room? What bothered you most was when they buzzed off your hair so they could stitch you up. You ended up having to get a crewcut and wore a baseball cap until it grew in—it looked like you were back in Little League. You started going out with that great guy from university security, cleaned up your act."

"I got shot in the back of the head," I told him. "That woman brought me back to life. I saw it all happen."

"Sounds like a really bad dream, man. Yeah, your forehead feels like you're running a fever. That is kind of what dying is like, though, a strange dream.

"I took you out to Brooklyn and outside of not remembering some stuff you were fine a day or two later. Like you will be once they treat you for the cancer."

The tumor was massive but they cut it out of me at Mount Sinai uptown. Even though I had ignored it for so long, I recovered. And when I did, I was in perfect health.

While all that happened, the alternate-worlds novel got bought and became the first thing of mine to be published. No corollary exists between having good luck and being good.

§

Many years after that, the daily walk from the library to visit Gerry at St. Vincent's was almost nostalgic. It reminded me of Gerry's miracle recovery in that hospital over a quarter century before. As in his prior time there, the doctors were surprised at the speed of his rebound and he got to go home.

This time, however, his life was a ruin. It had happened slowly and for a while imperceptibly before anyone understood that hepatitis was destroying his liver and filling his body with toxins. In the years after my cancer and before his illness became obvious, he would show up on Saturday mornings before I went to work, always with some beautiful lady with whom he was going out. This preceded his messy divorce.

His judgment had become erratic. He lost the house he owned out in Brooklyn, went bankrupt. He lived with an unstable, bedridden woman whom he insisted was the one who needed help.

Our sister, Lee, who owns a social-services company, hired him, kind of the way he had once hired me. But he quarreled with her and quit as he did with everybody he worked for. His temper had become very bad. Anger flashed at unexpected moments. He borrowed money from everyone he knew. From having a thousand friends, he went to having none.

Did I know all this? Yes. But I chose to ignore it. Was I a good brother? No. Not like he had been for me.

What was left was his family: our father was gone by then but he had our mother, our younger sisters, Lee and Polly and brother David. And, of course, me.

That story I'd been writing the morning he went into St. Vincent's stuck around on my computer. I took it out and fiddled with it on occasion.

FROM "THE TIMES OF MY LIFE" (A STORY IN PROGRESS)
The dance I'd interrupted when I jumped into the other world was part of a ritual. Worshippers danced in a circle, twisting, turning the way they saw the ones who leaped between worlds do. Most people can't do that leap between worlds, however hard they try. On the world where I landed, I was holy and scary, somewhere between a god and a monster.

In that version of reality, they called the little rips in the barriers between worlds Portals. When they found one, they built a temple nearby.

Wayfarers was what they called those of us who could make the leap. I got to wear linen robes, gold sandals and a white hat with a wide brim all around it and carry a symbolic staff. They were awestruck to see me and probably happy to say goodbye.

I got tired of them and their temple real fast. The robes cramped my style. The ceremonial wine gave a buzz but there weren't any temple virgins or magic mushrooms or anything like that.

The rest of their world sounded as dull as the part where I'd found myself. There was no way I could go back to my home world and that's where the portal in the sacred grove would take me. Trying to find another exit, I wandered the neighborhood looking for shafts of sun at midnight, slits of dark in the middle of the day.

Then, out of nowhere, over my left shoulder on a sunny afternoon, I saw a star in a slash of dark sky. Without even going back to the temple for my stuff, I turned towards it, turned towards it again and I was gone.

My sneakers and jeans are probably still back on the altar being worshipped. The big city where I found myself looked like Chicago but called itself Evening Star.

Despite the name, or maybe because of it, they had no great regard for Wayfarers. The business of Evening Star was business and I was just a kid in a dress who wasn't so good looking he could make a living that way.

But Evening Star was where I began to get some idea of how the worlds turn and how I could use that knowledge.

The city had a kind of demimonde where I got to meet other people who, when fire bit their ass or an angry mob closed in, were able to jump through a window only they could see.

My fellow Wayfarers had a kind of loose-knit guild where I became an apprentice, got taught a few basic ethical rules about trying never to do harm, sharpened my skills, learned how to make a living from them. One reality usually has something that another one needs and the world in need usually has something to offer in trade.

Not a bad life for a restless young man with no great powers of concentration. Because I was young and unattached and fairly stupid, I didn't fear much. One thing that had been drilled into me by the guild was to beware of places where there was another version of me.

"Two of a kind is one too many," as the saying goes. So, at first, when people would remark that I reminded them of some guy they'd met and that I looked a whole lot like him, I'd make plans to be somewhere else fast.

A lot of the time, though, I got homesick. For my parents, sure, and the rest of the family. But the one I missed most was Brad. He and I had been as one for most of my early life and all of his.

Gerry got well enough to go home from St. Vincent's once they solved his liquid build-up. But he never really got better and some months later he was admitted to Mt. Sinai on the Upper East Side where my cancer had been treated.

They had a liver-transplant program. The politics of transplants are as dirty and convoluted as any I've ever seen. My own doctors advised me not to volunteer part of my liver to Gerry. They said it might very well harm me and wouldn't help him.

My brother was in and out of coma that summer, his skin and eyes golden. He had several false starts when a liver was found but turned out not to be right. Then a liver flown in from Portland was pronounced good and transplanted into him.

By that Sunday, the change was remarkable. His color was normal. He was coherent. It seemed like a miracle.

Then late one night my phone rang: it was Gerry, sounding young, mad. "They're poisoning me, man. They're putting poison ammonia down on the floor. I can smell it. They're choking me. You got to come and get me out of here."

For the next couple of hours I felt like I was talking someone down from a bad acid trip. Later when I mentioned all this to him, he insisted they had been trying to poison him. Cracks like that revealed themselves, flaws in the recovery, or permanent damage from his illness. But he got better enough to go home once again that fall.

Stories, novels, even the wild chaotic ones, have more form than ordinary lives. Over the next year between stays at home, Gerry was in and out of various hospitals. He became part of my schedule: go to work, visit the gym, write, get together with someone I'd met, talk to Marty or Chris on the phone, and visit Gerry.

Once when I did I found he had another visitor. The years had softened Marixia. She looked more mundane than the austere woman in the lighted kitchen. Seeing her I actually remembered knowing her. She and her black boyfriend had been the supers of a building on Seventh and C in the East Village.

"You saved my life," I said.

She remembered me. "No," she said. "It was George, my partner, who talked them out of putting a bullet in your head. It was a cold night and you were left unconscious with just a shirt and cuts on the back of your head. I thought at first you were dead. We put you in the bath tub with hot water and you came around."

"Thank you and George."

"Ah, he's gone now. Your brother did us so many favors when he lived in the neighborhood. So I was glad to repay him. It breaks my heart to see him like this. He was always looking out for others."

She told me that she was still in the same building. "Everything else is changed but not that."

A few days later I walked over to Avenue C and Seventh Street. The neighborhood was gentrified almost beyond recognition. The place where I remembered her building standing was now a community garden.

It made me remember the bad night when my lover Pablo, the brother of a coke dealer, turned on me. In an East Village tenement hallway near where I now stood, he, the dealer brother and a couple of their gang emptied my pockets, forced me to kneel and shoved a gun down my throat. My ex-lover took my leather jacket and boots and put them on.

They yanked the pants and shorts off me because I was a filthy *maricón*, not a man. I felt the gun at the base of my skull and pleaded for my life while they laughed. Someone must have hit me on the back of my head and everything went black.

Thirty years later, I stood at the garden gate looking in at the greenery and the young trees. I wondered whether I had misunderstood Marixia or if she had been referring to some alternate worlds and if the kitchen where I'd been dragged without even a shirt on my back and a bullet in the base of my skull had been a place in Gerry's Amber. If so, I knew that the magic that had saved my life there was not to be found for him in my world.

When Gerry came back to consciousness a few days later, I mentioned that Marixia had been by to see him. He had no idea who she was.

His hepatitis C was attacking his new liver. One hospital stay melded into another. Sometimes Gerry was mobile for brief periods of time. Once he came by to visit me, very fragile and jaundiced. He was bright yellow. Heads turned on MacDougal Street as we walked slowly along.

Once I got a call at work from his girlfriend, who said I had to go out to Brooklyn and bring him to the Mt. Sinai emergency room. It was evening rush hour in the swelter of August. The cab trip to the Upper East Side took an hour and a half.

At one point we hit a pothole and Gerry bounced in his seat with his arms at his side, making no effort to catch himself. Holding on to him for a moment I thought he was dead and wondered at the complications that this would cause.

A few times he said he knew he was dying and told me how afraid it made him. I reminded him of how often he'd come back and how the things we fear are usually not as bad as we imagined when we actually encounter them. I changed the subject and talked about books we'd read, things we'd done as kids.

In truth, sanctity is a tough gig. I grew tired of the constant ups and downs, the death watch followed by the revivification, the madness caused by the toxic poisons from his failing liver, the begging me to smother him with a pillow, the calm after the storm, the return home, then the whole cycle again.

One night I went up to Mt. Sinai and he was in a four-bed room with a nurse on permanent duty at a desk right in the room.

This was a transgendered special duty nurse, named Helen, with rather unkempt long hair and a flat Tennessee accent, who told me she had been a male army nurse for thirty-two years and had learned that there was absolutely nothing she could say about whether a patient was going to make it aside from the fact that it had to do with genes and God.

The hospital had decided against a second transplant. I stayed with Gerry for a couple of hours. He told me he had seen death a few days before, felt he was close to it. He described death as a huge structure, an immense building made of flowers and lights. He was being drawn towards it and then escaped. Nearly thirty years before at St. Vincent's he had used almost the same words.

He was transferred out of Mt. Sinai into Beth Israel on the Lower East Side. There one night, with our younger brother David and me present, he launched into a mad monologue, a great barroom stand-up routine.

"The doctor this morning, when he came in, instead of a stethoscope, he was wearing a green lizard around his neck and I said, 'Doc, I hope you're not going to stick that on my chest.' And he looked surprised like nobody had ever told him that before.

"Last night, looking out the window, I saw this Mayan pyramid all on fire," he said. "And all these red bats flying in and out of the flames."

Briefly it felt like we were kids imagining a horror movie.

His bright yellow skin had turned to dull gold and then to something close to black. I'd never seen anything quite like it. From the hospital he was transferred to a nursing home. Then, on a lovely Saturday morning in spring, he died in a little hospital on the Upper East Side.

The funeral mass was up in Newton, Massachusetts, where our mother lived. My brother David and our sisters Lee and Polly were there, the whole extended Irish-American family showed up. The church has a handsome interior.

People sent flowers. My sister Polly and her husband Dennis are musicians and the music was beautifully handled. My nieces and nephews sang at the beginning. An amazing violinist played Massenet's "Meditation" from *Thaïs*, a favorite piece of Gerry's. I have trouble listening to it now.

Gerry's son, his ex-wife, his girlfriend were not present. One friend of his from long ago showed up. I didn't really feel Gerry's presence.

Afterwards, I had to get back to New York where I had my library job and a writing deadline. On the mostly deserted evening train, I took a pair of sunglasses out of my pocket and cried off and on across southern New England. His life wound in and out of mine and in his absence it winds still.

Writing is the place where I can be as bold and compassionate and wise as I choose.

FINALE: THE TIMES OF MY LIFE

People say a lot of dumb things like, "You can't take it with you," and "You can't go home again." But I've proven them wrong.

When I had made enough money trading between different versions of the world and when I was getting old enough that the games you can play with alternate lives and lovers began to get dull, I decided to settle down.

I knew how I wanted to end up and I had scouted out the possibilities. Most worlds didn't have either my brother or me. Some had one but had never had the other. I found a few where I'd existed but had left home or died young. Brad on those worlds was usually a sad kid who grew up to be a not very happy adult. But the damage there had already been done and I didn't think I could fit in.

So that left the ones where I had stayed and remained alive. On some of those the oppression of the Curfew Patrol had been just the beginning and the whole place was a concentration camp. On others, though, it had never existed or been a short and passing fancy. Those happy worlds were the ones I researched until I found one I thought was just about perfect.

Brad was in his late thirties, with a nice wife and a bunch of kids. The oldest boys were ten and thirteen, just about the same age difference as he and I had.

Brad's older brother was their godfather. A drunken failure but the kind of guy small kids adore. I scouted the situation out and decided it could be a perfect fit.

When people say, "Two of a kind is one too many," for once they're right. My drunken alter ego was a problem. But I had a solution that involved as little cruelty as possible. With the help of a pair of my fellow Wayfarers, I got the other me very smashed and hauled him off-world.

If the temple and the grove were not the same ones I'd found the first time I crossed through a portal, they were damn close. The worshippers, all dancing in a circle on a fine morning, were duly awestruck by our appearance in their midst.

I turned my double over to them, told them to take good care of him, keep him well—but not too well—oiled with wine, and said I'd be back to see how things went. When I turned at the portal to look back, he was dancing along with them and had a big smile on his face.

Taking his place, I began working a slow reformation, laying off the booze a bit, dressing better.

That pleases Brad, of course. But he gets a little worried about my inability to remember details of our past or to get chronology right. Once or twice I've joked about early onset Alzheimer's and while he smiles, he winces at the thought. And it's wonderful that he does.

The thing about a circle dance is you can join it at any place where the dancers will reach out and grasp your hands. And the thing about love is that, whatever its form, it's rare enough that if you lose it you'll cross a thousand worlds to get it back again.

Chapter Twelve

By night the view from the university library Science Reference desk was all about dark and light. You could sit there and look through the glass doors leading to the balcony, past the plastic shields and the illuminated atrium. The front of the library building has ranks of tall windows. Outside are the dark trees of Washington Square and beyond them the lights of the brownstones on the far side of the park and the skyscrapers towering behind them.

My decision to leave the university had kicked in. My finances were okay and I had given a year's notice that I would retire. The suicides had given me the push and Gerry's death had reinforced it but I knew my time was up anyway. A guy sitting at a desk answering questions was something out of the past in the internet age.

Lots of people seemed to see me for the first time as they prepared to see me for the last. Somebody who'd worked with me at the library for many years remarked that I knew where all the bodies were buried. She exaggerated, though I did know where one or two were located. And I'd done my best to see they stayed where they were.

In fact, a buried body was the reason I sat at the Science Reference desk late one night in my last weeks on the job and waited with curiosity and some dread for an old acquaintance to reappear. Twenty years before I'd sat at the same desk one night and waited for the same familiar figure. But I'd never imagined having to do this again.

Mostly in my last year at the university I enjoyed the freedom that came from no one quite knowing how to deal with me. Then my boss asked if I'd see whether there was anything of archival interest in the Office of Doom before it got renovated. She was very polite about it and I couldn't really refuse.

She didn't call it the Office of Doom, of course. She referred to it as Room 975, which is the number on the door. I was one of the few left who remembered the nickname.

The office was in a far corner of our floor and for many years it had been used for nothing but the storage of boxes of old university records. Those had been moved out but the dust remained. There were roach motels in the corners, a glue trap under the desk and strange stains on the rug. An old wooden hat rack was missing two of its hooks. The only thing on it was a gnarly woolen scarf in a rusty orange shade. The lock on one of the desk's side drawers had been broken open at some time in the past.

Even in a building as strange as this one, the room had always been especially creepy. I'd brought a rolling plastic trash bin with me and used it to keep the door propped open so as not to get shut in. Then I dusted off the swivel chair and sat at the desk.

Room 975 got its nickname among the lower echelon library staff because after the place first opened in the early '70s this windowless ten-foot-by-six-foot hole was where they stuck people who had fallen from grace and favor and were on their way out.

Pulling up the creaking chair, I went through the desk drawers, not expecting to find anything much after all these years but wanting to make sure. It was mundane stuff at first: jotted notes, a photo of an office party from a couple of decades back with some people who almost looked familiar, pamphlets and outdated fire-evacuation instructions. Everything went into the trash.

Then, way in the back of a bottom drawer, I found a small plastic nail manicure kit with the words 50TH ANNUAL CONVENTION OF THE FINANCIAL OFFICERS OF NEW YORK STATE in gold lettering.

The first occupant of the Office of Doom was a pale weasel of a man named Siddons. He had been the chief financial officer to the president of the university, William (Dollar Bill) Bradshaw, who built this very library and brought the school nearly to bankruptcy doing it.

When Bradshaw was abruptly axed by the board of trustees, Siddons found himself in this office. He spent his days whispering into the phone and doing his nails (which I must admit were quite immaculate and trim). Then one day he was gone to a new job where apparently his reputation had not yet traveled.

I tossed the manicure kit into the bin.

That set me looking for signs of the Office of Doom's next occupant, Dr. Harold Kassin. Known to us all as "Kassin the Assassin," he had been the hatchet man for a very aggressive Dean of Libraries. The Dean and Doctor. Kassin wanted to fire everybody.

But one morning the Dean was called into the office of the university president who succeeded Bradshaw and summarily dismissed for backdating documents. He was escorted off the premises by security guards as we all cheered. Kassin was in this office the very next day.

He had a face like an ax. At one time or another he'd confronted just about everyone in the library and told them he was watching them and they'd better straighten up or get out.

We practically ran group tours for all the people who wanted to look in and see his disgrace.

He too was gone without any forewarning one fine day. Word was that he'd taken a job as head of a small library in New Jersey. I pitied the staff.

The desk yielded no traces of Kassin, which didn't really surprise me. He was careful in the way of professional killers. I stood up and riffled through the file cabinet. Old folders full of invoices got tossed with scarcely a second glance. If anyone had been seriously interested in evaluating this stuff they wouldn't have given this assignment to me.

Then I found a stack of menus for long-gone pizza parlors, announcements of music acts at the Bottom Line and CBGB's, flyers from long-gone comic-book stores on Bleecker Street and horror film festivals at the Waverly theater.

After they ran out of disgraced administrators, the office had been returned to library use. For a few years it was where our student assistants got stashed.

Among the artifacts were a few scribbled notes and I recognized the handwriting. Joshua Watts was a film major who worked for us in the early '80s, a skinny kid who wore distressed leather and spiked hair and had an intense interest in Aleister Crowley, Roman Polanski, the Illuminati and role-playing games.

Even when you were face to face with him he seemed to be staring at you slightly askance from around some corner only he could see. Remembering him gave me twinges of guilt and regret.

Joshua and I got along okay. I'd achieved sobriety some years before, liked the kids and tried to be good to them. He and I shared a certain detachment and interest in the strange.

Judy Light by then had taken the name Judy Icon, was giving performances that mixed rock and avant-garde theater. The fact that I'd known her when she was Judy Finch meant Joshua thought I was very hip. When I told him the nickname we'd given the office he loved it.

As I riffled through the next layer of folders I realized the material I was tossing in the trash had been left behind by Frances Hooker, a librarian and the last occupant of this office. With that name her life in junior high school must have been a living hell. I felt not an iota of sympathy for her.

Miss Hooker was youngish but wore dresses that fell below the knee and blouses that came up to her chin. She never smiled and only discussed business.

The student employees lost their office when she arrived. For that and for reasons of temperament, she and Joshua hated each other from the start. To my shame I hadn't been entirely sad about this. She and I didn't get along either and Joshua kept her distracted.

Then, as if remembering those two had evoked it, I spotted an old Interlibrary Loan shipping envelope addressed to Joshua. Scrawled in black marker was *Necronom/Miskaton*.

Seeing that was a shock. Embarrassed by my superstition but careful not to disturb the envelope in any way, I quickly shut the drawer and got outside. If this was catalogued material it was supposed to be reported. Instead I locked the office and told everyone I was going to lunch.

My attitude with witches is that I don't believe in them except when I do. This is why I went to visit the *strega*, the witch who worked among us.

Her office was on the east side of Washington Square Park. Back before the university became an academic high roller, this was a gritty urban campus featuring a bunch of old commercial buildings converted to classrooms. I went through the side entrance of one of these, took a turn just inside the door, walked down a short corridor, descended spiral metal stairs and found myself in Central Supply.

Years ago the place had hummed. Anyone on campus who wanted anything had to get a requisition order and bring it here. Normally there was a line and three or four clerks behind a tall counter handling requests, making sure everything was filled out correctly and properly signed and dated and then piling your office supplies on the counter.

If there was a problem Ambrose was the one you saw first, a black guy built like a walking bunker who was always a little too busy to listen.

Central Supply was almost deserted now. Piles of dusty, broken furniture—tables, desks, chairs—sat where lines once formed. Ambrose was still at the counter but no one else was. He sat, older, bigger but somehow frail, absorbed in whatever was on his computer screen. I had to say "Hello" twice before he looked up.

"Is Mrs. Rossi, here?" Once upon a time only unusual requests from the highest university echelon or esoteric problems that defied clear definition got referred to Teresa Rossi.

Now Ambrose nodded without looking up and called out, "Teresa, someone for you."

"I know" was the answer, like she expected me. "Send him in."

With no more formality than that, I lifted a hinged section of the counter and walked back to her office.

The university locksmith many years ago was a tiny man with a large head and a beautiful face—like the ones on shepherds in Renaissance nativity paintings. He had come from Palermo and lived in Greenwich Village.

Once he told me that back when he first arrived here, Teresa Rossi's mother had been the neighborhood *strega*. He mentioned that her mother was a witch with great respect and added as an afterthought that her father had a hardware shop on the corner of Houston and Thompson Streets.

All else had changed but Teresa Rossi at first glance was just the same, dark hair with little highlights, nice but anonymous at-work dress and jewelry that caught the eye (was that a minute owl's face staring out from that earring?) but when you looked closely seemed perfectly mundane.

"You're still here," she said expressing no surprise. Part of her aura was that she was never surprised.

"For a little while longer," I said. "You too?"

She shrugged. "Each department orders everything online from Staples now. What we do is receive broken furniture and call for carting companies to come and haul it away."

"But you're still in business?" She nodded and waited for me to speak. "There was a kid working for us years ago who pulled a stupid prank with Interlibrary Loan."

"Joshua Watts," Teresa Rossi said like it happened earlier in the week and not all those years before. "That went way beyond being a prank. I thought it had all been taken care of." She showed a flash of irritation. At moments she could be chilling.

"Something connected to that turned up today." I told her what I'd found.

"You didn't touch it."

"No."

"It will have to be dealt with when there's nobody around."

"I work late tomorrow night."

"That will be good." And the session was over. I told myself this was what it was like back when the mafia operated in the neighborhood and it didn't do to know too much about what they did.

§

Back when he worked for us I had brought Joshua with me to help carry stuff back to our department. We were waiting in line when Teresa emerged from her office with the University Counsel and escorted him out as he babbled his gratitude. "Don't know how you found those letters. The secretary swore she'd discarded them years ago." She nodded as if this was nothing.

Joshua was fascinated by Teresa Rossi. Something made her notice him too. I stepped up to place my order and she motioned him over and spoke to him. Later I asked what she'd had to say.

"She wanted to know who I was. Said not to trust you too far but I think she was kidding."

Retailing workplace gossip, I told him what the locksmith told me and also stories of how she had some kind of control over lost objects and future events.

"People like her and you are the limbic system of this place," he said. "You know how in our brains behind all the recent flashy developments that gave us stuff like emotions and aesthetics and cosmic awareness there's this lizard brain. It's what makes the heart beat and what stays alert to odd noises and sudden movements in the dark while we sleep. Don't wonder where the dinosaurs went, there's a bit of one inside each of us."

"So Mrs. Rossi and I are ancient lizards?"

"Yeah man. You're the Old Ones and it's cool."

Thinking back, I can remember Joshua talking about H. P. Lovecraft and the evil book the *Necronomicon* and Miskatonic University, the accursed New England institution of higher learning that shows up in Lovecraft stories.

Lovecraft seemed more than a little silly to me and as far as I could see to Joshua. We joked about accursed universities not being that far fetched. I remember him talking about doing an Interlibrary Loan request for the *Necronomicon*. I even showed him how to search the huge print tomes of library holdings as one did in those pre-internet years, and as part of the gag I approved the ILL request for him.

He told me, months, maybe a year later that the book had arrived. I said, "It's probably something a Lovecraft fan produced."

"It's close enough," he said, peeking around the invisible corner, and I assumed he was joking.

By the time Joshua got the book, Frances Hooker had been hired. She apparently never slept, never went home and had no interest in life except library science. Even other librarians didn't like her but they agreed that she was excellent at her work and shut themselves in their offices when she was round.

I had to deal with her and found she hated me because I didn't have a library degree. I believe she hated everyone who wasn't a librarian. She thought that librarians should be addressed as "Curator" in the same way as physicians are called Doctor. No one went along with this.

Mad librarians were no novelty. The first one I worked for at the university was Alice Marlow. She had dyed blonde hair and, though somewhat pudgy, wore leather mini-skirts and mesh stockings. It was the early 1970s and stuff like that got worn by many but not by any other librarians that I can recall.

The main library hadn't yet been built and departments and collections were stuck in odd places around campus. We had been installed in a small office on the floor above the Gates of Eden Beer Hall, a student hangout on Waverly Place. There was a men's hat manufacturer on the floor above us in those dusty, far gone days.

Alice was erratic, sweet and zaftig one minute, insanely suspicious the next. I was no prize either, sometimes slipping down to the Gates of Eden to get drunk or over to Washington Square to cop drugs. Once she threatened to fire me for being habitually late to work.

She'd usually forget about things like that but I made it a point to come in early the next day. She never showed up and wasn't there the day after that either. I began to wonder what had happened.

That afternoon two people from administration came and took all her personal effects. It seemed she'd gone berserk in the West Fourth Street subway station two days before screaming that people were putting LSD in her coffee, and her family had her committed.

Hooker was unpleasant to me but she was hell on Joshua who was used to easygoing supervision. I assumed that was what made him increasingly twitchy. I tried telling him not to let her get to him. He stopped speaking to anyone and then stopped coming to work and going to class.

I made inquiries and his roommates said he'd gotten very moody and had taken off suddenly. "He talked about needing to go somewhere up in New England, man," one of them said.

Later I was told to go through his locker. There was the *Necronomicon* with leather binding and gold lettering that looked not at all cheap or new.

It didn't exude evil but what happened to Joshua had spooked me and I didn't want to touch it. While I stood wondering what to do, Frances Hooker walked by. I thought it was Fate.

"This looks like a rare book," I said, "It's from Interlibrary Loan and I don't know how to handle something like this." I didn't even have to say that was because I wasn't a librarian. She glared at me, gathered up the volume and stalked off to the Office of Doom.

Ms. Hooker's behavior over the next year or so grew stranger than Marlow's ever was. The cleaning people heard her shrieking in her office late at night. On one occasion she stood up at a faculty meeting and spoke in tongues.

The rare-books librarian said that once when she was talking to him, a tongue long and forked like a snake's lolled out of her mouth. But he drank and nobody believed him. Except me, kind of.

Then she disappeared, leaving a disjointed note about mountains and madness and needing to travel. I felt regret about all this and knew I should have handled it better. When I was ordered a month or so later to clear out her office, the book was in the top drawer of her desk.

Feeling stupid but not knowing what else to do I went to Central Supply and told Teresa Rossi what had happened. Like what seemed to be everybody at the University she'd known my brother Gerry when he worked there and loved him.

Because of that she just looked disappointed with me and said I'd caused trouble by letting Joshua borrow the book. She told me to stay at work late and someone would be there.

That someone appeared just before closing time. It was early fall and not that cold but he wore an overcoat, a wide-brimmed hat and dark glasses, and carried a leather satchel. Joshua had been gone less than a year and a half but from what I could see he looked twenty years older, gaunt, and stone faced.

To this day I don't feel proud about not having protected the kid. It's one of the reasons I tried to behave decently to Marco years later.

Without a word he went into the Office of Doom and came out with something in his satchel. "Joshua, I'm sorry..." I said.

"It's okay." The voice was faint and from far away. Then he was gone.

I was the one who suggested that the now vacant Office of Doom be used as a storage space. Everyone thought it was a good idea and so it had remained for better than two decades.

§

This is now the digital age; students and faculty don't much use paper books or journals. Yet the surroundings are pleasant enough and the computer facilities are excellent. So just before eleven o'clock on the night I sat waiting once again, the place was full of foreign doctors from around the world studying for their U.S. equivalency exams.

Busy, conspiratorial, they would jump up and dash downstairs to smoke foul-smelling cigarettes outdoors. And as always they watched me from the corners of their eyes convinced that I worked for the secret police and was going to turn them in.

Their names, Visascia, Yadaminia, sounded like obscure nineteenth-century diseases. The one thing they all wanted was to pass their exams and go work in American emergency rooms.

They barely looked up when Joshua Watts appeared. In fact nothing about him would have attracted their attention. Existence apparently had gotten easier for him. Except for a certain wariness, he looked like a guy you'd see in any suburban mall, balding, a bit overweight, a little pressed for time. He carried a satchel.

"You're still here." The voice was a breath, a whisper. He showed no surprise.

I let him into the Office of Doom, showed him where I'd found the envelope, then left. A guard walked by announcing closing time as he came back to the desk.

He peered at me from around his corner. "Some kind of errata sheet," he said. "Must have missed it the last time. I've gotten better over the years."

"Joshua, what happened to you?" I wanted him to say everything was fine now.

"Awful stuff at first. Mrs. Rossi, though, told me who to talk to, how to throw myself on their mercy. She said they always need someone to clean up little mistakes."

"What happened with you and with Frances Hooker bothers me..." I trailed off.

Joshua looked around his invisible corner, gave what might have been the ghost of a smile. Then he turned and was gone.

§

Everyone thought my retirement party was quite a success: a large crowd, plenty of sentimental and funny gifts. Kenneth, the poet I'd been going out with, and another ex-boyfriend or two who still worked at the university stopped by.

A surprise guest was Guard Robins, who shook my hand, smiled and presented me with an envelope. I opened it and found a grinning photo of a very young Charles Fortnum—a

Prince of the Big Night Hours. Magnets hold him on my refrigerator as I write this.

Godchildren appeared: Chris called me from Ohio. Selesta stopped by, my sister Lee sent my nieces Antonia and Dirrane by to remind me as kids do that life will continue.

Teresa Rossi showed up unexpectedly. People asked her when she was going to call it quits and she said, "Soon, maybe." At one point when we were alone, she told me, "An old friend wants you to know the case is closed and nobody holds any grudge against you." When I started to thank her she added, "It's not strictly justice. But ones like us don't always want that."

Chapter Thirteen

In my retirement I began keeping a dream book. I hadn't done this since my time with Dr. Lovell and my first dream was Maria Lovell herself, sitting in her little office, smiling and shaking her head. "You must understand, darling, that I am a ghost, now, a memory."

The dead appeared in my dreams: Gerry, Charles Fortnum, Mags in her long deterioration, Geoff, young, then ruined, Freddie Ayers and other partners. I wondered if my survival was fate or the more likely dumb luck. I wondered if I had paranormal powers or psychosis.

In a dream about my brother, Gerry was in his early twenties and we sat smoking grass at a sidewalk café in a city of our imaginings. "Ghosts are one way the past comes calling," he said.

He was right and I thought about it that summer as unfolding events made me try to establish a timeline of forty-year-old memories, monsters and murders. I scribbled phrases like "statute of limitations" and "déjà vu" on pieces of scrap paper, wrote "The idle mind occupies itself with inventing connections" on a Post-it and stuck that on my fridge.

It wasn't just me. The whole city, maybe the whole world seemed to be in a similar mood. Books were all memoirs; every rock concert was a reunion, every museum exhibition a retrospective, every Broadway opening a revival.

Nostalgia got my undivided attention one morning in June. I came out the door of my building on the corner of Bleecker and MacDougal Street to find it was the early 1960s again.

A few old places like the Figaro and Café Wha? had more or less survived and their signs could always be seen. But that morning long-gone café and bar signs, the Gas Light, the Fat Black, Pussy Cat, the Kettle Of Fish, and Rienzi had all returned. Even the Folklore Center poked its nose out. On the ground floor of my building, the San Remo had come back from wherever notorious old bars go after they die.

On warm, sunny mornings in this neighborhood, someone is always making a movie. MacDougal Street was choked with trailers, a breakfast buffet was set up on tables along the sidewalk, and a prop woman toted a set of bongo drums.

This film I'd heard about. It starred some television actors whose names meant nothing to me and concerned a young folk singer, just enough unlike Bob Dylan to avoid lawsuits, in Greenwich Village circa 1961.

That morning, I was on my way over to St. Mark's Church in-the-Bowery for a memorial service. And this had me in a reflective mood to begin with. All I could think was how, back in early 1964, I brought my secret crush Marty Simonson along with a couple of our fellow transfer students into the Village. I'd already visited the neighborhood a few times but knew almost as little about the place as they did.

The first bar we wandered into was the old San Remo. The grouchy bartender looked at our ROTC haircuts and asked, "You guys in the army? The army of the squares, maybe?"

We all had to show our draft cards to prove that we were over eighteen. But it was my card that got held under a light and examined to see if it was counterfeit. He made me plead to be served, which my friends found hilarious. I'd just turned twenty, a bit older than any of them, and was their ringleader.

Later I understood the bartender knew all that; guessed how I earned my pocket money and wanted to remember my face for future reference. On later visits we usually stopped in there.

When the place got crowded he'd chase us off our bar stools, saying "Beer heads stand back and let the mixed drink customers sit."

One night, one of the regulars pointed out Norman Mailer sitting at a table with a stylish lady and a guy who looked like he might have been a prizefighter.

That same barfly was the one who told us the bartender was Jonah Diamond, son of Max. As drama lit students, Marty and I knew that name. Max Diamond was a legend from the '20s and '30s: theater critic, Algonquin Round Table wit, scriptwriter for the Marx Brothers. His newspaper column *Diamond in the Rough* and later the radio show of the same name introduced first New York and then the nation to theatrical banter, celebrity interviews and bitchy book and movie reviews.

Some say that the homicidal radio personality in the movie *Laura* is based on Max Diamond. Famously, he once said, "My ambition is to die at the wheel of an expensive car that I don't own in the company of a beautiful woman to whom I'm not married on the grounds of a country club that doesn't admit Jews." And one evening in 1947 he managed to do exactly that.

Jonah Diamond was a surly Greenwich Village lowlife who, we were told, had been to jail. We found this fascinating, wondered if it was for possession of exotic drugs, for political activity or selling forged Jackson Pollocks.

When I discovered a few years later that it was for criminal assault and rape I knew enough about him that it was no big surprise. By then Jonah had said to me about his father, "The selfish bastard went out in high style and left me with nothing but his cigar bills and some half-assed gibberish about magic." Around then, Jonah also threatened to kill me.

As I recalled this on the summer morning so many years later, a minor dust storm swirled around my legs. And I remembered deciding with Barbara Lohr that the swirls of dried leaves and trash were ghosts and small gods, the spirits playful and malign of Manhattan.

§

The charm of St. Mark's in-the-Bowery is that it's an early nineteenth-century Episcopal country church complete with graveyard that finds itself located on Second Avenue in the dirty, dynamic East Village.

That morning the church hosted a memorial service for Robin St. Just. Born Robert Justin in Duluth, Minnesota, St. Just was the one who discovered subway graffiti artists and Blondie. Long years ago at a ballet intermission I'd attempted to walk off with his boy, "The Downtown Ganymede."

When St. Just died in a fall down the stairs of his building, obituaries and articles on the arts pages showed him in Avedon photos of Warhol's studio and in newspaper pictures of opening nights at the Met, in shots taken at CBGB's and Studio 54. The police found no evidence of foul play in his death and cited a lack of motive. That's because they didn't know St. Just.

Amid the crowd gathered in the cobblestone church yard, I recognized lots of faces. Wearing dark glasses and scarves were former hippies who were now successful entrepreneurs, men and women who had gone from experimental theater communes to roles as wise-cracking pals in long-running television sitcoms. Along with these were many who looked resourceful but a bit worn and who I knew still lived, apprehensive but wily, in old rent-stabilized apartments on ungentrified blocks in neighborhoods like this one.

My old accomplice and onetime employer, Frankie the Bug Boy, once everybody's favorite drug connection, was there with Gloria Starrett, the ancient dancer who, legend had it, pleasured JFK up at the Hotel Pierre when she was a call girl. They stood with Nick and Norah Grubstreet, my private nickname for a young couple who supplemented their trust funds with hack writing.

"Critic, performer, poet, painter, composer, Robin had his fingers in everything," said Nick.

"His fingers were the least of it," Gloria replied.

Then I saw Barbara Lohr straight and tall as a Guards officer in one of those wide-brimmed hats English ladies know how to find and standing under the portico with some friends.

As Major Barbara waved me over I remembered her saying when we cleaned out Eddie Ackers' apartment a few years before, "Ceremonies for the dead are the only real rituals left."

She smiled a bit sadly. For even longer than I'd known her, Barbara had been a friend, and a close one, of St. Just. Major Barbara's parents were actors. Her mother was Tom Brown's kindly mother and Bob Cratchit's wife in movies I saw on television as a kid. Her father played gallant young officers who died holding off the Pathans in the Khyber Pass or went down in Noël Coward's destroyer.

In reality he was a sadist and she was a drunk. Or maybe it was the other way around. All this I found out from others. They were the reason that Barbara left London and sought her fortune in America.

In the Major's big fantasy novels, romantic, fiery gay males toss their long hair and run their enemies through with cold steel, as unlike the behavior of the writer and her partner Marie, two very sensible women, as it is possible to be. St. Just gave her work serious attention, much to the envy of genre writers everywhere.

Jay Glass, critic, writer, Flying Dutchman survivor, looked furtive and bitter. "His age was reported as anywhere from fifty-eight to sixty-six," Jay was saying as I approached. Critics too have their pecking order and even dead St. Just was many cuts above Jay Glass.

The Major murmured, "He was sixty-five. I'm two weeks older than he was."

Then a side door opened and we began to move toward the church. St. Just had become an Episcopalian late in life, just like W.H. Auden. The obituaries described him as eclectic.

The word *plagiarism* was used privately. But it was said of St. Just that when he stole from you, it didn't seem like theft so much as affirmation.

Before going inside, I looked around at the trees and the sun, the world passing by outside the iron fence. A plain black car pulled away from the curb.

Instinctively, I identified the two male riders in sports coats as cops and was reminded of police monitoring a mafia funeral. I guess it was a day for memories and juxtaposition because I also realized that one of them was Jaime, an old lover of mine.

The Major and those of us with her had good seats near the front of the church, two rows behind St. Just's surprisingly plain daughter from his brief early marriage to the actress Katie Berlin. She sat between her nebbishy husband and St. Just's brother, a retired insurance executive from Chicago.

"Ah, Tanya Starrett," whispered Jay Glass, and I looked to see a handsome young African-American woman with her hair in a small afro come down the aisle. She nodded slightly to the Major and winked. When I looked at Jay for an explanation, he murmured with some bitterness, "The new Robin St. Just."

Tanya Starrett's good looks were lightly adorned. She had no visible tattoos or piercing. Her white top could almost have been a classic T-shirt. She wore some bracelets and on a chain around her neck was what looked at first like an ordinary plastic ring.

richard bowes

180

Because of what Jay had told me, the ring caught my attention. Not as ordinary as it first seemed. The piece evoked Jonah Diamond and his father.

Then the service began with Mozart's *Exsultate, Jubilate*, which St. Just had said he wanted played at his funeral. The daughter spoke briefly, and the brother.

Then an elderly curator emeritus at MOMA talked about him. "Robin came to us when he was twenty-two as an intern. Six months after his arrival, Jack Moore—who was then the curator of sculpture—took him on as an assistant. It was still that wonderful time when a bright young person could come to the city and get noticed quickly."

Jay Glass snorted rather loudly and the Major glared at him.

"Within a few years Jack was dead, as we all remember, and Robin—still in his mid-twenties—was able to take over and finish the catalog for the 1967 American Retrospective Show."

Songs with lyrics by St. Just, the one on the New York Dolls first album, the one Marianne Faithfull sang, were performed quietly. Somehow the fact the he had songs on a few classic rock albums was almost the last straw when people envied him.

"I'm not Saint Francis and he wasn't me" was one of the lines. "Children of the gods touched me and I'm a miracle man" was another.

Then the Major rose and walked to the microphone. "Robin and I both came to New York in the same week from schools in different parts of the world. It was 1962 and both MOMA where Robin worked and *Harper's Bazaar* where I got my first job paid about eighty dollars a week.

"But he had found a place he could afford, the wonderfully awful Hotel Betsy Ross on the outskirts of the old Garment District. And within days of meeting him, I moved there too—into a separate room, of course. Over the years we traveled in and out of each others' orbits, ending up as fellow parishioners here at St. Mark's Church."

Hearing the Betsy mentioned was a bit of a surprise. The Major talked about St. Just taking her with him when he met Jim Morrison and the Doors. About his finding distinctive graffiti and tracking down the artist Keith Haring.

"His final passing, the way it happened, was not fair, perhaps. He was kind. To me and to many others. And if he wasn't always kind to everyone, well, as he himself said, he wasn't St. Francis."

I watched as Tanya Starrett and the Major briefly embraced at the end of the service. The ring on Ms. Starrett's necklace chain made me remember Jonah Diamond, describing a very old amber ring with a dragonfly inside. I tried to get a closer look at this one and was aware of the Bug Boy staring my way.

At the end of the service as the crowd dispersed, I went with Major Barbara, Jay Glass, and few others through the gate, and down the stairs that lead to East Ninth Street. It was a fine early June day, warm but not hot. As we hit the sidewalk an imperceptible breeze caused dust to swirl in the gutter, apparently reminding the Major of small spirits.

"Oh, Robin, you can't come with us, I'm afraid," she sighed. "In his prime and sometimes later," she said, "Robin really was a kind of small god. And now he's a ghost." She nodded my way and gave a little smile.

The Major and Marie live in a rambling third-floor apartment in a building that overlooks the St. Mark's Church rectory yard. From certain angles in certain lights, the view from their windows evokes an English village.

Half a dozen of us sat in the dining room drinking tea as dark as the Major's old oak table, eating scones and talking about St. Just. Ceiling fans beat slowly and the open windows brought in the sun, the scent of flowers in somebody's garden, and the distant voices of children from the church daycare center.

"In the *Times*," said Jay Glass, "Someone mentioned all the influences on St. Just, everyone from e.e. cummings to Fats

Waller. Actually all he had was one really big dose of Jack Moore."

Jack Moore was the critic who discovered Jason Finch, Judy's father, among many other artists. I once heard him described as being like a broken-nosed Irish traffic cop standing at the intersection of the written word and abstract expressionism, of modern dance and the morning newspaper.

"Booze and boys had crippled Moore's ability to function," Jay Glass said. "St. Just was doing Jack's job long before he died. But I'm not one of those who think little Robin murdered him. Not at all!"

The Major shook her head wearily. Jack Moore had supposedly died in a hit and run, clipped by a car over on West Street late one night. I knew a bit of the inside story. Back then what went on after dark in the riverfront of the Far West Village never got seriously investigated.

The Major said, "Things were changing in the mid-sixties and Robin was more suited to function in that world. He understood the electronic media and the new music in ways Moore just couldn't. Robin did a lot for many new writers and artists. But as with Moore, the time had come for Robin St. Just to step aside."

"Step aside" seemed to me a thoughtless euphemism for an old friend's fatal tumble.

"Tanya Starrett has an inhuman ability to be in on any scene just before it becomes a scene," someone said. "Her Arts Zoo will be fabulous for the creative community."

"And I don't believe for a minute that she pushed St. Just," said Jay Glass.

Some in the room approved of Ms. Starrett and her zoo, some didn't. Quite an argument ensued. It wasn't something that interested me much and I guess that showed. When I took my leave, the Major saw me to the door.

"Having a steady job means you didn't have to worry about survival like the rest of us," she said. That made it sound like

I'd been stuck in storage for all those years. It bothered me enough to tell me this was at least partly true.

§

The Saturday after St. Just's memorial, I browsed the flea markets along Sixth Avenue. Not so long before, big raucous markets had sprawled for blocks on any weekend. Now ugly high-rise buildings stand on most of the lots and only small remnants of the great carnival remain.

In part I really did need to find a housewarming present for my goddaughter Selesta. Mostly, though, I was looking for Frankie the Bug Boy because I had certain questions about both Jonah Diamond and Jack Moore. Frankie had, it was said, gone from dealing *junk* to dealing junk.

Maybe it was symbolic that the Bug Boy set up in the small, crowded market in a parking lot on a corner of Seventeenth Street. The location tied in nicely with some things I was trying to get straight in my memory.

This lot was the former site of the Hotel Betsy Ross. I'm not sure when the Betsy got built and didn't notice when it disappeared. Decayed fleabags like it once stood every few blocks in Manhattan. In the late sixties before I moved in with Geoff and Mags, I had lived at the Betsy.

The hotel was full of people down on their luck: drunks, addicts, drag queens and the occasional kid new to the city. It was at the Betsy that I once spent evenings listening to the speed babble of Billy B, the young son of a famous junkie author.

In the Bug Boy's booth that day he had a drum set, an almost new bike and microwave, a speaker system, a vacuum cleaner, and a pretty good leather jacket.

"Old hippies rising from the dead and walking into my booth," Frankie said when he saw me. "I must be having acid flashbacks!"

The Betsy was where I'd met Frankie before I began running drugs for him. "Bug Boys" is what they called kids who were going to be jockeys. In his teens Frankie had gotten too tall and was so stoned he fell off horses that were standing still.

"As always, your stuff looks like the contents of some apartment you just ripped off," I said. He looked a bit offended. I'd been told that if you asked him just right, the Bug Boy would bring out from under one of his tables the tray of bootleg copies of brand new movies, many not yet released, that he had for sale.

Getting information from him could be a devious, sidewise kind of process. "Hey," I said and indicated the lot crowded with tents and tables, "This is an historic spot we're standing on."

He nodded. "Yeah, it was weird hearing it mentioned in church. I wondered if you still remembered."

"I hadn't even known that this is where St. Just and the Major stayed when they first came to New York. Maybe it was classier earlier in the sixties," I said. Then I threw in, "This must be where they met Billy B." It was no more than a hunch but I wanted his reaction.

Frankie paused then evaded. "Lots of people came and went back then, man. I can't remember who knew who." But he hadn't said no.

"Remember listening to Billy B rap?" I asked him. The son of the great man managed to be gaunt and puffy at the same time. He'd lie on his bed and talk endlessly. "Meth, man, is like a kind of vitamin that makes you smart and lets you see right through walls," he'd say. "That's why junkies are all old and dried up. My old man sleeps twenty hours a day. I haven't slept in a year and a half."

Billy B was a trust-fund baby. Both of us, me first, then Frankie, did little errands for him. One day, Billy told me how he felt a kind of mystic kinship for another son of a well known writer. This guy was looking for someone to do a simple chore for him.

The friend lived way west in the Village on a little side street over near the Hudson. When I paid a visit, the friend turned out to be Jonah Diamond.

I was surprised but he didn't seem to be. He looked at me with disgust and boredom the same way he looked at every-thing and said, "Billy told me he'd send the choir boy from Hell. You got some street marks on you now."

In the five or so years since I'd first seen him he'd gotten real bad looking. His face was thin and kind of blue, his neck bloated.

Weird encounters pretty much defined my life right then but this one made even me uneasy. He offered me a hundred dol-lars to be the bait and draw to a secluded spot a guy he needed to talk to about a ring of his the guy had. But I had some hid-den reserve of common sense and didn't take the job.

When I saw Billy B and told him what had happened, he wasn't happy. In fact he stood up and said, "There's a little gun I can keep under my belt in back with my shirt hanging out to hide it and it's not so good for shooting someone but it's a bad surprise when you think I'm reaching into my back pocket for my wallet to pay you off and I pull out the .22 and blow open your face."

I left before finding out if he could actually do that. From then on the Bug Boy ran his errands instead of me and shortly afterwards I left the Betsy.

All these years later in his booth at the flea market I asked Frankie, "Did Billy B ever send you to meet someone named Jonah Diamond?"

The Bug Boy looked really quizzical and shook his head. "I don't remember the name," he told me and I was certain he was lying.

I was tempted to ask him something else just to see him squirm again. But at that moment a woman with feathery green hair came into the booth and wanted to look at the drums. With relief, Frankie turned to deal with her.

Walking away, I thought about the wastrel sons of notorious writer fathers and it struck me that Max Diamond with his *Diamond in the Rough* newspaper column and radio show occupied pretty much the same slot in his time as first Jack Moore and then Robin St. Just did in theirs.

I might have carried this line of thought further, but at that moment, I spotted a possible housewarming gift.

§

That June my novel about time travel and Greek gods was published and I did readings and signings the week after I talked to the Bug Boy. The next weekend I had to go to a convention up in New England. There I appeared on some panels and was asked if I believed in time travel, which I don't. No one asked if I believed in old gods, on which I am quite ambiguous. It was a little while before I thought again about Jonah Diamond and company.

That summer Marty Simonson came into town to teach a summer course on stage direction at the university and took a sublet over on Abingdon Square in the Village. His career was in good shape. He'd just had a Tony nomination, was Creative Director at the Pittsburgh Playhouse and had directed some *Law and Order* episodes.

Our history as lovers and friends still meant a lot to us both. But one reason our relationship endures is that he doesn't write and isn't a rival and I'm not in show business and don't put the arm on him professionally. Some of the people we knew from the theater program at college are fairly desperate and ask him for favors he can't grant.

"At my age, in most businesses I'd be enjoying a certain security," he said. "Fortunately I like my work and still get hired. But my finances would be kind of shaky without teaching gigs. For a lot of my friends, though, the money situation is just plain scary."

That Sunday we had a leisurely brunch at Paris Commune on Bank Street and took a stroll. Because of something that was on my mind and certain memories that we shared, I led us over to tiny, quiet Weehawken Street. It's a single, short block between Tenth and Christopher but it was almost like I wanted someone with me when I walked there.

The west side of the street is the back of a bunch of old riverfront structures. These buildings face the Hudson. Over the years, stevedore bars on the river turned to leather bars, maritime supply stores became porn video parlors.

But on Weehawken little has changed. Amazingly, one or two rear roofs still have shingles and there's a flight of wooden stairs going up to a porch on a second floor.

"It has just a touch of an old New England shore town," I said.

Marty had grown up way east on Long Island and saw it too. "Not the quaint, scenic part with the views. These are the rented rooms where they stuck the town drunk and the summer kids who worked as waitresses and lifeguards."

I paused and looked up at that second-floor porch. The windows were dark and it seemed as if they might be papered over.

"Remember Jonah Diamond, Max Diamond's son? Tended bar at the San Remo?" Marty thought for a moment, then nodded. "He lived up there in an old rundown artist's studio. Years ago, I got sent around to see him."

"About what, his buying your soul, renting your ass? You had the face of an angel and the mind of Satan. I was in awe." Every man likes being remembered as a rogue in his youth. Marty waited for my story.

I recalled yellow stains on the walls and the way the place smelled of mildew and cats. Jonah was sprawled on a busted old couch, his eyes yellow and his hands shaking. It was the first time I'd looked at someone and knew they were dying. Behind him, through big, dirty front windows, the sun reflected off the Hudson and the ruins of the old elevated West Side highway cast shadows.

"Jonah talked about his father," I said, "about how when he was a little kid Max had called him a cheap glass diamond. Jonah didn't meet his critical standards.

"He said nothing much was left after his old man died but, in his words, 'Bad memories and lucky charms.'

"He said his old man was more superstitious than any of his admirers would ever have believed. 'Even Columbia University couldn't knock all the fucking Kabbalah out of him,' was how he put it.

"Jonah described to me a ring that was supposed to be amber and ancient but he thought looked like a piece of plastic junk. His father kept it on him all the time; believed his success as an arbiter of the arts depended on it.

"Jonah had no personal use for the thing, thought it was superstitious bullshit. But when it came to him he found a sucker and rented it out. The one who wore it had a major critical career but fell behind on the rent.

"Max Diamond had told Jonah that what looked like a dragonfly preserved in the ring was actually the soul of Callimachus, the first critic."

At that Marty laughed out loud. "Who'd have thought a critic's soul was such a magic and valuable thing?"

And right then on a bright, warm Sunday it did seem pretty funny. So I didn't tell him how Jonah said he had a way for me to make a hundred dollars. He was going to point out a man who frequented the neighborhood piers looking for trade. I was going to pick him up, see if he was wearing the ring. If he was I'd bring him to a place where he and Jonah could talk.

What I did say to Marty was, "It was about selling my soul and my ass. But in a rare burst of intelligence, I chickened out." I also added, "Right around the corner on West Street is the spot where Jack Moore, the critic, got run over a week later."

"Honey, you could do tours of the dark side of the Village!" Marty told me.

As we continued on our way, scraps of paper blew along with us. On the other side of the street a guy wearing a polo shirt and sunglasses sat in a car. I recognized him as a cop. I also realized that I knew him.

At the Christopher Street end of the block some really shopworn hustlers lounged on one corner near the door of Badlands, the video gallery. On the other corner, balding, grey-bearded bears, gay guys proud of their body hair and pot bellies, smoked outside the Dugout bar.

Marty paused and mimed his indecision at which way to go. The bears were amused and began beckoning seductively to us. So we stopped in there.

§

Talking to Frankie, remembering the Betsy and that world brought me some nasty dreams. In one of them Geoff, naked in sunlight streaming through a window, turned to me and said, "Look what you've done," and there were needle marks on his arms and his slashed wrists were bleeding.

Playing my godfather role took away some of the sting. Neither of Selesta's parents could be in town for her apartment warming a few nights later. Though I knew Joan had paid for a lot of the furniture.

I brought a couple of bottles of a good Sauternes, the turquoise-green goose lamp and book of illustrated Chinese folk tales from my apartment that the hostess has loved since she was a little girl. I also brought a half dozen rather old Chinese bowls and as an extra special present I brought Marty, who qualified as a celebrity in these circles.

Selesta and her boyfriend, Sammy, had just moved into a fourth-floor walkup on Ludlow Street in the Lower East Side.

Selesta now has a tattoo design on her throat that matches the green of her eyes. Sammy's full name is Samson. He shaves his head. The two have mostly been together since college.

It's a good match. In high school, he had an obsessive-compulsive disorder. She was bulimic. Now, and it almost seems to follow logically, he is an actor. she is an artist. Both have day jobs they never talk about. Selesta and Samson possess well-developed networking skills.

"Mathis, this is my godfather," she told a tall young man with a chin beard. "He writes wonderful speculative fiction."

"That is so cool," Mathis said. His eyes never stopped darting around the room.

"This is Marty Simonson. He directed Al Pacino and Claire Danes in *King Lear* at Williamsport last year."

"Awesome!" He focused on Marty.

"Mathis has a blog," she told us. The small rooms had begun to fill up rapidly.

"*Saturday Night and Sunday Morning*," Mathis said. Marty seemed impressed. I had heard of it, even looked at it.

Godparents, however beloved, arrive early and stay a very short time if they are hip. I sat for a while on the double bed and watched young people come through the front door and kiss Selesta and Sammy.

Marty sat next to me. Mathis said, "I started *Saturday Night and Sunday Morning* writing on Sunday the things I'd seen the night before. Now I do it every day. I've got advertising and everything. You'll be on it tomorrow. What's the most important thing you've done in the last three months?"

Before Marty could reply, the door opened again and a small entourage entered. At its center, simple and elegant, was Tanya Starrett. She smiled and hugged the hostess and host. I saw she wore a T-shirt with "Arts Zoo" lettered on it and a picture of the Mona Lisa in a cage.

"Tanya!" Mathis, awestruck, abandoned us.

Marty was curious, "The new St. Just," I told him. Ms. Starrett looked around the apartment and missed nothing and nobody. I was impressed by her absolute self-confidence. As Selesta led her toward us, I finally got a good look at the soul of Callimachus imprisoned in amber.

I hoped Marty wouldn't notice and regretted saying anything to him. I remembered Jonah Diamond saying he'd kill me if I ever told anyone.

§

Other events intervened in my life. A friend's mother had died the winter before and I went to New Jersey with him and used my cataloging skills to help inventory everything in the house. Marty and I spent a lot of time together while he was in town. So it was an August night with a big moon in the sky the next time I walked down Weehawken Street.

By then I had done some research. I'd learned that Jack Moore wrote his first important reviews in 1949, a month or so after Max Diamond and the wife of a Park Avenue society doctor were discovered wrapped around a tree on an exclusive Fairfield country club's golf course, in a car "borrowed" from a diplomat at the fledgling United Nations. Moore's own death had taken place, as nearly as I could piece the timeline together, about a week after my final encounter with Jonah Diamond.

As a writer, my insights and suspicions about what goes on around me tend to be retrospective. Forty years after the event, I was certain Jack Moore was the one Jonah Diamond had wanted me to bait. With all his booze and boy problems Moore must have skipped the rent on the ring. With him gone, Diamond obviously found someone else to take the lease.

Not long after Jack Moore's supposed hit and run, an artist, campy and obsessed, began a whole series of paintings of the death: the body sprawled on West Street, being loaded into an ambulance, on exhibition at Campbell's Funeral Home with mourners weeping. St. Just wrote a much-discussed piece for *The Times* arts pages on critics and publicity. The sixties were a mad and alien world when I looked back.

On Weehawken Street on a summer night in the early twenty-first century, voices rose and fell like waves, music blasted and ceased when doors opened and closed. A couple of young guys in shorts and tank tops that showed off their tattoos went past me arm in arm. If I was their age the night would have been magic. I stopped and faced what I still thought of as Jonah Diamond's building.

All around the front door and across the windows of what was once Diamond's apartment were strips of yellow crime scene tape. The cop I'd seen parked here the afternoon Marty and I walked down this block was Denny. Years ago when he was young and I was a lot younger than I am now, he was the first police partner of my boyfriend Jaime the cop.

That night on Weehawken Street I walked down the block and asked a hustler and then a bartender at the Dugout what had happened. They told me about the police taking out the floor boards the week before, lowering them down through the second story windows

That reminded me of the time twenty years back that I had first seen Jaime. It was on First Avenue in the East Village. He wore the uniform of a Police Academy cadet and we were both part of a crowd watching a crew from the Police Property Office at work dismantling the floor of a bar.

The Keg of Nails was the name of the place, a leftover from the days when those blocks were an outpost of Little Italy. The story that emerged in neighborhood gossip and later in the papers was that a multiple hit had taken place in there decades before.

They disposed of the bodies but hadn't washed out all the bloodstains. Much later in connection with another case someone confessed to seeing the murders and the floor got taken out to be used as evidence.

My immediate take was that back when Frankie the Bug Boy ran the errand for Jonah, he must have brought Jack Moore right to the building on Weehawken Street. Moore had not left the place alive. They'd killed him there and dumped the body on West Street to be run over.

§

One night the next week or a bit later, I got a call. "Denny tells me you're hanging around in bad places," Jaime said. It was the first time we'd spoken in years. He asked me to meet him at a place I knew.

When I came out the front door of my building a few minutes later, I found the August night illuminated and people standing silent and expectant like the witnesses to a miracle in a Raphael painting. In the crowd I saw Selesta and Sam and a group of their friends.

Under the lights, an actor wearing jeans and a T-shirt in the manner of the young Brando, paused in front of the Café Figaro and called, "Allen, Allen Ginsberg."

"Cut," someone said. The actor was hustled away, technicians began to move, the audience relaxed. Selesta came over and kissed me.

"We were going to call and see if you wanted to come out for coffee," she said and I was charmed by her polite lie. "Then we saw the film crew and Jared Michaels and realized they were filming that Kerouac movie."

Mathis of *Saturday Night and Sunday Morning* was with them, looking at the crowd in search of celebrities. He had referred to me briefly in his blog the day after we met. Mostly he wrote about Tanya Starrett and about Marty.

He reported Ms. Starrett as saying that the Arts Zoo would open in the East Village in September. She told him it was a chance for people to really see the artists in their midst. "Men and women willing to spend their lives below the poverty line because of their love for what they do."

Mathis had asked her if it was true that all the participants would be naked and in cages.

"In cages, yes," she had said. "But in the clothes they wear when they're working."

Marty had then described to her the crowd at the bear bar we had visited which contained a nice sprinkling of writers, musicians, visual artists. "The zoo should have a bear cage," he said and Ms. Starrett seemed interested.

When I had read the blog I remembered thinking the more I stared at the ring she wore, the more it looked like a plastic gumball-machine prize.

That night on MacDougal Street, the kids planned to stand there and wait for Kerouac to reappear. The Village was now a theme park: Beatnik World, maybe. I said good night and went on my way.

Jaime was parked in front of a hydrant over near Sixth Avenue. He was dressed in sweatpants and a Yankees T-shirt, bigger, beefier than I remembered. His hair was still dark but thin now on top. The smile was the same. We sat down in that coffee shop on West Fourth Street where the cops go.

I had iced tea. He used skim milk and NutraSweet in his coffee. We talked a little bit. I knew he had two kids. He told me that now it was four. I told him I was retired. Then he said, "Denny tells me he saw you a couple of times recently."

"I'm surprised he remembered who I was."

"It's something you learn to do in this line of work. He says that you're making his job more difficult by hanging around a site he's investigating and asking the bystanders questions."

"There's a building I remember from a long way back. Way before I knew you. I was thinking about a guy I knew who lived there and who was very mean and very crazy. Seeing it gutted reminded me of the time you and I first met."

"The Keg of Nails." He smiled thinking about it. His memory had always been good.

I remembered Jaime that night, an Hispanic kid in his early twenties, alert and aware of himself in ways a straight guy isn't. The police cadet uniform looked like a grey version of the one I'd worn in ROTC but he did more for it. He turned and saw me looking at him. One thing had led to another and we went back to the apartment on Second Avenue where I lived.

"That night on Weehawken Street, I figured they were looking for bloodstains," I said.

"From whoever you knew that lived there how long ago?"

"Maybe thirty-eight years."

"That'd be one cold case."

For a moment I thought of asking him why he had staked out St. Just's funeral a few months before. But Jaime rubbed his eyes and I saw how tired he was.

When he spoke it was in the tone of a cop telling a civilian to move along. "What's going on over on Weehawken's got nothing to do with whatever you're talking about. Denny works Lofts and Safes now. Stolen goods. Not homicide. Denny's a good guy. Knew a bit about us and never let it bother him.

"You know I thought about you and me quite a few times before he called. I don't tell anybody about it but I got no problem with what we did. And besides the fun you were nice, you know, showed me how to take exams, never spoke down to me or tried to twist my head around. You said you're retired now? I could use some of that. You maybe need something to do. Volunteer. Maybe teach.

"There's dangerous guys involved in investigations like Denny's working on. Stay clear of it. I'd feel bad if something happened to you."

§

On a September Sunday with the first hint of autumn the Major and I followed the signs and arrows down Saint Mark's Place to the Arts Zoo. It almost seemed stupid to wreck an old friendship with accusations of voodoo and murder. But I wanted to let her know what I knew.

The Major talked about her summer, a book-signing tour in the Midwest, a vacation in Nova Scotia with Marie. Then she asked how mine had been.

That was my opening. "I've been thinking about Jonah Diamond and the past ever since the day of the memorial service."

"The past is very alive right now," she said and indicated swirling leaves frisking about us like a playful puppy and "Look at the dust devils."

"We must have been very stoned when we made that up."

The Major looked a bit amused, a bit affectionate, at the tricks my memory was playing. "It wasn't a case of us making it up. You told me about those being local ghosts and small gods. You spoke about it very seriously.

"Looking and watching over time, I realized you were right. You were a drug-soaked young Celtic poet back then. I think all those years working at the library took something out of you."

Irritated, I said, "Did St. Just have that amber ring with the dragonfly on him when they found him at the bottom of the stairs? The one Tanya Starrett wears around her neck?"

Not showing even a trace of surprise she said, "No, but it was among his effects. Not many people knew this but St. Just had been sick for a while with early-onset Alzheimer's. I gave the ring to Tanya. And, yes, I'm sure it violates some protocol of his will. But she admired him a lot and it had no innate value. And it gives her confidence. She's very young. As St. Just was when his career started."

"Jonah Diamond called it the Callimachus ring. Max Diamond got it from God knows where. Jack Moore wore it until Jonah killed him and took it back. That's when St. Just got it. And you eventually."

Her expression changed to one of concern. We had reached Tompkins Square. The Actors Cage was set up on the east side of the park. The crowds were large. People bought tickets and stood around the old-fashioned zoo fences.

Inside on a large stage a dozen actors auditioned all at the same moment in a cacophony of Shakespeare and Mamet, Sullivan and Sondheim. A dozen others down near the fence mimed waiting tables: taking orders, carrying trays, picking up tips. Some were young but a lot were in their fifties and sixties. In a corner an older woman mimed coming down imaginary stairs to a real mailbox. She opened it and pulled out bills and an oversize eviction notice. I thought of Mags.

In silence we watched the performers and the crowd. Then the Major said, "When you first came to Manhattan you were like the rest of us, struggling to survive, to create. Some of us became casualties of drugs and sex. Some fell under the spells of various magics.

"I didn't think you'd survive. You did, though. Your brother got you that nice job, and you held onto it for all these years and have a good pension.

"Lots of the rest of us didn't have that luxury. We had to live by our wits and the grace of the local gods. Not pretty. Not nice in many ways. A lot of us haven't much to show for all those years. That's what the Arts Zoo is all about."

The Painters Cage on the west side of the park contained an art gallery and a big studio with a good north light. Both were open to the audience like theater sets.

Just inside the fence men and women sat on the pavement with their art works for sale. The prices were a few dollars for each. They had cardboard signs that read, *Please buy my work. I have no medical insurance and no home.*

The Musicians Cage was set up in a schoolyard on Avenue B. A steel band had just finished playing. As we approached, four musicians in rehearsal clothes scattered at kitchen tables and on folding chairs around the yard began to play Olivier Messiaen's *Quartet for the End of Time.*

The Major and I weren't walking as close as we had before. I said, "The ring was yours to give, wasn't it? Billy B felt an affinity for Jonah Diamond. I'll bet Jonah felt one for you. All of you were children of crazy artists. Did he give it to you and St. Just? Did you buy it from him? Jonah died in a nursing home. Someone must have given him money."

"I collaborated in witchcraft, robbery, and murder and what did I get out of all that?"

"St. Just's praise is what launched you."

Neither of us spoke or paid much attention as we passed the Bear Cage in a small vacant lot on Avenue B. The guys inside were singing karaoke disco.

She shook her head and looked disappointed. "If I'd ever thought of killing anyone, I'd start right now with you. If any or all of this was true, what would prevent me from eliminating you?"

"Because, if anything happens to me, there's a letter that will get delivered to a cop I know." It wasn't true but I thought it was a nice touch.

The Writers Cage was down on Houston Street. Balloon sellers and popcorn carts ringed the bars but this wasn't as popular as some of the other exhibits.

"I'm not afraid of the police," said the Major. "It's necessary that we part for a while." As she turned away, she added, "I think you might devote a little of your time to this project." The swirl of leaves was with us again. "It will please the gods and especially the ghosts."

The Bug Boy was there, wearing a hat that said *Zookeeper* and selling tickets. He obviously had overheard and understood the last part of our conversation.

From inside the cage came a clatter of keyboards. Writers in their pajamas or their underwear wandered around looking for grants in hollow logs. They'd jump up to try and grab the contracts hanging just out of reach on the branches of trees. Nick and Norah Grubstreet were in there dressed in matching Prada sleepwear and looking very amused.

Jay Glass in his boxers sat at a computer, spoke on a cell phone and seemed all business. But when another writer rattled the cage door and found it locked, his expression changed to a veiled anxiety that didn't seem rehearsed.

Along with everyone else, I'd heard how the Amazon numbers zoomed on Glass's essay collection from a small publisher after he'd been profiled on National Public Radio when the Arts Zoo opened.

Tanya Starrett stood near the cage speaking to a television reporter. The Major was at her side and the amber ring was at her throat. She was someone who could have pushed St. Just down a flight of stairs.

She said, "This is about the artists who are a major reason for this city's being a tourist attraction. While providing publicity and entertainment, we're trying at the same time to bring attention to creative people, many of them in late middle age and older who have minimum resources."

Leaves stirred in the gutter, spiraled and blew over my shoes. I tried to step away and it happened again. Paper blew against my leg. Out of the corner of my eye I saw Jaime's car drive past. I wondered if these might be the dangerous people he had warned me about.

The Bug Boy stepped up next to me and whispered in my ear, "You're going around asking questions, making everybody all uneasy. And look at how upset you got all the little spirits. You think they're angry that they died? Don't be crazy, man. They all prefer it the way they are."

We were next to a door in the cage. "The Major's even more pissed at you than she was with Jay Glass talking trash about St. Just. You need to do what he's doing to make her happy. Everyone wants you inside. For old times' sake I'm letting you keep your clothes."

A spiral of dust blew in my eyes. The cage door opened. The Bug Boy and someone else had my arms. Through dust and tears I saw Jay jump up. But I knew that before he could get out the door would clang shut behind me.

Chapter Fourteen

Tanya Starrett concluded her interview with New York Cable News. She and the Major walked off without looking my way. The Bug Boy and the cops were nowhere to be seen.

Suddenly a microphone got stuck between the bars of the Writers Cage. "Why are you in there?" asked the reporter.

For a moment I thought of telling her the whole twisted story from Jonah Diamond on. Then some kind of survival instinct clicked in and I said, "Everything in the arts depends on getting shown, getting heard, getting read, getting seen, but mostly getting attention. The news media is our oxygen!"

Later I saw myself on television. My hair was wild, my hands clutched the bars of the cage in which I was locked. Behind me clustered a crowd of mostly mainstream authors quietly seething that a lowly spec-fiction writer was soaking up camera time.

Their leaping to snare prop publishing contracts may have begun as an act but it became more real as the day progressed. They really seemed to want those prop contracts. Jay Glass actually appeared to be trying to write.

The other inmate besides me who was still in street clothes looked at first like a child in an old slouch hat. On second glance I saw an adult, aged and sardonic, with a face like a wise old monkey's. He seemed familiar but I couldn't quite remember why. When I asked later on nobody remembered him.

I only spent a late afternoon and evening on display. They let us out after nine PM. But the time served proved productive. I was on television for about twenty seconds and apparently got seen by everyone in the city. This helped me not think about the soul of Callimachus and my encounter with the Major.

Immediately a couple of editors asked if I had stories to send them. Andre, a hot youngish guy from my yoga class at the University gym whom I'd noticed but never spoken to, mentioned that he'd seen me. "What was it like?" he asked.

I was about to say something about the publicity aspect when I realized where his interest lay. "Frustrating," I said. "I kept thinking of writers I'd have liked to lock up. Maybe that's how animals in the zoo feel."

"You don't mind being the guy who holds the keys," Andre replied and I could tell the young man was impressed. In my late middle age this seldom happens.

We had coffee that afternoon at the Caffe Reggio on Mac-Dougal Street. He was in his mid-thirties, looked five years younger and had a French mother and Anglo father. Andre said the father was a bit cold and distant but I thought later maybe he wasn't quite cold and distant enough. Andre did freelance design and lived with James—a boring guy, I guessed—who had much more money than Andre and far less imagination than I do.

Around then I heard on good authority that the apartment on Weehawken Street had been dismantled by the cops in connection with a movie bootleg operation. This made me wonder if what I'd seen really had anything to do with Jonah Diamond and Callimachus. Then I remembered that the Bug Boy sold bootleg movies and he had worked for Jonah Diamond, which made me think there might be a connection. But the paranoid intensity had cooled.

§

Just after the Arts Zoo, mostly because I live in Manhattan and am available, I was asked to be a last minute substitute at the monthly *New York Review of Science Fiction* readings series. The scheduled author, a well-known fantasist and fabled hypochondriac, had come down with something. The reading was at the Melville Gallery at the South Street Seaport.

A paradox as the printed word fades into the electronic is that the reading—a live writer speaking in public to an audience—becomes ever more important. Television, radio, the internet are wholesale publicity venues. Potentially you can reach millions. Live readings are retail, not quite one on one, though I have done events with not many more listeners than that.

Many years ago, I did my first public reading for that same NYRSF series. Back then these events were held in a woman's loft on the Bowery. The audience sat around on couches and chairs and bought tea brewed right in the kitchen and cold drinks straight from the fridge.

Before that loft event I hadn't made a public appearance sober since I played Abe Lincoln's son when I was four. I fretted for months and at the event some said I read much too softly while others told me I was much too fast. The other reader, who has gone on to a large career outside the genre, was gracious enough afterwards to forget it had ever happened.

In the years since, I've gone from terror to nonchalance without, perhaps, ever achieving competence. The South Street Seaport is a small carefully preserved chunk of old maritime New York. The Melville Gallery on Water Street is a large first-floor space in a vintage building. Pillars hold up the ceiling. At that time the walls were decorated with paintings of disasters at sea.

richard bowes

I'd asked Andre if he wanted to come and listen to me. And since it was early in our acquaintance he was polite enough to invent a plausible excuse. It wasn't my being a writer that turned him on, but the idea of imprisonment and my desire to do it to others. We had begun getting together once or twice a week.

Last-minute substituting wins you the gratitude of the ones running the event but not necessarily of those who have come to hear someone else. The crowd was good sized and didn't seem violently disappointed. Again I saw the child-size figure with the old monkey's face from the Arts Zoo. He was seated among young writers who didn't seem aware of him.

Then I got distracted. "Saw you in the Zoo the other week," said a large, surly young man who previously had done no more than glower at me. "I'd like to get me some of that publicity. My novel is twelve hundred pages long—so big it frightens all those little editors."

"Maybe you should do some short stories," I suggested. "Make them feel warm and safe."

"It takes me twenty thousand words just to clear my throat," he replied.

"How did you get included in the Arts Zoo?" a young woman asked. "I inquired all over the place as to where I should apply and got no response."

"You don't apply," I said and was about to tell her how it had happened until I thought better of it. "It's like a real zoo—they shove you into a cage against your will." She shook her head and didn't believe me.

The other reader that month was Brockman, tall and crane-like, an old-time science fiction writer. Brockman was famous for having blown the fuses in his brain back in the Golden Age while writing too many paperback originals too fast on too much booze and amphetamine. He's bitter and disillusioned— it's his shtick.

"I'd never heard of you until I found out you were doing this reading," Brockman said staring down at me. "I read a couple of your stories that got some attention. I thought they were okay."

That's as close to a compliment as Brockman gives.

It must have been a subconscious connection that made me ask him about the monkey child. Brockman looked where I gestured. "Herzog," he muttered. "You can't keep a dead fraud down. He plagiarized a story of mine for an *Outer Limits* script"

That, I realized, was who the child/monkey was. Kinsey Herzog, legendary speculative-fiction writer, winner of everything from the Nebula to the Oscar and a legendary literary infighter. "Never forgives a slight or a favor," it was said of him. He had died in his late seventies some years before. Maybe feuds are a perverse way of preserving the past.

Brockman was a master of the genre feud himself. But that night he was flustered and stammering. From the corner of my eye I saw the monkey child give a little smile each time that happened. And I seemed to recall that it was Herzog who had accused Brockman of plagiarism.

When I was introduced by the reading's curator, I walked to the lectern. The wall behind me was lined with oil paintings of sailing ships capsizing in hurricane winds, trapped in ice, burning to the waterline.

"*The God of Thieves found himself in a vast hall, filled with people rushing about laden with packages,*" I began. Looking into the audience I saw no trace of Kinsey Herzog.

§

The next afternoon Andre came by my place. His schedule was loose enough that he had chunks of time when no one knew where he was. Retirement made it easy for me to arrange these diversions.

We talked for a little while about the art on my walls and then the game began. "I know your life, my friend," I said, "A rich man indulges you and you repay him by cheating."

He showed surprise that I knew this. "Are you with the police," he said looking a bit apprehensive.

This evolved into his being a young revolutionary in a country not quite like the one we were in. He fell into the hands of an enigmatic older man who stripped and handcuffed him. This improvisation was easy to invent and produced its pleasures. Andre would submit to just about anything once he was properly handcuffed.

Early Saturday morning a couple of weeks later, I went on the radio to promote a story collection that had recently appeared. At five AM from the southernmost tip of Manhattan *The Hour of the Wolf* was broadcast on WBAI: two hours of talk, music and readings centered on speculative fiction. This venue was a personal favorite of mine, one that existed only at a very odd hour in a part of the city all but deserted at that particular time.

Listener-sponsored WBAI was once the wild child of freeform New York radio, the place to go to for coverage of smoke-ins and protest marches. Now, in the pre-dawn, I arrived at an almost empty skyscraper, signed in with security in a silent lobby, went up to the shabby station where an engineer and a couple of other guys sat around gossiping.

WBAI as always was on the verge of some crisis: a takeover by dissident radicals or unpaid creditors. I got off on the combination of ritual and impending doom. Like every other time I've been on the air I wondered if it would be the last.

The transition from one show to the next is like the stunt where one guy slides into the driver's seat of a moving car as the driver bumps onto the shotgun side. The car doesn't even lurch. The prior show's host arose; his reggae music theme faded out. My host sat down and a wolf's howl faded in.

It was on radio, undisturbed by a visible audience, that I learned how to read aloud, to utilize the quiet library voice I'd acquired over decades at a reference desk. That morning I began: *"One fine May afternoon the Cinnamon Cavalier popped out of the baking ovens of the Giant King's castle. Since he was a cookie intended from the first for the King's only daughter and only child, no effort had been spared. The heat of the kitchen shimmered in the sunlight as he was brought forth."*

The great part of this particular gig came after two hours broadcasting to the world from a closed studio. It was when I would stagger into the lobby of WBAI and look out the windows at dawn on the silver Hudson River.

§

Books of Wonder in the West Teens just off Fifth Avenue has very nice cookies, shelves of children's books and classic cover art on the walls. They give lots of readings there and on a Sunday afternoon between Thanksgiving and Christmas they held one for the authors of a children's anthology in which I'd appeared.

In my time I've gone out with hustlers, medical students and actors, a cop, a masseur, a maître d', a security guard and an artist who made electronic sculpture out of dysfunctional picture tubes. But never with another writer or even someone much interested in books. I don't know why but I again asked Andre if he wanted to hear me read. He shook his head, said he couldn't. This time I saw he was a little put off by the invitation.

That Sunday in an open space at the back of Books of Wonder, the audience included more adults than children. The Major was also in the anthology and was present.

Even though things had turned out rather well in the Writers Cage and my suspicions about her connection with Callimachus had started to seem like a hallucination, I was still a bit angry and didn't trust her. But she nodded to me and I nodded back.

richard bowes

Half a dozen of us read—each was allotted ten minutes. Her story was a charming piece of derring-do in which a resourceful girl rescued her bully of an older brother who'd been turned into a frog. She then kept him in an aquarium in her room, fed him flies.

This reminded me of how much I'd liked the Major's work back when we were younger and on speaking terms. When I went to tell her that, something else caught my attention. Kinsey Herzog was in the audience, wide-eyed and amused.

Because we did share a certain understanding I mentioned this.

"Others have reported seeing him recently," she said lest I think my sighting was important. "Sad, a half-forgotten old spirit hanging around the living!" And with that she turned away.

When my turn came, I looked out at the audience of smiling adults and serious children, none of whom noticed Herzog, and said: *"There was never such a celebration as when the Queen of Summer wed the King of Winter. The Four Winds, their mutual cousins, in the excitement of the moment, blew open every door and window in the castle."*

Both my brothers Gerry and David became painters and in my life friends, lovers and others have been artists, photographers. Their work covers the walls of my tiny apartment. Andre on his next visit looked them over. He spoke quietly. "Some of these are valuable. Did you purchase them?"

"Each was a gift," I said and looked a little scornful. "As your art will be when the time comes for me to take everything from you." The plastic male chastity device I had put on the night table gave just the right effect. For reasons with which I've more or less come to terms, I like a dash of fear in the mix but I prefer that it be my partner's. Andre's expression showed his interest and the game was on.

§

Housing Works Bookstore lies on the vague frontier where SoHo meets the Lower East Side. The store has comfortable chairs and a nice café. It's run by a foundation that helps the homeless and people with HIV.

That January I took part in a reading there for an anthology of stories about gay elves. Andre, of course, was absent.

This venue attracted a glamorous crowd of best-selling YA authors which turned out for one of their number who was a reader.

In my story a young halfbreed describes mortal/fey love in the demimonde: *"The dollar boys and pillow girls when they boast about their protectors/lovers always talk of velvet tongues and cocks that know no rest and orgasms that ride on until you're hoarse with yelling."*

It was a good performance if I do say so. The audience reaction was strong. A couple of bloggers who covered the event gave my reading nice reviews.

Strangely, I felt bothered that there was no sign of Herzog. There was, however, a woman elderly and elegant in a long black dress with tiny silver buckles diagonally across the front. She had a halo of blue hair and small silver glasses through which she peered at me. When I looked again she had vanished. That gave me a mild chill, which I appreciated.

Small doses of fear keep horrible fear at bay. I'd learned that as a kid. I wondered if Andre, like me, had been introduced to the game when he was too young. But he always drew back when I pressed him. "Why do you need to think about something that works?" he asked. I snapped the cuffs on him.

I'd told him to wear throwaway stuff and bring a change of clothing. He shuddered when I cut his shirt and shorts off with a shears, cried out as I snipped his boxerbriefs in two.

§

The coffee house has a magic place in the legend of the written word from the time that Johnson and Goldsmith trad-

richard bowes

ed quips while Boswell scribbled them down, to the evening Ginsberg recited *Howl* at the Café Rienzi.

Think Coffee is a modern-style coffee house—large and well lighted. At dozens of tables, young people looked up from their laptops with polite semi-interest as I read: *"Salome's hand is the hinge and John the Baptist's head is the hammer on the door knocker at the Studio Caravaggio. I slam the brass head held by its brass hair a few times before the spy slot on the iron door opens and closes."*

The espresso machine came on at that moment and drowned me out, which the audience and I found kind of amusing. Herzog wasn't in the crowd but I did catch sight of the lady in the long black dress.

Around then I began writing a story about a not terribly distant future where the written word is dying away. The narrator, a very self-conscious writer, is involved with a partner who is post-literate and has never read a book.

They have little common but the sex. The sex however is quite hot ,which turns the narrator on and bothers him a great deal. The partner's name was Andre for the first two drafts, when I changed it to Marcel.

Our affair had slipped into a routine and we sometimes didn't get together every week. I wondered how long this would continue and like the Marschallin in the last act of *Der Rosenkavalier* I doubted there would be other young men after he was gone. Andre, unlike some others, probably wouldn't haunt my dreams and I had finished the story by the time I gave my next reading.

§

The bar on the second floor of KGB was already jammed when I slipped in the door. Everyone from Brockman to the Major was present. A friend waved at me and pointed to an empty chair. I made my way across the worn floor. The crowd at the bar was two deep. A picture of Lenin stared down from the dark red walls.

New York has every kind of literary venue from downtown poetry slams to uptown gatherings of PEN International. But on the third Wednesday of each month in a red-walled bar in what was once the left-wing Ukrainian clubhouse on East Fourth Street (the right-wingers met at the Ukrainian National Home over on Second Avenue) writers published and unpublished, editors, readers and critics come to hear speculative-fiction authors speak their words aloud.

On this particular Wednesday evening I was one of half a dozen readers at a fund raiser for a campaign for artists' co-ops. The owners of a half-finished apartment building had gone bankrupt. A move was afoot to convert it into low-cost artist housing. The campaign was to make sure space was allocated for destitute spec-fiction writers.

Anyone who's done enough live readings develops a stand-up routine. Twitches and quirks can be played for laughs. I once saw a much-lauded writer burn a pickle on a stick as a demonstration of some scientific truth in one of his stories. The visual effect was mesmerizing; the smell was disgusting.

When I got up to read there were sirens outside. I said, "The one great thing about getting old is that when I hear that sound, I relax because I know the police are no longer interested in me. Ambulances are another matter."

Then I began: "*Each time he finds me reading, Marcel watches me with a look of concern and distrust so slight that I would miss it if we hadn't been together for over a year.*"

I glanced around the packed tables, the line of faces at the bar, the people standing a few feet in front of the podium. Andre wasn't there, of course. But Herzog was and this time leaning against him was the woman with the silver glasses and buttons.

There was a long pause, a couple of people coughed. I shifted my gaze to my text. "*That night each time I elicited a sigh, a gulp, a sign of satisfaction, I murmured, to Marcel, 'I learned that from a book.'*"

After KGB readings are over, a large crowd always walks up to St. Mark's Place for dinner. It's in the building erected on the former site of the Dom, that huge Polish wedding hall where Warhol, the artist who knew everything about self-promotion, introduced the Velvet Underground to an unwary world.

The restaurant is Chinese and once had a Chairman Mao theme with menus designed to look like Little Red Books. Unobtrusive traces of that remain and form a strange symmetry with KGB's Soviet décor. On the way there that night someone talked about an Artists Circus in Tompkins Square Park to promote the artist housing.

I happened to walk next to Brockman, the first time we'd met since we read together at South Street. I described the thin old lady I'd spotted with Herzog.

Brockman displayed some amusement. "That's Melanie Anselm," he said, "very big in children's fantasy when she was alive. She and Herzog were an item back when his second wife threw him out of the house."

He gave a rusty laugh. "Many years ago the Major had a kids' novel everyone thought was going to get the Newbery Medal. But Melanie had connections—some say that she seduced one of the judges—and snatched it away from her. The Major is still furious about it."

We walked in the midst of a crowd of young writers and editors that didn't seem to pay much more attention to us than they did to Herzog and Melanie Anselm. Their talk centered on the circus promotion and how it would be a more positive statement than the Zoo.

The Major walked near us and from her expression I thought she might have overheard Brockman's and my conversation. It made me want to talk with the two of them about revenants and the past.

But it occurred to me that the three of us weren't that different from Herzog and Melanie. We were ghosts tagging along and trying to stay visible for a little while longer.

Then one young lady, the youngest editor in the city at that moment, turned to us. She had an idea for a lion=tamer act with a group of prominent speculative-fiction writers as the big cats and wondered what we thought. Brockman snorted, the Major looked dubious. But I told her it sounded quite interesting and wondered what the media coverage would be like.

richard bowes

Chapter Fifteen

Geoff and I walked one night amid a twisted New York of glass and steel, girls in witches' hats, boys in tutus. He turned to me with his angel face distorted by anger and said, "You're my Subway Man. What he did to you, you did to me."

The dream bothered me enough that friends asked what was wrong. A questionnaire from Tanya Starrett about my willingness to participate in the Artists Circus got ignored. On what turned out to be our last encounter, even the imperceptive Andre noticed that the enigmatic host of the lonely cabin where he was forced to seek refuge wasn't really paying attention to the game.

Then in the pre-dawn of a morning in April, I woke up from a violent and disturbing dream. In it, I was somewhere that I realized was the Southwest with three other guys whom I knew in the dream but didn't quite recognize when I thought about them later.

All of us were engaged in smuggling something—drugs as it turned out. We were tough. Or they were anyway, big guys with long hair and mustaches. There was, I knew, another bunch of guys much tougher than us with whom we didn't get along and there were cops.

The end of the dream was that I heard police sirens and was scared but relieved because they weren't as bad as the other guys. The last image in the dream, however, was the cops smashing two of the big guys' faces right into the adobe wall of the building we stayed in. And I knew, in the way one does in dreams, that the other guy and I were in for something as bad or worse. Then I woke up in my bed in my apartment.

From the time I was a small boy I've been afraid of the long marches of the night, the time in the dark when the lights inside me went out. The fear that would hit me as my head was on the pillow was that dreams would change me and that I, the one falling asleep, would not be the one who woke up.

Imagining the fragility of my identity always chilled me. I did fall asleep again though and dreamed once more.

This time, I saw the head cop with his short white hair and grey suit sitting in his car, smoking a cigarette, staring blue-eyed and expressionless at me. In the dream I was very young by my current standard, maybe in my mid-twenties, that bad time in my life.

In my dream, I realized that I had been looking at a computer and had viewed all this on some kind of a website.

When I awoke this time, the sun was up. Except for my having seen it as a website, the dream seemed like a fragment of a past when I might wake up and find myself in places almost that bad.

I felt sick, my stomach was upset, every bone and muscle ached and each move I made took an effort.

Nothing seemed to have led up to this illness. I'd been to the theater the night before with my friend and editor Ellen. We'd seen a show with music about abducted orphans and eighteenth-century boy sopranos played by women.

A few hours before that, my affair with Andre got broken off abruptly. James, the guy with whom Andre lived, called me up and said that Andre had told him everything. They both wanted me to stay away from now on. I told James that it was a-once-a-week thing that had become routine and boring over the last year or so, and asked him to say goodbye to Andre for me.

As a veteran of more than forty years in Manhattan, normally neither big, melodramatic Broadway shows nor sudden disruptions in my love life cause the kind of distress I felt that morning.

Even as I wondered if I should call my doctor, I was aware of a kind of web stream that ran constantly in a corner of my brain. The fever dream took the form of a perpetual Google search complete with web pages and blogs I couldn't remember looking for.

Pictures and stories with elusive contexts appeared. At one point, I found myself looking at the profiles of the members of a tough cop unit somewhere in the Southwest. It had short bios, photos of them with mustaches and holsters and mask-like sunglasses.

As I wondered why and how I had looked this up, I saw a familiar face with a white crewcut and expressionless cop eyes.

I remembered I wanted to call my doctor. As I dialed the number, I thought of the tune and lyrics of a song I'd been listening to recently. It was by John Dowland, a poet and composer who was kind of the Kurt Cobain of Elizabethan England. Something in the melancholy grace of the tune, the resignation of the song's lyrics had caught me.

> *Absence can no joy impart:*
> *Joy once fled cannot return.*
> *Now, oh now I needs must part,*
> *Parting though I absent mourn.*

Maybe this attachment had been a kind of harbinger, some part of my consciousness telling me I had started dying. I wondered how Dowland's song "Flow My Tears," had affected Philip K. Dick when he'd used it in a title.

Somehow the call to the doctor never got made. I couldn't remember what day it was. People who phoned me, friends, my godson Chris in Ohio, the woman who had called herself my work-wife before I retired from the University, seemed concerned.

Many things ran on the screen inside my head. The Macabres when I found myself looking at their site seemed like many a New York late '70s punk group. The photos showed the musicians—emaciated, decked in bondage accessories, with their hair hacked off at odd angles. A bit of one of their songs played. Then police sirens wailed just like they had when my companions in the dream and I had gotten caught.

I realized that the sirens were my phone ringing. A friend's friend who taught nursing at the University wanted the telephone number of my medical group and the number of someone who could take me there next morning.

§

That night was especially awful: a long confusion of dreams. Chris kept calling. He seemed almost frantic but I was too sick to talk to him for more than a minute or two.

When I looked at my inner computer screen it showed me palm trees and bright sun and elephants. The Macabres now worked naked in a prison chain gang. A woman guard with the face of a peacock seemed very familiar. I thought I spotted the policeman with the blue eyes that gave away nothing. He looked right at me and was about to speak

Then my doorbell sounded and it was my friend Bruce who was there to take me to the doctor's. With his help I got dressed and walked the few blocks to my medical group office on Washington Square. A very concerned doctor ordered me into St. Vincent's hospital.

Shortly afterwards Bruce escorted me to the emergency-room admittance desk. Then he hugged me and was off to another job and I was in the power of the hospital.

There was no waiting. I identified myself, was given a brief form to fill out and was shown right into the middle of the beds and gurneys, patients and orderlies. Numbers flashed on computer screens, and machines beeped. I thought of my brother Gerry when I'd seen him into this same emergency room.

Nurses and doctors clustered around an enormously fat, comatose woman, then dispersed. A social worker took the life history of an elderly black man who very patiently explained to her how he had lost everything he ever had and lived now in a shelter. A moaning patient rolled by on a gurney hung with IV bags. Two cops wheeled in a shooting victim.

Then an orderly threw back the curtains around a bed and told me to come inside. My clothes were taken away and I became completely passive. I was dressed in two gowns, one worn forward, the other backwards, and socks with skid-proof soles. I was bled and examined and hauled through cold corridors and X-rayed.

Tubes got attached to me. A catheter was stuck up my urinary tract; at one point a very new intern tried to stick a tube down my throat and I choked and gagged. A horrible brown goop came up my guts and into my mouth and nose. My hospital gowns got soaked and there was commotion. People talked about me as if I was dead or not there.

It reminded me of an accident scene. I heard police radios, saw flares illuminating a night time car crash. I saw a familiar picture on a computer screen. It was in black and white, a 1950s newspaper shot.

A kid in his late teens had been thrown onto the branch of a tree by the force of a collision. He hung over tree limb bent at the waist and barefoot, his loafers gone, his legs still in jeans that almost rode off his hips, his upper body bare. The cool striped shirt he wore now hung down over his head. That was probably to the good: the face and eyes under those circumstances are not something you'd want to see.

That image haunted me at fourteen. I had imagined myself dramatically dead in just that manner if only I could drive and had a car.

"That photograph was his own private version of the Albert Pinkham Ryder primitive painting, 'Death on a Pale Horse,'" I read on a screen in front of me and realized I was looking at a website about me and that I was referred to in the past tense.

Then the screen was gone and I was back in the tumult of the emergency room. "Intestinal blockage—massive fluid build-up," said a female resident. "It's critical."

"Rejected the drain," said the intern who had failed to get it in.

A male nurse spoke quietly to me like I was a frightened animal, put his hand on my chest to calm me and stuck the tube into my nose and down my throat in a single gesture. A tall wheeled IV pole with hooks that held my drains, feeding bag, urine bag and various meters was attached to me.

Doctors examined me further. I felt like my insides were grinding themselves apart. A bag hanging next to my head rapidly filled with brown goop that had been inside me.

It was very late at night when I was wheeled onto elevators and off them then down silent corridors. Still dirty and wearing damp hospital gowns I was brought into a ward on the twelfth floor.

A young Asian nurse named Margaret Yang took over. Before I was placed on a bed, she called and four orderlies appeared. Women talking in the accents of Puerto Rico, Ukraine and Jamaica brought me into a bathroom, sponged me off, put me under shower water and turned me around under it saying, as I tried to cover myself, "It's okay. You are as God made you."

§

Only when I was clean, in clean clothes and on a bed looking out at the night, did I remember that I had been in this hospital more than forty-two years before. When I was twenty-one this was where I awoke one night with no idea who or where I was.

The place then seemed vast, chilly and strange. The lighted windows in the brownstones across the street had revealed stylish apartments, silhouettes of the occupants, and I knew it looked like a *New Yorker* cover without knowing what that meant or how I knew it.

I remembered a nurse having told me I'd been found face down and half undressed in a hallway, bleeding from a cut on my head and without any wallet or I.D. I had lots of alcohol and a couple of drugs in my bloodstream. None of this had meant anything to me.

A very old nun, thin and stiff, her face almost unlined, came around late in that night. Even with amnesia I was still enough of a Catholic kid to feel embarrassed talking to a nun while sitting on top of the sheets in just a skimpy hospital gown.

She inspected the bandage on my forehead and talked about Dylan Thomas. "He was brought here not ten or twelve years ago after a hard night's drinking. He died from that and pneumonia on the floor just below this one. I thought of him when I saw you," I remembered her saying while looking at me calmly. That's when she said, "I wonder if you too are a young man who has an uneasy relationship with death."

Scared, I said, "I don't even know who I am."

"Time will reveal those things," she said. "You're still very young."

Then I found myself looking at that long-ago night on a computer screen. It was all conveyed in images: a *New Yorker* cover of figures silhouetted against the lighted windows of their brownstones, a figure of a nun that seemed almost translucent.

What appeared at first to be the famous drawing of the young Rimbaud unconscious in a bed after being shot by his lover Verlaine turned out to be a photo of Dylan Thomas dead in St Vincent's Hospital—and became me at twenty-one with my poet's hair and empty, blue, amnesiac's eyes.

I pulled back from the screen and saw all around me a vast dark space with green globes rotating through it. Then I squinted and saw that the globes were the glowing screens that monitored each patient in this hospital. Beyond us, further out in the endless dark, were other screens in other hospitals, stretching on into infinity.

I thought of Gerry, floating towards the light on his way to death.

§

Apparently I called out, because then Nurse Yang was speaking to me, asking if I was okay. The universe and the globes disappeared. St Vincent's, as I saw it all these years later, seemed a small, slightly shabby and intensely human place.

"I'm so glad," I told her. "You people have saved my life."

She was amused and said that this was what they tried to do for everyone brought in here but that it was always nice to be appreciated. When she started to leave, I got upset and she showed me how to ring for help if I needed it.

After she was gone I lay in the cool quiet with the distant sound of hospital bells and the voices of the women at the nurses' station. But I didn't sleep.

My fear that all trace of me would be lost while I slept was out and active that night. Lying there, it seemed likely that this person with a search engine installed in his head was not the me who had existed a few days ago.

Drugs and the tubes siphoning the liquid out of my guts and into plastic bags had eased my pain and I did drift off every once in a while. But nurses and orderlies came and woke me quite regularly to take my signs and measure my temperature.

At one moment I would be awake in the chill quiet of that hospital with a window view of the Con Edison Building and the Zeckendorf Towers at Union Square over the low rises of Greenwich Village.

In the next, I'd be looking at a computer screen that showed a map of the old Village—a vivid 1950s touristy affair with cartoon painters in berets and naked models, beatnik kids playing guitars in Washington Square and Dylan Thomas with drinks in both hands at the bar of the White Horse Tavern.

Awake again in the dark, I waited, listened, half expecting the old nun to reappear. Instead what I got was a moment's glimpse of the white-haired cop who had watched my friends get beaten. He looked at me now with the same deadpan.

§

I came out of a doze, awakened by a gaggle of bright-eyed young residents. One of them, a woman with an Indian accent, said, "We were all amazed by the X-rays of your intestines. It was the talk of the morning rounds."

"Why?" I asked.

"Because of the blockage they were extremely distended. You came very close to having a rupture, which would have been very bad. You could easily have died." All of them, a small Asian woman, a tall rather dizzy looking blond American boy and a laid-back black man nodded their agreement and stared at me fascinated.

"How did this happen?" I wanted to know.

"We believe it was from twenty-three years ago when you had cancer and they removed part of your colon," she said. "After all this time, the stitching began to unravel and adhered to the other side of your intestines."

Other doctors appeared: the gastroenterological resident spoke to me, my own internist popped in. They told me that I was out of immediate danger. Sometimes the blockage eased all by itself. Sometimes it required surgery. The surgeon would see me the next day.

My bedside phone had now been connected. I made some calls. People came by, friends and family, old flames and godchildren. They brought flowers and disposable razors, my CD player, a notebook, they gave me back rubs and went out and asked questions at the nurse's station. They established my presence, showed the world that I was someone who was loved and cared for.

Margaret Yang came and sat for a while, talked to my sister Lee who was visiting about this unique old hospital and how they were all devoted to it. I wanted to hang on to everyone, nurses, friends, family who was there in the bright daylight.

They had brought me the Dowland CD. The countertenor sang:

> Part we must though now I die,
> Die I do to part with you.

Gradually on that lovely spring day with the sun pouring down on the old bricks of the Village, twilight gave way to night. Lights in the hospital dimmed, the halls got quiet.

When I was operated on for cancer it was uptown at Mt. Sinai. The ward I was in overlooked Central Park and at night in the intensity of my illness and fear and the drugs inside me, I saw lights passing amid the leafless winter trees.

And I imagined an alternate world called Capricorn where people dying of cancer in this world appeared to the population as glowing apparitions.

The night before that operation, I awoke with the feeling I was falling through the furniture, through the floor and thought I was falling into Capricorn.

Remembering that, I saw a picture of myself, ethereal and floating amid a stand of winter trees in a hospital bed. The white-haired cop was showing it to me on a screen.

"When we spotted that, we knew you were in no way ordinary," he said. "Our seeing you like this confirmed an initial report from when you were in this place as a kid with a busted head and no memory. Someone spoke to you and said you had an uneasy relationship with death and the potential to see more than the world around you."

§

Some people have the gift of being perfect hospital visitors. The flowers my friend Marc brought the next morning looked like a Flemish still life, his conversation was amusing and aimless.

He sat beside my bed that morning and I told him about a book I'd once written.

"Back in 1984 I thought I was dying of AIDS but it turned out I had cancer which they cut out of me. *Feral Cell* was a fantasy novel I wrote during and after that. In it people dying of cancer in this world are worshipped in an adjacent world named Capricorn. They call our world Cancer and call themselves the Capri.

"The faithful among them find ways of bringing a few people who are doomed on our world over to theirs. To prevent us from drifting back here, they dress us in the skins of deceased Capri, make us drink their blood, the Blood of the Goat, and are objects of awe.

"But there are others on that world—decadent aristocrats, of course—who hunt us. They throw silver nets over us and drag us down. They skin us and drain our blood and use those things to cross into this world."

"That must almost have made getting sick worthwhile," he said.

I babbled on. "The future New York City I depicted in the book—turn-of-the-third-millennium Manhattan—was all open-air drug markets. Rival gangs of rollerskaters and skateboarders clash in the streets. What we got, of course, was gentrification and Disneyland.

"A lot of being sick is like one long nightmare. In my Capricorn everything was terror and magic. At night, patients in a children's cancer ward could be seen floating amid the trees of a sacred grove."

Marc walked with me as I pushed my IV stand around the floor. One of the hall windows overlooked Seventh Avenue.

Outside on a glorious day in spring, traffic flowed south past the Village Vanguard jazz club.

"The low buildings make it look like the nineteen fifties," Marc said.

"Time travel," I said.

It was a quiet Sunday. Later that afternoon, my friend Joan Mata was giving me a back rub when a dark-haired woman, not tall but with great presence and wearing a red dress suit, appeared. She introduced herself as the one who would be my surgeon if the intestinal blockage didn't ease. And I knew that it hadn't and wouldn't and that she would operate on me.

As night came and friends and family had departed, I thought of Jimmy when he was a patient at this hospital. Jimmy and I had met in the Garment District, been lovers briefly and were friends in the years of AIDS terror. He designed and constructed department-store window displays.

Since I'd first known him he talked about the little people inside his head, the ones he relied on for his ideas.

"Last night they put on this show with fireflies and ice floes. Perfect for Christmas in July," he'd say. "Sadly what I'm looking for is ideas for Father's Day which is, as always, a wilderness of sports shirts and fishing tackle."

Just before Jimmy died in this very hospital, I came into his room and found him in tears.

"They're all sprawled on the stage, dead," he told me.

§

Without being aware of a transition to sleep, somewhere in the night I became part of a Milky Way of bodies lying hooked up to lighted screens. I saw all of us, patients here and across the world, floating in a vast majestic orbit.

Then the cop, tough, his blue eyes giving away nothing, watched as I looked at the photo he'd handed me.

It showed me in my dream of the Southwest along with my companions who would later get arrested and beaten into pulp.

"How did you know these guys?" he asked.

"In the dream I had I was a friend of one of them. Carlo," I said.

"Friend, you mean like a boyfriend?" He displayed no attitude but past experience with cops made me wary. I shook my head.

Then he told me, "It must be tough for someone like you. Kind of comfortable, retired, having something like this from his past brought up after all these years."

"Nothing like that happened to me. It's just a dream."

"A dream, maybe, but made up of bits of your past."

Then I heard voices and he was gone. Lights went on in my room and curtains got drawn around the other bed. Since my arrival I had been the only patient in the room. That ended.

"In here."

"Easy."

The new patient cried out as they moved him. Through an opening in the curtain, I saw nurses and orderlies transfer him to the bed. Then they stood back and two young surgeons from the emergency room appeared. From their talk, I learned that the patient had been in some kind of an incident that had damaged his scrotum.

The doctors spoke to him. "We saved one testicle and your penis," they said. "But we couldn't save the other."

The patient asked a question too mumbled for me to hear and a doctor said, "Yes, you'll have full function."

Then they were gone and almost immediately the kid slept and snored. His name, I found out later, was Jamine Wilson and he was nineteen.

§

Dawn was just about to break. I opened the notebook and wrote out a will, divided my possessions among my siblings and friends. The will was a way of trying to hold onto my self, to indicate that I still knew who I was and what was mine.

That afternoon my sister Lee, elegantly dressed as always, visited me. I had named her my executor. Remembering Gerry, I dreaded the thought of prolonged illness and coma. I said I didn't want extreme measures to be taken to keep me alive if I couldn't be revived. She went out to the desk and informed them of this.

Then we talked and listened to Jamine Wilson in the next bed on his phone. He talked about buying hot iPods. He called a woman and told her to bring him burgers and fries from McDonald's.

He lived in a halfway house to which he didn't want to return. A social worker came by and informed him that he would have to be out of the hospital the next morning. He ignored her.

"Where are you now," he asked the woman on the phone. "Can't you get on the subway?"

My sister left when they came to take me downstairs for X-rays. They gave me barium and recorded its progress through my digestive tract. I was there for hours, lying flat on a cold metal slab while they took each series of shots, resting, sleeping sometimes on the metal slab, until it was time for the next pictures.

It reminded me of the esoteric forms of modeling. Hand models, foot models; unprepossessing people with one exquisite feature. "Intestine model, that's me," I told the technician who smiled and didn't understand.

I dozed and saw a screen that read, "An example of his early modeling work." And there I was, very young, kneeling in the sand in Frye boots and leather jacket, a kerchief tied around my neck but with my shirt unbuttoned, belt unbuckled, jeans and briefs pulled down to my knees, my hands cuffed behind me and my cock excited. It looked like some S&M scenario I might have posed for in my youth. But the setting was the Southwest of that dream.

Then they woke me up and took some more X-rays.

When I got back to the room, Jamine's hospital lunch was untouched beside his bed. I had taken nothing by mouth for days. He looked up at me dark and angry. Our eyes met and for a moment I saw a bit of myself: the kid in the nightmares, the kid who'd ended up in this hospital with his memory gone. And I think, maybe, he saw something similar.

"Where are you now?" he asked someone on the phone then said, "You were there five minutes ago."

Some time later, his caller finally arrived whizzing down the hall on a motorized wheelchair, the McDonald's bag on her lap. She was Hispanic with eyes that looked hurt or afraid.

She maneuvered her chair next to the bed. The two of them ate. He chewed noisily, talked while he did. "I was so scared," he said, "When I saw all the blood. And it took so long for them to call for help."

The cell phone rang and he talked to someone. Shortly afterwards a girl and a guy in their late teens came down the hall on their chairs. These were his friends from the halfway house. They seemed oddly impressed by whatever had happened to him.

Before the evening was over there were five wheelchairs in the room and I realized that Jamine too must have one. I was surprised by how quiet and lost everyone but Jamine seemed. At some point they were told they had to leave. My roommate turned off his phone and went back to sleep.

§

The room, the ward, the floor, the hospital grew silent.

"The place is overrun with ghosts," Randall, my old daddy, once said when I visited him in a very classy hospital uptown where he'd gone for major heart surgery.

"They came and talked to me at night, taunted me. An awful man I lived with when I was young and stupid and new to New York was cruising the halls like it was still 1925. He was a cruel bastard, physically abusive, and I'd walked out on him. He told me he was waiting for me, that sooner or later he'd have me again."

Before he got sick Randall was an easy gig. He protected me from myself at work, took me to opera and ballet and didn't demand much. He really got off on having a young guy around. Give him a chance encounter in his own apartment with a nude twenty-two year old and he was happy.

"I know when I pop off that awful sadist will be waiting for me, and I'm afraid," he said.

My own problems were all I could think about. I forced a smile like he'd made a joke. But he shook his head and looked sad. Randall died at that uptown hospital later that year. Only now did I understand he'd loved me as much as I'd let him.

Deep in the night the cop and I stood at the window and looked at the very late traffic flowing south on Seventh Avenue. I could tell by the car models that it was the late 1960s. The constant flow of traffic downtown was like the passage of time.

"We can do it, you know," he said. "Bring you back forty years to face trial."

"For what?" I asked. "What crimes did I ever commit that were worth that kind of attention?"

"Look at yourself." Again the screen came up and it was the three guys whose faces I could almost remember and myself all in boots and jeans and leather vests and kerchiefs around our necks. Like musicians on an album cover imitating desperados.

The one furthest away from me handed a cloth sack to the next guy, who handed a smaller brown paper package to the guy next to me, who handed me a white packet and I turned and handed a glassine envelope to someone not in the picture: like a high school textbook illustration of a drug distribution system.

"A kid died from something you sold," the cop said. The screen showed a girl, maybe eighteen, sprawled on the floor

richard bowes

228

of a suburban bedroom with a needle in her arm and a Jim Morrison poster on the wall.

"None of that ever happened," I said. "I never did anything like that." But I remembered Geoff in a dream calling me his Subway Man.

"We don't plant this stuff. It was inside you. Back in 1969 a family wants vengeance," he replied and I guessed Geoff's family once had.

I saw myself from behind kneeling naked with my hands tied at my back. All around on the sand, my clothes lay in strips where they'd been cut off me. My jacket and boots were tossed aside; the kerchief I'd worn around my neck was now tied over my eyes. Behind me the three other guys all hung by their necks from the branches of a tree.

The cop said, "You'll wish they'd hanged you too. What the family wants to do will make what happened to that black kid in your room a joke."

Then I saw myself frontally, my cock severed, bleeding to death into the sand, my mouth open in a silent scream. I remembered being taken down and turned out in the East Village stairwell.

That woke me and I lay in my hospital bed in the first dawn light. But I had trouble shaking the dream.

§

Greenwich Village was partly an Irish neighborhood in days gone by and St. Vincent's still reflected that. My nurse that morning was Mary Collins, an old woman originally from Kerry, with a round unlined face, the last of the breed. I'd established my credentials, told her about my grandparents from Aran.

After the policeman had mentioned that initial report, I'd asked Mary Collins about the nun I'd talked to. She looked at me and said, "You saw Sister Immaculata. I haven't thought about her in years. They said she roamed the halls and talk-

dust devil on a quiet street

ed to the patients. Some of them she comforted, others she frightened."

"But she was real."

She shrugged. "Well, when I first worked here, they told stories about catching glimpses of her. But I never did."

Behind the curtains around the other bed, Nurse Yang spoke quietly to Jamine. "No matter what our other issues, we need to eat healthy food. Try this orange juice."

"I'm not hungry."

"Try it for me." And we heard him slurp some orange juice.

"She has the patience of Job," murmured Mary Collins and turned to leave.

I said, "There's this guy I keep seeing in my dreams. He looks like a cop, shows me all kinds of things, threatens to drag me back to face punishment for crimes I never committed."

Nurse Collins paused. In the silence, I heard Margaret Yang say, "Would you try this cereal?"

"His name wouldn't be McGittrick would it?" Mary Collins asked.

"I don't know."

"Immaculata and McGittrick both—ah you are a rare one! If that's how it is, tell him to back away. While you're a patient in this hospital, you're ours, not his." She winked and nodded at me and I guessed she was doing for me what Nurse Yang was doing for my roommate.

Word came that my surgery was scheduled for that night. The exact time was not set. Jamine was on his cell phone. He was due to be released from the hospital that afternoon and sent back to his halfway house. I wondered about the pain he didn't seem to be feeling and the desperate moment that had left him partially castrated.

Lying there, I thought of people I knew who had come out of surgery with hallucinations attached to their brain like parasites.

A few years before, an old professor of mine was not doing well after heart surgery. He was incoherent. Things hung in the balance and then with his eyes shut and seemingly unconscious, he said quite clearly, "Surgeon Major Herzog of the Israeli Air Medical Brigade orders you to get off your asses and get me cured."

"Herzog straightened things out," my professor told me a few days later when he had rallied and begun recovery. "The first time I saw him was shortly after the operation. I came to and he was standing in full uniform at the end of my bed reading the computer screen. He told me I was someone they needed to have alive and he was going to save me. Then he changed some of the instructions on the screen."

No one on the staff had ever heard of Surgeon Major Marvin Herzog. The doctors attributed the now rapid recovery not to a series of crisp orders and clandestine changes in the patient's treatment but to the body's wonderful will to live.

A week or two later when I visited him at home, my professor told me, "Dr. Herzog said last night that usually they don't let people like me see him. But he thinks I can handle it. He explained how his unit oversees everybody who's under anesthesia…"

As he went on, I realized he was still talking to his imaginary Doctor and maybe always would.

Finally I was wheeled out for more X-rays. When I came back hours later, doctors, nurses and Jamine's social worker were in attendance. His motorized chair, a shabby, beat-up item, had been brought into the room. When he was helped into it, he screamed with pain. A hurried conference took place out in the hall. The patient was helped back into bed.

Late that night, he was still there, talking quietly into his cell phone. It had been arranged that he was to be sent, not back to his halfway house, but to a rehab facility. He seemed pleased. Was it for this that he or someone else had used the knife?

McGittrick had noticed him. Was that a first sighting, like Immaculata observing me all those years ago?

§

That night I waited at the window feeling very small and lonely and watched the tail lights of the cars as they rushed into the past.

A short time before I got sick my mother, in her late eighties, underwent a long and intense operation for cancer. During the hospitalization that followed she was well taken care of by the hospital nurses and orderlies and seemed to love them.

My mother walked with our help immediately after the operation as you're supposed to. Everyone was amazed at how quickly she moved, looking around impatiently, fascinated by the other rooms on the floor—the vacant ones with their empty beds, the locked doors that led to conference rooms and doctors' hideaways.

Later, when reminded of this, my mother remembered nothing of her treatment. All she could recall was a movie being made night after night in which her body was used to portray a corpse. The ones making the film were criminals, threatening and intimidating her. The hospital workers were helping them. This went on all during her time in recovery.

She wanted to walk as quickly as possible, she said, so she could escape. Her fascination with the rest of the floor was because those were places that figured in the dreams. She pretended to love the staff because she was terrified of them.

By daylight my mother found the place drab and ordinary, devoid of the desperate drama it held during her nights. Like the professor she never quite disentangled herself from the hallucination.

Then someone calling my name interrupted me. Word had come that the surgical team was ready and the gurney was on its way.

I went back to my room and the gurney was there. As I was loaded aboard and my IV pole was strapped to its side like a

richard bowes

flag, I saw my godchild and niece, Antonia, twenty years old but tiny as a child, come down the hall. Somehow she had gotten into the hospital at this late hour.

In that amazing place, it was quite all right with everyone that she accompany me down to surgery. "You'll have to leave before they begin the procedure," one of the nurses told her.

Off we went and the attendant sang as we rolled along and told me that I was going to be fine. Then deep in the hospital, far into the night, we were in the surgical anteroom. One of the young doctors who had operated on Jamine was part of the team.

He and the others seemed like college students as they joked with Antonia and me while we awaited the surgeon who was late. Then she was there in her red jacket and dress and greeted us all.

I thanked Antonia for being with me as they hooked me up. I held onto the image of her as everyone smiled at me and I was gone while wondering if I was ever coming back.

§

When I awoke a young man with a shaved head said, "Good morning, Richard, you're in surgical recovery, my name is Scott Horton and I'm a nurse. How do you feel?"

"Like I've just been hit by a truck but haven't felt the pain yet," I said and he grinned, nodded with approval, pleased I was coherent enough to attempt a joke.

Just before I had awakened, in the moment between darkness and light, I had been in the vast space with only the light of the hospital patients' computer screens revolving around me like suns in galaxies.

In the way it happens in dreams, I knew these were all the unconscious patients in all the hospitals in the world. Together we formed an anima, an intelligence. Most of us were part of this for a couple of hours, for a day sometimes. For a few it was for months and even years.

The policeman looked up from the computer with his white crewcut, his battered nose, his cigarette.

"Someone told me your name is McGittrick," I said.

"If that name gets you off..." He shrugged.

"In other words I'm making you up as I go along."

"Somewhere inside you knew someone oversaw the intersection of this world and the next. First you put a face on that one. Now you've found a name for me. Mostly I don't deal personally with people in your situation. I don't have to because they aren't aware of me.

"We could keep you in a coma for as long as you live. Instead we are sending you back a changed man," he told me. "You'll never be able to forget what you've seen and you'll never again accept the waking world as the real one."

I had been going to ask him what he wanted. Instead, I had awakened to find Nurse Horton.

In the bright early morning in the hospital, he showed me a new button on my IV stand. "You press that when you feel any discomfort and the painkiller is injected directly into your bloodstream," he told me. "You can do that at five-minute intervals whenever you feel you need to. I'll be back to see you very shortly."

I held his arm and said, "Please don't go away. I saw this guy just before I came to. The nurse upstairs called him McGittrick. He said they were using my mind while I was unconscious, that he could keep me in a coma for as long as I lived."

He smiled. "Well, you tell McGittrick to back off. You're my patient. We have you now and we're not letting go. We're going to get you cleaned up and I'd like you to walk a little sometime today."

An orderly came in and took my temperature. One of the young doctors who had assisted in the surgery came by. "Things went very well. We're confident we removed the obstruction. We opened you up along the old cancer surgery scar. We didn't find any cancer this time."

Another orderly took blood. Scott returned and the two of them helped me sit up and put my feet over the edge of the bed. "You're doing great," he said and the orderly agreed. I slid off the bed and my feet found the floor.

The orderly pushed the IV stand. Scott held me. I walked around the room. The sun was shining outside. "I think I can do this by myself," I said. They made me take hold of the handle bar. I pushed it out the door and into the hallway and back again.

"Very good," they told me and I lay down on the bed. I was sitting propped up when my sister Lee and brother-in-law Peter came in. My surgeon dropped by and talked with us. Everyone seemed very pleased.

When I was alone, Scott brought me some paper and a pen that I asked for. He sat with me for a little while, told me that he was thirty-three years old. That he came from a town outside Boston and lived now in Chelsea within walking distance of the hospital. I wondered who he lived with but didn't ask.

I wrote Scott a rambling thank you note/love letter and added at the end of it, *People who have hallucinations after operations sometimes don't seem to come all the way back. Part of them gets lost. The hallucination can be at least as good, as powerful and compelling and meaningful as real life. Especially since real life is being a patient, the victim of a disease. The hallucination is so engrossing that they don't want to leave it behind. I'm afraid that will happen with me.*

Scott had gone off duty by the time I finished writing. I spent a very bad night in the recovery ward. People were waxing the floor, cleaning the walls. The nurses were slow to respond. Being awake was a nightmare. I thought of Gerry after his liver transplant.

Then McGittrick was with me. "You're not supposed to talk about what I've told you, asshole," he said. "That other time, you wrote that book about the world where people dying of cancer could become gods. But you made it science fiction and anyway nobody read it so that was okay.

"That young nurse who thinks he's so tough? 'We have you now and we're not letting go,' he says. When his time comes he will be ours and he won't even know it's happened.'"

"What's the point of all this?" I asked.

"You know how people when dying feel themselves drawn toward some kind of glowing light? They find it comforting. Well, those globes floating in the flickering brain, the warm light of death and the promise of peace, are you and all the other assholes hooked up to machines, each contributing his or her little bit. Last night you were part of the light the dying souls were drawn towards. That's one of the things we do."

I thought of poor Gerry floating towards the light as he died. "Why an old cop, why not an angel with a fiery sword," I asked.

"You don't believe in angels. You have a thing for the law. Your kind usually shows that by being bad and getting caught. The cuffs go on and you swoon. You were too bright to get a criminal record. Our reports say you have promise."

"Before the operation you were threatening me with mutilation. Now..."

"I'm going to offer you my job."

"Right," I said. "But you don't exist. You told me so."

He seemed a bit amused. "That's not as big a deal as you make it seem."

"And the phony charges?"

"Could also not be a big deal. That depends on you."

§

Then he was gone and it was morning. The door of my room was open, the cleaning crew had departed and the hospital was waking up. Pain had begun to gnaw at my guts. I hit the button, waited a few minutes and then hit it again.

Scott walked by and I called him. He had just come on duty. He had other patients but he stopped for me. "How are you?

"Bad night." I wanted to tell him about the men endlessly cleaning the floor and the smell of ammonia but I didn't.

"Did McGittrick talk to you again?"

"Sorry I bothered you about that. I feel stupid." What I was sorry about was having brought him to McGittrick's attention.

"It's why I'm here. We're going to get you ready to return to your ward. I want you to walk before then."

Later when he was watching me push my IV stand around Recovery, I asked him, "Does everybody in this hospital know about McGittrick?"

He grinned. "If they worked with Mary Collins they do. I started out with her."

When they came to take me back upstairs Scott said good-bye and I knew it was unlikely I'd ever see him again. Unless, of course, I took McGittrick up on his offer.

When I returned to the twelfth floor, I was in a new room all by myself. Jamine was gone. Even Nurse Yang, busy with her current patients, barely remembered him. That's how it would be with me.

I hit the painkiller button, got up and walked. I needed the pole to lean on a little. Nurses and orderlies nodded their approval. I was a model patient, a teacher's pet.

When my phone rang it was my godchild Chris planning to come in from Ohio and stay with me after I got out of the hospital. Friends came by. Flowers got delivered. I fell asleep, exhausted.

It was getting dark when I awoke and there was commotion and a gigantic man was wheeled in. "Purple," he said. "Don't go far from me, girl." My new roommate had a private health-care worker. He called her Purple, which wasn't her name and which made her quite angry.

He sang Prince songs. He called people by names he'd given them. He told me he was an architect who had stepped through a door in a half-finished building he'd designed and fallen two floors because there was no floor on the other side. All the bones in his feet had been shattered. It took the healthcare worker and all the orderlies on the floor to help him change his position in the bed.

At one point I dozed off but awoke to hear a West Indian orderly whom he called Tangerine saying, "I do not have to take this. I will be treated with respect. My name to you is Mrs. Jackson."

"Oh, Tangerine!" he cried in a despairing voice.

I hit the pain button, got up and walked to the window over-looking Seventh Avenue. In the night, the streetlights turned from red to green.

A computer screen on a nearby station counter faced the window and was reflected on the dark glass. McGittrick's face danced on the window in front of me.

When I turned to look at the computer screen it was blank. I turned back and the face was there. It might have been the drugs or I may have been asleep on my feet. But as hard as I looked McGittrick remained.

Then Jamine's face appeared on the screen. McGittrick said, "He stands out kind of the way you did, flirting with death but afraid of it. Bear in mind that if you don't work for us someone else will—maybe him."

"What exactly would I do?"

"Be around; make sure all is running as it should. Be a cop," he said. "Think it over."

"Okay. But when I sleep from now on, you have to stay out of my dreams."

"You're not dreaming. It's just easier to reach you when you're asleep. But we'll give you a little time to consider."

When I came back into to my own ward, the nurses at the desk, as if they sensed something about me, looked up when I passed by. When I went into my room the architect was croon-ing a song to his caregiver who was telling him to shut up.

They stopped when they saw me and I wondered if I was marked somehow.

"Look," I said, "I'm recovering from major surgery. I need to sleep." They stared at me, nodded and were quiet. I hit the painkiller button and hit it again every few minutes until I drifted away.

§

I awoke and it was morning. The architect, quite deferentially, asked if I had slept well. "I made sure all these fine ladies kept very quiet so you could rest and get better."

This guy was a well-meaning lunatic with none of Jamine's vibes. I thanked him.

Then Mrs. Jackson helped me wash up and I was taken for X-rays. When I returned the architect was gone, brought to another ward for physical therapy, Nurse Collins said.

She was on duty and had come in to check on me. "You're doing well," she said. "They didn't get you this time."

"Who was Immaculata? Who is McGittrick?"

"I don't think she was any kind of angel and I don't think he's a banshee because I don't believe in them. Ones like that lurk in the cracks of every hospital there ever was. Most places they don't even know about it anymore. But they still have them. Give them the back of your hand."

I'd begun feeling that if I performed certain tasks—walked rapidly three times around the floor, say, then I was practically recovered.

That night I paused on my rounds and looked out the window. The Greenwich Village crowds on a Friday night in spring reminded me of the rush of being twenty and in the city. I thought of Andre and how I'd lost him just before I got sick.

McGittrick was reflected in the window "You know," he said. "That guy that got away might still be with you if you'd been well when his friend called. We can let you replay that scene." Cops offer candy when they believe you're beginning to soften and cooperate. But they still can't be trusted.

"I enjoy the sweet melancholy of affairs gone by," I said. "I'd like to be with Andre as if nothing ever happened. But I'd know that wasn't true and wouldn't be able to stand it." As I headed back to my room, I said, "Thanks, though."

As I hit the pain button, a young guy who'd had an emergency appendectomy was brought into the room. He lay quietly, breathing deep unconscious breaths. I passed into sleep remembering moments when someone with whom I'd made love fell into slumber like this just before I did.

§

The next morning was a Saturday. A resident and a nurse came in and drew a curtain around my bed. They detached me from the catheter, pulled the feeding tube out of my throat and through my nose.

That morning I ate liquids for the first time since I'd been there. Everything tasted awful. I forced myself to eat a little Jell-O, drink clear soup, apple juice, because that was the way to get better.

Dale, my roommate, cast no aura, had no vibes that I could feel. He was twenty-seven, a film editor who had collapsed in horrible pain on Friday night. He was getting out later that day. His insurance paid for no more than that.

After ten days in the hospital, I was a veteran and showed him how to push his IV rack, how to ring for a nurse.

Marc came by. I told him, "When I wrote *Feral Cell* I had the narrator drink blood. Blood of the Goat binds him to the alternate world, Capricorn. Blood of the Crab binds him here. As one world fades the other gets clearer. What I was writing about was being sick. It's like this other country. You get pulled in there without wanting to and have to haul your ass out."

He said, "Remember first coming to the city and how hard it was to stick here? Like at any moment the job, the apartment you were sharing with the best friend, the lover would all come loose and you'd be sucked back to Metuchen or Doylestown or Portsmouth. Kind of the same thing."

The roommate was on the phone. "It felt like a bad movie, waking up and finding all these people staring down at me. The guy in here with me is this amazing Village character."

He was still on the phone when his lovely Korean girlfriend came in with his clothes. She took his gown off him as he stood talking and dressed him from his skin out. It bothered me that he was getting out and I was still inside. As they left, he turned, waved goodbye and grinned because he was young and this was all an adventure. I had more in common with Jamine than with this kid.

That evening, I was served a horrible dish of pasta and chicken but it was a test of my recovery and I ate a bit of it.

That night McGittrick said, "If it's not love that interests you, how about revenge? The guy, the Subway Man, screwed you around sexually and mentally when you were just a kid. You wrote a story about that. We can go deep into the past. You could go back and make sure he never did that to you or anyone else."

I shook my head. "The one I most wanted to kill was myself. It took a long time to untangle that. This is who I am and I'm satisfied with it," I told him. "I'm turning down your offer."

He smiled and shook his head like my stupidity amused him. On the screen, I knelt blindfolded in the desert. "Did you forget about that?" he asked as I walked away.

When I hit the intravenous drug button, I thought about what I'd told McGittrick and realized it was true. Somewhere along the line I had come to terms with what had happened to me. Even though I, maybe, hadn't come to terms with what I'd done to others. I didn't hit the button again that night.

§

Sunday morning, as I tried to choke down tasteless jelly on dry toast, another patient was brought in. I looked up and found Frankie the Bug Boy looking back. He was thin and grey, old, I realized, like I was.

"You look like shit," the Bug Boy said. "You should have stayed in the Zoo where you'd be safe and warm."

"You don't exactly look like a spring dawn yourself," I said. "They have you watching me?"

"You got big ideas about yourself," he told me. "I'm in for kidney stones. What did they get you for?"

We talked a bit. "If you gotta be sick this is the place to be," the Bug Boy said, "I live way downtown but I gave a phony address so this is my hospital."

I'd heard somewhere that Frankie had turned state's evidence in a criminal case, served a very short sentence and disappeared. I'd wondered if the case had anything to do with the counterfeit videos and the loft on Weehawken Street. I wondered that again now.

He went into the bathroom and changed into a pair of gowns. He came out, drew the curtain between us and started watching television with the sound way down. His being there could just have been a coincidence, I told myself several times.

It was confirmed that I was going home the next day. At one point that afternoon my godchild Antonia walked the circuit of the floor with me several times. When we came to the window on Seventh Avenue, I looked around and realized there's no way that a computer screen could be reflected from the desk onto the glass.

"Thank you," I told Margaret Yang later. "You people gave me a life transfusion."

"We just did our job. You are an interesting patient," she said.

That night when I stopped and looked out, the traffic was a Sunday night dribble without any magic at all.

§

The next morning, I awoke with the memory of a visitor. The night before I had opened my eyes and seen Sister Immaculata. "I'm disappointed," she told me. "That you aren't willing to give others the same chance that was given to you."

"What chance was that?" I asked.

"You were a stumbling wayfarer," she said. "We helped you survive in the hope you would eventually help us."

"What is it that you do?"

"Hope and Easeful Death," she said with a radiant smile and I remembered why I trusted cops more than nuns.

That morning they disconnected me from the last of my attachments. The IV pole was wheeled away.

Frankie was about to go down to the operating room. He would spend this day in the hospital and then be released the next.

"See you around," he said. "The flea-market thing is over. I'm kind of retired like you. These days I'm spending time in Washington Square Park around the chess tables in the southwest corner."

Then my friend Bruce was there, pulling my stuff together, helping me get my pants on, tying my shoes for me. I was in my own clothes and feeling kind of lost.

Nurse Collins was on duty, "Good luck," she said as I passed the desk for the last time. She looked at me for a long moment. "And let's hope we see no more of you in here."

The taxi ride home took only a few minutes. The flight of stairs to my apartment was the first I had climbed in almost two weeks and I had to stop and rest halfway up.

I'd thought that when I got out of the hospital I would magically be well and had a hundred errands to do. Bruce insisted I get undressed again and helped me into bed.

"When what they gave you in the hospital wears off," he said. "You will feel like you've been hit by a fist the size of a horse."

He filled my prescriptions for OxyContin and antibiotics, bought me food we thought I could eat, lay on my couch and looked at a book of Paul Cadmus's art he'd found on my shelves. I dozed and awoke and dozed some more. People called and asked how I was. A friend brought by a huge basket of fruit.

Bruce taped the phone extension cord to the floor so that I wouldn't trip on it. More than any other single thing this spelled old age and sickness to me. It struck me as I fell asleep that Bruce was HIV-positive and taking a cocktail of drugs to stay alive, yet I was so feeble he was taking care of me.

The second day Bruce came by in the morning, watched to make sure I didn't fall down in the shower, helped me get dressed and went with me for a little walk. The third day when he came by I got myself dressed.

Late that night, I looked at myself in the mirror. It was a stranger's face, thin with huge eyes. This was a taste of what very old age would be like. I missed the large ever-present organization devoted to making me better. My life felt flat without the spice of hallucination and paranoia.

The next day my godson Chris came in from Ohio to stay with me. That year we were both up for Nebulas and the ceremonies were to be held in New York City.

We were in different categories, fortunately. It was on my mind that if I could attend the ceremonies and all the related events, it would mean I had passed a critical test and was well.

Chris was shocked at the first sight of me, though he tried to hide it. When one person is in his sixties and sick and the other less than half his age and well, their pace of life differs.

He adapted to mine, walked slowly around the neighborhood with me, sat in the park on the long sunny afternoons, ate in my favorite restaurants where to me the food all tasted like chalk now, read me stories.

The Awards were on Saturday night in a hotel in Lower Manhattan. All the magic of speculative fiction is on the pages and in the cover art. The physical reality is dowdy. Internet photos of the book signing and reception show Chris happy and mugging and me fading out of the picture. Like those sketches Renaissance artists did of youth and old age.

As the awards ceremony dragged on I realized I'd be unable to walk to the dais if I won. I needn't have worried. A luminary of the field, quite remarkably drunk, after complaining bitterly that he for once hadn't been nominated, mangled all names and titles beyond recognition, then presented the award to the excellent writer who won. When it was over I rode home in a cab and went to bed.

Chris had also lost and was nice enough to stay on and keep me company. One day as we walked into the park I saw the Bug Boy, looking as grey and thin as I did, sitting at a chess table in the southwest corner of Washington Square. The chess players share that space with drug dealers and hustlers.

I said hello and he nodded very slightly. Spotters in the park are paid to warn dealers if the heat is on the prowl or tip hustlers off that a customer is at hand. That seemed to be what Frankie was doing. But while I couldn't quite believe this was all a coincidence, I also remembered my mother and my teacher unable to escape their anesthesia dreams.

One evening I took Chris to see a play that was running at a theater around the corner from my place. As we walked down narrow old Minetta Lane, kids on motorized wheelchairs rolled past the Sixth Avenue end of the Lane.

For a moment I saw Jamine. Then I wasn't sure and then they were gone.

One day on the street we found a guy selling candid black and white photos that his father had taken fifty, forty, thirty years ago on the streets of Greenwich Village. One shot taken from an upstairs window and dated 1968 showed the Ninth Circle, a hustler bar with young guys in tight jeans and leather jackets standing on the front stairs. I felt a rush of déjà vu.

That night, on a website in my dreams, I saw that scene again, the street, the stairs, the figures. But this time there was a close up. The kid in the center of the group was me. The other guys were my partners in crime from the dream.

I clicked the mouse and the next picture came up. It was a figure in a motorized wheelchair rolling up Minetta Lane towards the camera. My face was a twisted mask. My hands were claws. I awoke with that image of myself ancient and partially paralyzed: the ultimate nightmare.

"You see how long we've been keeping an eye on you. And how long we'll keep it up," McGittrick said and I awoke in the dawn light.

That evening when Chris and I kissed goodbye at Penn Station and he went off on the airport train, I felt the most incredible loneliness and loss. He'd been sharing his energy and youth with me and now I was on my own again.

Back downtown, I sat on a bench in Washington Square in the May twilight. Dogs yapped in the runs. As the light went away a jazz quintet played "These Foolish Things (Remind Me of You)."

McGittrick stood studying me. "Why," I asked," was it necessary to screw my head around as you've been doing?"

"Think of it as boot camp. Break you down, rebuild you. Would the you who went to sleep the night before you got sick have sat in a public park having this conversation?"

"How did you get into this racket?"

He smiled, "Immaculata recruited me. Said I was a restless soul that wouldn't be happy unless I got to see a little more of life and death than others did."

"And now?"

"I'm ready to move on. You'll understand when you're in my place."

My guts, where they had been cut open and stapled back together, still hurt a little. I'd pretty much tapered off the medication but suddenly I needed to go home and take half an OxyContin tablet.

I arose and he asked, "Would you rather talk to Sister Immaculata?"

"That's okay. You're less scary than a nun."

"You've got a while to decide," he said. "But not, you know, forever."

I nodded and continued on my way. But we both knew how I'd decided.

Dowland wrote:

Sad despair doth drive me hence
This despair unkindness sends
If that parting be offence
It is I which then offends

I had seen death and didn't want to die. Maybe I was a restless soul or maybe I was too big a coward to face death all at once and forever.

From a little reading I'd done, some research on the internet, I knew that injury or illness actually can change a personality. What I'd always feared had happened. The one who had gone to sleep that night a few weeks before had awakened as someone else. And I didn't entirely sympathize with that person who now was lost and gone.

Chapter Sixteen

As I recovered that summer I woke up a couple of times feeling McGittrick watching me like a cop who wants you to know he's watching you. Once or twice I awoke with the image of Sister Immaculata and her chilling smile. I was bothered that my hallucinations lingered.

One lovely afternoon I sat with Joan Mata outside a café across the street from my house. I had green tea, she had a white wine. We laughed about Selesta and Sam's wedding with a lesbian minister presiding and even about cancer when we talked of Joan's breast surgery.

"You were so strong all through that," I told her.

"Like you were back in the day," she said. "I wasn't letting just anybody take care of my daughter. I recognized a survivor."

Then she said, "My God, who is that woman?" And I saw Teresa Rossi pass by like she owned the sidewalk. Someone had told me Teresa had just retired from the university. I half rose and bowed. Ms. Rossi noticed and nodded to me.

"The *strega*," I explained and described the Office of Doom to someone who really would understand.

Children, godchildren in my case, save us all. On a ride out to the Hamptons that weekend Joan and I discussed our mothers, both fiercely holding onto life. Each of us would be the oldest members of our family when they died. Not a distinction we wanted.

We arrived in the evening with a sea breeze and little sound beside the slow rhythm of the Atlantic; we could have been in one of the Mata paintings or an old family snapshot.

Adding to that illusion, there were children in the cottage. Joan's younger sister Catherina was taking care of her granddaughters aged four and five and had brought them to see great-grandmother Ruth.

The next morning, though, I stood on the porch with a mug of tea and realized the 1950s Hamptons were gone. The neighboring pond had been drained decades before and a summer mansion had been built on the site. A more recent and even larger vacation home now stood on the meadow. The House That Ate the World, by comparison, now seemed like a charming relic of the past.

Joan came out and sat on the porch swing. She talked on her cell phone with her business partner about a corporate logo they were designing. Then she got a call from Selesta, who was driving out with Sam.

Recently Selesta had told all of us that she was pregnant and she and Sam had decided to have the child. Her news was always in the background now. Joan and Ruth discussed obstetricians and hospitals with her. Selesta didn't understand why she might need a doctor who was discreet.

"Because you don't want to end up on the front page of the *National Enquirer*," Joan said. She shook her head when she got off the phone.

"Selesta once said it was good to always be a little scared," I told her.

"She won't know what fear is until she becomes a parent."

Two very busy young ladies returned from the beach with Catherina. Each carried a dripping pail. "These are living clams," they told us. Though the clams looked as dead as could be, we exclaimed over them.

Ruth sat out on the lawn under a large umbrella. Her great-granddaughters went to show her the living clams.

"I married the least cat-like man in the world," Joan said. "I really didn't understand that was what I was doing. That was his main qualification. Then Selesta was born and I saw it hadn't worked. I wasn't used to my plans going awry. Not even my unformulated ones."

"You told Selesta all this?"

"I've told her everything. Like you said."

"The vestigial tail?" Joan had to have one removed when she was a child.

She nodded.

Later that afternoon I sat with Ruth and the little girls who dug up the lawn and ignored us. "Richie, you'd think after I'd made such a mess out of my family's lives they wouldn't trust me with their offspring. But you'd be wrong. Someone always needs to dump their kids."

Neither Catherina nor either of her daughters had shown the slightest trace of the Margay. "It's right out of Mendel," Ruth said. "Poor Luis was at one end. Catherina's at the other. Joan is somewhere in between."

One of her great-granddaughters had come over to us and Ruth was rubbing the girl's neck. The child gave a great yawn and arched her back like a kitten.

Ruth looked at me with an expression that said, "You've got to wonder."

Later when Selesta and Sam appeared, I told them, "Selesta, much as I love you, you're grown up. You never want toys, you don't like musicals anymore. I mean, how do I justify going to lousy shows if I can't say I'm taking a child? I want to be the godfather, maybe the god-grandfather to your kid."

"That's the main reason we decided to have a child," she said and Sam nodded his agreement

She looked out at Ruth on her lounge chair with the children around her and said, "I want that for Joan."

§

When you visit a maternity ward you scarcely know you're in a hospital. It's about life instead of illness, about bedazzled adults and the tiny, red-faced dictators who are going to run their lives.

Selesta's child was a boy, the first male born into the family since Luis Mata almost seventy years before and named for him.

I got to hold Luis. It's nice but in truth I like kids better when they're standing up and talking. There's a wonderful stuffed ocelot that I'm planning to give him. It could as easily be a margay. Selesta will be good with that.

Ruth was there in a motorized wheel chair with her caregiver.

"A perfectly normal baby," said the very discreet doctor.

"Meaning he doesn't have a tail," said Joan quietly when the doctor left.

"Not yet, anyway," Ruth murmured.

Chapter Seventeen

That autumn the World Fantasy Convention was held up the Hudson River Valley at Saratoga. The town's not a long trip from Manhattan and Chris would be there promoting his first novel.

It was after the thoroughbred racing season and before the first snow, but Saratoga Springs, that aristocratic old resort in upstate New York, was still beautiful. Locations favored by the rich tend to be. The air was crisp, the foliage still turning.

For a long Halloween weekend the streets of the tiny, picturesque town were flooded with the floating speculativefiction community which assembles in a location, then disperses in all directions and reassembles at the next preordained spot. I'd been as one with it months before at the Nebula ceremony.

Saratoga Springs is Washington Irving country. He created a Hudson Valley folklore with just two short stories, "Rip Van Winkle" and "The Legend of Sleepy Hollow." One clear, chill evening that weekend I stood outdoors at sunset, looked at the Catskills and thought about Van Brunt and how Mimsey Friedman was in hiding to escape him.

Did this haunted location give an extra tang to the noise and gossip, rumor, self-promotion and booze? The first night at the hotel, bright-faced young writers fresh out of workshops gazed covertly at editors and agents who passed them by with that blank eye that acknowledges no one.

Older writers without publishers circled endlessly like raptors over a barren landscape while a well-oiled horror author strode by ensconced in an entourage comprised of his rigidly smiling wife and several adoring groupies.

Watching all this I told my friend Ellen, "I like writing but hate being a writer." An on-line magazine editor standing nearby said he'd buy an article on that subject at an attractive fee. And I told him I'd gladly consider it.

Moments like those are what brought me to Saratoga. At any properly run convention, readings and panel discussions go on from early in the morning to late at night. A panel I attended that first day was called "Promoting the Genre" and was chaired by Major Barbara and featured Tanya Starrett discussing the publicity success of the Arts Circus.

The Major gave a presentation with photos of the event. Tanya had been the ringmaster complete with red miniskirt and the soul of Callimachus.

Nick and Norah Grubstreet, the trendy young couple I'd last seen at the Writers Cage, were shown, she on stilts, he juggling books. Several shots displayed a tall young editor in a cat tamer's outfit, cracking her whip at writers in lion and tiger costumes who stood on stools and snarled. I kept thinking of Eddie Acker's *Man Eater* porn.

The next day I was on a panel called something like "Fantasy Appropriated (Stealing Our Tropes!)." The talk turned to E.T.A. Hoffmann, the early nineteenth-century German Romantic writer. Ballets like *The Nutcracker* and *Coppélia* and Offenbach's opera *Tales of Hoffmann* are based on his stories.

Actually, I brought up the subject and said, "Hoffmann often included himself as a narrator/character. He's one of the reasons I thought it was okay to do in my own work. The opera was important to me a kid. Yes, I was *that* kind of kid!"

Several of the panelists were academics and the conversation turned to Authorial Ideation or something. I'm easily bored and have an almost magical ability to go away while staying on the scene.

My gaze wandered and I found myself in eye contact with a guy in the front row, young in a world growing grey. He smiled, nodded and when the panel was over stepped up to introduce himself and say how much he enjoyed my stories—a young man of sensitivity and discernment.

He was a writer I'd heard of and much cuter than I'd expected. We walked to the hotel bar and he described a proposal he had for an anthology of stories about the destruction of New York City.

Its tentative title was *Godzilla Does Manhattan* and he wondered if I'd be interested. The proposed payment-per-word wasn't half bad. The kid was friendly and looked like he worked out. I said it sounded interesting.

We hung around for a while and he talked about recent New-York-Gets-Destroyed movies, none of which I'd found particularly compelling: *Cloverfield*; *Independence Day*; *I Am Legend*. When he described death and devastation, his eyes glistened.

Then he said, "Please. It wouldn't be a New York book without queer content. And I know you do first-person stuff." If not gay, the kid was certainly curious.

Anita Bonhill, the old dark-fantasy novelist, and a few others joined us. We found a place where we could all sit and order tea and drinks. "There's a convention somewhere in the United States every weekend," someone said.

"Sometimes several," said Anna Bonhill, "and plenty more abroad." Anna has been in the genre for years and years, a midlist writer driven to bitterness at never having won an award.

Almost an achievement: there are nearly as many awards as there are conventions.

She said, "Legends abound about (she named a once famous genre writer). People said that for a period of several years he lived entirely at conventions. He had no money and his domestic life was in turmoil. So he went from convention to convention, arrived a day or two early and crashed with fellow writers or fans. He'd stay a day or two after the convention and then scramble for transportation to the next town.

"It only worked because so many people considered him sexy," Anna said. Then she realized she was almost due to appear on a panel and left us. The little group began to drift away.

"Was he sexy?" the anthologist asked when we were alone.

"He wasn't to my taste," I said. "But conventions are duller without him hanging around."

Ten years before, I'd have gone out of my way to make sure this guy and I got alone somewhere. Now it felt like more trouble than it was worth. He seemed to get that. With the chance to think things over this probably was a relief to him too.

§

Sunday afternoon was the awards ceremony. For those of us not nominated Sunday noon was getaway time. I'd been mentioned in blogs. Convention pictures were already up on the net and I wondered if it was possible that my bald spot was really as big as it looked.

It was a bright and bracing day. Chris was the star of the convention. His first novel had just appeared to great reviews and rumors of award nominations. He was leaving early and I saw him off on the shuttle bus to the airport. Dutch New York hangs on in the Hudson Valley. The driver had a face right out of a Franz Hals painting. This was the townsman amused by the flight of Ichabod Crane, not above lifting a stein in memory of Rip Van Winkle.

As we kissed goodbye and the bus pulled out, an editor of my acquaintance was pushing his daughter in a stroller. "Don't think of it as losing a child," he said, "Think of it as gaining your freedom."

Then I walked through the hotel lobby to find my ride back to the city. The anthologist spotted me and asked if I'd given *Godzilla Does Manhattan* any more thought. Nothing is sadder than an old whore. Though I'd completely forgotten about it, I said it sounded great and he could put me down as a contributor.

Chapter Eighteen

Old feelings and memories are like items on a knickknack shelf. On occasion you rearrange the lot, polish a couple, wonder what it means and why you keep them.

One morning very late in winter I got reminded of the Velvet Underground song "New Age," in the live version, the one where Lou Reed sings about getting a funny call today.

In fact I got two funny calls. The first came before ten AM, early by my standards. The great luxury of retirement is staying up late and sleeping late. Marty Simonson said hello and asked how I was.

His career has been hot in the last few years. *Algonquin*, the play about Dorothy Parker and company that he directed, won all kinds of awards and he got to make the television movie.

Marty has, of course, an instinct for the dramatic tease. "An old friend of yours talked about you last night," he told me. "She's known you almost as long as I have." Then a slight pause while I tried to imagine what he was talking about and he said, "Judy Finch says hello."

That was a surprise. Judy and I hadn't spoken since Geoff, Mags and I hung around with her briefly forty years back. I'd seen her since, of course, like anybody might: in the famous scene in the Scorsese film where she shoots DeNiro, as Pirate Jenny when they did *Threepenny Opera* at Lincoln Center.

She was a dark star but one who survived and for a while took the stage name Judy Icon: hipper than Madonna, more famous than Patti Smith. I caught her show in a couple of incarnations. They were collages of monologues and songs, all improvisation, never done the same way twice.

But what popped into my head when Marty mentioned the name was that earliest memory of the East Village: Judy sitting on the front stairs of her parents' house waiting for Ray Light.

I asked him, "What's she doing these days? And how the hell are you and she so intimate?"

"She's writing, composing, doing what we all do later in life—trying to make it all make sense. She's got a stage work in mind and I'm helping her shape it. We wondered if you were free for lunch today."

This promised to be really interesting. Then Marty made it more so by adding, "I told Judy about a piece you showed me right after the murder/suicide when that whole scene exploded. You know the one? Do you still have it?"

It took a moment before I remembered what he was talking about. I told him I thought so.

"Could you bring it along? She was intrigued when I described it and I think this may be material she can use."

It was one of those mornings—maybe you've had a few of them lately—when money was tight and pressing dental bills meant that a couple of thousand dollars would not go amiss. I agreed to meet them at noon at Taxi Stand over on the Bowery.

I'd looked at the piece Marty wanted a few years back when I wrote my East Village story. It was in a storage box in my closet and it took a little searching, diving down among the scribbled rejection notes from long forgotten editors, the abandoned projects, old notebooks full of catty commentary,

photos of godchildren, aborted play and novel ideas, sketches
for board games I'd once designed, letters from lost lovers, before I found what I wanted.

The manuscript, typewritten on old yellow paper, was a
first-person monologue. Parts I'd adapted from memory and
personal experience but bits of it I'd gotten straight from the
mind of Ray Light.

The Kid with the Sun in His Eyes

The Kid hasn't even been given that name yet as
he stands on the corner of East Fourth Street and
the Bowery and tries to blink away the late afternoon sun because he's not used to it and because
his eyes are a bit pinned.

Just a couple of weeks before, the Kid rode
from Ohio to the city in several cars and a couple
of trucks always with lone drivers, guys who sometimes just wanted to talk about themselves and
their families and all he had to do was be there.
Other times along the way things got done with his
body and for that he managed not to be present, to
take a mental walk and come back to himself when
everything was over and he and the driver were
once more rolling towards New York. That ability to go away was the thing about the Kid, more
even than his hair and his clothes, that his parents
wanted to cut off of him.

In the city the Kid hit Times Square first and it
was bright and confusing and scary and then some
guy took him downtown to the East Village, which
was poor and rundown but easier to figure out and
the cops were mean but not so thick on the ground
as uptown and other runaways warned him about
where not to go and who in the neighborhood got
rewards or kicks turning in ones like him.

So the sixteen-year-old Kid stands on the corner
of East Fourth Street and Second Avenue leaning
on a brick wall with one leg up behind him in the

dust devil on a quiet street

classic pose and this mad boy who's taken the name Rimbaud is there with him, talking, making flowery gestures, saying. "Another place, another dimension or something is where that stud thinks he's going, man. That he thought I was the one who was going to take him there is what's so fucking funny and freaky. Like he's a cult leader but somehow he's trying to learn from me."

The Kid is coming to understand that it's drugs and hustling that keeps boys like him and Rimbaud alive and in contact with this world and he feels still in control of all that. Because he has a kind of skill sometimes with a mark or a john to know what they know as they know it and without them being able to tell he's hip to them. But with all that he finds himself this afternoon out on the block early because he slipped over some line and woke up just after noon with a nasty need.

Rimbaud says, "The stud is important in art stuff. He runs a gallery or something. He told me he could get me a job and he wants to see me tonight. But, like, he's the most weirded-out trick I've ever turned. One minute he's telling me to read his mind, the next he's ready to push me out a window so I can fly."

When Rimbaud's finished talking, the two of them pool their money to split a five-dollar bag of junk to hold them over until the night. Just as they're about to set out for East Seventh Street where they'll score, Rimbaud nudges the Kid and says, "There he is," and the Kid sees the outline of a figure, a guy crossing the street silhouetted against the October sun streaming down the long blocks.

Then I realized it was getting towards noon so I skimmed the rest of the piece. Thinking about it as I brushed my teeth and showered, I understood how it would be of great interest to Judy if the project was what I suspected it was going to be. As I finished shaving, the phone rang again.

"Hey, Daddy Mack," said a slightly raspy somewhat nasal voice, "You know where your string is this morning?"

I'm old and not so fast on the uptake these days. I'd almost hung up on a crank call before I realized I knew the voice and even recognized the reference. I said, "Lizard?"

He hung up and the number was blocked on my caller I.D. But that voice could only have belonged to Lizard Pavane. Thirty years ago, he and I designed board games together. Some sold and a couple of those did okay.

The game the Lizard referred to was called *Mack Daddy*, and, yes, each player was a pimp, sending a string of sex workers out onto the urban streets. The game pieces were garishly colored wide brimmed hats and linked pairs of platform high heels. The board was a city street map. It owed more than a bit to Monopoly. Players rolled dice, drew cards that brought rewards or the unwelcome attention of the cops.

When we'd worked on it, we were still dumb enough to think of ourselves as mad, bad and dangerous instead of as two assholes. No one could be persuaded to buy and produce it, which now seemed to me a very good thing.

But the uncanny nature of the Lizard struck me. After not having thought of it for years that game was one of the aborted projects that I'd just pawed through in my search for the story.

I left my apartment wondering why he called and thinking of the more amazing coincidence that he and Judy Finch would reappear on the same day. It's a sign of how addled I've become that I didn't remember that with the Lizard there were no accidents.

§

Walking east on Bleecker Street, stopping at a copy shop to get clearer reproductions of my fading pages, I remembered Judy on stage at the Fillmore, singing with the group Lord of Light.

The Fillmore East in 1971 was in the last months of its brief and glittery career. Rock groups were playing in sports arenas by then; the East Village was going very bad. Heading the bill that Saturday night was a frazzled hippy band whose last hit had been a year or two before. A canny old bluesman had second billing, with Lord of Light as the opening act.

Rumors of suicides and intricate kink washed around the band—they were part of its draw. But the Fillmore audience was tough. It took more than that to impress us. Joplin and Hendrix and Morrison had come and gone and left us with exaggerated memories of their performances here. In a paradox I was the junkie trying to stay clean but all the non-addicts I was with were ripped out of their heads on various mind-bending substances. The Fillmore was maybe two-thirds full.

Then the psychedelic amoebas of Joshua Light Show filled the back screen, the drummer and bassist laid down the beat, the group was on stage. Ray Light wore black from the neck on down. Judy had a blond crewcut—the little girl I'd seen on the front stairs was totally gone. The guy called BD wore long white robes.

Our world was all afire with Lord of Light stories. Ray, Judy and BD were almost openly an off-stage threeway. That would have been a fascination when I was with Geoff and Mags. Now it hurt.

No physical or emotional attachment manifested on stage. Ray and Judy came together to harmonize, then stepped apart. BD moved like a zombie while banging a tambourine. Everyone in the East Village knew he'd busted Ray and now was his boy squeeze.

"Revelation in a thousand volts," Ray Light sang. "Blowing you to heaven," sang Judy. A star can touch everyone in a crowded house, a stadium; a cult legend can touch a small percentage. But Ray Light's touch, I can testify, could be searing.

Those in the audience who were as susceptible as I was got sucked into his memory, passed with him through iron doors

that were locked behind them, went down institutional hall-
ways to a place where they were strapped to a table and had
their brains blasted with electricity.

When the song was over and I glanced around, I saw an audience mostly just mildly grooving. But I noticed a scattered
few who looked as disturbed as I felt.

After that, most of Lord of Light's set passed without anything similar happening and I was about to write off what I'd
felt as some kind of much delayed acid aftershock.

Then they sang "Just a Boy without Wings," a song where Ray
Light, yelled, *"Reach me, reach me, reach me or die,"* and I was
naked and handcuffed on a window ledge trying not to look
at the pavement eight floors below while trying desperately
to meld my mind with that of the man who stood behind me.
The nightmare lasted until the music stopped and I was shaking and wet with sweat.

I realized that Ray and I shared at least one very bad experience. And he could do what that nightmare man had tried to
force me to do.

As the reverb from the stage died down, Marty who was sitting next to me shrugged and said, "I give it a nine because
you can die to it." The rest of our party laughed but I was still
trying to get myself to breath normally. The window ledge was
a memory I'd taken some care to avoid.

§

So many years later, still thinking about that long-gone
night, I found myself on the Bowery in front of Taxi Stand.
Maybe you know the place. It opened a few years back just
up the street from CBGB's, which was still in business then.
Completely remodeled in aluminum and glass, trendy for a
while, Taxi Stand occupies a spot which had for decades been
a blowsy all-night cafeteria favored by cab drivers, cops, drag
and female prostitutes.

Wall murals of black and white photographs from the 1940s
and '50s caught the Bowery by night: neon signs with letters

missing, parties from uptown slumming, drunks with ruined faces singing, fat women with their garters showing dancing on bars, drunken college louts trying to be hip.

When I arrived right at noon the place was still almost empty. Marty saw me and said something to the woman with him. Judy Finch turned my way, smiled and spoke my name. She looked good: mid-forties instead of late fifties, ash blonde, no obvious work on her face. For an instant, I saw a flash of the blonde crewcut figure from Lord of Light. She stared at me and I kind of hoped she never saw the story I wrote about her.

"I can't believe it," she said softly, saving her voice, "We precious few don't die easily." She took a sip of the mimosa with which she had brought the morning to a close. "Marty tells me that you've got some amazing material."

He had ordered iced tea, which meant he was keeping his head clear. I did the same and Marty told me about the show they were developing. "It will be a little bit like cabaret, a bit like those evenings Elaine Stritch did and Bea Arthur. Great monster ladies of the American stage talk about breaking onto Broadway, sing a couple of Sondheim songs, reminisce about *Golden Girls* on television and then give you a few funny/painful glimpses of their lives."

"Their stage careers are kind of impressive," said Judy. "But I pretty much got those old ladies beat when it comes to the life story aspect. Living with the Lord of Light who turned out to be the God of Death *and* with the guy who killed him; they can't top that." She laughed at my startled expression and said, "Oh, honey, I'm going to talk *very openly* about Ray and BD and the deaths."

"We're going to use a bunch of Ray Light songs that Judy did originally," Marty told me. "There's a band in the show."

"Yeah, Ray's music has slipped out of peoples' memories," Judy said. "This maybe will bring it back."

"What she can't get is permission to use any kind of reference to Phillip Marcy—the one Ray Light used to call the Man—nothing he wrote, not a photo, or a mention of his habits and suicide," Marty said. "His estate threatens to sue if his name is even used."

"They're afraid we're going to defile his memory. As if that would be possible," said Judy. "We were kind of stuck. Then Marty asked if I remembered you. Like I ever forget anybody from back then in the East Village!"

Just the sincerity with which she looked into my eyes made me pretty certain she had. The waiter came with our drinks and took our orders.

"Can you show us what you have?" Marty asked. I brought out a copy of "The Kid with the Sun in His Eyes" and read aloud the opening section I'd looked over at home.

I finished and Judy said very quietly, "I didn't get to see the guy Ray lived with until the day he got snatched. All I knew was I hated the Man." Then she asked me, "You have more?"

The waiter came with our food. I put the oyster po' boy I'd ordered aside and read:

> At night East Fourth Street becomes the off-Broadway Rialto and the Kid mixes with boys and girls on the corner of Second Avenue, the glassy-eyed drag queens smoking in the alley next to the Club 82 where guys in dresses talk dirty and sing lewd songs in falsetto for the benefit of middle-aged Midwestern drunks in New York on business.
>
> He slips in and out of the intermission crowds at Truck and Warehouse and La Mama, pokes his head into Phoebe's on the corner of the Bowery looking for a daddy for the night. And there in the smoke and amid the crowd of dealers and at-liberty actors and lead-poisoned painters and playwrights dying for a break, the guy Mad Rimbaud pointed out earlier comes up to him and says, "The Kid with the Sun in His Eyes."

For a moment the Kid is in the john's head, a thing that once in a while happens with him, sees himself and Mad Rimbaud who since has made himself scarce as the guy saw them that afternoon. The guy starts buying him drinks, says that he has a gallery uptown like he thinks the Kid might be impressed. But the only things that the Kid pays attention to are the money laid out on the bar and something the john says. "You can read me, I felt you do it. I see you flying into the rising sun with your eyes wide open. And I'm tagging along."

The Kid understands what Rimbaud was saying about this being one crazy queen but he believes he can handle it.

Later with the crowd beginning to thin out the man says he knows the Kid is the one who is going to break through and he wants to find out tonight. By then the Kid's snorted enough junk in the men's room using the man's money that he's plucked off the bar and he isn't afraid of anything.

The Kid with the Sun in His Eyes can't remember the drinks and the junk, can't remember the ride in the creaking freight elevator or what had happened to his clothes or when his hands got cuffed behind his back. "Close your eyes and see into me," says a voice behind him. The Kid's bare feet are on a window sill. A huge window is open in front of him and eight floors down is the concrete sidewalk. The glimpse he briefly had into the mind of the one who'd brought him here is wavy and blurred. Reaching it now is like trying to see through a sun glare even though it's night outside and cold air is hitting him.

"Look at me," he hears the one who stands right behind him say and tries to but the guy has a grip of iron and holds the Kid's head so the Kid can't turn to see him. "Look into me," the guy says. "You did this once this afternoon when I first saw you and you did it for a moment in the bar. And you will do it again. You will look into me," he says. "I can teach

you how but I want you to be able to do it better
than I can. Once I had this boy. I found him on the
street and brought him here and he could see with
his eyes shut and could look into me but not at will,
only off and on. I taught him in the same way I'm
teaching you. And when he had almost reached the
point where he could lead me, they stole him away."
He talks some more and the Kid realizes he's going
to be trapped here and tortured until he sees or
dies.

Judy paused with a bit of salad on a fork but didn't put it
in her mouth. "Let me read the whole manuscript," she said.
"This is fascinating. I feel like the boy he talks about having
taught and lost is Ray. Something like this happened to you?"

I shrugged. "Something kind of like it. I certainly can't project my thoughts. Maybe I have some sensitivity I'm not con-
scious of or something and that's what Marcy detected when
he picked me up. For a few seconds when Ray sang at the Fillmore I saw what had happened to him and knew he was the
one Marcy had talked about."

"That's my story too," Judy Finch said quickly. "We both got
a touch of Ray." And she looked at me like suddenly she did
know who I was. "Was it after this you started writing science
fiction?"

"I write fantasy," I said, "And that began a lot later."

"I want to use this material," she told Marty

"We need to ask the lawyers but it never mentions Philip
Marcy by name and I think it will be fine." Marty looked my
way and smiled, "We'll work out a deal, and you'll get a writing
credit and some kind of really small percentage."

Judy said they'd be in touch. On my walk back home after
lunch, I remembered how after the Lord of Light concert at
the Fillmore I hadn't wanted to hang around for the other acts.
Instead I gave my friends the slip and went back to the Avenue
B apartment where I was staying.

On some blocks in the East Village back then you took a deep breath and tried to look hard and scary before you walked them. A big part of the story of those years was kids coming to the city, curious or desperate, and getting swallowed up. Cults were working the streets. That night I remember women members of the Children of God were doing what they called "fishy flirting" over on First Avenue, soliciting guys for sex and maybe conversion.

When I got home, nobody else was there. On the kitchen table was a newspaper opened and folded to a story that had taken place in that very neighborhood. "Art Dealer Dead in Eight Story Plunge" was the headline. I recognized the face in the accompanying photo. I read some sketchy details of Phillip Marcy's death and a few facts about his career.

And I remembered the morning a few years back when I awoke and saw the big windows that still had HAVERFORD BUSINESS FORMS, a long-dead company, written on them in gold lettering.

The windows overlooked a neighborhood where almost nothing was more than eight stories tall. The morning sun flowed in and half blinded me. It created a halo around the figure that appeared.

The night before Phillip Marcy had picked me up at Phoebe's Bar across the street. Upstairs I'd found he was bigger and stronger and far scarier than I'd guessed. But even fear of falling eight stories onto the cement wasn't enough to make me able to link my mind with his. He kept insisting I'd done it earlier.

That next morning when he approached, I tried to stand up and realized I was still handcuffed. He gestured and I rolled off the couch, walked in front of him to the door of his loft. On a stool were my clothes nicely folded and my boots lying on top of them. He pulled open the bar lock and the front door swung open. I cringed at the cold.

He picked up my clothes and tossed them into the hall, then took a key out of his pocket and unlocked the cuffs. He put one hand on my shoulder, propelled me out the door and tossed some wadded-up bills after me. Before I could scramble into the clothes, the door slammed. And because I was young and very stupid, I felt like a terrible failure.

I'd been a flop in Phillip Marcy's horrible world. Not the kind of boy he was looking for—one who fulfilled what I thought was about the deepest kink I'd ever been near. But the night after Marcy's death I heard Ray Light sing:

"You found me in the Meld and hid me in your cage."

Remembering Ray and looking at the newspaper photo, I sat down at an ancient Underwood typewriter in the East Village tenement and wrote "The Kid with the Sun in His Eyes." And almost forty years later, I was pleased with the fucked-up kid who was able to do that.

§

One reason I was the last person in Manhattan without a cell phone was that I cherished the excitement of coming home and finding a call light flashing on my answering machine. It happened on my return that afternoon. The Lizard had left a message. Without identifying himself he said, "I have news that will bring a faint ray of light into your dreary existence," and gave me a telephone number.

It took a few calls. The first couple of times I got busy signals. Then the receiver at the other end was picked up but all I heard was a woman yelling. She was too far from the phone for me to be able to tell what she was saying. But I knew this was the right number. Women were always yelling at the Lizard. And, in this case, I recognized the voice.

A few minutes later he called back, "I'm coming into the city immediately," he said. "We need to get together." He also told me the good news.

"There's an online site that wants to revive *Biting the Apple*, and is willing to pay for the privilege." This was a board game which he and I had produced almost thirty years ago for the brand new humor magazine *Cheep Irony*. That mag was supposed to meld the best parts of *Saturday Night Live* and *The New Yorker*. It had gone belly up after a few issues.

"But we got paid," the Lizard remarked. "We got a certain amount of attention that got us a few more game commissions. And they let the rights revert to us. No wonder the assholes went broke. The people who are interested now think it's quaint, an historic artifact. By the way, do you happen to have a copy of the damn thing?"

It so happened I did and even knew where it was. *Biting the Apple* was another one of the things I'd clawed my way past that morning while searching for my story.

"Splendid," he said when I told him. "Rumors of your senile dementia are clearly exaggerated." Then he gave me the address of a place where we'd meet in a few hours and hung up.

Maybe the rumors weren't exaggerated. For the second time I marveled at the serendipity of the day.

Looking at *Biting the Apple* I saw it had the same basic rules and design as *Mack Daddy*. It was about making it big in Manhattan circa the early 1980s—finding a rent-controlled penthouse, producing a disco musical, making a fortune with a videogame arcade, meeting Jackie Onassis, dressing like a circa-1955 nerd which suddenly was very hip, not wearing a mullet, visiting the backrooms at Studio 54, the Saint and Limelight. My head reeled.

In my years between booze and cancer the Lizard and I had drifted in and out of each other's lives, close at times, not even speaking at others. Somehow we'd fallen into the racket of designing games for toy companies, for ad agencies that thought games were nice promotional tools, for people who hired us because they believed that we were so weird we must be creative and maybe even wise.

I remember an account executive looking at my partner askance and asking him, "What kind of name is Lizard Pavane, anyway?"

"An invented one," he replied seemingly amazed that anyone could ask a question so idiotic. We designed a game in which one player got to commit a series of famous murders and the other tried to stop him, a game for a giant investment company in which the players were all brokers trying to sell as many retirement plans to corporations as possible, a game for lobbyists to play with members of the U.S. Congress to convince them to deregulate the airlines.

Demand had been hot for a little while and had then disappeared in a puff of smoke. I'd had a few other projects with Lizard Pavane after that. But we hadn't seen much of each other since he moved to New Jersey some years back.

Our meeting took me to the East Village for the second time that day. I'd seen the neighborhood go from gritty, working-class Slavic, to mad hippy, to drug-raddled hellhole. Now the blocks I went down were tree shaded and lined with gift shops, boutiques, small restaurants. The place I wanted was a little bar called Giga's Guillotine on 10th Street and Avenue C.

On my way, I thought about Lizard Pavane calling me on the same day Judy had reappeared in my life. The Lizard's connection with her had been a much more intimate and dramatic one than mine. We'd never talked about it but I'd heard plenty of stories, even seen it mentioned in a book or two. I debated telling him about what had happened to me that afternoon.

Only when I reached my destination did I understand there was little need to mention Judy and absolutely no chance that his reappearance in my life on the same day as hers was a coincidence.

Giga's Guillotine was someone's tacky dream of a 1950s Paris bistro, all quirky and intimate with a parquet floor and Yves Montand playing on the sound system and not at all the Lizard's kind of place.

Ambience, though, was not why we were there. Walking in, I realized that the site had once been occupied by Sid's, a place everyone called Ugly Sid's, a lowlife bar that always managed to stay open until dawn. And it was in Ugly Sid's, the Sunday night after his Fillmore concerts, that Ray Light had died with a knife in his gut.

The Lizard sat at a table sporting a crumpled yachting blazer, drinking an amber liquid that I assumed was Jack Daniels. A small suitcase and a grey raincoat rested on the chair beside him. Long sleeves and a buttoned-up collar hid the iguana tattoos.

I hadn't seen him in five or six years. But really, at five foot four with his black eyes gleaming and his head freshly shaved, he looked not very different than he had thirty years before when I met him for the first time.

Now he saw me and rasped, "You look kind of the same too, except old and confused."

I sat down and ordered a seltzer. "Was that Nina I heard in the background on the phone?" I asked.

"She does have a distinctive shrill scream," he said. "Doubtless your life is as cold and loveless as ever so you're interested in mine. I'm in the midst of civil insurrection, domestic upheaval"

"Nina tossed you out?" Nina is the long-suffering but not infinitely-suffering type. She has a management job with William Morris that bought the house they live in.

"If only she had! What a thrill to be picked up by a strong woman and physically tossed out a door! I would die happy. But she knows that's what I want so she never laid a hand on me: just screamed until I went away and no doubt is changing the locks even as I speak."

He looked at a table full of kids in their twenties and his lip curled, "Girls these days just have gym muscles. In my time there were women who did actual physical labor. Did you bring the game? Nina was whining because she couldn't win. She destroyed my copy after I won all three times we played."

"Is that what the argument was about, you insisted on winning a game you'd designed?" I didn't add, "Even at the risk of pissing off the woman who's supporting you?"

He looked amazed that I asked. "Of course," he said and without pause added, "I think we can get another couple of thousand for updating the game, making it relevant for right now. Any ideas about what that takes these days?"

"Having a blog that gets fifty thousand hits a day?" I said. "The ability to speak Mandarin plus English and two Chinese dialects?" I added. He looked bored. The game was the excuse, not the reason for my being here. Wondering what angle the Lizard was playing, I glanced around the room trying to catch some trace of Ugly Sid's.

"Yes," said the Lizard. "This piece of faux whimsy sits on the very spot where very late one night Bruno Delmar, AKA BD, put a knife into Ray Light before going home and hanging himself."

"I once heard that while those things happened Judy was with you at your loft," I said. I hadn't known Lizard back then, but the story was part of his legend and gave him a bit of the aura of a great lover. The very fact that his looks made that so improbable was a sly twist to the tale.

Some of that must have been obvious on my face because the Lizard cackled and said, "You're thinking to yourself that a gay guy who looked like me would live and die alone. You don't understand. Girls may want to talk to pretty guys who make nice conversation. But they end up having to rely on guys who look like me.

"Judy came by my place. She seemed desperate and afraid, obviously wanting to stay with me. Who was I to refuse? The next day we found out what had happened. 'She was with me all last night,' was all I had to tell the cops when they came around. The guy I shared the loft with, his girlfriend and a couple of other people corroborated.

"At that point, the lawyers descended. Her parents both had money. All they were interested in was showing she had nothing to do with the murder and had no idea BD was going to do what he did. After a few weeks or so her family took her away somewhere to recover. That was practically the last I saw of Judy."

"Had you and she been together for long before that night?"

"We'd just met a couple of weeks before the Fillmore gig. Lord of Light was laying down tracks at Electric Ladyland. Bruno Delmar got Judy and me together at a party. I was already doing okay at that point; had that reviewing gig at *Rolling Stone* and was doing PR. She and I dug each other as the saying went. Until the fateful night, though, we'd done nothing more than talk and exchange glances.

"Apparently BD repeatedly told her that if anything happened I was the one she could turn to. Bruno and I went way back. He trusted me. Maybe I was the only one he trusted."

"You knew BD?" This was a surprise.

"Bruno Delmar and I met in grade school. We were the two smartest boys at Saint Martin de Tours in Canarsie. He liked to be called BD and when I first knew him was a really decent kid. Gallant, you know, stepping into fights and standing up for you if you were his friend.

"After that I went to Brooklyn Polytech, got a scholarship to Cornell. BD got caught in family problems. His mother was badly crazy and when his father died he had absolutely nowhere to live. He ended up in a halfway house and the army and we lost touch.

"A few years later I was back in the city after college hanging around the East Village. And there was BD. He didn't say what he was doing and I didn't ask; that's the way we'd been brought up. But he was still the Bruno Delmar I'd gone to school with. Then one day his picture was in the underground papers and I found out what he'd been up to. He disappeared before I could speak to him."

"I saw him just before his cover got blown," I told Lizard. "Judy Finch confronted some guy at a party. It was all very spacy, everyone ripped. But I do remember how when she turned and walked away he stared after her all lost and in love.

"The next day the story broke and he was gone. Not long afterwards, Judy disappeared. Later I found out they were both in a band with Ray Light."

"You're right about BD being in love," said Lizard. "Come on, I got to meet someone." He threw money on the table, picked up his bag and coat and headed out the door.

"The next time I saw Bruno Delmar he was with Lord of Light," Lizard told me, "in some kind of relationship with Ray Light and Judy. At that moment you couldn't be wingy enough to satisfy the fans.

"But he and I could still talk. The gallantry was still there. He obviously loved Judy even though she didn't much like him. It was what made him find a way of giving her protection, providing cover."

"Why did she need cover? He killed Ray Light in front of a dozen witnesses."

We went up gentrified Avenue C with warmly lighted bars and restaurants every few doors. Lizard Pavane now walked a bit slow and stiff legged but something I remembered about him was still true. He hated to have anybody get in his way or walk faster than he did. Each time someone passed us, he'd kind of growl and make a move like he wanted to hit them with his bag.

"Asshole," he said to me, "It's my guess she knew Ray Light had killed people and wanted BD to off him before Ray did the same to her. BD made sure she had the alibi. And the way he did the deed took all the attention off her."

He looked at me hard and gave his cackling laugh. "You don't believe little Judy Finch could have arranged such a thing, do you? Boy, did she have you conned!"

We were on the corner of Fourth Street when he stopped and said, "Thanks to Nina, I found out Judy's doing a memoir show and your old boyfriend is directing it."

"I only found out about that today," I said.

The Lizard looked like he didn't believe me. Along with the game I'd also brought a copy of my story. On an impulse I handed that to him and said, "She's interested in this thing I wrote the day after Marcy died and the day before BD and Ray did."

"I'll get back to you," he told me and stuffed everything in his bag. Before he crossed the street and headed into the green lawns and neat brick apartment houses of Stuyvesant Town, the Lizard told me, "If Nina calls, you don't know where I am or where I went."

Walking back to my place, I felt like I was always on the periphery of great events, never quite on the scene. Like when I saw Ray Light and BD getting into a van on the north side of Tompkins Park on their last night alive.

BD had washed the makeup off his face and wore black jeans and leathers. He looked much more like the guy I had seen at the party a few years before.

Ray had a red kepi cap pulled down over his face, his collar turned up and his hair in a ponytail. He didn't want to be recognized. But the eyes and the way he got into my head were unmistakable.

He looked at me and I got a flash of what he saw in dim lights and shadows: a guy a bit battered and forlorn walking on the park side of the street in derelict leather jacket and boots.

It took me a moment to recognize myself. I felt Ray Light inside my head seeing the lust and awe on my mind as I watched him. He found "The Kid with the Sun in His Eyes," which I'd spent a chunk of the weekend writing.

And he found my actual encounter with the Man. I could feel his contempt, felt he held my breath and heart in his hand and could snuff me out if he wanted. It lasted just a few seconds.

BD touched Light's shoulder and broke the connection, shook his head and gestured for me to move on. In retrospect I knew he didn't want me messing up his plans. Looking back, he'd saved my life.

§

When I got home from meeting the Lizard I got a call from Nina. We exchanged tentative greetings and marveled at how long it had been since we'd seen each other. Then she said. "Where's Lizard?"

"I don't know."

"He talked to you before he left. You agreed to meet at that idiotic Guillotine bar. There's someone he sees who lives in Stuyvesant Town. I need to know if he's staying with her."

"I couldn't tell you."

"You just did," she said and hung up.

§

A few days later I sat alongside Marty in a small rehearsal space in the bowels of the Public Theater listening to Judy talk about being a kid living on St. Mark's Place with her father the artist and her mother the critic; about becoming a teenager the year Kennedy was shot. The guy who would be music director of the show played piano and Judy sang a snatch of Sam Cooke's "A Change is Gonna Come."

She stood leaning on the back of a chair and said, "I was fifteen in 1965 and going to the Quaker School. A few blocks away from me another tale played itself out. An old friend of mine, who knows a bit about these things, wrote this version."

She enacted parts of "The Kid with the Sun in His Eyes" and ended with this section:

> The Man held the Kid's fingers to a lighted can-
> dle and told him, "I'm teaching you as the one who

taught me did. He brought me to the point where I could meld with certain other minds and I can do that with you. He would have taught me more but he was taken from me. I will not leave you until you can go into every mind and meld with anyone."

Unless you've been writing for the theater for a long while and had it happen to you hundreds of times, I believe it's hard to resist when someone with talent reads your words aloud. Judy understood this material, had the attitude and stance down.

I liked the dumb street-kid vulnerability she projected. This section was my guess as to what had happened to Ray Light. She and I had talked it over and agreed that it felt real.

At first the Man never let the Kid With the Sun in His Eyes out of his sight, kept him tethered and tied when he went out, got him off drugs cold turkey. With the Man the Kid could not just go away and hide in his own mind. The Man could go there and bring him back and the kid stopped fighting it because he was learning to get inside other peoples' minds, not most of the time or with most people. But he could look down at the street below, look inside certain people, and he wanted to learn how to do that with everyone.

After the first night the Man no longer suspended him in front of an open window to force him to communicate. After a couple of weeks, the Man trusted him enough that when he went off to work one morning, he gave the Kid a dollar, let him out on the street and told him to be back at six o'clock. It was a test. And it worked. The Kid was fascinated enough that he did come back even though he hated the Man. Given how things were there was no hiding that.

Judy relaxed, lost the Kid's stance and speech and said in her own voice, "I met him on one of the first days he was out. I saw him on St. Mark's Place looking a little scared. He said his name was Ray, Ray Light. I found out later that it was actually Jonathan Duncan—too mundane for the life he wanted to lead in this city.

"Right then, out of nowhere and all in a rush, I knew just what he was feeling, I knew without our even talking that he was a runaway, that he was afraid of being reported to the cops, that he lived with someone he thought of as the Man.

"At that same moment he knew everything about me. Since he was my first boyfriend I thought that was what it was like to have one. Raised by parents in the arts in this city in the nineteen sixties and I was that naïve.

"We spent that afternoon together until he had to go back to the loft. After that he'd meet me when I got out of school; we'd get together on weekends when the Man let him out.

"We were like that for maybe two months. Then one day private detectives hired by his family snatched him off the street right in front of me. No other boyfriend I found was like him. I didn't see him again for another few years. But I thought of him every day."

After that she took a break and we all sat together drinking coffee. Marty had some notes that Judy glanced at and nodded. It was all kind of comfortable, reminding me of sitting on front steps in the East Village long ago.

Then she looked at me and said thoughtfully, "After a while, even with someone as big and great and wonderful and scary as Ray, one's memories become very set—like a series of old photos. Your piece gave him back to me, let me see him from a new angle."

"And gets us around the Marcy problem," said Marty.

"You know," she said, "A few years after Ray and BD had gone, a very creepy old Englishman, into Satanism, a friend of Aleister Crowley, talked to me about Phillip Marcy."

As she spoke, she fell into an imitation of the man's speech. He sounded amused, sinister, a bit absurd, a bit chilling. "When young Phillip was in college, one of his professors was a man with remarkable mind control and an ability to teach the skill to others, not always with the best intent, not always by the gentlest methods.

"Phillip Marcy fell completely under his spell. Then one day the teacher disappeared. He was never found. The police, of course, were useless. Dear Phillip had learned enough of the gift for it to obsess him but not enough to control it. He spent his days trying to learn, trying to teach. Again, it wasn't always by the gentlest methods. No great surprise when he met his end."

Then Marty asked, "So Ray Light really did have some kind of gift?"

"Yeah," I told him. "I encountered Ray the last night he was alive. He looked at me that last Sunday and I saw myself through his eyes. It was like a knife going into me, but…"

I caught anger in Judy's eyes and shut up. I'd told her about being in Ray's head the night of the concert but hadn't mentioned that last meeting.

Maybe she was angry that I'd seen her lover alive after she had. But maybe she was bothered because I might have seen a little too much for her own good.

What I'd been going to say was that if Ray Light showed that kind of contempt to a harmless fan boy who'd blundered into his path, what must Phillip Marcy have been shown? One look at himself as Ray Light saw him and Marcy would willingly have gone out the window where he'd tortured God knew how many.

§

"Thanks, buddy," said the Lizard on the phone. "You gave the bloodhound just enough information so that she could track me down." He said it sarcastically, but he was calling from home and actually did sound kind of like he was thanking me.

We talked a bit about updating the game. "Well, what do kids do when they come to the city, these days?" he wanted to know.

"Hang on and wait for someone to jump-start the economy," I suggested. We were old and this particular spring of inspiration had run dry some decades ago. "I have no more idea than you do."

Then the Lizard got down to the real point of his call. "How's Judy's show going?"

"Really well. They let me see it again a couple of days ago. There's quite a bit of music. Judy can still sing. It's taking shape as a kind of cabaret. Next week is a run-through for friends in the business to start a little buzz." I didn't mention that she no longer spoke to me.

He paused then said. "I thought that story you wrote was a real acute guess about what Phillip Marcy did to Ray Light. Maybe a bit more than a guess?"

"Just a bit," I said.

"You poor kid," Lizard actually sounded sympathetic. "From what I remember BD telling me, Light had an obsession with the one he still called the Man. Whenever they were in New York, he'd try to approach Marcy because there was a lot he hadn't been taught. But the guy didn't want to see him."

I said, "Phillip Marcy created a monster and the monster was out to get him."

"Ray wanted BD to get himself picked up by Marcy and then let Ray into the loft to join them. Bruno and Light's relationship was deeply complicated but Bruno didn't want to do that."

"Eventually BD must have gone along," I told Lizard. "But if he was as gallant as you say, seeing even someone who deserved it as much as the Man go out the window must have bothered him a lot. Something I wonder is how could Ray

Light not read BD's mind that last night and know what he had planned?"

"From what Bruno told me, Ray would pick up a vision of the future or something from his head. It was part of what Light found so fascinating about him. Mostly, though, Ray had no idea what BD was thinking."

Lizard paused, then said, "Okay, I gave you all that, now tell me when the performance is."

So I told him and was quite curious as to why he wanted to know.

§

Judy sat backwards on a metal café chair on a low stage and spoke. "When Ray and I got together again it was a few years after he got taken away from me. 1969 was a much different world from 1965, dark and full of fear. If you don't understand that change you didn't live through that time in this place."

"An informal workshop" was what they called this. It was held on Monday night in a rehearsal space at the Public Theater. "Nothing was absolutely clear in that world," she said. "When Ray Light came back to me, he brought with him BD, Bruno Delmar, the one who had helped snatch Ray off the street. Everyone thought of him as a monster, a pig. We'd chased him out of the neighborhood. Now he and Ray were lovers.

"I became part of that and we started playing together." She sang the old Lord of Light song "Just a Boy Without Wings." It was a quiet song now, not scary as much as lost and more than a little sad.

The quartet on the stage had worked with her before and was tight with a nice jazz inflection.

Marty was happy. The show had word-of-mouth to spare. Old theater friends of Judy's, people from various production companies, someone from a foundation that did arts funding and a couple of documentary film producers, seventy or eighty in all, sat on folding chairs.

Tanya Starrett was there with the soul of Callimachus on a gold chain around her neck. My goddaughter Selesta's friend Mathis who ran the arts blog *Saturday Night and Sunday Morning* also was present. I nodded to him but he looked puzzled by me.

One chair with a "Reserved William Morris" sign was empty. I remembered that Nina worked there and kept my eye on it.

"Oh, there were rumors," said Judy, "stories that various people who had given Ray trouble; a psychiatrist, his father, had died by their own hands. But that kind of legend surrounded other bands and a lot of personalities in those days. And there were lots of moments when the three of us, Ray and BD and me, were one. But the dynamic maybe couldn't endure."

She tuned the guitar and said, "This is something I started many years ago and finished just recently." The song's lyrics were all about the night of the murder/suicide. It had the lines:

One who loved me and one I loved
Went out one night and never returned.

When she finished, I looked over and Lizard sat in the empty chair I'd noticed earlier. He stared at Judy and, as the crowd applauded, he stood up and took a couple of steps toward the stage. She noticed him immediately and paused where she was.

"BD did more than love you. He saved your life and left you free to live it," Lizard Pavane said.

People in the audience were giving each other "Is this part of the show?" glances. Marty who sat next to me was on his feet. Judy's pianist looked like someone who'd handled a few drunken customers in his performing career. He started to rise.

Judy looked right at Lizard. She gestured for the others to sit down. "One night I guess BD decided to liberate himself and me and especially Ray from a trap we'd fallen into, a kind of magic that had gone very bad. But before he did that, he put me in the care of a childhood friend of his, this wonderful man right here."

She came down off the stage, reached out, touched Lizard's cheek and for a moment became the desperate twenty-one year old who'd come to his door begging for help.

Judy spoke to him quietly for a moment. Lizard seemed mesmerized. Then she sat him down, climbed back on stage and sang a hard driving version of the Ray Light song "Revelation in a Thousand Volts." It was a select audience but even given that the applause was intense.

The last part of the show dealing with the decades of Judy's life since that famous night seemed more than a little anticlimactic. The next time I looked his way, Lizard was gone.

"If we could just get him to stand up and do that every night," Marty muttered at the finale.

After the performance was over and she'd thanked the audience and the band, Judy turned to Marty and said, "Get me contact information for Pavane." She never looked my way at all.

§

It was a few days later that I got a call from Marty. "Lots of interest in this show," he said. The immediate word is we're doing weekend cabaret at Joe's Pub for the month of March with the intention of moving to one of the Public Theater stages in late September and then who knows.

"Everyone liked the first part and we're going to make the whole piece just about the Ray Light years. You'll get a contract sometime before we open. You have my personal guarantee that it won't be generous."

I thanked him. Later that same day, Lizard Pavane called me. "They still want *Biting the Apple* and they'll pay, maybe, two grand for it. But they got a couple of kids to do the modern-day equivalent. I think they believe we're a little stale."

"No argument there," I said.

There was a pause. "I've been talking a lot with Judy," he told me. "About BD. She says I've given her access to him, made her think about him and remember him in ways she hadn't. We're getting together again this afternoon. It almost feels like old times."

"Nina won't be happy."

"Nina will have to learn to get over it."

I wanted to tell him he'd been right about Judy. She wanted Ray killed and got BD to do it for love. She was able to murder someone who could read her mind because animal instinct required no prior thought.

I could have told Lizard that the minute she got what she needed from him for her show, he'd be dropped cold. But he was having fun and the past is magic at our point in life. So I said it sounded good and to keep me informed.

A writer's life only becomes clear to him after he writes it. And I sat waiting for the phone to ring.

Chapter Nineteen

That summer as the economy collapsed, Judy Finch's show *Revelation (In a Thousand Volts)* was in rewrite and rehearsal. Just after Labor Day it opened at the Public Theater. Joan Mata was my guest opening night. When Judy did my monologue to big applause Joan whispered, "This is what half-human friends are for," turned in her seat and applauded me.

In November it opened on Broadway with strong word of mouth and fine reviews. Lizard Pavane had a minor heart attack around then. His disappointment that Judy never called was so sad it humanized him.

§

Marco reappeared in my life, first by email and then in person. He was involved in computer animation and turning manga into movies. My head spun when he tried to explain. He and his fiancée, Celia, went to New Jersey to meet her family. Celia looked quite lovely online. She gave Marco a day off and we two stopped in a student bar he remembered.

He'd told Celia about Terry and Eloise. "I told her about you too. How you saved, maybe not my life but you let me get through those days without being afraid I was going crazy."

"Or at least, that you weren't the only one."

"Yes! You saw ghosts and just kept on going." We were laughing. He said, "I don't see that stuff much anymore," and shrugged, a little happy/a bit sad.

"You got to see my ghosts. I'm afraid I didn't do very well by them."

"When they looked at you they weren't angry. It was more, 'Is that him? Sorry we can't stop.'" I must have shown I didn't know what he was talking about. "When you turned to me and told me, 'Be smarter than we were,' they glanced back like they were sorry to leave you."

Marco, it seemed, was being nice to an old revenant. Before we parted he said, "Celia said to give you this," and kissed me.

§

In June, for the fortieth anniversary of the event, an old friend asked me to reminisce about the Stonewall Riots for his blog.

It was a last-minute request but a title and opening paragraph came to me immediately and the assignment gave me immense pleasure. I wrote:

> IN HISTORY'S VICINITY
> It's odd to be old enough to remember history.
> The Stonewall Riot always makes me feel like a
> citizen of Concord awakened by musket fire on that
> crisp April morning and wondering what the com-
> motion was.

Writing this took me back to the New York City of the 1960s. I wrote about walking down Third Avenue with its bird bars and discreet cruising, passing through the world famous chicken run at Fifty-Third and Lex with its boy hustlers hanging around corner coffee shops. Bars and the street pretty much delineated gay life back then.

The first gay bar I ever went to was one in Boston called—maybe—the Sugar Bowl. I was sixteen and the drinking age there was twenty-one. They wouldn't serve me but didn't care if guys gave me their drinks.

The Sugar Bowl was also the first place I got tossed by the cops. I'd been slapped around once or twice for loitering where nice boys didn't venture. But this was a raid and a cop gave me a bloody nose. He let me go when I gave him the name of an uncle of mine who was on the force. My life was hell when I got home.

Compared to Boston everything in New York was big and open. It was like everyone in the city knew what boys did at Fifty-third and Third. In Boston it was all dark corners and whispers.

Those bars, those coffee shops, were criminal enterprises subject to police raids and being shut down. The men cruising and boys loitering could be arrested on a whim. Serving minors, serving as a place minors could be had for cash was no bigger a crime than catering to a gay clientele.

Mart Crowley's *The Boys in the Band* was the first American play to deal overtly with gay life and the kind of men who drank in the Bird Bars. It opened on April 15, 1968. By the time the movie came out in 1970 its world of gay self-hatred and closeted sex looked like a period piece.

Between the play and the movie's openings the Stonewall Riot had occurred. If I'd known the Stonewall was going to become an historic site I'd have paid more attention. In fact it was one bar among many. Gay kids poured into Greenwich Village from all over the city, the country, the world. The nation was all on fire and every oppression but ours got protested.

The Stonewall Inn was badly ventilated, crowded, and filthy, the toilets were an abomination, the bartenders were hostile and the drinks were watered. But that was true in all the Village gay bars. Manhattan ran on methedrine and speed was easily obtained there, the drags danced like furies. The crowd was young. The scent was beer, sweat, amyl nitrate and cheap cologne.

Mags couldn't stand the place. Geoff and I put on a show of ennui but shared a fascination. He wouldn't go there unless I went with him. Until I wrote the article I'd forgotten that.

My grandfather from Ireland used to say that if every man who boasted he'd fought in the Easter Rising of 1916 had actually stood at the Dublin Post Office, James Connolly and Pádraic Pearse would be sitting in Buckingham Palace at the moment he spoke.

In my case, around three o'clock on that famous Saturday morning I was walking down St. Mark's Place with Geoff looking for the Bug Boy. Mags was elsewhere. A kid we both knew rushed up and gave us a garbled story about the Stonewall. That's when we became aware of distant sirens.

In that time and place civil disturbances were what bullfights were to Hemingway's Madrid and we were all aficionados. The kid ran off to spread the news. Geoff and I headed west, crossed Astor Place and went down Eighth Street, which was still the heart of the Village.

The book and music stores were dark but the bars were just closing, the after-hours clubs were opening. The street was full of people all looking west.

Near the corner of Sixth Avenue was what we recognized as the rear area of the riot. In the doorway of the Nathan's, a blond kid in short-shorts and mascara held a bloody towel to his forehead and a friend held him. From the upper floors of the massive, darkened Women's House of Detention across the Avenue, some inmates were yelling, "The fucking pigs are killing all the faggots."

Police cars with flashing cherry-tops barred the way. All along Sixth Avenue, firemen hosed down piles of burning trash. Paddywagons and Tactical Patrol buses were parked two deep and the riot cops were angrier than I ever saw them.

Here coherent memory breaks down. From Sheridan Square I looked down Christopher Street and caught a glimpse of the front of the Stonewall Inn. Broken glass was everywhere. A car had been turned on its side.

A lot of us discovered how angry we were that weekend. Geoff amazed me. He was red-faced, furious, spitting out "Kill the fuckers" every time cops rode by.

The riot had broken down into guerilla tactics: roving bands of kids chanting slogans, burning trash. I heard people shouting from their windows at the cops to go away. I saw a cop smash his club across the back of a guy who I think was just coming home with groceries and smash him again when he dropped his bags.

That did it. Too much speed in his system, a short lifetime of swallowing insults and accumulating anger: Geoff moved towards the cop and his partner. I grabbed him, threw him against a parked car, and dragged him down a side street before the police came after us.

I concluded the piece:

> By Monday it was over. But as with 9/11 decades later, events in this tumultuous city in that time of war and turmoil began to be defined as having happened before Stonewall or after.
>
> And it was kids like the ones on Fifty-Third and Third, not the suit johns in their uptown bars, who had given us those nights.
>
> Men with powdered hair and silk britches could have signed declarations and petitions to King George forever. But on that Concord morning it was men and women, not the most attractive or socially poised, not with the purest of motives or the loftiest of intents, people like me and perhaps like you, who found themselves pushed one unendurable time too many.

Geoff was the one I thought of when I wrote that last line. But in the article, I gave him another name, left him out of the narrative because I felt things weren't easy between his ghost and me. But when I remembered dragging him away from the cops I thought I'd done a bit better by him than the Subway Man ever did by me.

§

When I told Marty this he said, "The day I met you, my life was over. Stepdad had skipped out and that crazy school with late registration was all Mom could afford. They'd made me strip and put on a uniform. Suddenly this cute little wise-guy is talking, making me laugh. Doesn't saving my life balance out Geoff? I'm sorry he and Mags are gone but, honey, I'm glad we're here!"

Revelation (In a Thousand Volts) won a couple of Tony Awards for Judy Finch. Marty won for director. That year I got some lovely little checks. I wanted to add "playwright" to the hundred-word bio/bibliography that gets included each time I publish a story.

"Judy," Marty told me, "is every inch a professional and as total a monster as I've ever encountered."

Mostly that year Recession was the story. Not so much a crisis as a chronic illness. Everyone seemed to get poor at the same time. The legendary St. Vincent's Hospital where my brother and I had been patients was bankrupt and threatened with closure. Some part of me believed so much in Nurse Collins and the hospital staff and even in McGittrick and Sister Immaculata that I anticipated a last-minute rescue.

Chapter Twenty

On the frontier of old age small incidents and dreams produce grave thoughts. Is my repeatedly losing the remote control that operates my CD player or my blank stare at the computer screen as I try to remember why I logged on just now explained by head injuries I took when I was young? Or is this just the natural course of things slowly getting worse as time dances on?

The feeling I'm approaching the end of my personal road always lurks. Waking up some mornings I feel my brother Gerry is in the room, open my eyes and see the empty daybed. Towards the end of the chase, I understand he was the person in whose company I awoke to most often in my life.

Surfing a mild S&M website full of vintage black-and-white snapshots from the '50s and '60s I found one I've seen online before under a variety of titles. This time it was called "Daddy's Home."

In it a crewcut American boy, thin in the way of kids back then, stands naked in a suburban living room. He looks sixteen though I know he's nineteen. Tanlines on his arms and legs show that it's summer and he's spent lots of time in T-shirts and shorts. His dick is semi-hard and his palms are resting on his buttocks like maybe he expects to get spanked.

This was before Will started doing that. The pose is probably because I was used to having pockets and didn't know what else to do with my hands. I hated compulsory ROTC and gym. But the hours of close-order drill and wind sprints had produced good definition.

I even recognized the couch behind me and the photo on the wall from when Will picked me up on the Fire Island Ferry in the summer of '63. I've wondered how this shot got into circulation. Did Will give it to someone or sell it? Was it among his effects when he died? Did he live long enough to get online?

The kid in the shot is cute enough. But the eyes are what I notice. He's gazing away from the camera and they are blank, like he has no soul.

I know he's gone away and won't be back until this session is over. "Do what you want" is the message. This is what the Subway Man and other guys saw.

The ability to go away and leave my body behind was something I'd probably developed early, maybe had from birth. But I really noticed it in Boston when I was sixteen, going on thirteen, and was getting picked up, sneaking booze, dropping Benzedrine. My parents didn't want to know what I was doing but wanted very much for me to stop doing it.

Schoolwork didn't interest me at all, my grades slipped and I ended up in summer school. One Saturday night I snuck out without telling anyone and came home late, with a bloody nose and stinking of beer. I'd been caught in a police raid on the Sugar Bowl, though I kept that secret.

My father was waiting. My pants got taken away and my bare ass got beaten, things I'd thought didn't happen anymore.

For the foreseeable future if I wasn't at school, my part-time job or Sunday Mass, I would be at home in pajama pants (sissy clothes—real boys slept in their Jockeys). This guaranteed that

I couldn't leave the house. I was to do my homework and be in bed with the lights out by eight o'clock.

Leaving for school each morning, I'd plot an escape; imagine I could find some guy who'd take me away with him. But each evening like I was under a malign spell I lay awake in the hot dark listening to kids my age out on the street, hoping none of them would discover what had happened to me.

For once instead of being afraid I'd wake up as somebody else, I wished it would happen. From a distance, I watched this hopeless boy shorn of all his pride and was glad I didn't have to share his agony.

Eventually my mother became concerned or maybe bored. Friday night she let me get out of bed and watch a movie with her on the Late Show. It was then I saw the strange, ballet-drenched English film of the opera *Tales of Hoffmann* about which I'd known little.

In act one a drunken Hoffmann falls in love with an automaton. In act two he loses his soul to a woman who's the Devil's pawn. In the opera Hoffmann gets his soul back by breaking a mirror with a key. It looked easy enough if for some reason I ever wanted mine again—though it seemed a useless encumbrance.

§

Well after I'd forgotten all about it, the young *Godzilla Does Manhattan* anthology editor I'd met at Saratoga found a publisher and reminded me of my commitment. Writing a story has always been like wrestling in my sleep. This time it seemed worse than ever but it always seems worse than ever.

New York is one of my primary subjects and apparently I have a superstitious fear of writing *finis* to the place. Obviously some story is going to be the last one I write. But would my constructing a story about the destruction of New York City be a form of creative suicide?

I considered natural catastrophe; envisioned the streets awash in hurricanes and tsunami. But New York as New Or-

richard bowes

leans or Japan was too obvious. So was New York as Baghdad and the image it brought to mind of tanks moving slowly down a ruined Fifth Avenue supported by infantry with weapons at the ready and helmets shaped like black falcon heads.

I saw burning towers but that had actually happened and I'd already written about it. My own New York was in the grip of a massive financial whammy. I imagined barefoot American kids begging from well-to-do foreign tourists. In fact I was pretty confident that if things ever came to that New York kids would be wearing the rich tourists' shoes.

I thought about a sudden appearance in every phase of city life—on the street, in government, business, the arts, at clubs and gyms, online and on screen—of thin, elegant people with gimlet eyes and chilly laughs.

They would seem to be everywhere exuding the ultimate New York sexual allure of money and power. It would be said they were a cult and/or clones, that they were telepaths, tireless in bed, LGBT or straight as the mood was upon them. They conquered and looted us at will. For a moment this seemed like my story idea.

Then I realized that my aliens were just the yuppie bankers who had actually done most of those things over the previous decade. And the city had, in the way of New York, changed and survived.

Each of those plots was a gambit, a game, a lousy disaster movie invented by one without a soul. For a city's destruction to be tragedy it has, like an individual's, to be fate and not just a meaningless accident. The end has to come from within.

§

Thinking about this, I went to a gallery opening—a retrospective of Downtown New York art from the early '70s through the late '80s—the time of Basquiat and Haring, graffiti and punk. I'd been on the periphery of that scene and a friend who'd been far more central to it took me as his date.

Opening night, a generation after their great moment, the survivors, artists and performers, gallery owners and critics, reminded me of the Waxworks scene from *Sunset Boulevard*.

Raddled, shell-shocked, they looked at the paintings, the sculptures and collages but more at the photos of amateur drag performance at the Pyramid club, obscenities scrawled on gallery walls, the dirty, bombed-out background of garbage-strewn vacant lots, the emptiness of lower Broadway after dark, the abandoned cars, gutted buildings and broken glass of a dying city, and told each other they'd do it all over again.

In fact, that New York was no place for people now aged and infirm. It was scary day and night. Everybody knew somebody who'd been shot. Lots of us had severe drug and alcohol problems and unbreakable sexual addictions. But at moments in the show the perverse beauty of certain faces in those photos was breathtaking.

Scattered among the opening night crowd were students, kids in their late teens and early twenties, marveling at the wonder of it all—not the art but the ruined city that spawned it, and how cool it would have been to live there and then. Looking at them, I didn't think they'd have lasted an afternoon.

Afterwards my friend and I walked as he railed about the clothes the students had worn. "Just things they throw on without any message or thought. I had more suits than any man I knew, as many dresses as any woman." I was waiting but he didn't say "We had faces, then."

One thing I'd looked for in the exhibit was photos of friends lost and gone and I did find some. I also wondered if I'd see myself but that didn't happen.

One of the resurrected faces belonged to Hal Danzig, the kid of extraordinary beauty who had been dubbed the Downtown Ganymede by the critic St. Just in the meth-fueled mosh pit of youth and androgyny that was New York in the late '60s. And the title had stuck.

Hal used the women's rooms in clubs and bars. Women did not object and he wouldn't have been left alone long enough to take a piss in a men's room.

Hal and I first met in the lobby of the Metropolitan Opera House at Lincoln Center. American Ballet Theater's *Coppélia* with Carla Fracci and Erik Bruhn was the attraction. The lobby buzzed with the news that Bruhn's Tartar lover, the premier danseur Nureyev, was in the audience. The crowd parted before Lincoln Kirstein, bisexual founder of the company, manic-depressive, patron of the arts.

Coppélia is based on a Hoffmann story, which the opera also uses, in which an enchanted youth falls in love with an animated doll. Surveying the crowd, I saw older men, rich and powerful, and the cleverly animated boys, amazingly lifelike to the casual glance, whom they escorted.

That, of course, wasn't the case with me. I had merely lost my soul and I thought of Randall, who'd brought me, as a patron, not a sugar daddy.

Randall introduced me to the critic St. Just, who in turn introduced us to Hal Danzig. For the rest of the evening I was aware of nothing else. Hal was small but with perfect features in the way of certain movie stars like Ladd and Newman, unblemished skin, dark hair that swept down to his shoulders and a bright, wicked smile he could flash on and off.

We stepped aside and I slipped a pair of Black Beauties, the amphetamine of the gods, into his palm. "Oh, sir, you are too generous to me, a simple streetwalker!" he said as our keepers dragged us apart.

Doing research afterwards, I found that Hal came from a well-to-do family in Missouri who paid small bribes to keep him away. He may have been an automaton but I didn't care. We slept together on occasion over the next few years. Then, as he hovered on the far side of his celebrity, we became lovers.

It was after Mags and Geoff and before I got mugged by my boyfriend. By then I already looked banged up and used. There were no more nice old patrons and the guys who picked me up did it expecting to get a rough time. I was trying to go clean and sober. Recovering my soul turned out to be harder than it had been for Hoffmann.

Hal could still earn money on his looks but he had an oil burner of a coke habit. I knew the connections and he didn't. I suppose it never amounted to much, our affair. He was beautiful and I copped the drugs. He did them and I tried not to. On drugs he was an automaton. Mostly I watched us from a distance.

Before he walked out he smiled as brightly as he had six years before in the Met lobby and said, "I don't think you're really here and you don't think I'm really human."

§

Hal was on my mind when I got a text message reminder: the *Godzilla Does Manhattan* deadline was near. For me a problem with the project was that the editor saw Japanese horror movies while I saw E.T.A. Hoffmann and Oscar Wilde.

The day before, I'd gone to the opening of a photo exhibit by the late Stan ("Add an 'a' and he's Satan," said St. Just) Brabant. An abused kid, a street hustler, a talented, ruthless photographer: he showed up in NYC in the '70s and was part of the scene if not a big star.

Brabant had witnessed the marriage of punk and bondage, leather straps and shaved bodies, figures wrapped head to toe in duct tape, young guys in bustiers plucking their eyebrows before they went out for the night, ladies in nothing but nurses' hats displaying their clits.

When Brabant died, he died hard in the AIDS ward at St. Vincent's. He made a darkroom in the lavatory, lay in bed and took pictures of his visitors. Hal and I both appeared in the retrospective but not in the same shots, not at the same time. I'm trying to smile and it looks painful. His smile is automatic.

It made me remember the last time I saw Hal. By 1990 or so, I was settling into middle age, had my library job, was writing, had long ago kicked drugs and booze, avoided situations in which I wanted to leave my body. It was kind of like having a soul.

One afternoon I was eating lunch in Washington Square Park. It was a clear and breezy day with psycho skateboard boys circling the fountain where there sat Madonna hookers and River Phoenix street waifs in from the suburbs.

New York was in the last phase of a lawless time and the park was a center for all manner of trade. A slender figure in a fine suede jacket appeared near the fountain. He looked like Hal but seemed too young. From a distance he looked the age he'd been when we first met.

As far as I knew no one had heard from Hal in some years. He'd disappeared and was rumored to have returned home which only happened back then when you were ready to die.

But I watched as he walked right up to a Spanish guy sitting on the steps and spoke to him. The guy, whom I'd seen before and guessed was dealing coke, seemed a little distant, distrustful, shook his head. I was amused by this: someone who looked too good to buy drugs.

But the more I watched the more sure I became that this in fact was Hal—the height, the color, the tilt of his head all matched my memories. I thought of Dorian Gray. Hal made eye contact with a tall cinnamon-haired kid who nodded. Together they walked south and passed not far from me.

What Hal was doing was insanely dangerous. The tough Rockefeller drug laws were in full effect and the park swarmed with undercover cops. I stood up and tried to catch his eye.

Then I saw just how thin and drawn he was, saw the years and caught the flat desperation in his eyes. I sat down as he and the dealer passed by and out of the park. Later the dealer came back but not Hal. For a time I thought about trying to make contact with my old love but I never did.

It seemed to me that this patch of memory without a resolution might be a story. But could Hal Danzig destroy New York? Dorian Gray didn't destroy London. How would this work in *Godzilla Does Manhattan*?

§

That night Hal himself gave me the answer as we walked down the center of a Bleecker Street utterly deserted except for us. Every storefront was empty and all the windows were broken. We were right near where I live. Some buildings were gone. The one on the corner opposite mine had partly collapsed. Grass and young trees grew in the empty spaces. Besides us, nothing moved but fluttering newspapers and swirls of dust in the gutters.

Hal turned to me and his face was a doll's with empty eye sockets. He said, "I died and you lived—two meaningless events. Do you think I didn't see you in the park, gaping at me in horror that last time? Of course I did. You were almost translucent but I saw you. Like a ghost.

"When your parents humiliated you, took away your clothes, instead of leaving home like Satan Brabant, like even I did, you lay in the dark and imagined you had a soul to lose.

"Brabant when he was dying didn't want your mournful expression. He wanted me coming through the door, superficial and doomed like we all were.

"Your yuppified, genteel New York is a dream. Your world doesn't exist. What you see around you now is how New York ended. AIDS was only the prelude to a world of infectious diseases.

"My city is the one that everyone will remember. Mine is the one so many of us died for. Do you think anybody will ever lay down their lives for the New York you imagine you inhabit?

"It wasn't a soul you lacked, it was courage and timing, darling. You didn't know when it was your moment to die."

§

Nothing has the clarity of a dream. My first reaction, opening my eyes in the pale light of dawn was that I'd awakened in Hal's city.

The noise of New York outside my windows put that idea away. I thought about Hal saying my survival was nothing but bad timing and cowardice. I remembered Hoffmann in the opera ending up drunk and face down on a beer-hall table and the 1940s film with the hideous Ivan Le Lorraine Albright picture of Dorian Gray hidden in a closet.

For a moment, like old times, I stood apart and looked at myself, a dreary old man lying in bed. Then I realized I had my story—a parting gift from the Downtown Ganymede.

Chapter Twenty-One

As I slow down, life around me speeds up. It seemed a short time later that I was sitting in the park on a fine spring evening going over the proofs of my *Godzilla Does Manhattan* story.

Urged by family and friends I'd gotten a cell phone. Joan Mata called and told me about Luis saying real words. We talked about our mothers who were very ill. "You heard about St. Vincent's," I said. That morning it was announced the hospital was shutting its emergency room, shifting patients to other hospitals, a victim of bankruptcy and changing times.

The conversation ended, the light was fading. Jason who worked at a neighborhood massage and reflexology parlor and I were having a low-key affair. He was due by my place in a little while. I like a bit of danger and mystery in the mix and much as I enjoyed Jason he gave little of either.

As I got up, a familiar figure stood before me in the twilight.

"You missed your chance," said McGittrick. His image wavered slightly.

"Seems more like I avoided a bad post-life career choice." I waited for a reply but there was none. McGittrick nodded sadly as if he kind of agreed and as I watched he faded into the dusk.

So the whole incredible place was gone. The young nurses like Scott Horton and Margaret Yang would doubtless find jobs in big soulless hospitals.

But what would happen with old Nurse Mary Collins? All she knew would fade away along with Sister Immaculata and Mc-Gittrick himself. And I realized that in some twisted corner of my mind I'd believed until today that I could take McGittrick's offer, delay death a bit and go direct traffic at St. Vincent's.

§

As you get older you've seen it all before. The seasons pass faster, there's less to differentiate them. One sunny, breezy day in August I walked up MacDougal Street. Chris had called me earlier from LaGuardia. He and Tony, my godson-in-law, would be staying at a friend's place in the West Village while she was out of town. I was on my way to meet them and give them her keys. Dust kicked up in the gutters as I turned onto narrow, ancient Minetta Lane.

Crossing Sixth Avenue I thought about *Godzilla Does Manhattan*, which had just been released. The first reviewer on Amazon was apparently the one who'd complained about Hoffmann stealing from the genre. He made the same complaint in his review and savaged my story. So the game continues and life goes on.

West of Sheridan Square the breeze picked up and the neighborhood gods were alive. At the end of the block, crossing Bleecker Street as it winds its way through the Village, were two figures with long hair and flowing clothes. I thought of the Witch Girls and of late '60s hippie fashion.

One turned slightly and I saw Mags. The other was Geoff, smiling like I was an old memory, an amusing déjà vu. I started to trot amid eddies of dust, candy wrappers and crushed coffee containers. On the corner, I looked where the ghosts had headed. They were gone. I trotted in that direction looked up and down the cross streets, paused out of breath on a corner.

My phone was buzzing. Chris wondered where I was. I turned and headed his way, small gods and spirits dancing around me. As I turned onto the block where he waited, a tabloid page flew past me, grit got in my eyes. Chris and Tony stood on a stoop and waved as I approached.

Posters of dead firefighters swirled, Sister Immaculata smiled, a dead teen was slung half naked over a tree branch, lighted pumpkin faces looked out a coach window and a suicide caught my eye on his way to the marble floor.

I was confused and doubtless looked it. Chris rushed forward and hugged his crazy old godfather. At dinner that night I told them what I'd seen. "I'm hallucinating," I said. "It's all just dreams."

"But they're real dreams," Chris told me. "Nothing is as real as dreams."

richard bowes

Epilogue

On WBAI Radio on the tenth anniversary of the World Trade Center attack, I read my story of the days that followed 9/11. Or rather I sat in the studio and listened to a beautifully produced and edited reading that I'd done for the fifth anniversary show.

It was a bright New York Sunday though not quite as lovely as the weather ten years before. After the reading, a psychoanalyst and I discussed on the air the day, its impact and aftermath.

I'd been leery of this story for the last few years because of my feelings about Mags and Geoff and myself. Hearing it this time I thought of Marco describing their expressions of fond recollection when they saw me. I wondered when we'd meet again and if a swirl of dust would mark our passage from this city.

Perhaps it's insanity, brain damage or both but I found myself smiling. And I'll end my story here.

RICHARD BOWES was raised in Boston, went to school on Long Island and has lived in Manhattan for most of the last forty-seven years. He wrote fashion copy and plays, sold antique toys in flea markets, worked on library information desks and got into an amazing amount of trouble along the way. For the last thirty years and more he has written speculative fiction and published six novels and two short-story collections (with two more due out this year). He has published seventy stories and won two World Fantasy, a Lambda, an IHG and Million Writers Awards.

AUG X 2013

CPSIA information can be obtained at www.ICGtesting.com
Printed in the USA
LVOW060046290613

340697LV00004B/863/P